Richard Henry Thomas

Penelve

Among the Quakers

Richard Henry Thomas

Penelve
Among the Quakers

ISBN/EAN: 9783337404765

Printed in Europe, USA, Canada, Australia, Japan

Cover: Foto ©Andreas Hilbeck / pixelio.de

More available books at **www.hansebooks.com**

PENELVE;

OR

AMONG THE QUAKERS.

AN AMERICAN STORY.

BY

RICHARD H. THOMAS, M.D.,

AUTHOR OF "ECHOES AND PICTURES," ETC.

ORIGINAL ILLUSTRATIONS BY OSMAN THOMAS.

LONDON:

HEADLEY BROTHERS,

14, BISHOPSGATE STREET WITHOUT, E.C.

PHILADELPHIA, U.S.A.:

J. C. WINSTON & CO.,

718, ARCH STREET.

1898.

HEADLEY BROTHERS,

PRINTERS,

LONDON AND ASHFORD, KENT.

TO THE MEMORY

OF MY BELOVED BROTHER,

JAMES CAREY THOMAS, M.D.,

WHO, AFTER THE DEATH OF OUR FATHER, BECAME AS A

FATHER TO ME,

This little Book is Dedicated.

HIS WARM APPROVAL OF THE PURPOSE OF "PENELVE,"

AND HIS HEARTY INTEREST

IN SUCH OF THE CHAPTERS AS HE WAS ABLE TO HAVE READ

TO HIM DURING HIS LAST SHORT ILLNESS,

HAVE BEEN A GREAT ENCOURAGEMENT AND

SATISFACTION TO ME.

PREFACE.

Richard H. Thomas, of Baltimore, is already known to a wide circle of English readers by his book of poems, entitled, " Echoes and Pictures."

The following story is intended to portray home life among the Society of Friends in the Eastern Middle States in its influence upon a serious minded man, fresh from the New York world and agnostic in his faith. The singular charm of Quaker home life has appealed to many novelists, but their descriptions have almost always been wanting in completeness for lack of that fulness of knowledge which can alone come where there is close sympathy with the essentials of Quakerism. Richard H. Thomas has this sympathy. He has written a story, which while imaginary in plot is, I believe, entirely truthful in spirit. The Quaker setting and atmosphere of the book are painted from the life ; so also are the characters ; and the account of the hero's growth into spiritual light is derived from actual acquaintance with similar experiences. I feel sure that all who read the following pages will be grateful to the author for having introduced them to the lives of plain living and holy thinking which he has described.

WM. CHAS. BRAITHWAITE.

Banbury,

31st March, 1898.

NOTE.

The author wishes to explain that while the picture presented in the following pages is, he believes, an accurate one, an equally truthful picture of Friends of other branches and in other sections of the country might be very different from the one here given.

CONTENTS.

CHAPTER.	PAGE.

ILLUSTRATIONS.

PENELVE;

OR

AMONG THE QUAKERS.

CHAPTER I.

THE BLIZZARD.

LATE one February evening, in 189—, a sleigh with a single occupant was moving rapidly along a lonely road in Northern New York in the direction of Flumetown. No other vehicle was in sight, and only the jingling of the horse's bells broke the profound quiet.

The full moon had just risen above the mountains, and their slopes still lay in deep shadow, while far away on the other side of the valley the silvery whiteness of the unbroken snow on the clearings stood out in strong contrast to the dark reaches of pine forest, which covered the greater part of the hills. The valley itself was mostly open land, and but thinly settled, so that, except for a few scattered buildings and some tall trees, which cast their long shadows across the snow, the whole of the nearer landscape presented an almost unbroken sheet of white, and with the moon shining in a cloudless sky the scene was almost as bright as day.

Robert Strongwood, accustomed to the narrow vistas of a great city, looked out upon the landscape as upon fairy land, and, exhilarated by the atmosphere, so dry and cold and absolutely quiet, he realized a thrill of fresh life, and a joy of existence such as he had not felt since he left college.

But many matters of importance were weighing upon his mind, and even the beautiful prospect could not long hold his attention, so that it was with a start that a little later he awoke to the fact that the moon was over-clouded and that the wind was rising with a chilly coldness that seemed to pierce through all his wrappings, and to reach his very bones. A few moments later, the storm burst in its fury upon him, bringing with it driving snow and thick darkness.

He was still several miles from the town, and there was no sign of any shelter near by. In what seemed an incredibly short time the road became impeded with snow-drifts, and he was obliged to trust entirely to the horse to find the way. He felt he could thoroughly understand how a farmer, in attempting to go the few yards that lay between his house and barn during a blizzard, had been lost in the snow, and frozen to death. Strongwood was congratulating himself that he was not on foot, when a cry for help reached him.

"There's some one lost in the blizzard," he said, and reined up his horse.

The cry came again.

"Help!"

As the young man peered into the gloom he dimly discerned what he took to be a human figure, standing black against the thick darkness which enveloped it. It was very near, but in the roar of the storm the voice was scarcely audible.

"Help!"

It was a woman's voice.

Strongwood was afraid to leave the sleigh, lest the horse, already excited, should bolt.

"Madam," he shouted, "if you can come to me, I can help you."

The owner of the voice made her way, more by sound than by sight, and stood by the sleigh.

Strongwood gave her his hand, and she attempted to climb in, but her foot slipped on the wooden step, and she fell so suddenly that in a moment he lost both hold and sight of her. He was out of the sleigh in an instant, and was helping her up, when the horse gave a sudden start and galloped off. The unexpected tug pulled them both over in the snow, and the young man was dragged some yards by the reins, which, in order to have both hands free, he had slipped over his arm. When he recovered himself, he was alone in the mad, whirling storm. Horse and sleigh and young lady were out of sight. At last, however, in a momentary lull in the wind, he heard an answer to his shouts, and the two made their way to each other. The situation was desperate. But the knowledge that his companion depended upon him for help called out all his energies, and he exerted himself to the utmost. He threw his cloak over her, and supported her as well as he could. The storm made words impossible, for they needed all their strength to pull through the snow. They guided themselves by a fence at the side of the road, but whether they were going away from succour, or towards it, they had no means of knowing.

Exhausted, and all but ready to sink down in the drift, they at last saw a light, and found themselves at the door of a wayside cottage. The danger was not over, however, for it was long before the old woman within distinguished their knocking from the rattling and blows of the wind, and when finally she opened the door, she had almost to drag the wanderers into the cottage.

CHAPTER II.

BANISHMENT.

"WELL, doctor, what is your verdict?"

The speaker was Robert Strongwood. He was seated in the consulting room of a New York specialist. The May sunshine, sifting through green leaves and lace curtains, filled the room, and was more favourable to a study of Strongwood's personal appearance than the blinding snow of the blizzard in which we first met him three months before. Seen thus, he was a man of medium height, with dark hair, high forehead, deep set thoughtful eyes, and a moustache not heavy enough to hide the movements of a sensitive mouth ; in short he had an interesting face with plenty of possibilities in it either for good or evil, although its prevailing expression was somewhat worldly and cynical. He was carefully dressed, but looked weary and harassed, and awaited with ill-concealed nervousness the doctor's answer.

The famous physician paused a moment, as if to give added emphasis to his reply, and then said :

"I will be perfectly frank with you, Mr. Strongwood. I have great hopes of your recovery ; but I must tell you that such a result depends largely upon yourself. You need great care, for there is certainly commencing trouble at the top of your left lung, and the microscope has confirmed the diagnosis. You should go at once to the mountains, to some place at a moderate elevation, where you can be a large part of the time in the open air, and where you can have good food, regulated exercise, and pleasant society."

"But, doctor, it would be exceedingly awkward for me to leave the city just now. My business needs me."

"You are not able to give it your attention, and it is a matter of great importance for you to get away before the depressing heat is upon us," returned the physician, and he proceeded to name several suitable localities, and to give further directions.

It was a beautiful morning in the second week of May. Even in the great city one felt the freshness of spring-time. The public squares were in all their first beauty of leaf and flower, as yet unspoiled by the dust and glare of the summer. There was exhilaration in the air and sunshine; but it was all lost upon Robert Strongwood, as he walked down the street, and wearily mounted the steps of the Elevated Railway to take the train down town.

The physician's opinion was a great blow to him. He had not supposed that there was anything seriously wrong, and he had only consulted the celebrated Dr. Sanders at the repeated and urgent persuasion of Mr. Hansen, his partner.

As he entered his place of business, that gentleman greeted him and succeeded, though with some difficulty, in eliciting what the doctor had said.

"When do you think you'll go?" he asked.

"I think I'll stay where I am."

"In face of what you have heard this morning?"

"Yes. Doctors are not infallible any more than popes. I can take care of myself in town. I can't leave the business."

"That is what I said when I broke my thigh last winter; but I had to do it all the same."

"That was quite different."

"I know it. All the difference between having you at the helm or me."

Strongwood smiled.

"I did not mean that. The business is safe enough; but you were unable to work last winter; while, now,—I am quite able."

"Look here, Strongwood, you're a sensible man. It is better for the business for you to be away six months, or even a year, than to break down permanently."

"I am not going to break down."

"The doctor thinks you will, and I have long thought so. You should have gone to Europe with your mother and sisters."

"Thank you, I don't care for sight-seeing. It tires me."

"If you're too weak for pleasure, you're not strong enough for work," said Hansen, with a smile at the antithesis; and he continued so urgently to persuade his partner to act on the doctor's advice, and promised so faithfully to keep him well informed of the progress of the business, that finally Strongwood yielded enough to say that he would think it over.

*   *   *   *

Robert Strongwood's father had died from the effects of an accident when young Robert was only four years old; but the son retained a vivid remembrance of the affection which his father had showered upon him. All his life since he had been hungering for it; for his mother, though she did not mean to be unkind, was so absorbed in her fashionable engagements that she had neither time nor energy left to do more for Robert than to see that he was well clothed and cared for; and when he came to her with his childish interests he was oftener than not met with a rebuff. He soon learned what to expect, and withdrew very much into himself. To this day, however, when some special pleasure or difficulty made him forget, he would sometimes claim her sympathy, but only to leave her presence angry and wounded at her want of response.

Mrs. Strongwood also had had her trials. Most of her husband's income had ceased with his death, and in her efforts to keep up her former style, she was in danger of running through the property. Her financial troubles came to an end, however, by her marriage with Mr. McPherson, a wealthy New York banker, who suited her, at least in this, that he delighted in seeing his wife shine in society. Although there had been little in common between the rich man and the sensitive, thoughtful boy, the banker had treated his step-son not only justly but generously; for he had assumed all the expenses of his education and sent him to college, and afterwards established him in business, and induced Mrs. McPherson to place what remained of her late husband's property in the hands of a trustee for the benefit of her son.

Robert had made good use of his advantages, had gone through college with credit as a student, and had excelled in sailing and rowing, having been one of the crew of the winning boat in the inter-collegiate boat race of his senior year. At twenty-eight he found himself, partly as a result of his own energy, and partly by the death or the unexpected withdrawals of senior members of the firm, at the head of a substantial wholesale business in drugs.

Mr. McPherson had died about three years before this story opens, leaving his wife and two daughters—Lucy, who was nearly twenty-one, and Mary about nineteen. They were both, especially Lucy, very fond of gaiety of all sorts, and sometimes plagued Robert a good deal with the numerous engagements to which they expected him to be ready to accompany them. They were far richer than he, and Lucy now and then made unpleasant remarks as to his indebtedness to her father. Even his mother irritated him by references to how much he owed to "poor dear Mr. McPherson," till he almost wished he had been left to fight his own battles, and he had actually begun to lay by money every year in hopes of paying back what was such a source of annoyance.

With this exception his life, until that spring, had been a great success in all outward matters, and even at home things had improved. There was a growing friendship between his younger sister and himself ; and though Robert could not easily throw off his habit of reserve, nor make her the confidante of his deepest thoughts, they had arrived at a good mutual understanding, and would read and discuss together their favourite philosophical theories and authors.

The blizzard, of which I have spoken in the previous chapter, seemed to mark a turning point in Strongwood's fortunes. He had been overworked before, and the cold and exposure of that night had told heavily upon his strength. In fact, he had been longer in recovering from the immediate effects of the storm than had Miss Isabel Galway, whom he had rescued. She was as cheery and bright as usual after a day's rest, but it was a fortnight before Strongwood was fit to return to New York. Mr. Galway had had him to his own house, and had loaded him with attentions. The intimacy thus commenced had been a very pleasant one ; the teasing he had undergone in regard to Miss Galway being the only drawback. Why he did not at once fall in love with her none could say ; for, from a worldly point of view, she was an excellent match as the daughter of a wealthy man, and besides this she was a sweet, attractive girl.

Robert's health had never fully recovered, and when Mrs. McPherson decided to spend eighteen months in Europe with her daughters, Mary had urged him to go with them for the summer, but neither her mother nor Lucy very strongly backed up the proposal, and Robert was unwilling to leave the business. Then Mary offered to stay with him : but no one would hear of that, and so the house was let furnished to a distant relative of the family, with whom it was arranged that Robert should board.

Mrs. McPherson and her daughters had now been gone about ten days. Robert was beginning to feel very lonely, and his interview with Dr. Sanders had not helped matters.

"I think the doctor meant more than he said," thought he, as he sat in his room that evening. " Why can't he speak out plainly, and not torment one with hints. It's probably all up with me, just as I'm beginning to make headway too. I believe this is the worst possible world—I might as well have died outright in the blizzard. A loving God indeed ! Just as a fellow thinks he is over the hard places and success is assured, something happens to dash everything to the ground. It's worse than if there had been no hope from the first. If there be a God, what does he care about the top of my left lung, or whether it is a little weaker than the right one ?

" Well, after all, one must go under sometime. I suppose it might as well be now as forty years hence. But I should like to have had a little more of the sun and air first.—Pshaw !" he said after pause, " what am I thinking about ? My dinner must have disagreed with me. The question is, What is to be done ?"

"How blessings brighten as they take their flight. I feel it would do me good to see even a contemptuous toss of Lucy's frizzled head. To think of spending the whole summer among absolute strangers! Not even Hansen, nor any of the club. But I suppose I must."

He lit a cigarette and settled himself in an easy chair. The evening was warm, and through the open window he gazed mechanically at the houses opposite, looming up before him in the fading twilight with their monotonous walls of brown stone, roofs all of the same height, and windows exactly corresponding.

"If Mr. and Miss Galway were only not going to Alaska, I think I should invite myself to pay them a visit." Then he relapsed into thought. After smoking one or two cigarettes, he started up, and saying, "That's the very thing, and he lives among the mountains too—I'm sure it's as good as any place Sanders recommends," threw away his cigarette, closed the window and shutters, turned up the gas, and wrote as follows :—

"No. —, —th Street, New York.

"May 17th, 189—.

" Dear Charlie,

"What an age it is since we last heard from each other, and yet how we used to talk over all our plans together at college. It's too bad that we have drifted so far apart.

"To-night I want to have a talk with you, for I'm quite alone ; my mother and sisters have gone to Europe, and I, being in a quandary, have naturally remembered you, and have decided to appeal to you as I should have done in the old days. Don't be frightened, I'm not in debt, and don't need a few dollars to set me straight. But I am run down and am ordered away from the city at once. As I was thinking over the matter I remembered the hearty invitation you gave me in your last letter of forgotten date. I think it ran something like this, ' Whenever you feel inclined, etc.' This seems to give a wide margin, and on the strength of it I thought I might presume on our old acquaintance.

" Seriously, would it be perfectly convenient to you to have me come for a week or two ? I need cheering up and a rest. But I feel sure that you will be as frank with me as I am with you, and not let me come if it is not perfectly convenient.

" Hoping that fortune has smiled on you, as it has, except in the matter of health, upon me.

"I am, old fellow, yours as ever,

" ROBERT STRONGWOOD."

" P.S. Perhaps I should add that the doctor thinks my lungs are slightly affected."

" I can stay with him a week or two," he thought, " and see how the mountain air suits me, and then go on to some regular resort. I do wish the doctor would have let me go to the sea shore. The water is my element. However, I've got to submit. This place will answer as to elevation and pleasant society at any rate. Hello ! what's his address ? Strongwood racked his brain, but could not remember.

" I declare it must be nearly ten years since I wrote to him. I wonder whether he's alive. Let me see ; he went to live at Pen—, Pen—, Pen Mar ?—no—, Pendene ?—no. Well, it was in Pennsylvania anyhow, and in the mountains."

The next morning when he awoke, the name came to him. It was—Penelve.

CHAPTER III.

IN the shortest possible time Strongwood received a reply from his friend at Penelve, first by telegram and then by a letter, characterized by all the old-time heartiness, urging him to come at once, and remain as long as he could.

The fact was that Charles Bruce was himself delighted at the prospect, for he was not only sincerely attached to his old classmate, but he cherished as well a deep sense of gratitude. Just before Bruce had completed his third year at college, his father had died, and, although he left enough for his family to live upon with economy, there was not sufficient to enable his son to finish the college course. At this juncture Robert Strongwood had, of his own accord, induced Mr. McPherson to advance the needed funds. Principal and interest had long been paid, but Charles Bruce had always hoped for some special opportunity, like the present, of showing his gratitude.

Strongwood was greatly cheered by the letter, and set off as soon as he could make his arrangements. The day was very hot, as days in the latter half of May often are, and the journey was a long one, so that the sun was nearly setting when, thoroughly wearied, Strongwood stepped out on the platform at Penelve.

His first impressions of the place are perhaps best described in extracts from his letters to his sister Mary.

"My last letter will have told you of my intention of leaving New York. It was hard work to make up my mind, I can tell you, and had the doctor been less positive, I certainly should not have moved a step. I was too down in the mouth to care much for the scenery we passed through the day before yesterday, although in itself it was very fine— had I been in the mood to enjoy it.

"Charlie met me at the station—looking just the same jolly old fellow he always was ; curly brown hair, honest eyes and thick-set figure ; and for a moment his hearty hand-shake and welcome made me feel ten years younger.

"He introduced me to a Miss Grace Wildmere, a friend of his sister's, who lives near them, and who had come by the same train, and he was soon driving us both home in his light carriage.

"I left the conversation to them, for I was very tired, until I caught them using the word 'meeting-house' several times ; then I roused myself and said :

"'Why, Charlie, what have you to do with a meeting-house? Are you a Methodist ?'

"'No, a Quaker.'

"'A Quaker !' I exclaimed. 'You certainly were not one at college.'

"'No, but many things can happen in ten years.'

"'I thought nobody ever joined Quakers now-a-days,' I remarked, hardly knowing how to take the news.

"'I suppose you consider Quakers a case of *Nascitur non fit*, like poets,' remarked Miss Wildmere.

"I saw she was disposed to chaff me, and I made matters worse by asking Charlie why he had not told me of the change.

"'It is such an old story,' he replied, 'that it never occurred to me. I hope it would not have discouraged you from coming.'

"This question rather floored me. I could not say 'Yes,' and not caring to say 'No,' I dodged, and said that I could not imagine him a strait-laced Quaker.

"'Do I look strait-laced?' said he, turning about in his seat, and looking at me with such laughing eyes, that I felt rather disconcerted, and added:

"'No, you don't. I should never have taken you for a Quaker. I thought all Quakers wore broad-brimmed hats, and said "thee."'

"'Why Rob,' he returned, 'You're behind the times,' and he proceeded to explain that those peculiarities had been practically discarded, though some still wore the dress from habit, and the 'thee' and 'thou' were retained among themselves as a matter of friendliness, with something of the same feeling as the Germans use 'Du.'

"'I only wish we used it grammatically,' he continued. 'I am sure it would enrich the language.'

"'Why don't you,' I asked.

"'It does not sound natural,' said Charlie, 'But here we are at home.'

"We had driven through the town and now, about a quarter of a mile beyond it, we turned into very attractive, but not extensive grounds, in which stood a substantial stone house with a wide piazza around two sides of it.

"On the lawn some ladies were playing croquet. One of the younger ones, Miss Bruce, as I afterwards learned, on seeing us, immediately dropped her mallet and ran to the porch to welcome us as we drove up. Another young lady, who proved to be a cousin to the Miss Wildmere who was with us, followed, more slowly, while the third player, an old lady in the Quaker dress, went on playing, only stopping to call out, 'So thee's come back, Charlie, I'm glad thee's brought thy friend. I'll come in a moment.'

"Having finished her turn by going through several hoops and croquetting one or two balls, she, too, came up, her flushed face wreathed in smiles, and her cap strings flying loose, and welcomed me most cordially.

"'I suppose thou wilt think that an old woman like me should not get so excited over croquet, but thou sees I was behind-hand in the game and wanted to catch up. These girls are very good to play an unpopular game for my sake.'

"The 'girls' asserted that they enjoyed it themselves. As the three stood there they formed a striking group. I think they would have attracted notice in any circle, if only by the indefinable something—I suppose it was the Quaker in them—that made them with all their refinement so different from the people one generally meets in society. But I was beginning to wonder whether there was an ideal Quaker in the family, when I suddenly saw one before me in the person of Charlie's mother-in-law, Mrs. Leslie ; tall, straight, neatly dressed in the traditional costume, with the thin, calm face of an ascetic, lighted up with a smile of friendly cordiality. She was as different as possible from Mrs. Compton, Charlie's aunt, the old lady who was playing croquet, who is short and stout and wears her garb as if it were not a part of her. She is evidently a character.

"I soon found out that Mrs. Bruce has been seriously ill, and is not yet downstairs, and I was beginning to feel that my visit was inopportune, when Charlie explained that all danger was over, and that my presence was no inconvenience. There are three children, nice, bright little things, but I have not seen much of them yet.

"Charlie took me at once to my room and insisted upon my having tea upstairs, which in due time he brought up himself. It was exceedingly good. Among other things there were fresh strawberries and soft shell crabs. When I expressed surprise at seeing them, especially the latter, he replied :

" 'Oh, a friend of ours purchased them in the Baltimore market this morning.'

"So you see what pains they had taken for me, for Baltimore must be nearly two hundred and fifty miles away.

But, oh Mary, to think of being among the Quakers, when I came in hopes of lively society. I do feel blue in spite of a day's rest and the lovely panorama of mountain and valley that lies before me as I sit by my window. If I were only well I should not mind it. It would be an interesting study. But I am not well. You will say, 'Why not read your favourite books?' To tell the truth I have no heart to do it. What's the good? My only refuge is in stoicism, and I shall be fortunate if it does not end in cynicism, which, if of a lower order is certainly more entertaining, at least to oneself."

A few days later he wrote :

" Uplands,
"Penelve, Pa.,
"May 28th, 189—.

" My Dear Mary,

"It was pleasant to hear of your smooth voyage and safe arrival. I almost feel as if I too were in a foreign country.

I wonder if I am as much of a curosity to the people here as
they are to me. I make some *faux pas* every day, and we often
find that we are talking at cross-purposes, for they and I use
the same words with such different meanings. However,
they understand me better than I do them, for they are well
read, while I am quite ignorant of their special vocabulary.
Thus, 'having silence,' means silent grace before meals, and
they call family prayers 'reading.' Sunday is 'First-day,' and
all the other days have different names from ours. By the
way, two of my mistakes have to do with these very things.
I had noticed that they said no 'grace,' and so the next meal
I began to talk the moment we were seated. It was really
very inattentive of me, for they bow their heads devotionally,
but I had been pre-occupied and had not raised my eyes.
However, I spoke, and was much mystified at the evident
surprise on every one's face. Charlie immediately apologized
for not having told me before, and explained their custom.

"'What is your objection to words?' I asked.

"'None whatever,' said Charlie, 'if they are spontaneous,
but it is so easy to fall into phrases without life.'

"I wondered what he would think of many of us city
folks, who say grace very much as we unfold our napkins.

"'Still,' I replied, 'it's a good form, and it is certainly
very pretty to hear children repeating "grace" with their
little voices.'

"'Very pretty,' said Mrs. Leslie. 'It pleases the parents
and entertains the guests, if that is the object.'

"I asked if it were not a pity to make everything so serious.
But I have since found that such a remark always rouses them
to show why the particular matter under consideration is
really serious, and in this instance they showed how the

silence allows each one to direct his thoughts as he feels best, and Charlie quoted some place, from Acts I think it was, to show that the words spoken by Christ at the Last Supper were at first understood as referring to the daily meals. You know I don't take much stock in such things, so my attention wandered, but I wished afterwards that it hadn't, for I might have saved myself from the mistake I made this morning when I was down to breakfast for the first time.

"When the meal was over they had their 'reading.' I supposed it was the same as prayers, and, wishing to conform to custom, as soon as Charlie had closed the Bible, down I knelt. Almost immediately, I saw out of the corner of my eye that no one else was kneeling, so I leave you to imagine how quickly I resumed my seat. No one except seven-year-old Bertie in the least changed countenance, and he did his best to restrain himself. I was exceedingly mortified, especially as I noticed, when Charlie prayed a few moments later, that they all bowed their heads just as they had done when I knelt. They had actually thought that I was about to pray. Charlie confessed as much when I taxed him with it afterwards, but said it made no difference. They all understood it was a mistake. He went on to explain that they by no means always have prayer, nor do they have any arrangement as to who should pray, for they lay great stress on reality, and want nothing said for the sake of saying it, and they feel it very important to emphasize this with the children.

"Do you know, Mary, that these people really think God cares about everything in their lives. I asked Charlie if this was a peculiarity of the Quakers, and he almost laughed in my face, and asked me where I had been brought up. Of course, I knew it was a Christian doctrine, but really I have never come into close contact with people who actually believed it. Perhaps the Galways did, but the terrible danger of that blizzard would have roused the least faith, so that their ascribing our escape to Providence did not surprise me. It seems to me preposterous. We are in the hands of a blind set of laws which are utterly remorseless. I confess this view is not so pleasant to me now that the laws are dragging me down, as it was when they were helping me on. Still, it's a fact, nevertheless, and, this morning, if I had felt more at home, I should have expostulated with Miss Bruce for telling one of the children that God would help him to bear his toothache."

CHAPTER IV.

"ROB," said Bruce, at breakfast one morning a few days later, "I hear that Professor Swift has come to Penelve for the summer. You know, he is one of the great authorities on lung troubles. Would it not be a good thing for you to see him?"

Strongwood agreed, little thinking how much his visit to Penelve would be prolonged in consequence; for the great man first wished to keep him under observation, and finally told Bruce that his friend could not do better than stay where he was for the summer. This did not suit Strongwood's ideas, though no polite excuse for leaving occurred to him; neither did it quite fall in with the wishes of the rest of the family; but Charlie so seldom really set his mind on anything of this kind, and was so evidently enjoying the renewal of his old college friendship, that they made no objection.

Bruce accompanied Strongwood on his first visit to the doctor, and as they were going, one of those apparently trivial events happened which have an important bearing on the future. Just before they reached the hotel where Dr. Swift was staying they turned a corner and almost ran against a young man.

"Why, Mr. Hardynge," said Strongwood, "what brings you to Penelve?"

"Oh, I'm travelling for a Philadelphia firm;—and you?"

"I am here recruiting for a few weeks."

"Recovering from the effects of the blizzard, I suppose?"

There was something unpleasant in Hardynge's tone. Besides, how came he to know anything about the blizzard?

However, Strongwood smiled, said he must be off to an appointment, and, with a formal bow, rejoined Bruce, who was waiting a yard or two farther on, and they entered the hotel together.

Ralph Hardynge returned the bow, stood a moment or two as if uncertain which way he should go, and then slowly followed Strongwood into the hotel. He learned from the clerk who Bruce was, and with this information was able without attracting notice to find out all about the family before evening.

The motive which inspired his curiosity was a sinister one. He wished to injure Strongwood, because, as he supposed, Strongwood six years before had done him irreparable harm, just as his fortunes seemed to be most promising. Instead of the success that had been almost assured, ruin had suddenly stared him in the face, and his whole life had been clouded. Neither time nor absence had softened his hatred, and now that he had again met his enemy, the old passion leaped up. His slight figure, fashionable attire, and cigarette, his blue eyes, light hair and almost ennuyéd expression seemed to present nothing dangerous ; and yet a good judge of character might have detected below the smooth exterior a great power for underhand scheming. But in the nineteenth century men do not often pursue revenge for its own sake, at least, if there is any risk to be run. Hardynge, of course, had as yet no plan ; but that day he learned enough of Strongwood's present surroundings, and of Miss Bruce, to

"CROQUET JUST ABOUT GIVES ME THE EXERCISE I AM FIT FOR, AND I REALLY ENJOY OLD MRS. COMPTON'S ENTHUSIASM IN THE GAME."

suggest an idea to him, from which he might work out a scheme, which whilst injuring Strongwood should at the same time put money into his own pocket.

In the meantime Strongwood had almost forgotten the meeting, and was writing to his sister. Could Hardynge have looked over his shoulder, he might have concluded that he had not yet found his clue.

" I am really improving," the letter ran, " and Professor Swift and Charlie together have persuaded me to stay on here for the present. Nothing could exceed the kindness of every one, and it is rendered so pleasantly as to make me feel perfectly at ease. The only limitation put on me is that Charlie asked me, with many apologies, not to smoke in the house when the weather was fit for me to be out. I know that it would be more polite for me to stop altogether, but really I cannot. But I do smoke less, partly by the doctor's advice. I spend most of the mornings on the shady side of the porch, or in a summer house in the garden. After dinner I rest, and later on I drive with Charlie, or play croquet. I have not till now been strong enough for lawn-tennis even, and croquet just about gives me the exercise I am fit for, and I really enjoy old Mrs. Compton's enthusiasm in the game (I had almost called her ' Aunt Mary,' as every one here does—relation or not). I am generally her partner, and very often either Miss Grace or Miss Amy Wildmere drops in and takes the other side with Miss Bruce, or Miss Bruce takes two balls. You ought to see Mrs. Compton waving her mallet in the air in triumph when we win. She is the greatest combination of strong good sense and real childlikeness (I don't mean childishness) that I have ever seen, and she is beginning to take a very motherly interest in me.

"But I believe I have never told you about the three young ladies. They are all alike in this, that they all dress simply, and all have that indefinable Quaker air about them that I first noticed. With a slight exception in regard to Miss Amy W., they seem perfectly natural in their manner, and yet are by no means merely country cousins; but would be able to hold their own anywhere. Miss Grace is tall and dark, with a square face and decided features. She is very pleasant and intensely practical, with a tendency (she would, I suppose, say 'temptation') to make caustic remarks. Miss Amy is blonde and *petite*, and a little inclined to be sentimental. Miss Bruce (whom they call 'Bessie') is the opposite of this. She is rather tall, with an abundance of rich brown hair arranged very simply. She has an oval face and bright eyes which are constantly changing in expression. If it were not for her nose and mouth, which are too large, she might be beautiful, for her complexion is clear, and her teeth perfect. Of course, as she lives here, I see more of her than of the others. She rather tires me, for she is always throwing so much energy into everything that she does.

"I could imagine Miss Amy quite ready for a flirtation, but Miss Bruce never—Diana would be more susceptible than she. Her treatment of me is perfect—too perfect. I am her brother's friend, here for his health, and she treats me accordingly,—perfectly frank, but beyond simple kindliness, perfectly indifferent. She is ready with repartee and amusing anecdotes, in which, generally, more of a moral is meant than meets the ear. She is at her best with the children, and I must say, in spite of her many engagements, she always seems to have leisure for everybody.

"The Bruces are well up in modern literature and on

the questions of the day, and we have many discussions. I
will give them credit for not continually forcing their
Quakerism on me, and my fears that they would try to
proselytize me have proved groundless; but their religion
crops out at most unexpected times, and their first thought in
regard to any new question is to compare it with the teaching
of the New Testament. One day I remarked that it must be
a very great effort to bring everything to such a high test,
and to have so many scruples, and Miss Bessie answered, ' It
is no effort to wish for fresh air, or to avoid pricking one's
fingers with thorns, or to wish the same for others.' I really
believe this is the way they look at it, and I don't understand
it, but I must acknowledge that they at least try to live up to
their creed. What's more, they seem to enjoy it. How they
can is more than I can fathom. Speaking of enjoyment, I
sometimes feel that I shall never really enjoy anything again.
To be sure I am improving, and the doctor professes to have
great hopes of my recovery, but I believe that it is only
temporary, and he won't *promise* anything; of course he
won't. He knows too much.

"This is a lovely country. But what are the beauties of
nature to a hopeless man? Do you remember those lines
we came across and which you liked, and I did not?—

> ' No music of birds or of ocean
> Finds echo in musicless hearts,
> The glory of sunrise is dreary,
>   When gladness departs—
>
> Then man must himself be creator;
> All nature his coming awaits;
> She gives him the outlines and colours;
>   He, glory creates.'

I agree with them now. Hope is gone—the creative

touch is gone. So farewell for the present. I must go for a game of lawn-tennis. It is the first time I have tried it."

The cheerfulness of consumptives is more proverbial than real, for it is not infrequently assumed, and when real often alternates with times of deep depression. Robert Strongwood was an active man, and enforced idleness was no ordinary trial, especially as he had little faith in its doing him any permanent good. In addition to this, he was homesick not for what he had lost, but for what he had never had ; for he now saw a picture of home-life that made him feel how barren his own had been. Even his intimacy with his sister seemed superficial compared with that which he saw between Bruce and his sister Bessie. It was never obtruded, but no one could be long an inmate of the house without discovering it. The relations between the younger and older members of the family also were those of simple, spontaneous affection. Each took it for granted that the others would be interested in his interests, and he was never disappointed. I do not mean to say that the family machinery never creaked, or caught, for it sometimes did. It was hardly possible that such decided characters should live together without occasional friction. Yet although Strongwood noticed this, it did not much mar the general impression of a household where love and sympathy ruled. He sometimes thought bitterly to himself that Mrs. Compton showed more real sympathy with him than his own mother had ever done. At the same time he could hardly blame Mrs. McPherson for not showing more in the present instance, for in his first letters he had spoken lightly of his illness, and had given the impression of being simply run down and suffering from a severe attack of the blues.

CHAPTER V.

A QUAKER MEETING.

"DID you have a good meeting this morning, Charles?" asked Lydia Leslie, on the following Sunday evening after tea, as they sat all together in the library.

"Yes, mother," and there was a good attendance both of members and strangers."

"Who spoke?"

Now it happened that both Charles and his sister had done so, and Bessie felt as if she did not care to have the matter discussed before a stranger, so utterly ignorant of Friends' ways as Strongwood was ; so she answered that they could enter into particulars another time, and Mrs. Compton, whom we shall hereafter speak of as "Aunt Mary," seeing that she wished the subject changed, said :

"What place of worship, Robert Strongwood, dost thou attend in New York?"

"Wherever there happens to be the best music."

As he said this he glanced towards Miss Bruce, for, notwithstanding his stated annoyance at her intensity of manner, he generally looked at her when he made a startling remark, and noticing that she looked rather astonished, he quickly added :

"Did I shock you, Miss Bruce ? What else should I go to church for ? "

"I think each one must answer that question for himself," replied Bessie.

"Oh, I forgot, you Friends don't believe in music in worship, do you? You wait till the Spirit moves you. By the way, does the Spirit ever move you to speak, Miss Bruce?"

The question was put in the airy way of one who wishes to keep up an entertaining conversation. Bessie knew this, and that he expected her to say "No." To have the subject come up in this way was very trying. She spoke very quietly, but with a blush that did not escape Strongwood's notice.

"I sometimes feel it right to speak."

It was now Strongwood's turn to be disconcerted. He hardly knew what to say, and replied drily:

"Indeed, how interesting."

An awkward pause followed, which Bruce put an end to by looking at his watch.

"It's nearly time for us to be going, Bessie. Shall we go to the mission meeting, or to the regular meeting?"

"I think I prefer our own to-night," Bessie replied as she rose to get ready.

Strongwood did not like the way the conversation had ended, and the next morning, seeing Miss Bruce in the garden gathering flowers, he went to her and said:

"Miss Bruce, I really must apologize for being so thoughtless last evening. I forgot how seriously you regard these things."

"That's all right, Mr. Strongwood," returned Bessie with a smile, "I quite understand. Our ways must seem very curious to you."

"Yes, to tell the truth, they do. Of course, I'm used to hearing people say that the Spirit inspired the Apostles, but it is strange to find any one thinking that it does so now."

"We believe," said Bessie, "that He does so as truly now as ever He did in the past."

"Then one would hardly expect that you would pay so much attention to such an antiquated book as the Bible."

"We pay attention to it because it is not antiquated. Every fresh insight into our duties or privileges finds its suggestion and proof in the Bible. It is the newest book in the world. It is the book of progress, the book of the future."

As she spoke, Strongwood was struck with the deep earnestness of her eyes. The colour came into her cheeks, and the sunlight falling through the leaves lightly touched her wavy hair and white dress. Altogether she made a very charming picture, which was all the more attractive from her total unconsciousness of the fact.

" But how can you prove," he continued, " that the Holy Spirit has ever spoken to men at all, or in fact that there is any such thing as the Holy Spirit ? "

He expected her to be shocked, but was disappointed. She simply answered :

" By experience."

" But suppose I have none ? "

" Excuse me, you have."

" How ? " replied Strongwood, beginning to be interested.

" Have you never felt lonely, and longed for something you did not know what ? never striven after higher ideals ? never been distressed at failing to reach them ? never wished to help others ? never ——" She paused, afraid that she had said too much.

The words touched him more deeply than she knew, but he was too proud to show how he felt, and said with an assumption of carelessness :

"Suppose for argument's sake that I have felt in the way you describe, how do I know they are not simply natural feelings?"

"In a sense they are natural feelings; but they are aroused in you because your true nature can be satisfied with nothing short of God, and because His Spirit is arousing you to long for Him."

"How am I to know that?"

"By the fact that others who have been in the same contion, have found, as they yielded to this call and came to God, that He satisfied them with the life and power they needed."

Strongwood suppressed an incredulous laugh.

"How am I to know where God is, or how to come to Him? Every one has a different recipe for the Unknowable."

Bessie ignored the scoff, and replied simply :

"You will find what God is, and what He thinks about you, in Jesus Christ. If you are willing for it, He will show you His power in your own heart."

Strongwood so far forgot himself as to answer :

"So that is your recipe, is it?"

Before Bessie had time to reply, the gardener came up with the letters, and she hastened off to distribute them.

Strongwood was interested in spite of himself, for the line Bessie took was not just what he had been accustomed to hear.

"Charlie," said he, as they drove together that afternoon, "How came you and your sister to join the Quakers?"

"I hope," said Bruce in reply, "that the real reason was deeper than the apparent, but that was very simple. My father was brought up a Friend, but left the Society after his marriage. Aunt Mary here, his sister, always remained a

Quaker, and when I graduated, her husband offered me a place in his business. Their own children had died young and I lived with them as their son, and naturally attended meeting with them. After mother died, Bessie made her home with us, and we both became Friends."

"You Friends hold a great many peculiar notions, don't you ?"

" We certainly differ on a number of points from other Christians."

" Don't you think it a little ' cheeky,' as we used to say at College, for such a small body ? "

" Why ? Do *you* swallow everything tradition teaches ?"

Strongwood laughed. " No, indeed. But I'm a free lance. You Quakers are not."

" We desire to be free to accept truth. As Whittier says :

' The windows of my soul I throw
Wide open to the sun.' "

" I grant," he continued, " that Friends have sometimes been a little conceited, at least some of them, but I believe that now we are more inclined to be ashamed of not living up to our ideals."

Strongwood's fear of being made a subject for proselytizing had given place to a little sense of pique at the entire absence of any effort of the kind. He thought that they did not consider him large enough game for them. They never even invited him to meeting, and had contented themselves with telling him that he would be welcome if ever he inclined to go, or that they would introduce him to some church people if he wished to attend church.

He made up his mind to go to meeting—if possible without their knowing it ; for his talk with Bessie had aroused his curiosity, and, as he had learned that Bruce and Mrs. Compton were " ministers," he thought he should be more likely to get a fair specimen of the usual service if he attended without their knowing it.

How he succeeded, the following portion of a letter to his sister, written immediately on his return from meeting, will show. When he came to read it over the next day, however, he decided, for reasons that will be sufficiently obvious, not to send it.

It was as follows :

" Uplands,

" Penelve. June 20th, 189—.

" My dear Mary,

" Yours of the 8th inst. came duly to hand. I am glad you are having such a good time, and have fallen in with such pleasant people. What a contrast your summer is to mine ! However, I have some new experiences even in this little corner of the world. Attending Quaker meeting this morning was one of them.

" I wanted to attend it unknown to my hosts, and so did not start till some time after the family had departed, supposing that, of course, I should as usual stay at home. I was in fact almost too late, for the congregation had gone in and the doors were shut. But just as I was turning away, three or four young men came up, and I went in with them. I found myself in a company of sixty or seventy persons. Except for a few peculiar bonnets near the front of the meeting, there was nothing distinctive in the assembly : some of the ladies were even fashionably dressed ; but, on the whole, there was a general air of simplicity. The men and women were not strictly separated from each other, but most of the men sat on my side of the aisle. On a platform in front of the congregation was a row of men and women. Among the men I noticed Charlie, who looked younger than the rest. Mrs. Compton occupied a seat towards the centre. I was glad I was too far back in the room for Charlie, who is rather near-sighted, to recognize who I was ; and when I was seated, Mrs. Compton was hidden by the man in front of me. There was no pulpit or desk, but a railing ran along the front of the platform. The rest of the room was neatly carpeted, and seated with benches and a few chairs.

" My first feeling after completing my survey was one of amusement. It seemed so queer for all these people to be sitting there doing nothing. Then I remembered that Charlie had told me, that in the silence they 'waited on the Lord,' whatever that might mean. He might as well have spoken in Choctaw.

" Just then, a working man near me arose, and said, ' Jesus said, " Where two or three are gathered together in My name, there am I in the midst of them." Friends, this is not a promise but a fact. If we are truly gathered in His name, He's here. No mistake about that. He is here to bless us, friends, each one of us, and to show us ourselves and Himself.'

" Then he sat down, so suddenly that I almost jumped. I was still mystified, for though the text was familiar, the application was unintelligible to me. But it made me realize that to these people the silence was not just an empty form, and I remembered another remark of Charlie's, about our being shown our ' true condition.' I wondered what my true condition was, and, as I thought about my life, I was not as satisfied with it as I wished to be. It seemed so small and selfish, and little misdeeds, and some grave ones came trooping through my memory, till I felt exceedingly uncomfortable.

"Presently I noticed the people near me were bowing their heads. I bowed also, and I heard a voice, which I recognized as Miss Bruce's, although it was quite different from her usual one. I never listened to such a prayer. Had God been present in bodily form, words and tone could not have expressed a greater sense of His presence, or of her expectation of a gracious hearing. Earnest as it was, it was also calm. There were no protestations of belief, but a taking for granted that God was true. As she prayed the hush over the congregation became deeper. Of what she said, I remember only the last sentences :

"'And now, Lord, bless that heart, which is lonely, and longing for home and rest, and does not know that Thou who art both our father and mother, art the true home for us all. Draw him to Thyself, that seeing his sin he may forsake it, and turn to Thee as a little child for forgiveness and new life, through Jesus Christ.'

"Mary, I have been restless and homesick, and these words made me wonder whether, after all, my homesickness could be that I was longing for God. Was He really so close to me as these people seemed to believe ? I could not answer the question then. I cannot now. I cannot accept their theories ; but I do see that they afford a strength and a rest I know nothing about.

"The silence that followed the prayer was so deep as to be almost oppressive, and I was glad when the next speaker arose and said : 'Behold the Lamb of God which taketh away the sins of the world.' Nothing in his remarks impressed me, but his manner did. He spoke with the same

air of absolute certainty, without any pride, or self assertion,
but with the certainty which comes to a man who feels that
he has once seen, and still sees.

"After him Charlie preached. I was much interested in
noticing the striking improvement in his manner over what it
used to be in our society debates at College. He made no
effort at display, and although in his earnestness his voice was
louder than was pleasant, and his gestures, when he made
any, were forcible rather than elegant, there was a serious-
ness of manner, and a dignity which made one feel that he
himself was impressed with his subject, and felt that he was
speaking from the divine impulse. Naturally I listened with
the closest attention.

" He spoke of Jesus Christ, and said that there must be
much in God which man can never understand ; but that it
is possible to understand Him to a satisfying extent, as His
Spirit within us illuminates our hearts to understand His
revelations. As character is higher than anything else, so the
highest revelation of God comes to us through this channel.
We can fully learn the character of God as it affects us, only
through a perfect human character. This we have in Christ
Jesus of Nazareth. There we see righteousness, power,
tenderness, love, a heart that sympathizes with us in our joys
and sorrows, and that would save us from our sins; a heart
that yearns over us. The death of Christ was an event that
outwardly is not to be repeated. But that one event, since
God is unchangeable, reveals for all time God's unending
sorrow over sinners, and how He continually suffers with
them and for them. His resurrection reveals and proclaims
to all men the victory of life over death, the victory of love
over sin, of light over darkness. God's attitude towards man

has always been such as has been unveiled to us in Christ. But it is only through Him that we know it, and learn how His undying wrath against sin is but one aspect of His undying love for each sinner. There is that in God which is akin to man, and that in man which responds to God. 'Oh friends,' he said, ' we can each know God for ourselves. He works for all men by His Spirit, however sunk in ignorance they may be. But to us has come the light that shines through our crucified Lord. Let us receive it and submit ourselves to Him. He will take us as we are, will purify us, and comfort us and give us His own life, and enable us to begin to live in fellowship with Him, and to grow into His own likeness. He is His own best evidence.'

"He spoke about twenty-five minutes, and I have, of course, only given the merest outline of what he said. When he sat down, another deep silence followed, which was broken by a young man singing—

> ' My Jesus as thou wilt,
> Oh, may my will be Thine.
> Into Thy hand of love
> I would my all resign.'

" He sang quite alone in an untrained but very sweet voice, and with much feeling. Some evidently did not like it, but I think most were impressed. Soon after, the two who sat in the middle of the platform shook hands, and the congregation dispersed.

" I felt that in the hour I had been in the meeting I had lived a long time, and got an insight into things I had never dreamed of before.

" In the vestibule I encountered Miss Bruce and was pleased to note her evident surprise at seeing me ; for I wanted to be sure that the words of her prayer had not been intentionally fitted to suit my case. However, she recovered herself quickly, and introduced me to several of the Friends whom I had not yet seen. It appears to be the custom among them to stand about and converse with one another after the meeting is over, and so it was quite a little while before we got off.

"I walked home with Miss Bruce and ——"

Here the dinner bell rang, and Strongwood put his letter aside, and, as I have said, never finished or sent it. He could not let any eye see such a revelation of his inward feelings; but he had really shown more yet to Bessie on their walk from meeting.

As soon as they were well out of earshot of the rest he had said :

"Miss Bruce, I understand now that when you speak of the presence of God you mean something which is very real to you."

"Of course. Is not that the case with all Christians ?"

"Perhaps. But I never met any who seemed to have such a realization of it. If one could only believe it, it would certainly make a difference in one's life."

"It does, and such a difference. It is the joy of life."

"I believe it is to you."

"I wish you knew it as well."

"Miss Bruce," he said, "when you used those closing words this morning, you did not know I was present, did you ?"

"No, not in the least. Yet, perhaps I ought to tell you that the words had not passed my lips, before I felt a very strong desire that they might be answered for you, wherever you might be."

"I'm sure I need it," Strongwood answered almost involuntarily.

"Then won't thee let it be answered in thy case?"

That little word "thee" thrilled him. He saw that she used it unconsciously; but this very fact showed how in her earnestness she had for the moment ceased to regard him as a stranger, and was speaking freely.

"How is it possible?" he asked.

"Cannot thee understand that the Lord Jesus wants thee? Can thee not submit to His rule, and in thy helplessness trust Him to forgive thee and to give thee new desires to follow and obey Him?"

"It would mean a pretty thorough change in me to do that."

"Of course it would. It means a turning from all that is against His will to a life of obedience and self-sacrifice as a child of God."

"And to be a Quaker?" he added half smiling; but was sorry the instant he had said it. But she was too engrossed with her subject to notice, and replied seriously:

"No, not unless you should be led to be one."

"But don't you think you are asking a good deal of me, who do not even theoretically accept Christianity as true?"

"Your mind doubts, but your heart accepts it, and cries out for Christ. I will not press you," she continued, "nor do I make any further request than this: When you are alone with God, don't refuse what you then realize to be His call."

Strongwood was silent, and nothing further was said till they reached home.

CHAPTER VI.

AFTER Bessie had left Strongwood to go to her own room she thought of so many helpful things she might have said to him, that she was almost discouraged, but on the whole she concluded not to attempt to re-open the conversation, but to leave it as it was. Had she but known it, she had taken the very wisest course in not saying more than she did, for Strongwood was not ready for persuasion. He began to laugh off the impression he had received before the day was over. But he did not tear up his letter, and that looked as though he were at least willing to keep a record of what he had felt.

The hour at meeting enabled him to understand the attitude of the family better; for while the beauty of the home life at Uplands more and more impressed him, he had not fully seen what the essential difference between him and the Bruces was. The strong purpose that controlled them was accepted among them as a matter of course, and seldom spoken of unless occasion demanded. Even then, though he was able to describe it, as we have seen, he did not really understand it. But now he began to see that the difference between them and himself went far deeper than questions of custom and policy, or even than the acceptance or denial of the hypothesis of a personal God. The difference was intrinsic, and was as real when they appeared to agree with him as when they differed ; for though sometimes on secondary questions they reached the same conclusion, it was always for different reasons.

To him God had been an abstraction, chiefly useful for purposes of discussion ; to them God was a living reality, who had manifested Himself in Jesus Christ, their Saviour—who now really lived within them and gave them His life and power. This belief of theirs Strongwood rejected as anthropomorphic ; but he ceased to sneer at it ; for their lives, in spite of occasional failures, gave too clear evidence that their under-lying purpose was to know God and to be obedient to Him in everything.

Their manner towards him also disarmed him. They were always ready, when asked, to explain their convictions and to give their reason, but they did not press their views on him, and they always put the best interpretation upon what he said. As a result of this he more and more dropped his cynical manner, and became natural and unrestrained.

Bessie would have been greatly astonished if she had known that she had had anything to do with this change, for she saw comparatively little of him, and was so taken up with her many engagements and duties, that it never occurred to her to think what opinion he might be forming of her. She neither sought or shunned him, but was always glad to help or entertain him, as she was every one.

Strongwood noticed this indifference and was rather piqued by it. But, because it was real and not feigned, it kept her free from self-consciousness, so that he had an opportunity of observing her true character. Now attractive people are never so attractive as when they make no effort to be so, but are just their own delightful selves. This was the case with Bessie, and Strongwood soon modified the rather unfavourable opinion which we have seen expressed in his letter.

He was not in love with her. Of this he was quite sure ; for, he had begun to realize her attractiveness too clearly not to question himself closely about the matter. The answer was negative. But he had spoken to her of the inmost feelings of his heart in a way he had never spoken to any one else ; and she had understood, and had answered his thought rather than his word. Still the fact remained that she was a Quaker, and he a man of the world. It would never do at all. Nevertheless he enjoyed being with her as far as circumstances allowed.

This, however, just now was even less than usual, for Bessie was very fully occupied. In addition to household duties, which during Mrs. Bruce's illness and convalescence were heavier than usual, and her regular engagements in various forms of mission work, she was one of the committee to make arrangements for the approaching Bible school picnic.

After many consultations as to where the picnic should be held, the strong wish of some of the younger people prevailed, and a small, level plateau on a mountain side about fifteen miles from Penelve was selected. Except for the trouble of reaching it, it seemed an ideal picnic ground ; for it was a delightful spot in itself, with a cool spring of water, and sufficient shade, and commanded a splendid view of the fertile plain and of the mountains beyond.

Hearing it so much talked about, Strongwood became interested in the project, and finally asked if the picnic was open to the public.

"Not to the general public, certainly," Bruce answered.

"Might I for instance be allowed to attend?"

"As far as the school is concerned, yes. But on your own account I should advise you not to go."

"I hope Robert will understand," Mrs. Compton put in, "that he will be entirely welcome. It is always understood that guests who are visiting our members are specially invited."

"Then I shall certainly go. I never refuse a good invitation."

"But Rob," said Bruce, "it means a thirty miles drive, and a good deal of exertion beside. It might set you back."

"Well, Charlie, if that's the only objection I'll ask Dr. Swift."

Dr. Swift, seeing that Strongwood very much wished to go, and not knowing how bad the roads were, or what such a picnic involved, consented, on condition that he should not make an early start. This was easily arranged, and Strongwood felt highly elated over the doctor's favourable opinion, which he considered indicated a prospect of speedy return to health. In fact he was already greatly improved.

As he was to be the guest of the school, he thought that it would be no more than polite to make the acquaintance of his host before enjoying the hospitality. Accordingly the following Sunday he attended the Bible school, which was held before meeting, and which gathered in a smaller room of the meeting-house. He found it largely composed of members of the meeting, and not unlike an ordinary Sunday school, except that there was no singing or formal prayer. He attended one of the Bible classes, and afterwards remained to the meeting which followed.

The impression created on this occasion was very different from that of the week before.

"I say, Charlie," Strongwood asked rather abruptly as they walked home, "wherever did that old curiosity come from?"

"That is Ephraim Breener, a minister from another Yearly Meeting."

"What's he doing here?"

"He is on a religious visit to Friends."

"How can you allow such preaching? Last week I almost wondered why every one was not a Friend. This week I'm almost surprised that any one is. Why that man preached an hour, if he preached a minute, and I defy anybody to give a rational account of what he said. The last important word in each sentence started him on a fresh point in the next, and he raised and lowered his voice to such an extent that at one moment he was splitting your ears, and the next he was speaking so low it was difficult to catch what he was saying. But he made one remark that I'm sure was perfectly true."

"What was that?"

"When he assured us he had not brought his sermon to meeting with him, and that when he had begun to speak he did not know what he was going to say. But I almost laughed when he bellowed out in stentorian tones, ' I have been made willing to lift up my feeble voice.' If he could have been rung down in ten minutes it would be as good as a farce."

"Come now, Rob, that's enough. The sermon was, I imagine, a greater trial to me than it was to you. But it was not a farce. Could you not see, that, mistaken as the man was, he was yet in earnest?"

Strongwood recognized the force of this, and said, "Excuse me, Charlie, I did go too far. The old man was in earnest, and some of his references to his own experience did impress me as both genuine and touching."

"That's just it," Bruce answered. "Sometimes when he speaks briefly and quietly I have known him to be most helpful. I believe that he has, as we say, a real gift, but he gets carried out of himself. I have been at his home, and there he is very useful. Every one respects him, and the neighbours come to him to have their disputes settled."

"I wish he'd stay there then, and not come here giving us headaches. I'll cheerfully contribute towards sending him back."

"He's a product," said Bruce, "of an extreme school among us, who believe in following nothing but the impression of the moment, and who forget that the whole man is to be animated by the Spirit of God."

"Have you many such?"

"Far fewer than when I joined Friends ten years ago."

"I should think you Quakers would often be troubled by people speaking who have no business to. What's to hinder me, for instance, from preaching?"

"Have you felt inclined to?"

"No."

"Do you think it would be easy?"

"Well, I've often spoken at club meetings."

"Then you think this would be the same thing?"

"No, come to think of it, it would be a profession of religion, and then, I imagine it must be pretty hard to break through the silence when no one expects you to speak."

"Exactly; there is something that restrains people.

They know that when a person speaks in meeting it is on the understanding that he believes God has given him a message to deliver then and there.   Still we do have trouble sometimes, especially from strangers.   But that is the price we pay for our liberty, and, though it is sometimes a trial, as to-day, the liberty is so precious that I feel it is worth while."

"Have you no means of restraining people ? "

"Yes, we have elders, a kind of standing committee on the ministry.   They are often a great help."

"I'd like to be an elder for one day, and I'm sure I'd be a help, I'd say : 'Friend Ephraim——' "

"Now, Rob, do be serious."

"Well, I will, and, seriously, I think that your Aunt Mary's prayer at the end of the meeting just hit the nail on the head."

Bruce smiled ; his friend was certainly not up in Quaker phraseology.

When they reached the house, Strongwood left Bruce and went to his room.   He hardly understood why the meeting that day had so depressed him.

"Why should I care if the Quakers do choose to allow their preachers to carry on like mad," he thought to himself. "It's nothing to me."

This was true enough in a sense, but the meeting of the week before had left an impression deeper than he supposed ; and though he had tried to laugh it off, there was one thing that remained.   He knew that some power had met him in that meeting.   What if it were God Himself !   What if prophecy and inspiration were not merely theological terms for phenomena of a past age, but realities in the nineteenth century !   In that case Christ was more than historical, and the evidence for him did not depend upon the accuracy of Bible documents alone—nor even upon history. But to-day's experience seemed to destroy even the slight foundation of faith that had been laid.

Going downstairs a little while before dinner, he found Bessie alone in the parlour.

" Miss Bruce," he said, " what did you think of the meeting this morning ? "

" I felt sorry for a good deal of it."

" It's rather rough on your doctrine of guidance, isn't it ? "

" How do you mean ? "

" Why, the sermon this morning."

" We do not claim," she said, " that we may not mistake our guidance."

" Well, I don't understand it," Strongwood answered. " Here comes a man who is as much in earnest as you are, and who lays claim to being under the immediate guidance of God. Yet he preaches in a way that you don't approve of, and that would soon empty the meeting-house if he kept it up. Even if there be such a thing as guidance, what good does it do, if earnest and sincere people can make such mistakes ? "—

" Would you deny the value of electricity because in working with it some have made mistakes, even fatal ones ? "

" Is not that rather different ? "

" Not enough to spoil the comparison. You are convinced of the value of electricity, and therefore you attribute all the accidents that happen with it to the mistakes or ignorance of the workmen. Now I believe just as firmly in the power of God to guide us, and so in the same way, I attribute the failures to the workmen."

"That may be well enough for you, Miss Bruce, but it hardly meets my case, for I have not your faith."

"Very true, Mr. Strongwood. But what would you say to me if I asserted that electric lights were of no account because the lamps in our house would not work?"

"I should take you where you could see them in good working order."

"Then you would not have me dwell on the failure?"

"No, except to have it corrected. I quite understand your meaning, Miss Bruce," he continued; "but you must admit that the parallel hardly holds, for it is not difficult to correct a fault in the mechanism of electric lighting, whereas in the other case, what I regard as a mistake you may consider a success." Here he suddenly recollected that his remarks might be understood as personal, and he stammered: "I don't refer of course to present company but apart from you people here."

Bessie smiled at his confusion.

"You mean that if my position were correct, there should be overwhelming evidence for the truth of it?"

"Yes," Strongwood answered, relieved by the way she had taken his remark, "especially as you claim that spiritual influence is universal."

"There are two intrinsic difficulties," she replied slowly. "A man's spirit is more delicate and his will and passions are very much harder to deal with than any mechanism that we can contrive. Very few, to carry out the illustration, are willing to be prepared by God to show forth His light and power, or to submit to the necessary insulation from the worldly spirit, or to be so shut up to dependence upon Him, as is required for thorough success."

Strongwood did not understand more than half of this
mystical language, but he answered :

"Then even you admit that from your own standpoint
this question of guidance is very difficult ? "

" Yes, but it is worth far more than the difficulty."

" I am afraid I don't follow you," Strongwood replied, as
they went in to dinner.

The dinner was a happy one, for Mrs. Bruce came downstairs for the first time ; and her husband with great delight
led her to the head of the table. On her way she stopped to
be introduced to Strongwood, whom she had not yet seen.

" It has been a great regret to me that I have been unable
to assist in thy entertainment," she said, " though I know
that the rest would not allow thee to want for anything."

" I have wanted nothing, I assure you, Madam, except
your presence."

Mrs. Bruce smiled and took her seat. As they sat with
bowed heads, Bruce very feelingly gave thanks for his wife's
restoration. It was evident how deeply all united with him,
and Strongwood noticed tears trembling in the eyes of more
than one, and he realized for the first time how serious an
illness she had had.

But as soon as the meal was fairly begun, all solemnity
vanished, and Bruce and his sister were almost as excited as
the children, till Mrs. Leslie was scandalized and showed her
feelings by sundry deprecatory remarks at such doings on the
First-day of the week. On this the family would assume an
air of unwonted gravity for about a minute, after which the
gaiety would break out once more.

Finally Bruce said :

" It's no use, mother, we can't keep quiet, we're too glad,

and really it can't be wrong to be merry on such an occasion."

" If it is done in a suitable manner, Charles. Thou must remember thy influence with the children."

" Oh, father, please don't. We don't want to be influenced ; we like thee just as thee is," cried Bertie.

" That's rather hard on me, Bertie," said his father smiling.

" No, it isn't, father. It means thee's just as nice as thee can be."

Here some one remarked that Mrs. Bruce looked wearied, and after that the excess of spirits moderated at once, and the rest of the meal was spent in a way more satisfactory to Mrs. Leslie. At its conclusion, Mrs. Bruce was quite ready to return to the quiet of her own room ; but she was not over-tired, and from this time she rapidly recovered strength.

CHAPTER VII.

STRONGWOOD MAKES A DISCOVERY.

THE days till the picnic passed quietly enough. Mrs. Compton, whose younger son, had he lived, would have been about Strongwood's age, and as she said, in the fondness of her heart, "very much such a man too," began more and more to assume a motherly attitude towards their guest. He seemed so lonely in his ill health, with his mother and sisters across the ocean.

"When dost thou expect them back?" she asked on one occasion, using the Friends' language correctly, as she always did when she remembered, which she seldom did, and never when she became interested.

"In about eighteen months, I think."

"Nonsense. They won't let thee be alone all that time."

"I don't think they will come back sooner, Mrs. Compton."

"Has thee written thy mother exactly what is the matter with thee?"

"Not fully; she knows I am out of health and discouraged."

"Now, Robert Strongwood, I consider that thee is treating thy mother very badly. She is sure to find out some time, and she will be greatly grieved at thy not telling her."

Strongwood put the matter off. But the old lady was not satisfied and returned to the attack, and insisted so earnestly and with such quaint good nature, that Strongwood finally agreed, and wrote, almost hoping that her cheerful prediction that his mother and sisters would be home within three months might be verified.

All this time he had no suspicion of his real feelings towards Bessie, though the frequency with which he found himself proving to himself that he did not care for her might have convinced him. But at present the very thought of such a thing amused him greatly.

One day, as he sat reading in the porch, he happened to think of the matter, and fancied how he should look as a Quaker. Then the picture changed, and he imagined Bessie as his wife attending her first ball. How would it all impress her? How would she act? Forgetting where he was, he broke out into a hearty laugh.

Mrs. Leslie, who was sitting near him, looked up, and said :

"Thou seems to find thy book very entertaining."

"Yes," he answered rather absently.

"Well," she replied, a little severely, "I have known many persons who have read that volume, but thou art the first who has found it amusing."

Then Strongwood recollected himself. He had asked Mrs. Leslie for a book explaining Friends' views, and she had lent him that sheet-anchor of ancient Quakerism, Barclay's "Apology."

He was somewhat confused, for to laugh aloud over such a book not only seemed rude to the lender, but also reflected unfavourably upon himself.

“Excuse me, Mrs. Leslie,” he said, “I really did not understand your question.   I was not reading at the moment, and I happened to think of an amusing situation, and forgot where I was.”

“I am not surprised,” Mrs. Leslie answered, “ at thy finding it hard to keep thy attention fixed on such a work.   I should not have given thee Barclay to begin with. If thou wilt let me have it,” she continued, stretching out her hand, “ I can find something else, not so full perhaps, but more attractive.”

Strongwood saw that he had fallen very much in her esteem ; but he had no thought of allowing it to be said that he was not equal to any book she might lend him. So he declined her proposal. “ Oh no, Mrs. Leslie, I must finish this first.”   Then, looking at his watch, he added : “ Why, it’s almost time for our drive, I must go and get ready ”; and so saying, he beat a hasty retreat into the house.

A day or so after this he had again been driving with Bruce, when, just as they were entering the gate on their return, he caught sight of Ezra Seward, one of the active Friends of Penelve meeting, talking with Bessie under the trees. To be sure they had only been consulting whether to order an extra half-gallon of ice-cream for the picnic, and were now looking grave over a black cloud that seemed to threaten a wet day on the morrow. But Strongwood did not know this, and even if he had known it, it would not have altered his feelings.   He could not see Bessie’s face, but Seward’s manner seemed unmistakable, and the sight acted upon Strongwood with magical effect.   He could no longer deceive himself as to his own real feelings, and he instantly regarded Seward as a rival. In vain he called himself a fool and assured himself that Bessie was not for him, nor he for her. It was of no use.

"I do love her," he said to himself, as he sat alone in his room that evening. " I need not become a Quaker, nor she a woman of society. What do I care for fashionable life? I shall not interfere with her work. She'll have no difficulty in finding all she wants of that in New York, I'm sure. Besides, we can surround ourselves with literary and cultured people; and she will more than hold her own among them too. We are just made for each other. What has possessed me to waste all these weeks. I only wish I was to drive her to-morrow. What a chance it would be!"

I must here explain, that with cruel disregard to his feelings, as he now felt, it had been arranged for Mrs. Compton to start with Strongwood at ten o'clock in the buggy, about three hours and a half after the rest, who were going in large phaetons. Now Mrs. Compton being an active old lady did not appreciate this arrangement any more than he did, for she wanted to be with the young people.

"Why cannot Robert Strongwood go with Charlie?" she had urged.

But Charles was going on horseback, because he might be detained by business till very late. The family was also seriously afraid lest Aunt Mary would be over-tired by the early start. The old lady at last rather reluctantly consented; but, in the vague hope that something might turn up to alter the plan at the last moment, she came down to early breakfast with bonnet and shawl all ready.

Fortune favoured her, though not at first; for when Bruce went off directly after breakfast to superintend the starting of the carriages she gave up hope. But shortly before the phaeton that was to call for them drove up, a confused message from the confectioner obliged Bessie to go in person to see that all the arrangements were understood.

"Ask them to wait for me, I shan't be long," she cried, as she hurried off.

While she was gone the phaeton arrived.

"Come on Aunt Mary," shouted the young people, as they drove up ; for seeing her in bonnet and shawl they supposed she was to go with them.

"Where's Bessie ? "

One of the young men jumped out and lifted the children in, and stood waiting to assist Aunt Mary.

"Bessie was called off to the confectioner's," she answered. "She'll be back presently. How nice you all look in there ; I wish I were going with you."

"Why, isn't thee coming with us? that's too bad," answered the young people ; for Aunt Mary was a great favourite.

"Oh no, I'm to come in the buggy at ten o'clock with Robert Strongwood."

"Excuse me, ladies," broke in the driver, "can't wait. It's late now, and I must follow the other teams ; for I don't know the way—unless some of you 'uns knows it ? "

No one did.

"I'm very sorry then," said the leader of the party, Dr. Storey, a young medical graduate, "I'm afraid we can't wait for Miss Bessie."

They all objected to this, but soon yielded to what seemed unavoidable.

"Then thee must get in Aunt Mary," they cried. "We can't lose both of you."

And so Aunt Mary climbed in, not without some sense of compunction. "I can get out if we meet her," she said ; a contingency that was not very probable, as the confectioner's lay in the opposite direction to the picnic ground.

They drove off in high glee, and Aunt Mary quickly resigned herself to the enjoyment. She was surprised to see a young man in the phaeton whom she did not know. He had light hair and a small moustache, and was introduced to her as Ralph Hardynge.

Scarcely had the carriage disappeared, when back came Bessie out of breath with running.

" Has not the phaeton come yet ? "

" Come ; yes, and gone," said Mrs. Leslie.

" Gone ! what, didn't they wait ? "

" The driver said he did not know the way, and had to hurry off, so as to follow the others."

" But I know the way, I could have directed them."

" So thee could. But we all forgot it at the moment. What made thee so long ? "

" The stupid confectioner was not ready to see me, and I had to wait till he came down. Where's Aunt Mary ? "

" She took thy place ——"

" That's really too bad," said Bessie, thoroughly vexed ; " She might have known I should not want to drive fifteen miles with Mr. Strongwood. All three of us could easily have gone in the dayton. I've a great mind to stay at home."

" Would they not miss thee a good deal at the picnic ? "

" I suppose they would ; but some one will be sure to tease me about Mr. Strongwood, and I hate it."

" I do not think they will, Bessie. They all know thee intended to go in the phaeton."

Bessie, still unmollified, went to her room to be quiet.

A little before nine o'clock, Strongwood, who had had breakfast in his room that morning as a precaution, and who therefore knew nothing of what had occurred, came down-stairs ; and began studying the road map on which Bruce had marked the route. Presently he heard a step, and looking up was surprised to see Bessie.

"Why, Miss Bruce, I thought you had gone these two hours."

"No, I was called off on an errand, and the phaeton came before I returned. The driver was in a hurry and would not wait, so off they went with Aunt Mary and the children. It was very disappointing."

Strongwood was delighted.

"Excuse me, Miss Bruce, if I am too selfish to agree with you. But I see the man has brought the buggy up very early. If you are ready, why should we not start before the day gets hotter ?"

Bessie agreed, and having brought out a supply of small tools and other sundries that might be useful at the picnic or in case of accident, she took her seat. Strongwood followed her, and they started off.

CHAPTER VIII.

THE MOUNTAIN DRIVE.

BESSIE had recovered her spirits, and was prepared to make the best of everything. As for Strongwood, he was exultant. Nothing could have served his purpose better. He was not nervous with thoughts of how to speak to her of his love; for it was, of course, much too soon for that. Besides, he knew that he must proceed very carefully, for never by the slightest sign had Bessie shown that she cared for him. But that did not trouble him at all, for he was only commencing to lay siege to her heart.

A more charming day could not be imagined. The dark cloud that had seemed threatening the evening before had broken elsewhere, but the air was the fresher for it, and everything in nature was at its best. It was still early, and the trees cast their shadows across the road, so Strongwood let down the top of the buggy that they might have nothing to shut out the views of mountain and river.

The road at first descended with many windings which afforded lovely vistas, now of rich farming land, now of the forest-covered Alleghanies, or again of a "gap," through which still more distant ranges were visible. The richness of the foliage, its diversified shades of green, lighted up with the luxuriant blossoms of the wild laurel, made a beautiful foreground for the mountains, which showed through the clear atmosphere with sharply defined outlines against a sky whose blue rivalled that of Italy. Here and there floated clouds in small masses, white as snow in the sunshine. Their shadows as they passed over the landscape only brought out more strongly the brightness and glory of the scene. Both Strongwood and Bessie felt the inspiration of the freshness and beauty around them, and were soon chatting gaily.

The road, quite new to Strongwood, was one of which Bessie never tired, and they both enjoyed discussing the various places of interest, and the events and persons connected with them. Never in his life had Strongwood felt so happy, and he wished the fifteen miles were fifty.

Suddenly at a rather sharp bend of the road, as they were ascending the mountain, they came upon a scene of desolation which explained the meaning of the dark cloud the evening before. For twenty or more yards in front of them the road was filled with fallen trees and branches. All down the side of the mountain they saw how the cyclone, as if it had been a Titan mowing, had cut a path for itself. In its track no tree, however large, or shrub, however small, had been spared, while on either side everything had been left absolutely unscathed. There was something awe-inspiring both in the completeness and in the limitation of the devastation, and something touching and pitiable in the life and freshness of the leaves and blossoms on the fallen trees, which danced in the sunlight as though the sentence of death had not passed upon them.

Bessie and Strongwood sat silently contemplating the scene. But the practical questions, What is to be done? and, Where is the picnic party? presented themselves, and were soon answered; for securely attached to a branch of one of the prostrate trees was a part of a paste-board box, evidently sacrificed for the purpose, on which, written in large characters was a notice that those who belonged to the Friends' picnic should turn back, and take the first road on the left, and that afterwards they would find further directions as needed.

"I suppose, Miss Bessie," remarked Strongwood, as they turned back, "that your explanation of that cyclone would be different from mine."

"I think it more than likely."

"Yes," he continued, "to me it is simply the result of well-defined natural laws, but I imagine you would consider it as the direct act of God."

"You are quite mistaken, Mr. Strongwood, if you think I underrate the laws of nature; but to me the term is but an expression for the orderly working of God in His universe. Your position reminds me of a story. A coloured minister, while preaching on the creation of man, said : 'When de Almighty created man, He made him out ob de dust ob de earth, and set him up agin a fence to dry.' Someone in the congregation called out, 'I say dere, who made dat ar fence?' The minister at first took no notice, but as the man continued refractory, he stopped and said : 'Now, brudder, you jest shet up ; don't yer know that a few such questions like dat would spile de best system of teology?' Now, Mr. Strongwood, when you talk about the action of law, I ask, Who made the law?"

"That is something I know nothing about. But what difference does it make, if the laws are invariable, whether they are maintained by an intelligent creator or by blind force?"

"It makes a great difference. For example, our bodies are subject to certain laws, yet we have great freedom of action. Why should not God have as much freedom in His universe, which in a sense is His body? I believe that He has, and it is a great comfort to feel that I am not the sport of irresistible fate, but am in the hands of a father who loves me, and loves all men."

"All that, Miss Bessie, implies a belief in special providences, which I consider impossible. I heard a poor man once praise God that he was able to pay his milk bill, as if the Almighty cared for such trifles."

"Why, Mr. Strongwood, is not one of the most wonderful things in nature the perfection of its minute details? The poor man's milk bill was certainly more important than a gnat's wing. Nothing gives me a greater sense of the power of God than the knowledge that He cares for every little thing in our lives. I believe in special providences so much, that I regard everything as a special providence, if we only take it in the right way."

"How do you mean?"

"I mean that if we are in harmony with God, we are in harmony with His universe, so that everything that happens to us is weighted with blessing."

"Even suffering, loss of reputation, death?"

"Yes."

Strongwood smiled—

> "'No man ere felt the halter draw
> 'With good opinion of the law.'"

"I shouldn't think your doctrine of special providences would be very popular. Would you, for example, tell the sufferers of the Johnstown flood, which, I understand, was the result of criminal carelessness, that that was a special providence?"

Strongwood was not arguing for argument's sake, but brought up what he felt to be a real difficulty.

Bessie recognized his earnestness, and said :

" Is not the fact that the innocent suffer for the guilty a necessary result of all men belonging to one family ? There is a bright side also, for the progress of one is the progress of all. It seems to me that this truth gives us a very strong motive for right conduct, and also that it supplies a clue to the deeper meaning of the crucifixion, which from ——"

Here she was interrupted by an involuntary exclamation from Strongwood ; for he had turned into the side road, and was looking with dismay at a " wash out " in front of him.

" We must have made a mistake ; we can never drive into a hole like that."

" Oh yes, it's all right," laughed Bessie. " See, there are the fresh carriage marks."

" It will break the buggy to pieces."

" Don't be uneasy. The buggy's used to it."

" Well then, I had better help you out first."

" Oh no, I'm used to it too. If you can stand it, I can."

So, reassured, Strongwood drove on carefully, and it really was not so bad as he had thought.

But for some time all sustained conversation was impossible ; for frosts, freshets, and heat, season after season, had been allowed to work their will on the mountain road, if road it could be called.

Now the buggy would nearly spill its occupants out on one side, and now on the other, and now it would jolt over the stones in the dry bed of a mountain torrent. At best the way was so narrow that Strongwood wondered what they would do if any other vehicle should meet them. Fortunately none did, and as Bessie took all the joltings as part of the fun of the picnic, Strongwood, who, accustomed to the smooth drives in Central Park and to the turnpikes near New York, was at first inclined to be nervous, soon found himself almost enjoying it.

At length, as they reached more level ground, the road, much to his relief, improved, and they proceeded more rapidly, till they were within a mile of their destination. Here they came upon a few scattered log houses. Bessie, who had always gone by the main road, was surprised to find people living so near to the picnic ground, which she had supposed to be much more isolated.

At the further end of the settlement, and separated from it by a considerable distance, stood a small house, which had evidently from the fresh look of the logs and whiteness of the plaster been newly built. As they were passing, there came from it such a wail of sorrow and despair that Strongwood, in spite of his city habit of minding his own affairs, involuntarily stopped the horse and readily fell in with Bessie's suggestion to get out and offer assistance.

CHAPTER IX.

THE BABES IN THE WOOD.

THEY found the door of the cottage open, and, within, a stalwart woodman, standing beside his wife, whose face was buried in her hands, while a lad, about thirteen years old, sat near her crying. All were so plunged in the depths of distress that it was only with much difficulty that their story could be made out.

At last, it transpired that the husband had but recently completed the cottage, and had been joined the week previous by his wife and three children. The day after they had moved in, the two younger ones—boys of eight and six—had wandered away into the woods and had not returned. The father and the neighbours had searched for them night and day in vain, but only on the nearer side of the stream which ran by the house, for it was far too wide and deep for such children to cross it, and there was no bridge. The night before, however, the mother had dreamed that she saw her children lying on the ground near their cottage, on a particular spot on the opposite side of the "creek." The husband at first had scoffed at the idea, but finally, at her persistent entreaty, had thrown some unsawn logs across the stream and told the boy to run and look, but to be sure not to go beyond the sound of his chopping wood. The boy had just come back with the report that he had found his brothers, but that they were quite dead.

Strongwood suggested that the lad might be mistaken.

" In that case," said Bessie, " we may be of some use. May we not come with you ? "

The poor woman, catching at the straw of possible comfort, readily assented, and the five started out. They crossed on the logs, and less than two hundred yards brought them to the place, though the undergrowth prevented them from seeing it, till they were close to the spot.

There before them were the children. The elder had taken off his jacket and covered his brother, who was lying as if comfortably asleep. The other, whose eyes even in death were earnestly fixed upon him, was sitting against the trunk of a tree, while his hand grasped a stick, evidently intended to drive off any wild animals. They were haggard and wizened from hunger and fatigue ; their hands and mouths and cheeks stained with the wild strawberries they had eaten ; the soles of their shoes were gone, and their stockings worn through, while their clothes, ragged and torn with the briars and snags of the forest, revealed deep bruises on their bodies and limbs. They had clearly been dead several days.

With a wild cry the mother threw herself on the ground beside them, and lay there moaning, the boy clung to her, weeping passionately, while the father leant on his stick and tried to stifle the great sobs that shook his frame.

Bessie wept in sympathy, and Strongwood required all his self-restraint not to do the same.

Presently the man said :

" How they must have walked ! look at their feet ! They must have gone on till the creek was so narrow they crossed it without knowin'." After a pause he continued : " To think how they must have heard us shoutin' and been too weak to answer. We'd 'a seen 'em if it weren't for the underbush. To think of it ;—so near home, and lost," and he sobbed afresh.

For some minutes they stood in painful silence, and then Bessie knelt down beside the mother and prayed for them. Her simple, earnest words soothed the mourners. Then the father said : "Come, Liza, we must go now. I'll carry Willie, you take Georgie." So saying, he lifted the elder boy. But his wife was much too overcome to do anything, and so Strongwood volunteered :

"Won't you allow me to carry him ?"

The man hesitated.

"You're not used to such work, you'd better not. But I'm much obliged to you."

Strongwood, accustomed as he was to New York ways, and to everything that art can do to make death beautiful, thought that the father simply meant that he was not able to carry the body, and replied :

"Oh, yes, I can do it easily. I only wish I could be of greater help."

But he soon found he had undertaken more than he had bargained for. It seemed impossible to go on. Bessie noticed him growing pale, and said in a low tone :

"It's not really necessary for you to carry him. We can watch till the man comes back."

This speech roused him, and he felt he could not run the risk of hurting the feelings of these poor people in their sorrow, and so summoning up all his resolution, he walked on with his burden.

Bessie understood, and turned back to help the poor mother, but her look was not lost on Strongwood, who felt well repaid for what he was doing.

By the time they reached the house several of the women and children from the neighbouring cottages were standing about the door, curious to know why a buggy from town should be there, and why none of the family were at home. When they saw the sorrowful procession they literally lifted up their voices and wept. Strongwood laid down his charge and walking to a little distance bared his head to the refreshing breeze.

As he stood looking down the road, he saw a man on horseback approaching. It was Ezra Seward coming to the picnic. He stopped to inquire what was the matter, and, while Strongwood was explaining, the father of the children came out and asked to speak with him.

"It seems rather sudden-like, but we ain't got any place to keep 'em, I guess we'll have to bury 'em to-day. You see?"

"I understand," said Strongwood, "and I quite approve, if it can be done."

"Well, sir, you see, I thought there might be a preacher at that Sunday School picnic, who might be willing to come over. Perhaps you could find out."

"It's a Quaker picnic," said Strongwood, "and this is one of their Elders. I'll ask him."

Several of the women by this time had gathered about them.

Ezra Seward had no doubt that some Friends would be willing to come over, but thought they could hardly proceed without an inquest.

"Don't yer trouble your heads about that," broke in one of the women. "My boy's after the coroner already. He'll be here in no time."

"Over such a road?"

"Law sakes, man, he don't live on that road. He's not far off. He was over yesterday helpin' to hunt for McKendry's children. He's at home to day, cultivatin' his corn."

So it was agreed that the funeral should take place at one o'clock, if the coroner did not object. McKendry said he would dig a grave and would knock some boards together for a coffin. The time was short, but they wished to have it when the men of the settlement should be able to come before they went back to work after dinner. Strongwood, who knew that country folks make great account of a funeral, was surprised at the roughness of the preparations, but he saw that both McKendry and his wife were thoroughly crushed. Then an idea struck him.

"I doubt if you have time," he said, "to do all that is necessary; I used to be good at carpentering. I see you have a pile of boards here. Let me do that for you."

The poor man consented gratefully and supplied him with tools and nails, and Strongwood got hammer and tacks out of the buggy, and told Bessie of his purpose.

She warmly approved, if it were not too much for him, and she fetched from the house some milk and bread which she made him take.

His great pleasure at her approval was, however, a good deal damped, when it was proposed that Bessie should drive on with Ezra Seward in the buggy, and leave him the horse. But it was too late to draw back, and he saw them go off with a heavy heart. If only he knew what Miss Bruce thought of that man.

"Elizabeth," said Seward as they drove off, "this is a very solemn occasion."

"It is indeed, Ezra Seward."

"I wish we could do something to comfort those poor people."

"I hope we may."

"This funeral is an important opportunity. Might it not be well to bring the children to it? It might make a lasting impression on them."

"I hardly think we ought to."

"Why not?"

"It's scarcely fair to the children to break up their picnic to attend the funeral of strangers."

"But this is almost brought to us."

"It would be very trying to the poor parents."

"I think not; people of this class like crowds at funerals."

"Well, Ezra Seward, I may be wrong; but it seems to me that the terrible circumstances of the case, might make attendance at the funeral a very serious thing for the more sensitive, nervous children. Does thee not think it would be much better for thee to come to Bible school next First-day, and draw the lesson from the story then?"

"Perhaps thou art right, Elizabeth. Thou generally art."

Although Bessie knew she was right, she was touched and a little confused at the humility of a man whom she regarded as a leading Friend in the meeting, so she answered:

"Oh no, Ezra Seward, thee does not know how many foolish things I say and do."

"I know thee better than thou thinks, Elizabeth, and to me thou art never foolish."

Bessie began to feel embarrassed. There was something new in the tone in which Seward addressed her that made her heart beat faster, and she was glad that their arrival at the picnic cut the conversation short.

Ezra noticed her blush and felt encouraged.

In the meanwhile Strongwood worked at the box, which was made large enough for the two little bodies. The coroner came and, knowing all the circumstances, declined to hold an inquest, and gave authority for the funeral to proceed. He was a kind man, and helped Strongwood with the heavy part of the work. When this was done, they procured a sheet and lined the box throughout, making a little pillow for the head and cushions at the sides by stuffing in straw. The outside was unsightly, and the happy thought, possibly suggested by the old story of the Babes in the Wood, of covering it with fresh leaves over-lapping each other came to Strongwood. Fortunately the tacks held out. When it was finished and the boards entirely covered, the effect was exceedingly pretty, and Strongwood was touched with the surprise and gratitude of the parents.

CHAPTER X.

THE picnic party had been having a merry time of it. All were in the highest spirits, and after the line of phaetons had left the city, there was much laughing and singing, but without uproariousness; and many jokes, good humoured if not witty, passed from one carriage to another. The necessity of turning into the side road only added to the enjoyment, and each heavy jolt was hailed with shouts of pleasurable alarm. Even Aunt Mary, though she found the bumping rather painful, entered into the merriment.

The party passed McKendry's with no suspicion of the tragedy that was going on so near, and reached the picnic ground not much later than they had expected.

After a careful warning to the children from the superintendent not to wander off, or to go out of sight of the grown folks, the pleasures of the picnic began.

Beyond some projecting rocks was an open space suitable for base-ball, and to this a number of the young men and boys resorted. Hardynge joined them, for he belonged to that rather numerous class of young men who, although they do not play the game themselves, have made such a study of it as to understand all its intricacies perfectly. This made him a valuable acquisition as umpire.

His presence at the picnic is easily explained. Business had again brought him to Penelve, where he had arrived the

"

previous day. In the course of a business call on a young man, who was a Friend, he had learned that several of the men he wished to secure orders from could not be seen the next day on account of the picnic.

"What picnic?" he asked.

"Our Friends' Bible School ——"

"Oh, a Quaker picnic. As I shall have to wait, I might as well go. What does a ticket cost?"

"It's not that kind of picnic. There are no tickets. But I guess I could take you. I think you said you knew Mr. Strongwood who is staying at Mr. Bruce's?"

"Yes."

"It'll be all right then; I'll introduce you."

The young man had only lately joined the Society, and did not know that he had quite overstepped his privileges. He received a caution at the picnic from the superintendent, to be more careful another time. But as the guest was already there, of course, they had to make the best of it.

Ralph Hardynge knew nothing of this, and was highly elated at the opportunity of following up a clue which he thought he had discovered, and which would, he hoped, lead to something that would at the same time injure Strongwood and help himself. It seemed rather mean to have used Strongwood's name to gain his invitation, but he was too much accustomed to such things to feel much compunction, and, without losing sight of his object, he now threw himself heartily into the business and pleasures of the day.

On reaching the picnic ground, Bessie and Seward found themselves in the midst of a scene that was so out of tune with what they had just left, that they felt almost shocked, and had to remind themselves that the gaiety and fun around them were in entire ignorance of the sorrow that was so near.

The smaller boys and girls were marching round in a ring and musically proclaiming the genealogy of " King William " and the " royal race he run." Further off, the older children were playing " hide and whoop," while frequent shouts came from the base-ball field. In the centre the more elderly Friends sat conversing, and not far off was a group of young people setting a long table, made of rough boards and tressels, but now attractive with its white cloth, bouquets of flowers and Japanese paper napkins. The work of arrangement was not progressing very rapidly, for there were many little practical jokes and much laughter. The same might be said of the cooking preparations, which were being carried on around a large camp fire, built at some distance, where the wind would drive away the smoke.

As Bessie stood watching, her first feelings changed, and it almost seemed as if she were the heartless one to bring a story of such distress to damp the innocent pleasure before her. " What a picture of human life," she thought. " Could we ever laugh, could we even live, if we truly realized all the sorrow that surrounds us ? " She might well ask the question ; only One has ever done this, and He died with a heart broken under the weight of it.

She was not long left to herself, for the children, as soon as they saw her, ran to her tumultuously.

" Oh, cousin Bessie (a term of affection merely), how long thee's been. Won't thee show us a new game ? '

" Presently ; I must say a few words to Aunt Mary, and then I'll come " ; and she went off to consult about the arrangements. This done, she so threw herself into the pleasures of the children that she seemed the gayest of them all, until the time arrived for leaving, when she started them on a fresh game under the charge of Grace Wildmere, and slipped off almost unperceived to join Aunt Mary, Ezra Seward and about six others to go to the funeral.

Quite a company of neighbours was already gathered about the door of the little log house when the Friends arrived. The two little bodies, dressed in white, with all the stains removed from their faces and their hair brushed and hands folded, lay in the box with their heads on the pillow as if asleep. The upper half of the lid was removed, and as the neighbours gazed there were many whispers, not only of pity, but also of admiration and wonder at the beautiful box. Strongwood, when he thought how different it would have been had he left the rough boards exposed, felt well repaid for his trouble. A few words from Bessie also pleased him.

" Is this your work ? " she said in an undertone.

" Yes, with some help——"

" It is lovely. I only hope you have not overtired yourself. It will be a great comfort to them."

Then she went forward and laid a bouquet of flowers on the coffin, and said to the parents :

"Some of our Friends asked me to bring you this."

Then she placed a white rosebud in each little hand, and another rosebud so as to rest against the cheek of one of them and hide a small discolouration. As she looked up, it was no small satisfaction to her to see that her brother had already come. He had got off from the store sooner than he had expected, and, being on horseback, had been able to make good time.

CHAPTER XI.

DUST TO DUST.

THE closing of the coffin was, as it always is, a painful time, but it was over at last, and four men carried the light burden on poles to the grave which had been dug in the further corner of the small plot of ground. The procession formed, and followed two and two. At Bruce's suggestion planks had been laid across chairs, so that all might sit down.

After a moment's pause, Ezra Seward arose, and, taking off his hat, said :

"Friends, I hope we are here to do more than sympathize with this family in its sore bereavement. No one can comfort them but the Lord ; but if He enable us, we can pray for them, and help them. Without Him our words are nothing. Therefore we have no arranged form of service, for we desire to wait on the Lord, who can use silence or speech as He sees best. May we only have words of His prompting, and may we all be willing to receive His message in our hearts. Let us be silent that He may speak to us."

A solemn hush fell upon the little company. No sound broke the stillness except the breeze among the trees, and the stifled sobs of the mother and her occasional low words, uttered almost unconsciously : "So near home, so near home,— and lost."

Presently Dr. Storey rose with the words: "Yes—so near home,—and lost."

Strongwood felt that if he could only get at the speaker he could pull him down for his bad taste. But the young man, quite unconscious of this mental criticism, went on to draw a parallel between the present event and a soul wandering from God. "You may think you are far from the Lord," he continued, "but you are not. Your self-will, like the undergrowth of the forest, hides Him from you, and your sins are as a broad stream you cannot cross. But you are not hidden from Him, and, if you are willing, He will bring you home. Why will you insist upon remaining in the wilderness under the wrath of God against sin?"

This last sentence was caught up and applied by McKendry in a way quite unintended by the speaker.

"Yes, Liza, that's it," said the poor man. "That's why we've lost our children. God's angry with us." At this both he and his wife broke into loud weeping, which the boy joined in out of sympathy, while some of the neighbours nodded their heads in sorrowful approval. It was most painful; but, as the weeping became less violent, Bessie, kneeling down, began:

"Oh Lord, show these dear people that this sorrow is not from Thy anger, but in Thy love." She continued in the same strain for a few sentences, and thus restored the meeting to its former solemnity; and soon after Bruce spoke of the sufferings of Christ:

"When Christ was crucified, it seemed to be the triumph of sin over good, it seemed as if God must be angry with Him to allow such unmerited suffering. But, as our minds are enlightened to understand the meaning of it all in the light of His resurrection, we see the divine side of it, and that that which seemed all wrong has become our blessing and salvation. We are to read all suffering in the light of Christ's suffering; for in that alone is set forth both the human and divine side of sorrow. All suffering, if borne in a spirit of trust and submission to the Lord, becomes full of the light of life." Then followed a few words of special application to the mourners, in which he spoke of the strength and comfort Christ gives.

Finally, Aunt Mary spoke, and referred to the story of "The Alpine Sheep," * which tells how, when summer comes, and the shepherd wishes to take the flock to higher pastures, he sometimes finds it impossible to make the sheep cross some place of difficulty, till he takes their lambs and carries them over. Then the parent sheep follow.

"May it not be, dear friends," she concluded, "that the Good Shepherd has taken your lambs, that you may be willing to follow Him, so that He may lead you to the home where they are!"

After a further pause, the men, at a sign from Ezra Seward, lowered the coffin and filled up the grave, after which Bessie laid the bouquet of flowers on the mound, and the company dispersed.

McKendry pressed Mrs. Compton's hand. "Yes, ma'am," he said, "you're right. That's just what we've done. We've forgotten the Good Shepherd. How can we come back to Him?"

This was a welcome opportunity, and before they left the Friends who talked with him felt that he had really

---

* This story is beautifully told in a poem by the wife of J. R. Lowell.

turned his face to the Lord. As for his wife, she was too much stunned to do more than dumbly assent to what her husband said. Bruce felt there was an opening for further work, and at McKendry's suggestion agreed to come up the next Sunday afternoon and hold a meeting.

By this time most of those who had come from the picnic had left. Ezra Seward was obliged to return to town in consequence of a business letter which Bruce had brought out to him. Bruce himself proceeded to the picnic on horseback ; Aunt Mary was carried off in another buggy by one of the young ladies who was specially devoted to her, and so Strongwood and Bessie once more found themselves driving alone.

There was something indefinable in her manner which made Strongwood's heart beat fast with hope, nor was he altogether mistaken in thinking that the morning's experiences had altered her feelings toward him ; for she had seen a new side of his character, and realized something of the true man that lay beneath the not altogether attractive exterior. She felt she had unwittingly judged him too severely. There was nothing in the words they said that showed any difference, but both felt it, and were consciously brought nearer to each other.

"I can understand, Miss Bessie," he said at last, "that it must be a great satisfaction to be able to assure those poor people that their sorrow has come to them in God's love ; I wish I could see how you make it out."

"When I look at Christ," replied Bessie, speaking in a low tone, "I see righteousness and love,—not merely general love, but personal love. God cannot be less than Christ, and so Christ becomes the key to all the works of God. He is

God expressed in human terms. This I understand, and I can trust where I don't understand."

"That is your reason then in a nutshell, I suppose?"

"It is one side of it, but it would be of little effect if it were not for personal revelation and experience."

"Your own, that is?"

"I mean the experience of all who have tested it, including myself."

"I am afraid I hardly know what you mean by personal revelation," he answered, and relapsed into silence.

The first person to meet them on their arrival at the picnic was Ralph Hardynge, who had heard nothing of their morning experiences. He came forward smiling.

"Why, Mr. Strongwood, how are you? How late you are. I've been expecting you these three hours. Found the drive through the woods too pleasant to cut short, eh!"

"The detention was unavoidable," replied Strongwood stiffly.

"Naturally it would be with such a companion."

Strongwood bit his lip.

"I hardly expected to find you here," he remarked as he helped Bessie out of the carriage.

"No," Hardynge replied, and added audaciously: "Yet I am here on the strength of your name."

"Indeed," and Strongwood proceeded to tie the horse to a tree. He hoped this action would obviate the necessity of introducing Miss Bruce, and Bessie, seeing his want of cordiality, helped him by moving off. Hardynge, however, had no intention of being balked, so he said:

"Perhaps you will kindly introduce me."

Strongwood, not caring to go to extremes, did so rather coldly.

"Miss Bruce, this is Mr. Hardynge, of ——. Excuse me, where are you from just now, I really forget?"

It was now Hardynge's turn to be angry. He did not believe that Strongwood had forgotten, and he saw that the studied coldness had had the intended effect on Miss Bruce. But he controlled himself, and said: "I am from Philadelphia."

"Oh! Mr. Hardynge of Philadelphia; Mr. Hardynge, Miss Bruce."

Bessie bowed in acknowledgment of this introduction, and Hardynge said:

"Delighted to see you, Miss Bruce. What a charming day for a picnic, what a delightful place, what charming people."

"I am glad you find it so."

"I assure you, Miss Bruce, there has been nothing to mar the delight of the occasion. One would almost think that you Quakers, oh excuse me, you Friends, had no care in the world. I suppose it is because your lives are so quiet."

"Is that your idea of our life, Mr. Hardynge?"

"Yes. I imagine you Friends going calmly through life, never ruffled with anything, while the great stream of the world rushes by you, and all the time you——"

"Sit high and dry out of it," laughed Bessie.

"Oh, no, not that way; more like an oasis in the midst of a desert."

"I never heard that great caravans rushed by an oasis; I thought they generally stopped."

"Oh, Miss Bruce, you're too quick for me. By the way, I hope you were not offended at my speaking of you as Quakers. It was quite an accident."

"It was no offence, I assure you, Mr. Hardynge. We often use the word ourselves."

"You are sometimes called Shakers, too, are you not?"

"No, they have no connection with us whatever."

"Oh, there is a difference then, is there? We outsiders, you know, can't follow all these divisions."

Here Strongwood, who had kept with them in rather moody silence, broke in:

"The Shakers are not a division of Friends. They live in celibate communities, and pay divine honours to the woman who founded them, and they have many grotesque practices. I hope you will never confound them with Friends again."

Strongwood's manner was almost rude, and it naturally made Bessie feel inclined to take Hardynge's part, so she said pleasantly:

"The mistake is not unnatural, for the words seem to have very much the same sense as well as sound, though in this case they mean such different things." Then, before Hardynge could speak, she changed the subject: "I believe you said that you live in Philadelphia?"

"Yes, that is, as far as a commercial traveller without a home in the world can be said to live anywhere."

"It must be very lonely sometimes."

"Yes, if one were not too busy to feel it."

"And you must find constant variety in meeting so many people."

"Not so much as you think. After the first, the variety is all in one groove."

"Including Quaker picnics?"

"Oh no, indeed. You can't imagine what a treat such a day as this is to me."

By this time they had joined the crowd about the table. The first set had finished their dinner, and the second were taking their places. Strongwood, who had been fuming at Hardynge's presence, managed in the slight confusion to conduct Bessie away, and quite naturally to find a seat by her. Bessie, however, did not wish to sit down, but proposed to help attend at the table. The other young ladies, who knew what she had been through, would not hear of this, and she had to yield.

When all were seated, a rap on the table gave the signal for a time of silent thanksgiving, after which Bessie said to Strongwood in a low tone :

"Were you not rather hard on Mr. Hardynge just now?"

"I don't know. But he had no right to use my name to secure an invitation."

"Would you not have allowed him to use it, if he had asked?"

"That's not the question," Strongwood answered evasively. "He and I are not sufficiently intimate for him to take such a liberty."

"Is he not a suitable person to come to the picnic? He seems a harmless fellow,—perhaps a little shallow."

"Well, I may have shown my annoyance too plainly. I did not mean——"

Here he stopped, for at that moment Bruce came up, and laid his hand on Bessie's shoulder, and Strongwood saw by his pale face that something serious had happened.

CHAPTER XII.

THE SEARCH.

"BESSIE," said Bruce, "when did thee see Bertie last?"

"Just before we went to McKendry's. He was with his teacher, Frank Adams, who promised to look after him."

"Frank says that Bertie went off with three or four of the Bible Class fellows. But they have come back, and did not even know he was following them."

"If that's the case," said Strongwood, rising, "we must look for him at once."

"Yes; but you must not join in the search, Rob," Bruce replied; "you are tired already."

"Charlie's quite right," interrupted Aunt Mary, who had come up. "Thee just sit down and eat thy dinner; I'm afraid thee'll be laid up as it is."

"But, Mrs. Compton, really I want to help."

"Why, man alive," she continued, "what's thee thinking about? Thee must keep still, and go home by the first carriage. Come, don't be a goose."

In spite of their anxiety, they all laughed at her grandmotherly manner, and Bessie added:

"There's really no need for you to go. There will be plenty who will enjoy doing it, and Bertie can't have gone far."

In fact many volunteers were already coming up to offer their services; most of them evidently looking upon the search as an unexpected piece of fun. No one outside the family imagined that a delicate boy of seven could be really lost in so short a time. Strongwood, seeing he was not likely to be needed, consented to resume his seat at the table. But neither he nor the Bruces could forget what they had witnessed in the morning, and they pictured to themselves possibilities they dared not speak of.

The search party divided up and went off two and two in various directions. Signals were arranged, and, after an hour, a great farm horn, which had been brought to warn any stragglers of the close of the picnic, was to be sounded at regular intervals till all had returned.

Aunt Mary, who by this time was very tired, became more and more uneasy.

"Oh, Bessie," she said, "why did we both go off to the funeral? How careless Clara will think us."

"But, Aunt Mary, if we had been here, thee would have been talking to the Friends, and I should have been helping at the table. He would have gone off just the same."

"How could it have happened?" Aunt Mary continued, "I'm sure he'll fall down some precipice, and, if he isn't killed, he'll catch his death of cold, or be bitten by a rattle-snake."

Bessie did not attempt to disentangle this jumble of dangers. She knew too well that any one of them was very possible. She simply said: "I wish we could help to find him."

"Yes, it almost distracts one to be forced to do nothing."

The conversation continued in this strain for some little while longer, till Bessie saw that their grave looks were casting a gloom over the party, while the little brother and sister, Clarence and Esther, were almost crying.

"Aunt Mary," she said at last, "we must really try to be cheerful. We are spoiling every one's pleasure."

"I don't know how thee feels," Aunt Mary interrupted, "but I'm very uneasy about Bertie, and *I'm* not good enough yet to act as if I didn't mind it."

Having thus delivered herself, however, the old lady suddenly quieted down. "I know it is wrong," she said. "I won't do so any more"; and she immediately went over to a circle of Friends, and began to speak cheerfully, and, changing the topic to ordinary matters, soon put them at their ease. Bessie kissed and comforted the twins, and took them to the other children, and presently all were merry again over a game of "catcher."

In the meanwhile Strongwood from his seat had carefully noted all that had passed, and had observed that there was one direction in which the searchers had not gone. They had thought it would be useless to look there, for it was known that Bertie had started with the young men from the opposite side of the grounds. But the experience of the morning had not been lost on Strongwood, and he determined that the child should not share the fate of the little McKendrys through a similar oversight. He felt rested, and so, putting some sandwiches into his pocket, for he knew the little fellow would be hungry, he quietly walked off past the empty phaetons.

He was not used to woods, but he recalled a newspaper paragraph which he had lately seen, explaining how to use a watch as a compass * in finding one's way, and he promptly

* The reason why a watch can be used as a compass is that at noon the sun stands south. Between that time and the next noon the hour hand of the watch makes two revolutions, whilst the sun (apparently) makes one. Therefore at any hour of the day, except noon, if the watch be held horizontally and the hour hand pointed to the sun, a spot on the dial half way between the end of the hour hand and xii. will point south. At six o'clock in the morning, for example, if the watch be held properly, the figure ix. will point south. At six o'clock in the afternoon iii. would point south. The results are sufficiently accurate for practical guidance.

"HELLO, BIRDIE!"

acted upon it. He took frequent observations, and pressed on rapidly for about three quarters of an hour. At the end of this time he thought he heard a faint answer to his shouts, and stopped to listen. It came again, and he hastily took out his knife and, having "blazed" a young maple that stood by itself, hurried in the direction of the sound. After considerable uncertainty, and by dint of repeated shoutings and replies, he found his way to the edge of a cliff, and, looking down, saw Bertie in a rather insecure position, about twelve feet below. He had evidently, in some way, fallen over the edge, but had lodged on a projecting fragment of the cliff. It was easy to see how the child could have had his fall broken by the bushes and branches, but it was not so easy to decide how to get him up again.

" Hello, Bertie !" cried Strongwood, " how did you get on such a perch as that ? My, but it's steep ! Hold on whilst I go and fetch some one to help."

" Don't leave me," wailed the boy, " the sun's so hot, and I'm so tired, I can't hold on much longer "; and he shuddered as he looked down to the tops of the trees that waved forty feet below him. " I thought no one would ever come."

" But what can I do for you by myself without a rope ?"

Bertie had not sat on the rock for half an hour for nothing.

" There's a place here where I could get across if I was only a man, and there's a path too," he said.

He pointed to the spot, and Strongwood, after considerable search and not a few scratches, found it. He wondered that there should be a path in such a place, and was not surprised to find that it was only a channel grooved by water after heavy rains, and far more difficult for climbing than moss or turf. He saw, however, that there was, as Bertie had said, a narrow ledge, the distance from which to the rock where the child was, was only a long step.

Strongwood was no mountain climber, and difficulties which might not have seemed great to an expert, were to him almost insurmountable. Should he miss his footing, there was nothing to save him from falling to the bottom. He gave several shouts for help, and then cautiously, with the aid of branches and bushes, made his way down. Towards the last these failed him. What should he do? He sat down and thought. Then he removed his coat and waistcoat, and, taking his suspenders, tied one end firmly to the stem of a small fir-tree. He tested it and found that it held, and by bearing his whole weight upon it he was able to secure a foothold in the slippery bed of the dry torrent, and to reach the ledge. Here by placing one foot on Bertie's rock, and holding on to his braces with his left hand he could lean far over and just grasp the child's arm with his right. In this rather awkward position he heard a distant halloa! and paused :—

" Shout, Bertie."

Bertie did so, but his voice was weak ; then Strongwood tried, but his breath soon gave out.

" Jump, Bertie."

Bertie jumped, and Strongwood helped him with a sudden pull, more forcible than a more experienced man would have used. The result was that either his left foot slipped, or the ground gave way, for the next moment he fell heavily on his breast on the hard earth, his feet hanging far out over the precipice, and his breath knocked out of him ; but his left hand still grasped his support and his right hand held Bertie's arm.

The boy, of course, had also fallen, but in the fall they had swung round, so that he lighted upon a bank of soft moss, and was more frightened than hurt.

The position was a critical one but it was some moments before Strongwood recovered himself sufficiently to realize it. At last he was roused by a slight sense of slipping, and looking up, he saw that there was not a moment to lose. The strain had loosened the roots of the fir-tree and they were beginning to give way. By a desperate jerk he was just able to plant one knee on the edge of the precipice before the tree fell. This gave him some purchase, and by clutching at the moss he was before long able to reach a place of safety. Bertie also did his part manfully.

Strongwood and Bertie rested in the shade of a tree before continuing their climb. The child eagerly devoured the sandwiches, and was soon revived, and began to ask questions. But Strongwood felt too exhausted to talk, and so got Bertie to tell his adventures.

" Well, young man, how did you come to choose such a strange hiding place?"

" It wasn't a hiding place at all," Bertie replied in an injured tone. " I did'nt mean to do it. They told me not to go where I couldn't see the grown up people, and I didn't. When the big fellows started for a walk I thought 'twould be fun to go with them. But they went so fast, and I fell down and lost my hat, and my knife and pencil dropped out of my pocket, and when I picked 'em up the others were gone. I called and ran after them, and then I came to a path and I thought it was the right way, and I ran, and ran, and fell over a bank and went down, oh, so far through the trees and bushes, till I got to that rock. It was so lonely, I thought of Robinson Crusoe."

" How long do you think you waited there ? "

" I think about ten hours, and I was so hungry and thirsty—and I'm so thirsty now."

" Here are some peppermint lozenges, perhaps they'll help you."

Although Strongwood was thoroughly exhausted, and could not get rid of the almost distressing oppression on his breathing, he was extremely happy at his success and in the thought of having served Bessie. It had cost him no little effort, but, especially after the events of the morning, it was certain to be appreciated at its full value. His heart warmed at the thought of her delight and surprise, for he was sure she had not seen him start on the search, and he metaphorically thanked his stars, or whatever unknown powers presided over his destinies, for the happy chance that had come to him. He could hardly wait till he was sufficiently rested to proceed, and he congratulated himself that his shouts had not been heard, for now he would have the entire credit of the rescue.

CHAPTER XIII.

A SNAKE IN THE GRASS.

THE search parties had worked hard, but unsuccessfully; the great field horn had sounded out its dolorous notes at regular intervals for nearly half an hour before the earliest of the searchers returned. As two by two they all came back without the child, Bruce being the last, they became very seriously alarmed. What could have become of Bertie? Could he have fallen down a precipice or into a well, or a pit? This last seemed the most likely, for there are many natural pits in that limestone region. It was now nearly five o'clock and Bruce, unwilling to waste more time in discussion, which promised no result, jumped on his horse and galloped off to McKendry's to ask the men of the settlement to come and help him in the search, hoping much from their experience in such matters.

The children had had a long day and were getting tired, and so it was agreed that all the party except the Bruces and those directly engaged in the search should return to town. Then first they missed Strongwood. No one seemed to know anything about him. The superintendent of the school was sure that he had not gone in any of the early phaetons, but as finally one or two said they had seen him walking in the direction of the road to Penelve, it seemed most likely that he had chosen to go a little way on foot till he should be overtaken by one of the carriages. Aunt Mary had told him to go home early, and she thought with some compunction that he might have been offended at her freedom of speech and gone off without telling them. " Besides," she added, " he was very tired."

This explanation seemed satisfactory to all except Bessie, who knew better, and to her anxiety about Bertie was now added the thought that Strongwood was perhaps sustaining life-long injury through his exertions. She said little however, for she reflected that, as the woods were to be searched again, it was more likely for a man to be found than a boy.

As the phaetons filled, Bessie tried in vain to persuade Aunt Mary to go.

" Whatever should I say to Clara ? " she objected.

" Thee might prepare her mind."

" Why should I prepare her mind for what I hope may not happen."

Bessie shook her head. She herself had little hope.

" Well, I haven't given up yet," said Aunt Mary, " and in any case it's better she should not know anything till she has to ; besides, if Bertie has been hurt, I may be needed. I can just sit down here with Esther and Clarence, and take a rest."

So a comfortable place was made for the old lady under the trees, but it was some time before she could settle down, for every few minutes her active mind would invent some fresh suggestion. The twins took their places by her and soon fell asleep, and at last she too closed her eyes, and Bessie sat alone thinking. She had wished to go off with the second search party herself, but felt she could not leave Aunt Mary and the children.

Ralph Hardynge, having business letters to write, excused himself from the second search, and went back in one of the phaetons. By a little manoeuvering he managed to take his place between Grace and Amy Wildmere on the seat by the driver.

Every one had learned something of what had happened at McKendry's, and, as they came near, all fell into respectful silence, and the carriages were driven past at a walk. Bruce was at the door and stopped them to ask that no word should be sent to his wife about Bertie. Just then McKendry came up with the neighbours, who had readily agreed to help in the search, and the picnic party drove on, heartily wishing Bruce success in his efforts. The conversation naturally turned on the events of the day.

"I wonder," said Amy, "if Mr. Strongwood has really gone home."

"Bessie thinks he is in the woods looking for Bertie," said Grace.

"I should think Miss Bruce ought to know," Hardynge remarked with a meaning tone.

Grace disregarded the tone, and went on : "She thinks he would hardly have left without telling them, and I agree with her. I don't think he would be so rude when they have all been so very kind to him."

"But I suppose he pays them well for it ?" said Hardynge. "He's rich enough I'm sure."

"No he doesn't," said Amy. "They are old college friends, and Charles Bruce would not let him pay for anything, though Robert Strongwood tried to persuade him. In fact they only came to an agreement after ——"

"Amy," said Grace, "I think thee ought to be careful what thee says about other people ; we only heard it by accident and I don't think they wished it repeated."

Hardynge was highly pleased at information which he could perhaps make some use of later, so he said gravely :

"You need not be uneasy, Miss Wildmere, I'm deep as a well." Then as Amy said nothing more, he changed the subject, and added : "If Mr. Strongwood is really searching for that child, I believe he'll find him."

"Why ?"

"Because he has such luck in those things."

"How do you mean ?" asked Amy.

"Haven't you heard of his adventure last winter ?"

"No, do tell us."

"Well then, last February he was in Flumetown, New York, and, one evening late, he was driving back to town from one of the villages, when he was caught in a blizzard. Of course, you know, I only give the story as it is told. Some people think that his having been out to a village on business was all humbug, and that everything, except the blizzard, of course, was all arranged. However, some people are unkind, and their view is probably wrong. But be that as it may, the story goes that when the storm was at its height, he heard a cry for help, and, reining up his horse, found a young lady standing there, too weak to climb into the sleigh."

"I shouldn't think he would expect her to climb in," said Amy, "Why could not he get out and help her ?"

"The whole story turns on this. He was afraid to do so, so it is said, for the horse was almost frantic. But as she could not get in, he had to get out, and, while he was helping her, off goes the horse, and they fell together in the snow."

"What a terrible thing it might have been," cried Amy. "Still, as we saw him to-day, I suppose I need not ask if they died."

" No, indeed.   He chafed her hands, and rubbed her face with snow, and half-carried her to a deserted house on the road side.   Here his luck did not fail him, for he had matches and was able to light a fire, and he boiled water in an old tin cup, and the next morning they came into town on the top of a sledge loaded with logs.   My informant saw them."

" How romantic. They ought to have married each other."

" Well, to tell the truth, some said they did, others claim that they only agreed to."

Grace Wildmere did not relish the turn the story had taken, and said severely : " In a small town, everybody's private affairs are so well known, that the truth would very soon be found out."

Hardynge replied by saying that his informant had left Flumetown a few days after the occurrence.

" Then perhaps it might be as well not to repeat reports that may be unfounded, and are calculated to do harm."

Ralph Hardynge coloured, not at what he had done, though he had shamelessly distorted the facts, but at the rebuke.   He was not used to be taken to task by young ladies. But he laughed it off.

" I never knew before, Miss Wildmere," he said, " that it was a disgrace to a man to be engaged to, or even to marry, a wealthy young lady.   But I don't understand you Quakers."

Then turning to Amy, he added :

" Perhaps you have heard Miss Bruce speak of his having a wife, or being engaged ? "

" No, I have always supposed him to be a single man without any definite prospects of changing his position."

" Then you think, Miss Wildmere, that Miss Bruce knows nothing of this ? "

" I'm sure I don't know, Grace is her great friend.   Does thee know, Grace ? "

" I know nothing about it.   We have other things to talk about than idle gossip."

" Yet, as he lives there, one would think he would have told some of them," said Hardynge.   " Unless indeed, he had reasons of his own for not doing so."

" Yes, provided there was anything to tell.   Is a man required to marry any girl he manages to save from a blizzard ? If that were the case, I think some of us would thank them for leaving us alone," replied Grace with some warmth.

" Still you know, it often happens."

" You have no evidence in this case whatever."

" But people say ——"

" Yes, people say a great deal that is not worth listening to."

But Amy did not share her cousin's dislike to gossip, and said meditatively :

" I should like to know whether Bessie has heard of this."

" I cannot see that it is any business of ours," said Grace ; " and we'd better be careful, for Charles Bruce is very fond of Robert Strongwood, and would not thank us for interfering."   Then with the uncomfortable feeling of having said too much, she became silent.

Hardynge saw that Amy was piqued, so with a show of taking the blame on himself, he said :

" You must excuse me, Miss Wildmere, I meant no harm. I see I should have said nothing."

" I don't see why." said Amy, evidently feeling injured ; " the story naturally suggested itself, and I think we should be perfectly justified in speaking of it to Bessie.   She probably knows it already, and could clear it all up."

"Yes," said Hardynge, "and one never knows ; if she is ignorant, it might be a friendly thing to tell her."

Grace bit her lip to keep back a stinging retort, and Hardynge, seeing her face, thought that he had gone far enough, and could leave what he had said to work. So he raised his voice that the other occupants of the carriage might hear, and choosing a safe topic for conversation, kept the whole party in a lively mood till they reached town. Grace, however, did not join in the fun. The previous conversation had troubled her, and the anxiety of the Bruces, to whom she was closely attached, weighed on her mind. She had wanted very much to stay with Bessie, but had consented perforce to leave, when she found that the search party and the family would fill the phaeton and buggy.

The grounds seemed very lonely after the phaetons had left. Aunt Mary and the twins were asleep, and the driver of the remaining phaeton was some distance off with his horses. Bessie sat looking at the splendid view. The sun had gone behind a passing cloud, and the shadow cast upon the scene that had been so brilliant seemed typical of the sad ending to the beautiful anticipations for the day. Would this also prove to be only a passing cloud ?

Presently Aunt Mary woke up, and then the twins, and they began to talk over the position of affairs. But conversation flagged, and, as is often the case among Friends, they fell into a silence, and Aunt Mary offered a prayer full of earnest entreaty, yet full also of trust and submission.

Then Aunt Mary, seeing that Bessie looked tired, undertook to keep the children entertained while Bessie busied herself with the easier task of arranging some supper for the search party when they should return.

CHAPTER XIV.

WAS IT A RESCUE?

AS soon as Strongwood felt at all equal to the exertion, he and Bertie started. The climb to the level ground was a short one, yet he found considerable difficulty, for, besides the steepness, the oppression on his chest continued, and he was more tired than he had supposed. By the time they reached the top he had to make a long pause to recover breath, and to stop again several times before he reached the maple tree which he had "blazed." Again he used his watch as a compass, and pushed on, but very slowly and with frequent rests. Sometimes he felt that he could go no further; but the thought that Bertie's life as well as his own depended upon his exertions made him struggle on. In this way an hour passed; but there was no sign of nearing the picnic ground. Another half-hour,—what could be the matter? Had he mistaken the direction? He thought he recognized landmarks, but it might be that he was deceived by false resemblances. More than twice the time he had taken in reaching Bertie had been consumed on their return walk, and their goal seemed no nearer.

At last he sat down in despair.

"Bertie, I don't know where we are, and I'm too tired to go on."

" Are we lost then ? " Bertie asked with quivering lips.

Strongwood tried to speak hopefully. " Perhaps I may be rested in a little while."

The child understood the tone better than the words, and was silent. Presently he kneeled down and said : " Heavenly Father, we are lost. Help us to get home, for Jesus's sake." Then, as if remembering that the Lord's will must be done, he added in a lower tone, and with an evident effort, " if it be right."

In spite of himself, Strongwood could not help smiling at the addition ; but the evident honesty of the words showed him how far the prayer had been from a mere form.

" That child really believes that he is speaking to God," he thought to himself, " Well, he's been taught to do so." But Strongwood felt that environment did not altogether explain it ; besides, how could such an environment have been produced without a succession of persons who honestly felt that they knew what intercourse with God is ? This was positive testimony. He had nothing to meet it with but theories, based upon the testimony of men whose personal evidence went no further than to say that they knew of no such experience.

The situation that Bertie and he were now in seemed desperate. Apart from his weakness, he was afraid that every step might lead them further away and so lessen the probability of their being found.

" Bertie," said he, " Perhaps some one might hear if we shouted."

They tried ; but the effort made Strongwood cough so violently, that he had to stop for hoarseness.

" My voice is gone," he said, " but you must do the best you can. Here's my watch. Every time the little tiny hand reaches sixty, call out."

The boy was delighted, and followed the directions carefully ; but his companion had not much hope that the shrill little voice would carry any distance, and he made one more effort to shout.

This time more than a cough resulted, for Strongwood, putting his handkerchief to his mouth found it stained a bright red. He moved his position a little that Bertie might not see the hæmorrhage which seemed to take away the last ray of hope ; for, though the bleeding was not really severe, it was the only one Strongwood had had, and he shared the common notion that all hæmorrhages from the lungs are of necessity immediately dangerous. Bertie, however, noticed nothing, for his whole attention was turned to timing his shouts, which he did with conscientious accuracy.

For the second time that year Strongwood found himself face to face with death. That night last winter in the snow and storm came before him in a series of pictures like the dissolving views of a magic lantern. On that occasion, before they reached the shelter of the kindly old woman's cottage they had come very close to death, and he had contemplated it as one does the entrance of a strange cave, not knowing what lies within the black mouth. A dread, colder than the piercing wind had chilled him, but he had clenched his teeth like a man and faced it. Now, in the beautiful summer evening, death had again come near ; but it was quite different. Then he had felt that the mystery of death was unsolvable, and must be faced. Since that time he had lived with those who rejoiced in the faith that light had shone through the mystery, and who looked forward, through Christ, to glory beyond. The glory they saw made his darkness blacker by contrast. He saw no light, but he no longer felt satisfied with his former theory, that there was no light to be seen. They had told him that their light did not come to them through clear knowledge of the life to come, but through an individual experience of a Saviour and a Father. How lonely he felt. If every one were orphans, then each one had to bear the inevitable. But if there were a Father who cared for all, then to live as an orphan was a needless loneliness.

As the hæmorrhage continued, the situation seemed to grow more hopeless. He bitterly repented his foolishness in going off on the search without telling anyone.

The reasons which had seemed so good,—fear of being prevented from going,—fear of being laughed at for going in so unlikely a direction,—now seemed flimsy enough ; while wounded pride and chagrin added their sting.

He disliked to be helped, and always preferred to carry out what he undertook single-handed. But now he was at his wits' end. Even in the blizzard he had struggled till they had reached shelter. Now, for the first time in his life, he acknowledged himself beaten. He should never get Bertie home,—he should never see Bessie again. It seemed so hard just to miss success after all his efforts. He had willingly risked his life to rescue Bertie, but he was to lose his life, and yet not rescue him. Some day they would be found, and their friends would guess the story, and Bessie would know it all. This was a comfort. But to lose her just as he had learned to love her, before he knew if she loved him, or had spoken to her of his love, and all because he had told no one whither he was going—was bitterness indeed. He felt that if he could only see Bessie once more, and receive a smile and a tear from her he should be satisfied.

" If there be a Helper, I wish I could find Him," he thought. And then he remembered Bessie's words, that our sense of need is the echo of God's call. If so, the call seemed to be a loud one.

" After all," he thought, " I can't go much on that idea, for any one in my position would feel the same as I do. But then, I suppose, Charlie would tell me that this only shows the need to be universal ; and he always insists that to doubt the supply of a common need of mankind is infidelity to nature. I must say that in my present circumstances there seems to be a good deal of force in that argument."

But he was too honest a man to persuade himself that he believed when he really doubted, or to suppose that if there were a God, He would accept unreal prayers. Strongwood could not pray, but he had ceased to be antagonistic. He was humbled and wished to pray, and was willing to learn. He did not know that this change, if continued in, is the crucial one in a man's experience, and that the very wish to pray is in itself more than half a prayer ; for God is very near every honest heart that gropes after Him.

And now he thought no more of himself but of Bertie. If the hæmorrhage proved fatal, what would the child do ? To be sure Strongwood was of little help, as it was ; but if the bleeding would only stop, he might after a rest be able to do something. He racked his brains to invent signals, and finally, as his cough and hæmorrhage became less he got Bertie to collect some dry leaves in an open place and to light them, in the hopes that the smoke might attract attention. When this was done, he called the tired little fellow to him and made him lie down and go to sleep, with the promise that when he woke up he might go, and pick berries. Bertie had been much frightened at the hæmorrhage, but as he did not notice it till it was subsiding, Strongwood was able to reassure him.

"Poor little man," said Strongwood to himself as he watched the boy's quiet sleep, "I've done all that I can to get you home; I suppose it will end by my covering you with my coat, as the McKendry boy did his brother."

CHAPTER XV.

Rescued, But—

STRONGWOOD by surrendering his antagonism to the thought of a personal God, had done no more than become a true agnostic, one who admitting his ignorance, is willing to be taught. But the step from false to true agnosticism is no slight one ; it had involved a real humbling of himself before the requirements of truth, and it had been followed, as all such experiences are, by a quickening of the moral sense. The faults of his character stood out before him in such bold relief as to startle and trouble him. If by any chance he and Bertie should be rescued, he resolved to live differently, to be a better son and brother, to be more unselfish—in short, to be a truer and nobler man. Then as his eyes fell on the sleeping boy, and he thought of the anxious friends, he began again to revolve plans in his mind for finding the way home.

"If it only were not for this wretched weakness," he thought, "I'm sure I could do something."

While he and Bertie were lying there, Bessie at the picnic ground continued her preparations for the tea she intended to give the search party on their return. She was more and more perplexed as to what had become of Strongwood.

The rest had been so sure that he had gone home that for a time she had felt she must be mistaken. But now that

she was alone with her thoughts, it seemed impossible to her
that one who had shown such sympathy with entire strangers
in the morning, could leave his friends in their anxiety in the
afternoon. Yes, he must be somewhere in the woods looking
for Bertie ; doubtless, he had gone off quietly to avoid being
hindered. But if so, he had been absent a long time. What
if he should himself have become bewildered in the forest ?

As she thought it over, a very natural suggestion occurred
to her.

*   *   *   *

" Wake up, Bertie ! Wake up !" cried Strongwood a few
moments later. " There's the horn ; we are saved."

They were really not far off. He had not missed his
way at all ; but had simply failed to realize how very slow their
homeward progress had been ; for every step had been an
effort ; and his eyes, unaccustomed to forest sights, had failed
to recognize land-marks.

Hope lent new strength, and, though the exertion caused
renewal of the cough and hæmorrhage, he pressed on.
Success was assured. Bertie was saved ; he himself alone
had effected the rescue, and should himself have the triumph
of restoring him in person to his friends—and to Bessie.

But as soon as they were near enough to see the top of
the phaeton over a slight rise in the ground, and the tension
was over, Strongwood again felt weak ; his head swam, and
leaning against a tree for support, he said :

" Bertie, do you see the top of that carriage ? "

" Yes."

" Run towards it, and you'll find your Aunt Bessie."
Bertie hesitated.

" I don't like to leave thee when thee's so sick."

"Go quick, and send somebody," and Strongwood sank down to the ground.

Bertie needed no second instruction, and a few minutes later, Bessie, looking up, saw a dust-begrimed, hatless little boy with very torn clothing, running towards her. Aunt Mary and the twins saw him also, and they all surrounded him eagerly.

"Why, Bertie, where has thee been?" they all asked at once.

"I fell down a steep place," said Bertie, as soon as he had recovered breath; "and Robert Strongwood got me up, and ——"

"The dear man," said Aunt Mary. "But where is he? I don't see him."

"Oh, Aunt Bessie, do come quick; he's on the ground, and blood's all comin' out of his mouth, and"— Bertie added, in an awe-struck voice—" I guess he's almost dead."

This announcement cut short any further demonstration over Bertie.

"Here Bessie," said Aunt Mary, as the former started off, " Here's a bottle of Valentine's beef, and thee'd better take a pitcher and fill it with cold water at the spring as thee goes, and stay, here's a shawl."

"Yes, Aunt Mary," said Bessie, as she gathered up the articles. "And I'll send Bertie back directly to tell thee how Robert Strongwood is."

So saying, she followed Bertie. They found Strongwood sitting on the ground with his back against a tree, his head fallen forward, his face deathly pale, and stained with blood about the mouth, while the tell-tale handkerchief in his hand and his dusty clothing completed the ghastly picture. He did not answer their call, or show any signs of life.

" Is he dead, Aunt Bessie ? " asked Bertie solemnly.

" I hope not," Bessie almost gasped out.

" He'll have died for me," said the child softly. "Something like Heavenly Jesus, only here there were no wicked men, nor ——"

But Bessie, who had no mind to improve the occasion just then, had already laid Strongwood's head on the ground, loosened his collar and cravat, raised his feet by placing them on a log, and was dashing cold water on his face with her hand.

After a few moments of suspense she had the satisfaction of seeing him draw a long breath.

He opened his eyes, saw her and Bertie, smiled, and closed them again. Bessie felt his pulse. It was weak, but regular. In a little while it was perceptibly stronger, and his breathing became natural.

" Bertie, can thee find the way back to Aunt Mary ? "

" Oh, yes."

" Run to her then, and she will give thee something to eat. Tell her Robert Strongwood is better, and, as soon as father comes, be sure to send him to me."

He left her, and presently the signal of successful search sounded out—three short blasts of the horn in rapid succession, repeated in half a minute. How thankful Bessie felt, and yet,—the tears came in her eyes as she compared what Strongwood was now, with what he had been as he helped her into the carriage that very morning—that morning ! It seemed a week ago.

Moistening her handkerchief with fresh spring water, she gently bathed his forehead and washed the stains from his mouth. He was by this time quite conscious ; but lay with his eyes shut, feeling very weak, though very happy to have her so near him and to feel her soft touch.

Presently she said :

"Mr. Strongwood, won't you take this?" and she held a glass containing some beef juice to his lips. He assented, and so she raised his head and he drank it.

"Let me put something under your head now ; I think, as you are better, it would be more comfortable for you"; and suiting the action to the word, she made a pillow of the shawl and placed it in position.

" Is that more comfortable ?"

"Thank you, yes." His voice was feeble but clear.

" We came as quickly as we could," he continued. " I'm afraid you were very anxious about Bertie."

" Yes, and about you too, Mr. Strongwood ; nobody knew what had become of you."

" Please excuse me, I ought to have told you I was going."

" I think you were very wise not to ; for we should never have allowed you to go. But now, you must not talk, it might make you worse. You must lie perfectly still till Charlie comes. You see, I am your nurse, and must be obeyed."

The last words were intended to be spoken half playfully, but a little tremble in her voice showed Strongwood how deeply she felt, and opening his eyes, he saw her's full of tears. He felt that she cared, and it satisfied him—he had no wish to speak. Her presence, her sweet voice and gentle touch were like a delicious dream. He only hoped that assistance would be long in coming.

CHAPTER XVI.

WHEN, half an hour later, Bruce came up with Dr. Storey, McKendry, and others of the party, he found Bessie anxiously looking for them.

"How is he?" asked Bruce, pressing her hand with an expression of mingled joy at Bertie's safety and of solicitude for his friend.

"I hardly know." He has been coughing, and the hæmorrhage has started again.

"Doctor," said Bruce, "I'm very glad thee stayed. This is a case for thy skill."

The doctor smiled. His sympathy for Strongwood could not altogether spoil his pleasure that his friends, who had not yet ceased addressing him as Joe, should have occasion to recognize his professional character. He knelt by the patient, noted all the characteristic features of the hæmorrhage, felt his pulse, counted the respirations, etc., administered a hypodermic injection of medicine to check the hæmorrhage, and asked if they had any ice.

"Only what is in the freezer," said Bessie, "but there's some ice-cream left, if that would do any good."

"The very thing," said the doctor. "Let him have some. Be careful not to give him very much at a time."

Then he called Bruce aside.

"It is clearly a case of hæmoptysis," he said with the natural fondness of young doctors for long words. "That is," he added, "I mean bronchial hæmorrhage ; he is also thoroughly exhausted."

"Does thee consider the bleeding dangerous ?"

"Not of itself. I should judge that it is not due to the erosion of a blood vessel ; but that it comes from the bronchial mucous membrane. His weakness is not due to loss of blood, but to overstrain."

Bruce, not interested in the medical remarks, came at once to the practical question :

"What can be done, doctor ?"

"That's the difficulty. A drive over a road such as we came by is out of the question for him."

"There is another road. It is better, but very much longer."

McKendry, who had been watching them, and who fully took in the situation, now came forward and said :

"Excuse me, doctor, I've been a thinkin' that it wouldn't do to carry him back to town as he is. If my cottage would be of any service, he's welcome to it. We won't soon forget what he did for us this mornin'. The house is small, but it's clean and dry, and it's quiet. There ain't no children now to"— and his voice broke down.

"Would it not be too great a strain on your wife ?" asked Bruce.

"No, sir, I think 'twill do her good to have her mind distracted like. Leastways, our house is at your service."

"We are greatly obliged to you, I am sure," said Bruce. "What does thee think, doctor ?"

" The very thing. Perhaps if thee and our friend McKendry here would go forward and prepare Mrs. McKendry, you could have the room ready by the time we can get him there. I think he had better be quiet a little while longer. I'll spend the night with him."

So Bruce and McKendry departed with a few others, and, before the phaeton with Strongwood drove slowly up to the door of the cottage, the arrangements were complete. The bedstead had been taken from the upper room where it was close under the roof to the more airy room below in front of the kitchen. Mrs. McKendry boasted not only of a new, husk, cotton top mattress, but also of that joy of the country folk in that region, a large feather bed, and her hospitable soul rebelled at the doctor's refusing it; she only consented not to have it used on his insisting that it was not suitable for persons with hæmorrhage. The linen was coarse, but spotlessly white, and everything looked very inviting as Strongwood was carried in.

" We're rough, but you're welcome to what we've got," said the woman heartily.

" Thanks," whispered Strongwood. " You have made everything beautifully comfortable."

" Good bye, Rob," said Bruce. " I shall come up in the morning to see how you are. How can I ever thank you for what you've done ? " and he pressed Strongwood's hand, and leaving him before he could answer, joined the party in the phaeton, which soon drove off.

Meanwhile, at Uplands, Lydia Leslie and Mrs. Bruce had been spending a quiet day. The latter, as she wished to sit up to welcome the party home from the picnic, did not come downstairs till late in the afternoon. After a seven o'clock tea they sat together in the porch. The sun had set behind the mountains, and twilight was rapidly closing in. They listened for the sound of wheels, and watched the fire-flies rising from the grass and shedding forth their light, as if they were little stars that had fallen to earth and lost their way, though, unlike stars, their light was intermittent.

"They are staying rather late, I think," said Mrs. Leslie. "I hope nothing has happened."

"Oh, I think not, mother; it has been a very hot day, and they have been waiting for the cool of the evening to start for home."

So they talked on, and waited without uneasiness. But ill news flies fast, and too many people by this time knew of Bertie being lost for it to be kept a secret. About half-past eight, one of the servants having finished her work, went out to call on an acquaintance, who was cook in another Friend's family, and while there had heard of the occurrence, and hastening home, blurted out the news with many sobs and incoherent sentences, and not a few touches which her Irish imagination added.

When she had left them, Clara and her mother sat for a long time without speaking. Neither of them were able to find relief to their feelings in words; for both, unlike Bruce and Bessie, were naturally silent.

At last Clara said :

"If Bertie is lost on the mountains, I know he is as much under God's care, whatever happens to him, as if he were in my arms, but it's hard to believe it."

"Yes, Clara ; and it makes it so much harder that we can do nothing."

"I don't think so, mother. To be so utterly helpless as we are makes it easier for me to trust."

After a pause, Mrs. Leslie said :

" How could they have let him wander off ? However, I don't believe they were careless either, dost thou ? "

" No, mother, I don't ; and we must be careful not to let them imagine we do, for they will blame themselves. I know that they love Bertie as much as I do." Then her mother heart made her correct herself—" I mean, as truly."

" I am so thankful, Clara, that thou canst keep so calm."

" I'm not calm at all, mother, I'm all trembling— but I don't want to choose my own way," and she gave a stifled sob.

Her mother made no reply, but came and sat beside her, and drew her head down on her shoulder, and there they remained, each absorbed in her own thoughts, till the sound of wheels crunching on the gravel caused them to rise up, and with trembling steps go forward to meet the carriage.

" Here we are, Clara," cried Charlie. " All the chicks are safe ; I hope you haven't been anxious."

Clara could not trust herself to speak, but as soon as she saw Bertie she clasped him in her arms—

" Oh, my boy, my precious boy ! "

" Mother," said Bertie, " I've come back. I guess I'd have died, if Robert Strongwood hadn't got me off that rock, and he almost died doin' it."

" Don't be so quick, Bertie," said his father. " We'll explain all when we get in the house." Then turning to the other occupants of the phaeton, he said :

" Farewell, friends, and thank you very much for all your help."

" Farewell, we wish we could have done more," they called out as they drove away ; while Bruce shouted back :

" Don't forget to leave word at Dr. Storey's that he won't be back till to-morrow."

Perhaps Friends are less demonstrative than others, but it is due to no lack of deep feeling; and when the Bruces sat down, an unbroken family, in the sitting room, Clara grasping Bertie's hand as if afraid to let him go, they fell into silence, and presently her husband, in a brief prayer of only two or three minutes, thanked God for the preservation, and remembered the friend who had risked himself on their behalf, and remembered also those whose children had not returned.

" Father," said Bertie, as he kissed him good-night, " I think Robert Strongwood is the best man in the world—but 'cept thee."

As the door closed on the children, Bruce remarked :

" If my influence goes for anything, this will be the last picnic held on the mountain."

CHAPTER XVII.

THE CONSPIRATORS.

IF any one could be called the favourite of fortune, certainly in the eyes of his companions Fred Emorie at the age of twenty-one was that person. His parents idolized him, gave him every advantage that wealth could procure, and after he left college, sent him to travel for a year in Europe. On his return he studied law and was admitted to the New York bar. In addition to his fortune, his talents were decidedly above the average, and his friends prophesied a brilliant career. Whether it would be a useful one or not was a different question; for with all his engaging manners he was so supremely selfish that there was little prospect of his becoming useful except by accident.

This was Fred Emorie at twenty-one. At forty he had lost nearly all his money, his parents were dead, the better class of his friends had left him, he had no practice, and he considered himself the most ill-used man in the world. The cause of it all was that even from his school days one evil habit, that of gambling, had mastered him, and had now brought him to the verge of ruin; for, although he sometimes gained a good deal of money, when he had a stroke of luck, as he called it, it never lasted. He was also dissipated, and several times in a year he would go on a "spree." But, as a rule, he could control his appetite for drink, and when necessary for the purpose in hand he could keep from liquor for months at a time. He still retained enough quickness of resource and readiness of wit and good judgment to make him, while incapable of originating a plan for plucking the unwary, invaluable in carrying it out.

He was sitting in what he styled his office, and feeling peculiarly "down on his luck," when a rap on the door aroused him, and Ralph Hardynge entered.

The face that turned towards the visitor, though somewhat disfigured by excesses, had not lost all evidence of refinement. The thick, black hair was unkempt and the heavy moustache was untrimmed, but the eyes had some of their old brightness, and they now sparkled with pleasure, as he rose to meet his old comrade ; for Hardynge was not very often in New York, and he never called except to propose some scheme.

" Well, Hardynge, glad to see you, how are you?"

" All right, old fellow, how's yourself? Hard up, as usual ?"

" Yes."

" Want a job ?"

" Will it pay ?"

" Sure's you're born."

" Well, out with it."

" Wait a week, and I'll tell you. You know, or perhaps you don't, that I'm hard up myself. My last venture didn't pan out as I thought it would, and I lost the little pile I had saved. So I've got a scheme. You know Bob Strongwood, and that I owe him a grudge ; the sneak that he was to go blowing on me to my boss and my girl. I've a chance now to be even with him and get something out of it for my own advantage too, so that'll be killing two birds with one stone, won't it? Understand!"

" Exactly—well?"

" Well, Strongwood's at Penelve in Pennsylvania, spend-the summer, for his health, you know, staying with an old college chum of his. Said chum has a sister, quite a charming little Quaker, and old Bob, playing the invalid, goes courting said sister. A few days ago they had a picnic; and Bob he spent half the day driving her about, and the other half in a romantic search for her small nephew. It was awfully cleverly done; put up job of course; but we were all taken in, and there was a time hunting, I can tell you. But I soon saw through it all, and, of course, the next morning I hear the child is all safe, and old Bob reported nearly dead with his exertions. You see his little game; but I'm going to spoil it, or make him fork out a neat sum."

" Are you sure he's rich?" said Emorie, doubtfully.

" I don't think he is very, but his mother's rich as Crœsus, and awfully proud, and wouldn't stop at anything to save the reputation of the family, and she ——"

" Whatever are you driving at? Can't you come to the point?"

" Well," said Hardynge, "the point's just this. I go to Flumetown, New York, in the way of business, and have got to know a Mr. Galway, a leading man there. Last spring his daughter was rescued from a blizzard by Strongwood. There was a good deal of talk about their going to be married. There's nothing in it really, but that's all the better. His health has broken down, and they are off to Alaska this week, to be gone three months. She has two brothers; one, Ephraim, who lives in New Orleans, and the other, Jonathan, who's been off in Europe for years. They expected Jonathan home to go with them, but he gave out at the last—I suspect to the governor's relief, for he's rather wild they say. Now my plan is for you to go to Flumetown, and ——" Here his voice dropped to a whisper.

. Emorie listened to him very attentively, and then broke in : "I can't do it. It's dangerous and impracticable. Do it yourself."

"I can't. I'm known there. Besides you're the man— you're the right age, have been to Europe, have a dissipated look——"

"Thank you."

"Don't mention it. It's quite true ; I don't flatter. Then you've got brass."

"Yes, but I am perfectly ignorant of how to play the role."

"I can post you sufficiently. You'll find that you'll not be expected to know much."

"He'll suspect blackmail," said Emorie. "It's too barefaced to succeed. I tell you it's no go."

"On the contrary, it will go because it is so barefaced. Come, it's worth trying."

"Yes, but it's about the meanest trick I ever played."

"Which is saying a good deal."

"What do you mean ?"

"No offence, I assure you. I meant it as a compliment."

Emorie looked at him, hardly knowing what to make of the remark. But he had already determined to fall in with the plan; for he wanted the money, and he could not afford to quarrel. So he returned to the subject, and the two men were soon engrossed in minute details which need not now be repeated. In all their schemes Hardynge assumed the role of leader, without question ; for long experience had taught them that success followed their efforts most certainly, when Hardynge, who was very weak in executive ability, was the head, and Emorie the hands.

The conversation lasted far into the night, and they provided for every conceivable contingency. As he left, Hardynge said :

" Now then, you remember ; I've made arrangements to be informed when the Galways have really started, and I'll let you know. You wait for the first Atlantic liner that comes in after that, and then start. Of course, you'll have come in the steerage and have had a rough voyage. Be sure and have all your linen re-marked. Here's my address." And he gave him a slip of paper with an assumed name and a special address. " Remember our one chance lies in being prompt."

Business detained Hardynge in New York for several days after his conversation with Emorie. During this time an opportunity unexpectedly presented itself for starting a report of the financial unsoundness of the firm of Strongwood & Hansen. He calculated that the " Flumetown scheme," as he styled it, would be settled and the money paid long before any result of the report could be felt, and therefore he did not hesitate to seize the occasion for injuring Strongwood in this way. Accordingly he made use of information, accidentally gained, that the firm had asked for an extension on one of its notes, and of the fact that Strongwood was spending the summer quietly with a friend in the country instead of going for a few weeks, as was his custom, to some fashionable resort, to make it appear that his ill health was due to worry over business and that his going to Penelve was from motives of economy.

CHAPTER XVIII.

FIRST SUSPICIONS.

NOTWITHSTANDING the fatigues of the day before, Bruce made an early start, so as to see after Strongwood and get back to business as soon as he could. The buggy was loaded with necessaries, and, as he declared, un-necessaries, for the invalid. But Aunt Mary, who was the family authority on all matters of sickness, sent down directions, which Bessie fully carried out, and even added to herself, till her brother put his foot down and said that he had enough, and that the rest of the things must wait till McKendry should build a new room to hold them. Whereupon Bessie laughed, slipped one more article into the buggy, and sent him off.

Arrived at the mountain he found Strongwood had passed a fairly good night. There had been no hæmorrhage since nine o'clock the evening before. He had had only a slight rise in temperature, and had taken some nourishment. Altogether the doctor seemed quite satisfied with his progress, and felt that he might return to town for the day, leaving the patient under the care of the McKendrys.

Bruce gave a good account of Bertie, and brought warm messages of thanks from all to Strongwood. The latter, enjoined not to talk, only whispered a few words, and smiled his appreciation of their kindness in sending so many things for his comfort. But his smile was such a weary one that Bruce was greatly touched, and left him much concerned. Dr. Storey, after giving minute directions to Mrs. McKendry, and promising to come up the next day, got into the buggy with Bruce and they drove off.

"Doctor," said Bruce, "what does thee think of him? He seems to me a very ill man."

"I feel hopeful. He has had a severe strain; but with rest and good food, he'll be up and about before long."

"I hope he has all he needs."

"Everything, and they are most attentive. By the way, Charlie, I believe that McKendry is a thoroughly changed man. Last night he had family prayer for the first time. We heard it all through the board partition. He read the 118th Psalm, and quite broke down over the words, 'The Lord hath chastened me sore.' Then he prayed, such a prayer—homely, uncouth and sometimes laughable. But it was straight from his heart. He confessed his sins, prayed for himself, his family, for you, and for the invalid in the next room. I was where I could see Robert Strongwood's face. His eyes were closed, but when the man prayed for him, I thought a tear trembled between his lids. I believe it will be a great blessing to him to be there. I know McKendry's prayer this morning uplifted me."

Dr. Storey was quite right in thinking that Strongwood would feel the influence of the change that had come upon McKendry. It was the first time he had ever seen any one actually turn to the Lord. As the days passed he could not help feeling the power, and from what he heard the neighbours saying to Mrs. McKendry about her husband's former life, he soon gathered enough to show how great the change that had come so suddenly had been. To a man thoroughly aroused like Strongwood, what he saw was a practical illustration—in a sense, a demonstration of the living power of Christ. Not that he was conscious of its full importance, though he was consciously impressed. At times he explained it away, as merely emotional, but in his heart he felt it was something deeper.

After Bruce had left for McKendry's, Bessie went into the garden, and was busy among the flowers, when Amy Wildmere entered the gate. The click of the latch made Bessie look up.

"Oh, Amy, is it thee? Glad to see thee. Come in."

"No thank thee. I just thought I'd stop and ask how Bertie is this morning. We were so glad to hear he had been found."

"Yes, Amy, we are all so thankful. Robert Strongwood found him. But we fear it has been too much for him."

"Who—for Bertie?"

"No, Bertie seems all right. But Robert Strongwood. I'm afraid he's very ill. He had a hæmorrhage, and Dr. Storey had to stay with him all night on the mountain."

"On the mountain! Didn't he come home?"

"No, he stayed at McKendry's, the man whose children were lost, thee knows. Charlie has just gone up there to see after him, and to take some things."

"I hadn't heard he was ill at all. I am very sorry. Isn't it curious that he should have two such experiences in a few months?"

"Has he?" said Bessie simply. "I have not heard of it."

"Why, didn't he tell thee?"

"No. Did he tell thee?"

" Oh, dear, no. Mr. Hardynge told us all about it as we drove down last evening."

Amy saw that at the mention of Hardynge's name Bessie's interest began to wane, and she hastened to add :

" It was most romantic. They, I mean Robert Strongwood and the young lady. It was at Flumetown, New York. Oh, what was I saying? Oh yes. They were out in a blizzard alone, on a dark night, and had to take refuge in a deserted hut, and the next morning they came in on a sledge with logs, and I don't know what all they did; and Mr. Hardynge thought they were married, or perhaps only engaged, he wasn't quite sure. Perhaps thee knows ? "

" I know nothing about it. Mr. Strongwood does not make me his confidante."

" Well, I thought I'd ask thee, and if thee didn't know, it might be better to tell thee."

" Why ? "

Amy, who had expected Bessie to show some embarrassment, was considerably disappointed at her coolness, and hardly knew how to proceed, the reason for speaking of it seemed so obvious.

" Oh, I don't know," she said. I thought it was better thee should know it."

" I don't see why."

" Well, thee knows you are so much together and ——"

Bessie gave a merry laugh.

" So, little Amy, thee was afraid I should fall in love with him, was thee ? and thought thee would warn me ? It's very good of thee, but I think there was no need. That was a pretty story. Perhaps he'll give us an opportunity of congratulating him some day."

Bessie's tone, if not her words, were unmistakable, and romantic Amy, while she was too kind not to be glad that her friend was indifferent to Strongwood, could not help feeling a little chagrined at the sudden descent from poetry to prose. She began to say good-bye, when Bessie added :

" Oh, don't go yet. Let me give thee some Maréchal Niel roses for thy mother. I know they're her favourites."

Amy's strongest point was her affection for her mother, and she soon forgot, for the time being, her little romance, in discussing her mother's health, which, always delicate, had lately begun to show signs of increasing feebleness.

The story Amy had told did not make much impression upon Bessie. Of course, Strongwood was not married. That was clear enough. But he had spoken of having been exposed to a blizzard, and he might be engaged. Bessie had seen nothing in his actions towards any of the young ladies, or towards herself, inconsistent with this. It was very probably true ; and her mind turned to other things.

Had Hardynge known the first result of his scheme, he would have been a good deal disappointed.

CHAPTER XIX.

STRUGGLES AND DOUBTS.

IT is a common mistake for persons in health to suppose that illness is a good time to think. As a rule it is not, and, provided there is no overmastering desire or dread, the mind is often as idle as the body, or the same thoughts go through it again and again. But, although this is the case, and the patient feels rather than thinks, flashes of insight do from time to time break in upon him, and I suppose that no thoughtful man ever recovers from a serious illness without having his character and views of life deeply affected by it.

For several days after the picnic, Strongwood lay in McKendry's cottage in a listless, half-dreamy languor. He was perfectly himself, and would rouse when spoken to, but for a large part of the time he merely rested. McKendry's earnestness impressed him from the first, as we have seen; but the significance of it dawned on him only gradually. That a character so unlike Bruce's should be profoundly influenced by the same Gospel seemed to illustrate its adaptability to different classes of minds. As he lay there he saw that McKendry was finding comfort in the midst of his sorrow, and he envied him, and longed to discover the secret; yet he could not. His arguments against Christianity had not been categorically answered, and were too strong to be discarded. At the same time he could not use them as he had done before.

The quiet influence of lives lived in the power of God had been undermining his fortress, and no weapon but self-will could successfully turn away the inward word of God, even when it was only partially recognized.

The first day that he was able to be up, he was sitting in an armchair in the shade in front of the cottage expecting Bruce, for it was his day to come. What was his surprise, when the buggy appeared, to see, not Charlie, but Bessie.

"Charlie was called away on business just as he was starting," she said as she came towards him, after tying the horse to a tree, "so I've come instead. I hope you are better. I'm glad to see you able to be out."

The memory of her care of him as he lay helpless in the forest—or rather the memory of herself and all she did for him—had been the bright spot through the weary days that had followed. Now as she approached him, with her bright smile, her hair just enough disarranged by the wind, and her white straw hat blown sufficiently awry to give a slightly jaunty look, which her fine bearing saved from being undignified, Strongwood thought he had never seen a girl who at the same time was so splendid and so lovable.

They were quite alone, for McKendry was away at his work, and his wife had gone with their son on an errand.

Bessie gave him the letters, and carried the delicacies she had brought into the house. While she was thus engaged, it came over Strongwood that here was his opportunity. Not that he thought of making a formal proposal, but he could feel his way, and, if she should respond to his first advances, he could go further. At least he would let her see that he cared for her. If he did not, Seward might step in during his absence and carry her off. He was still weak, and the excitement of deciding so quickly to take the step almost unnerved him ; but by the time she had come out of the cottage he had his opening sentence all ready. Then he stopped.

She stood a moment in the low doorway, which framed her as if she were in a picture. The simplicity of her attire only set off her personal charms. And yet he paused, the words checked, almost as they were leaving his lips, by the thought of the contrast between himself and her. He, a man in consumption, rallying temporarily from a hæmorrhage, with no further work before him. She, in perfect health, and, unlike the fashionable girls of his acquaintance, who had no true object in life, working strenuously for noble, unselfish purposes. What had he to offer her in exchange for all the sacrifice he would ask her to make on his account ? Money ? He had seen enough of Bessie to know that she did not care for that. Then he thought, " She is free to choose. That is not my responsibility."

Bessie, as she looked at him, was startled at his sudden paleness.

" Are you in pain ? " she asked.

Strongwood nodded.

" Let me help you into the house, so that you can lie down," she said, and suiting the action to the word, she tenderly helped him to rise, and supported him as he walked. Then she fetched a restorative and administered it.

" Can I do anything more for you ?" she asked.

" Yes," he said almost involuntarily.

" What is it ? "

" Don't ask me, don't ask me," he answered, suddenly sitting up. "I have said too much already." He fell back exhausted, and added, as if to himself : " It's hard, so hard ; but it's right."

Bessie saw that the last words were not addressed to her, and, supposing they had reference to something in the letters she had brought, judged it safest not to ask questions, but busied herself in arranging the room more tastefully.

Strongwood watched her in silence, with a deepening realization of his loss. He longed to speak, but his very love kept him silent. As soon as Mrs. McKendry returned, Bessie left. On her way home she could not help thinking of the strange scene she had witnessed. What could have caused it? Could it have anything to do with the Flumetown story? All the letters for the household passed through her hands, but none ever came to Strongwood directed in a lady's writing, except from his mother and sisters. She did not believe he was the man to jilt a girl; but in any case, whatever the question might be, he had determined to do right about it; so that it must be in the way to be settled. She wished she could help him, but, as she could not, she tried to dismiss the matter from her mind.

On his part, Strongwood had all the pain and none of the joy of self-sacrifice, and was much worse for several days. Then he began to improve again, but it was not unnatural that he should grow restless. In spite of his good breeding and of his desire that his hosts should not feel that he looked down on their homely ways, he could not help sometimes being peevish and cross, and was greatly abashed one evening at hearing McKendry and his wife discussing him as they approached the house.

"Never you mind, 'Liza. My mother used to say, When sick folk air gettin' well, there ain't no livin' with 'em. It's a good sign."

"That's all well enough, Abe, but if you had the nursin'

of him like me, you'd know what it was. It's 'I want this,' or 'I don't want that,' or 'This pillow's uncomferble;'—he's jawin' the hull time, till I'm 'most tuckered out."

"I guess you air, 'Liza. I tell yer what's ailin' him. There's somethin' weighin' on his mind. We've just got to pray for him."

Here their voices were lost as they went behind the house; but that evening Strongwood heard through the door, for McKendry always unconsciously raised his voice at family worship, his own shortcomings confessed with considerable frankness, and yet with so much kind feeling that he could not be offended. He was touched at the prayer that he might be comforted, and in the days that followed was better able to control himself.

About a mile off lived an old man, an exhorter among the United Brethren. Hearing that there was a sick gentleman at McKendry's, he came over to see if he could be of any help. He was a tall man, with his beard shaven, except a little under his chin and far back on his cheeks, where it grew rather long and formed a kind of frame for his face. His hair was silvery-grey, and his eyes, which beamed upon all, illumined his homely features. Every one laughed at his simplicity in ordinary matters, and every one loved and respected him.

Brother Peterson often came to sit by Strongwood, and would begin to talk of indifferent matters. But whether he began on the crops, or weather, or politics, it was sure to lead naturally to the one subject that was uppermost in his mind. His theology was crude, and Strongwood could not help an inward chuckle now and then to think how easily he could involve the old man in a maze of contradictions. But

in matters of personal experience, Peterson was a seer,
and would let fall aphorisms almost startling in their simplicity
and appropriateness. Sometimes his companion could not
grasp their meaning, but he felt they had a meaning, and
treasured them up for future consideration.

It was not very long before Strongwood was able once
more to sit for a little while out of doors. His favourite place
was near the grave of the little children. He chose it partly
for the associations and partly for its view. It was here that
on one occasion Dr. Storey found him and handed him several
letters, one of which was from his mother, the first that had
come since the picnic. He had been longing for it, and, in
his eagerness to read it, quite forgot to inform the doctor that
he now considered himself well enough to return to town, as
in fact he was. But, being one of the young doctor's earliest
patients, he was perhaps treated a little over cautiously.

As soon as he was alone he tore open the letter, and
read :

> "Chamonix,
>
> "Savoy, France,
>
> "July 3rd, 189—.

"Dear Robert,

"You must think me a poor correspondent, but we
have moved so rapidly from place to place that there has
really been no time to write. I began a letter to you last
week, but, as it is only begun, I commence on a new sheet.

"Your letter giving us the doctor's opinion about you
came the day before yesterday. We are all shocked and hope
it may prove to be a mistake. I'm sure there's no consumption
in my family, and I never heard your poor father [all people
who had died were 'poor' in Mrs. McPherson's vocabulary]

speak of there being any in his. It must be a mistake. In the meantime, it is a satisfaction to think of you as in such good hands; only don't let that Quaker girl set her cap for you.

"We have been having a most delightful time, and have met charming people, some of them several times. Among the latter are a Lord Southliegh and his sister. They are well acquainted with Lord Martington, to whom, you know, we have letters of introduction. 'Quite by accident,' of course, their names appeared in the Visitors' Book the day after we arrived at Chamonix. It really is rather exciting, for Lord Southliegh is a peer of the realm, or at least will be on the death of his father, and he has certainly taken a great fancy to Lucy. I think, indeed I hope, it is more than a flirtation, and I quietly manage to throw them in each other's way.

"Last evening I was afraid Mary had spoiled it all. There was quite a little company of us in our private parlour. During a lull in the conversation some one remarked to Mary that she looked grave, and what does she do but tell about your health and that foolish doctor's opinion. I could have boxed her ears.

"I saw Lord Southliegh's face fall, and I knew what he was thinking. So to make the best of it I hastened to say that of course we were dreadfully anxious about you, but after all it was only an opinion of a doctor you had picked up in a country town (which was *literally* true, you know), and I didn't believe it; for there was no consumption in my family; and that even if the report about you were true, you must have got it from your father's side of the house; and I added that it was a relief that Mr. McPherson's family was clear. His Lordship looked relieved, and I heard him say to Lucy, ' It's your half-brother then?'   So the matter passed off, but it gave me a fright, I can tell you.

"Yesterday we went up La Flégère to see the sunset glow on Mont Blanc.   It was truly superb.   To-day I have been a little under the weather, and decided to stay at home and write to you, and have not gone with them on the Mer de Glace.   Fortunately the party is sufficiently well chaperoned without me.

"As I am writing I hear their voices outside the windows, and from the tones I imagine that they have had, as usual, a delightful excursion.   They are coming in and I must stop.   I shall keep you informed as to how Lord Southliegh's affair progresses, and you must write and tell me you are better.

"Your affectionate Mother,

"EMILY McPHERSON."

The letter fell from Strongwood's hands.   He knew he had no right to expect anything else; and yet unconsciously the change in his own feelings towards his mother and the influence of Mrs. Compton's bright anticipations had made him hope for much more.   He felt that if there had been one sympathetic word he could have been satisfied.   But even Mary, who seemed to be sorry, had sent no message.   He did not know that she had written a loving note, proposing to join him in the autumn; but that his mother had quietly destroyed it.   She did not mean to be cruel; but she would not believe that her son had consumption, and she had other plans for her daughter.

A sense of exceeding loneliness oppressed Strongwood. Never for a moment since Bessie's visit had he faltered in his decision that in his state of health he could not honourably think of winning her affections, but he mourned over the loss. He had only once seen her since, when she had come up with Bruce to the meeting on a Sunday afternoon at McKendry's, and the effect of seeing her had been to make him feel that it would be wise for him to get away from Penelve as soon as possible, lest he should unintentionally commit himself. Whither he should go he did not much care, and he thought bitterly that no one else cared much either. His business ambitions were crushed. To be sure he was getting better now; but he felt that he had nothing to look forward to but a year or so of invalidism with alternate periods of illness and improvement, each illness more severe than the last, each respite shorter and less complete, till the end.

There was very little on the mountain to distract his thoughts, and, as he now required no nursing, the McKendrys left him necessarily very much alone. Old brother Peterson's visits had also been interrupted by his wife's illness. In his depression, the glimmering of light that had come to Strongwood seemed lost. This life and the next (if there was a next) seemed enveloped in darkness. His health suffered, and when the doctor paid his next visit he found his patient laid up again, and decided that a removal to Uplands should be effected as soon as possible.

The next day Bruce drove up with a minister from Philadelphia who was on a "religious visit" to Friends in the neighbourhood, and who had expressed a "concern" to visit Strongwood. Bruce was much disappointed at finding him so poorly, and for a short time they talked about his case and on indifferent subjects, till Bruce said:

"Rob, our Friend here felt it would be right to come up

to see thee, and would be glad if we could have a little quiet time together."

Strongwood politely acquiesced, and as the silence began, watched the old man with interest. He wore the most correct cut of Quaker garb, his thin hair was brushed straight forward and an expression of deep introversion rested upon his somewhat heavy-featured, but fine countenance.

It was certainly a novel feeling, to say the least of it, to know that this old Friend had come up to hold a Quaker meeting just with him, and was now waiting in silence to receive a direct word from God for him and for no one else. Strongwood thought to himself that if he could only be sure that Charlie had not primed the preacher, he would now have an opportunity of testing the Quaker theory of guidance. He did not know that the old Friend, with a feeling common to his school, had declined to receive any intimation as to Strongwood's condition.

The old man sat, and sat, till all suspicion as to any one having suggested his message to him vanished. And then Strongwood began to hope for some word that in his loneliness and disappointment might enlighten his darkness. It was just what he wanted, and here was a man, believed to be possessed with a prophetic gift, come to him under a direct sense of God's call. He began to be anxious for the Friend to speak. But no word came. Ten minutes passed, fifteen minutes, twenty minutes. Still no word. He glanced at the minister. It was clear that a great conflict was going on in his mind. Strongwood wondered if he was to receive some denunciatory message, and felt in his discouragement that it would not be undeserved, and that, if it brought certainty, it would be better than the mist that at present bewildered him.

THEN HE STOOD FOR A FULL MINUTE, WITHOUT SPEAKING AND WITHOUT MOVING, WITH HIS EYES FIXED ON STRONGWOOD.

The minister was really going through no slight struggle; for he had, to himself, been remarkably "led" that morning to feel that he must go up to the mountain to see some one, he did not know whom, who had not been there long and who was in spiritual need. On telling Bruce of his feeling, he had pointed in the direction of McKendry's, and had let fall remarks which convinced Bruce that the person must be Strongwood; and he had, at some inconvenience, driven him up. After all this, the old Friend was human enough to feel humiliated at having no message, and was even tempted to question whether he had been guided at all. This last thought was almost agony to him; for he had tried all his tests and had felt sure, and, if he were mistaken here, did it not throw a doubt on his whole method and belief? But, come what might, he would not pretend. If nothing were given, nothing should be said, and with more heroism than persons who have not been in his position can easily comprehend, he at last silently motioned to Bruce that the "sitting" was over.

Bruce arose quietly, shook hands with Strongwood, and left the room. The old Friend also shook hands, and without a word, followed him, leaving Strongwood discouraged, and more hopeless than ever.

"Either there's no truth in their theory, or God don't care for me," he thought, and, whichever it is, the result is the same.

Just then the door opened. The old Friend re-entered the room, and, removing his hat, stood silently at the foot of the bed gazing at Strongwood, who felt strangely awed. Then the preacher drew himself up to the full height of his more than six feet, raised his right hand as high above his head as he could, and pointed upward. There he stood for a full minute, with his eyes fixed upon Strongwood, without speaking and without moving. Then he slowly lowered his hand, took his hat, and without a word departed.

At first Strongwood regarded this as merely a Quaker vagary, and felt deeply disappointed, but during the night the memory of that prophetic figure, pointing upward, returned to him, and came as a message. He knew that it had been intended to point him to Christ, as the One who loved him, and who knew the right path for him to take, and who was waiting to save him. He tried to look up. What he saw was very little, very indefinite, but a sense of divine compassion did come, and in so far as he saw it, he believed.

CHAPTER XX.

MACHINATIONS.

ON the Thursday of the week after the conversation between Hardynge and Emorie, a well-dressed middle-aged man in a travelling suit of Scotch cloth, grip-sack in hand, and a somewhat worn steamer rug on his left arm, alighted from the train at Flumetown, New York. His portmanteau was of English make, rather shabby, and well covered with old labels of Continental and English towns.

"Just landed from Europe," was the remark he overheard from the bystanders, as he hailed a carriage, and entering it, told the driver to take him to Mr. Caleb Galway's.

As the driver's seat was on the same level as the back seat, and was not divided from it, the new arrival finished his directions after he was in the carriage.

" Family ain't home sir," said the driver. " Went off four days ago."

The stranger appeared surprised and troubled.

" How very awkward," said he.

" Did you write to them you were coming, sir ? "

" They expected me more than a month ago, but I could not come then, and this time I hoped to surprise them."

In a small place like Flumetown customs are still somewhat primitive, and there is a freedom of intercourse between different classes unknown in cities, and people's private affairs become almost public property.

Emorie had counted on this, and was not surprised when the man turned and looked at him, with the question :

" You ain't Mr. Jonathan Galway, are you ? "

" Good guess ; I shouldn't have thought you'd have seen the likeness. I don't think one in a hundred would."

The driver, much flattered, continued :

" Just think o' that ! Why your father's been looking for you weeks ago, and misses you at last by four days. Well, if that ain't too bad. Howsomever, I'll drive you to the house."

By a skilful combination of asking for information and appearing to make confidences, Emorie succeeded, before they reached the Galway mansion, a country seat a little east of the town, in making a valuable ally of the driver; who immediately did him a good turn by announcing to the old woman in charge when she opened the door,

" Good day, Mrs. Henderson. Here, I've brought you Mr. Jonathan Galway, come just four days too late to see his folks."

Had Mrs. Henderson stopped to think, she would have remembered that the driver had no better means of knowing who the stranger was than she had. But a good deal depends on first impressions, and the man's confident tone created just the impression Emorie wished.

" Good afternoon, sir," she said, " I'm sorry you've come too late, and they were so disappointed to start without you."

" Yes," said Emorie, " I couldn't come as was at first

arranged, and afterwards, when I found I could come later, I thought I'd surprise them. The steamer was delayed. But I thought they did not start till the 18th."

"They were to leave New York on the 12th; that's Tuesday. To-day 's Thursday."

"I wonder if I could catch them anywhere?" said Emorie, meditatively.

"Well, if Mr. Galway was poorly they intended to spend Sunday in Chicago. I should think you might catch them there."

"I'll just wire them. May I leave my valise here till I find out what time the train goes?"

"Certainly," said Mrs. Henderson, relieved at the prospect of his speedy departure, "and I'll have something ready for you to eat when you come back."

"Thank you very much," replied Emorie, and he asked the driver to take him to the telegraph office, where, as previously arranged, he found a dispatch requiring him to remain in Flumetown. Apparently much disappointed, he telegraphed to "Galway, Union Hotel, Chicago," announcing his arrival, and regretting he could not join his father and sister. Of course, the message never really reached the travellers, who were far west of Chicago by this time, but was received and answered by a confederate, for whom he had himself often rendered similar services. At six o'clock he returned to Mr. Galway's, and with a disappointed air said to Mrs. Henderson :

"I've just received bad news by telegraph."

"Nothing happened to Mr. Galway, I hope, sir," said the housekeeper in alarm, forgetting that if there had been news, it would not have come to him.

"Not so bad as that," said Emorie; "but was father really poorly enough to make you expect bad news?"

"Well, sir, I can't say that; but he was weakly and ailin'. But Miss Belle, she has great hopes, and says I to myself, let her hope on; she'll find it out soon enough, poor thing, and so I keeps my own counsel."

"And very wise of you, too, Mrs. Henderson. Belle has a tender heart."

"That she has, sir."

"Were they much disappointed that I did not come?"

"Well, to tell the truth, sir, Mr. Galway was real cross about it. And Miss Belle, she was a good deal cut up, too. But she tried to cheer him up and told him you'd be comin' home, certain, when you heard how bad he was."

Emorie appeared much moved. The old housekeeper pitied him, and acting on her motto—"Nothing comforts folks like eatin'"—she showed him upstairs and told him supper would be ready in a few minutes.

As Emorie entered the dining-room he saw over the mantelpiece a large portrait of a fine-looking, elderly gentleman, and caught a glimpse of a companion portrait opposite of a gentle-faced lady. He knew that Mr. Galway was a self-made man and not likely to have family portraits, and besides, the dress was modern. The risk of mistake was very slight, and was rendered almost nothing by a peculiar expression of expectancy on Mrs. Henderson's face. He paused suddenly before the portrait and said:

"Why, that's father. It *is* good." He stood contemplating it a moment and then added, "But he's older and looks broken. Is there not a portrait of mother?" Then, pretending to discover it, and walking nearer, he exclaimed:

"There it is."

After a pause, during which the housekeeper observed him with ever-increasing sympathy, he said softly :

"She must have been very delicate when it was taken. I don't remember hearing ; but it must have been shortly before ——"

Mrs. Henderson noticed his hesitation, and came to his relief.

"Yes, sir," she said, "only three months before the end."

"I am afraid," said Emorie, with a hesitation that was not assumed, for his better nature was asserting itself enough to make him feel that he was committing sacrilege, "I am afraid she troubled herself very much over me."

"Now, sir, don't dwell on that. Maybe she knows now that you've come back."

"I should be willing to have my life shortened by ten years, if I could only blot out the last ten," Emorie answered remorsefully.

"Well, sir, you know the Good Book says, ' I will restore unto you the years that the locust hath eaten.' "

"Yes, but we can't undo the past."

"She died praying for you, sir," said Mrs. Henderson, wiping her eyes, "and, who knows," she continued, "whether even now she may not know if her prayers are answered ? "

Emorie had played the game too well for his own comfort. He thought of his own mother. If she had not prayed, she had at least hoped for him, and loved him, and believed in him to the end. The words of the simple old woman beside him made him feel that he was a brute. He almost decided to give the whole scheme up and return to respectable life. But no, the present bait and old habits were too strong. But he felt that this conversation must be stopped ; yet for once he lost his presence of mind and did not know what to do next.

To Mrs. Henderson, however, his continuing to stand before the picture without saying anything was the most natural thing in the world, and she waited respectfully, trying to appear not to notice the evident signs of his strong feeling.

After what she thought a suitable time she said, in a deprecating voice, as if to show she was sorry to disturb him :

" Your supper is ready, and I'm afeard it'll be cold."

Emorie blew his nose softly, and, Mrs. Henderson thought, furtively wiped his eyes, and sat down at the table quite himself again. He ate his meal in silence. When it was finished he pushed back his chair, and rising, remarked :

" As I told you, Mrs. Henderson, I've had bad news. Look at this," and he handed her the telegram Hardynge had sent him. She fumbled for some time for her spectacles, and then read :

" New York, July 14th, 189—.

" To Jonathan Galway, Flumetown, N.Y.

" Important business may require you to return to New York ; or go to Buffalo at any time. Await further dispatches.

" Berghen & Co."

" That *is* a disappointment, sir."

" It is indeed. Can you direct me to a good hotel ? "

" Hotel, sir ? What would Mr. Galway say ? "

But Emorie, wishing to be on the safe side, insisted.

" I feel that I have grieved father so much," he answered, " that I should rather not stay here till he says so. I have telegraphed to him *en route*, you know, and an answer will be coming to-morrow. Besides, it's rather late for you to prepare a room for me to-night."

"Well, sir, all I can say is that you're just like Miss Belle; always thinkin' of other people. Perhaps your way's best, but I don't half like it. You'll leave your valise here, won't you?"

"Thank you. Then I'll just take my grip-sack for the night." So saying, he left the house.

Emorie had calculated rightly on Mrs. Henderson's loquacity, and by the next morning a romantic story of his return, his tears over his mother's picture, and his repentant refusal to sleep at home till his father should give the word was on every one's lips.

CHAPTER XXI.

"JUST read this, Mr. Jonathan," said Mrs. Henderson triumphantly, as she opened the door for Emorie about noon the next day. "Didn't I tell you Mr. Galway wouldn't want you to go to a hotel?" and she handed him a telegram directing her to give him the best room and to spare no pains for his comfort.

And so Emorie settled in.

After dinner the gardener came in to pay his respects, and thought Mr. Jonathan might like to see a letter that had come from Mr. Galway that morning. "Mr. Jonathan" was very glad, and retained possession of it, and determined to go to the post office for all letters in future.

As soon as he was alone he went to Mr. Galway's study and began to examine the note. It was short, and simply contained some final directions as to plants, etc. It was written on a portable typewriter. Emorie thought he recognized the variety and, as he could procure one like it at a small outlay, he determined to do so. The rest of the afternoon was spent in learning to copy the signature, a kind of work that Emorie was only too well accustomed to.

Next morning he called at Mr. Galway's store, and, of course, found them expecting him. He carried off his ignorance of family matters so well, and was so affable that, especially as he asked no favours, no suspicions were aroused. He learnt, to his relief, that practically all who were really intimate with the Galways were on their vacation, and that Mr. Galway had left positive directions that, as he needed rest, no business letters should be sent to him. Finally the manager grew communicative, and told Emorie that he believed Miss Galway was really engaged, though the fact was not yet announced, and that the happy man lived in New York, and that he (the manager) shrewdly suspected him to be none other than the hero of the blizzard.

Emorie left the store, and proceeded to hunt up the old woman at whose cottage Miss Galway and Strongwood had spent that eventful night.

She was delighted to see him.

" Laws now," she said. " But Miss Belle will be cut up not to be at home when you came."

" I want to thank you for your kindness to her, Mrs. Smith."

" Thank me ! That night was the best day's work I ever done in my life. Jest look here. I was as poor as Job's turkey—cottage tumblin' down, and I was jest makin' up my min' to let Jennie, my grandchild here, go to the 'sylum. Now, ain't this a nice place for an old woman—new floor, new roof, walls strengthened, new paper, pretty pictures, new stove, and ——"

" I'm sure you deserved it, Mrs. Smith."

" And there's Jennie," she continued, " still with me ; bright as a button and happy as the day is long. Come here, Jennie, and shake hands with Miss Galway's brother."

As the child did so, rather shyly, Mrs. Smith continued :

"And when I had rheumatics last April, didn't Mr. Galway send the best doctor in Flumetown to me, and get everything I needed !"

" I've no doubt he was glad to do it."

" Yes, indeed, he's that generous ; and so's Mr. Strongtree—no, Strongwood, I mean, I allus get the name wrong—Here's his photograph. He sent two. Miss Belle said one was for me, but she never let on who the other one was for, and I didn't ask—I *knew*," and the old woman chuckled to herself. " I says to Miss Belle that she and he were just made for each other."

" What does Belle say ? "

" Oh, she says, ' No such thing, Mrs. Smith,' but she blushes and smiles all the same.   I know young girls."

" You must have had a great time that night."

" I should think we had.   I was gettin' ready to go to bed, when through the noise of the wind I heard a knock. ' Whoever wants to visit me this time o' night,' says I, and I opens the door, and there, if there weren't two people as nearly froze to death as ever you saw in your life. They could hardly speak. 'Twas as much as I could do to keep them from going near the fire ; I guess they didn't know no better. But it weren't five minutes till Mr. Strong—Strongwood—begins to direct matters, and she obeys him like a lamb, and he soon has me take her off to my room."

" Did they seem to be very fond of each other ? "

" Fond of each other ! Why, he didn't even know her name till the next mornin'. But I reckon he was fond of her before the week was out. You see, he didn't get over the effects of the blizzard for some time, while she was as chirpy as ever in two days."

"HE OPENS THE DOOR, AND THERE, IF THERE WERE NOT TWO PEOPLE AS NEARLY FROZE TO DEATH AS EVER YOU SAW IN YOUR LIFE"

"Then you think they will be married?" asked Emorie.

"Well, I can't say as I knows, only I have my views, you see; they cut a gold dollar in two to remember the night by, and she wears it on her watch chain, and the last time she called here, only a week ago, she took off her gloves to help me in somethin' I was doin' and, lo and behold, there was a new ring on her finger. She tried to turn it round so as I shouldn't see the pearl in it, but I was too quick for her, and I taxed her with it."

"What did she say?"

"She just laughed and was going away, but I called out: 'Is it him?'

"Still she laughed. But I weren't to be baulked, so I cried out; 'Is it Mr. Strongtree?'

"'No,' she says, 'it's not Mr. Strongtree,' and hurried off, still laughing.

"Then I remembered that I had got his name wrong as I allus do when I'm in a hurry. But I believe it's him."

Emorie by this time had obtained all the information he wanted and soon after took his leave, much disgusted at the turn affairs had taken. There was no ground whatever for scandal, and in all probability Mr. Strongwood was really the man who was engaged to Miss Galway. He went home and wrote Hardynge an angry letter, saying that he had successfully hoodwinked everybody, and gone to all the trouble only to stir up a mare's nest.

He waited however for his chief's reply, and did so the more readily as another method of reaping advantage from his stay in Flumetown occurred to him, for he had got access to Mr. Galway's private drawer.

After a few days, a letter came from Hardynge, saying that Emorie need not be so hot, but had better write a letter of brotherly congratulation to Strongwood and see what came of it.

Emorie had by this time fully established himself in Flumetown in his assumed character, and was warmly received in what little society was left in the place. He felt no fear of detection ; for no one was likely to telegraph ; and, unless detained on the road, Mr. Galway could receive no information by letter until he should land at Tacoma after his trip to Alaska.

He made himself specially agreeable to the officers of the bank.

CHAPTER XXII.

PENELVE ONCE MORE.

DR. STOREY, convinced that Strongwood was receiving no further benefit from his stay on the mountain, had his patient removed as soon as possible to Penelve. The better road had long been re-opened, and Strongwood bore the journey remarkably well. When, a few days later, Dr. Swift examined him, he gave the encouraging report that the disease had apparently made very little, if any advance ; but he refused to allow travelling to be thought of for the present.

Strongwood rapidly improved, and spent most of the day out of doors, where he soon became an invaluable acquisition to the children.

" Let's play ' Lost,'" they would cry ; and the three would gravely stand before Strongwood, while he, as superintendent of the supposed school, would say :

" Now, children, be very careful not to get lost. It's a dangerous place, and don't wander away."

This speech would always be delivered in a part of the garden near a clump of trees and some rocks, and pretty soon Esther would come to Bertie and ask if he had any idea where Clarence was. Then would follow solemn but very short consultations, and blowing of tin horns, and a searching until

Bertie could be seen bringing Clarence out from among the rocks. Strongwood never allowed them to do more than this, or to travesty the more serious parts of the experience in the forest.

At other times he would be giant, and pounce on them, to their great delight. But this game was too tiring for him to play long, or often, and he preferred "Lost," for in it after his speech he had nothing further to do, beyond presiding at the consultations over the search.

He saw comparatively little of Bessie, who was very busy getting her work into good shape before leaving Penelve for an absence of several weeks. As he regarded his improvement as only temporary, he still felt that from this point of view his resolution taken on the mountain was binding. But he inwardly chafed under the restrictions, and finally almost persuaded himself that he might be doing Bessie a wrong in not speaking. What, if she cared for him!

He set himself to observe her. She was certainly pleased when he came into the room, and would look up with a bright smile. This was encouraging, but then she had the same smile for any of the neighbours that called in. After a few days Strongwood had to admit that it would be egotism to suppose that she had any warmer feeling for him than pleasant friendliness. He felt a little troubled at it, but his better judgment made him admire her all the more.

"I hate girls who are all the time thinking of men," he thought, "but I believe I should have a good fighting chance, if I were only well enough. What a wretched thing this consumption is, and what a trick it has played me. It was the means of my knowing her, and now it's the means of my losing her."

He watched her drive from the house to the train with a sense of final loss, which made life seem very flat.

"I shall be gone before she returns," he said to himself, "and I shall not see her again. This is the last of my hopes. Is this a 'special providence,' I wonder? I suppose it is, according to her definition, only I can't see it in that light."

Bessie, to her surprise, found that she really felt the prospect of not seeing Strongwood again. She had become more interested in him than she supposed, for, since his illness, he had been showing the better side of his character.

A week before this a letter had come which had made little impression upon him at the time, beyond passing amusement. Bessie had brought it, and as she carried it to him had noticed with a little start that it bore "Flumetown" on the postmark. She could not help glancing at his face as he examined the envelope. It expressed nothing but pleased interest, and she felt satisfied that there was nothing in the story Amy Wildmere had told her.

The letter was as follows:

> "Creekside, Flumetown, N.Y.
>
> "July 20th, 189—.
>
> "Robert Strongwood, Esq.
>
> "Dear Sir,
>
> "On returning home somewhat unexpectedly last week, I found, as of course you know, that my father and sister had gone on a trip to Alaska. I seem to have missed several home letters while travelling, and this must be my excuse for not writing sooner to congratulate you on your engagement to my sister, of which I only learned since my arrival. There are few men whom I consider worthy of Belle, but from all

I have heard of you, including your gallant rescue of her last spring, I feel sure she has made no mistake in her choice.

"As I expect to return to Europe late in the fall, I cannot but hope that the happy day may be fixed before I leave.

" Hoping your stay at Penelve is benefiting your health,

" I am, my dear Sir, yours very sincerely,

" JONATHAN GALWAY."

Strongwood read the letter, and laughed.

"What a queer fellow Miss Galway's brother Jonathan must be. The idea of his coming home just after they had started. It's just what she declared he'd be likely to do. But who can have been playing practical jokes on him and making him think we are engaged." He sat down and wrote a pleasant letter, congratulating Mr. Galway on his return, and setting him right as to the mistake he had made. This done, he thought no more of the matter.

As he grew better, his desire for reading returned, and remembering Mrs. Leslie's implied slur on his powers of comprehending Barclay's " Apology," he looked up the work and commenced reading it. It certainly was difficult, and had not his pride been a little touched he might have laid it down after the first few pages. But when he had become used to the style, the closely reasoned arguments, and the fairness of the method impressed him.

"Charlie," said he one afternoon as they were driving, " I've just finished Barclay's ' Apology.' "

" Have you really, Rob? I should not have thought you would have got through with it. Whoever advised you to read it ? "

" Mrs. Leslie."

" Of course. She thinks there's no book like it. None of the rest of us would have dared to put it in your way."

" Why not ? "

" We should have been afraid it would be too stiff for you."

" Mrs. Leslie hinted as much, and that spurred me on ; but after the first I did not want to stop. It was so surprising and so interesting. It's a wonderful book."

" Barclay was only twenty-eight when he wrote it."

" So it naturally appeals to my age. I suppose it's your standard book ? "

" It undoubtedly was till thirty years ago. Since then, many have discarded it ; many regard it as unsound, and few really read it."

" I can quite understand the churches calling it unsound," said Strongwood. " And its style is certainly too scholastic ever to be popular. But, I tell you what, Charlie, you Quakers are making a serious mistake if you are discarding its teaching on the Bible."

" How do you mean ? "

" I mean this ; the general idea is that Christianity rests on the Bible, and that the Bible's claim to reverence depends on its absolute infallibility. Barclay maintains that neither of these suppositions is true. He says, what you are always urging, that every man carries the evidences of Christianity in his own heart, and he teaches that all good anywhere, even in heathen countries, is from Christ. Now a Christianity as free as that is a very different thing from current Christianity. It allows for new truth and welcomes progress. It has nothing to fear from discoveries, and, as to Higher Criticism ; if all Christians held Barclay's theory, Higher Criticism would create interest, but no alarm."

"That's what I tell our people, Rob. In proportion as we take up a more literal view of the Bible, we lose our position and our testimony, just when they are most needed."

"You certainly do. You have no small advantage in being able to say that your Society did not wait till necessity forced you to take new ground; but that you freely took it long ago, because you saw that it was the true one. I quite retract my former opinion that Quakers are a narrow sect."

"I am very glad, Rob, to hear you say so."

"Well, I do say so. Of course, I do not say I'm convinced; but Barclay very largely demonstrates that the stock objections to Christianity are due to misconception, and he goes far to narrow the issue down to the critical one between materialism and revealed religion. But what is most striking to me is the light Barclay's book throws on one's own half-understood thoughts."

Bruce, who was more interested in Strongwood's personal position than in his opinion of Barclay, was in hopes the conversation would turn in that direction; but he felt it wiser not to push matters.

After a pause, Strongwood added:

"But I don't see why Barclay makes so much of Christ and His work. It strikes me as a useless addition to his theory, which is that of the universal and saving Light."

"It doesn't seem to me, Rob," answered Bruce, "that Barclay lays any too much stress on the death of Christ; but I must confess his presentation of it does not satisfy me. To my mind two facts are abundantly plain; one is, that in every nation those that fear God and work righteousness are accepted with Him; and the other, that blessings so great as to be absolutely unique, are known only to those who have access to the history of Jesus Christ, and who profit by it. There is no contradiction between these two statements, because the same Jesus who lived and died in Palestine is He, who by His Spirit has always been working in the hearts of men."

" I remember you preached about that once ——"

" Yes, I believe I did. My view is that humanity is akin to God, and that God is akin to man. In order for this there must be something which we may call a human personality in God. This is Jesus Christ of Nazareth, and His coming as a man was not a change in His nature ; but a self-limitation, a self-emptying. In this way God's attitude towards us was shown in a focus of light ; told in human words ; revealed in human suffering. The full revelation comes to no man through the inward work of the Spirit, until the Spirit has this human revelation to work on, and it comes to no one through the human revelation, unless he submits himself to the Spirit."

" I'll think it over," said Strongwood. And during the last twenty minutes of the drive neither spoke.

On the hall table, as they entered, Strongwood found a letter waiting for him.

It bore the Flumetown postmark.

CHAPTER XXIII.

THE ATTACK.

STRONGWOOD'S thoughts as he sat down to open the letter were still absorbed in the subject of the conversation he had been having with Bruce. His notion of Christianity had been formed solely from the descriptions of its enemies and the assertions and practices of its worldly friends. What had recently been presented to him was quite fresh to his mind, and the teaching that all that was best in him was really from Christ seemed in itself to open a new world.

He cut open the envelope and read :—

" Creekside,

" Flumetown, N.Y.,

" July 29th, 189—.

" Robert Strongwood, Esq.,

" Sir,

" Your astounding letter reached me duly. I thought best to delay answering until I could communicate with my father and sister. So, to avoid publicity, I went to another town and telegraphed. The dispatch caught them at Tacoma before the steamer left. I inclose my father's letter which he asked me to forward to you. It speaks for itself. I have only to add that I shall, after waiting a reasonable time for your answer, proceed to carry out his directions.

> "Yours, etc.,
>
> "JONATHAN GALWAY."

The letter enclosed was as follows :—

> "Tacoma, Wash.,
>
> "July 21st, 189—.

"Sir,

"My son Jonathan, returned home since we left Flume-town, telegraphs me that you deny your engagement to my daughter. I can hardly credit the statement. If it is a joke on your part, it is certainly a cruel one ; for poor Belle has been utterly prostrated, and we have had to give up our trip.

"The doctor fears an attack of brain fever. She lies moaning, now looking at the half gold dollar, now at your photograph, and keeps saying how much kinder it would have been if you had let her perish in the storm.

"She is ready to forgive, if you will still be true to her. If not, she feels that it is right that you should be taught that you cannot trifle with affections with impunity. She will therefore demand heavy damages, and she urges me for the sake of the young lady who seems now to be engaging your attention, to instruct my son to inform her immediately of your perfidy.

"I have forwarded to him documentary evidence ; given him full instructions, and constituted him my attorney in my absence. You will therefore communicate with him, as we shall probably have left here before you receive this.

> "CALEB GALWAY.

"To Robert Strongwood, Esq."

Strongwood read the letter twice. He recognized the peculiar character of the typewriter used by Mr. Galway when away from home. The signature appeared undoubtedly genuine, but still he felt sure there was some mistake, and he wrote a curt note to " Jonathan Galway, Esq.," saying that he should take no notice of the matter.

The next day another letter came from Flumetown, enclosing a note which purported to be from Miss Galway. It was brief and written in a trembling hand, as if the writer were ill. But Strongwood had no doubt that it was genuine, for it showed the peculiarities of her style. What to make of it he could not tell. Could she have lost her reason? But then it was hardly likely that both she and her father could have gone out of their minds at the same time. They had never seemed to be people who would conspire to injure him. The whole thing was a mystery, and a most unpleasant one. The true explanation never occurred to him, for he had no reason to doubt that his correspondent was really Jonathan Galway. Emorie's proceedings had been in keeping with Jonathan's known character, and the fact that his letter paper bore the printed address of the Galway's residence and the family crest, showed that he was living at home.

The reference to documentary evidence sorely perplexed Strongwood ; and he racked his brain in a fruitless effort to think what it could be.

In the course of a day or two another letter came from Flumetown, saying that Strongwood had continued his trifling too long, and that the writer would allow him three days; after which, if he were not prepared to come to terms, a letter of warning would be sent to Miss Bruce, and he must expect to stand suit. "Coming to terms" meant, the letter explained, the payment of $20,000.

Strongwood feared the pecuniary loss that might arise from a suit for damages much less than the social stigma. It seemed so vulgar, and he knew that for one who would remember his acquittal fifty would remember that he had been sued. Worst of all was the thought of Bessie. What would she think? It was one thing for him to put restraint on himself, and, because he loved her, keep back the secret of his love, and even deny himself the joy of her society; but it was quite another thing to feel that she would look upon him as a deceiver unworthy even of her acquaintance.

Should he forestall his persecutors by writing to Miss Bruce? He felt he could not do so without giving her an intimation of his feelings. He seemed to be in a trap from which the only escape was by giving "hush" money. Yes, and lose his self-respect. He lay awake the whole night thinking it over. Who would ever believe that a well-to-do young lady, a church member, and one actively engaged in charitable work, would bring a suit against him for breach of promise of marriage, unless he had at least been indiscreet, and therefore unreliable?

The lawyer whom he generally consulted was spending the summer abroad; but a friend of his, a rising young man in the profession, was taking a short vacation with his family at Cresson, a summer resort on the Alleghanies not far off. Strongwood telegraphed to him and he came promptly.

The lawyer, after reading all the letters carefully, said, with a scrutinizing gaze at his client's countenance:

"Exactly how much truth is there in all this, Mr. Strongwood?"

" None whatever, Mr. Herrick."

" None whatever ? "

" None whatever."

" You rescued the young lady, as stated ? "

" I did."

" You divided the gold dollar with her ? "

" Yes."

" You exchanged photographs ? "

" Her father sent me a photograph of the cottage, and photographs of himself and daughter. In return I sent him two of myself, one of which I asked him to give to the old woman."

" That seems harmless. Has there been no correspondence ? "

" With Mr. Galway ? Yes ; in regard to repairs to the cottage, and an annuity for the old woman. On one occasion when her father was laid up, Miss Galway wrote and I answered."

" Were they purely business letters ? "

" They were."

" What is this 'documentary evidence' Mr. Galway speaks of ? "

" I have not the smallest idea."

" Have you Miss Galway's letter ? "

" No, I think I destroyed it."

" But you consider this note, which Mr. Jonathan Galway forwarded to you," continued Mr. Herrick, "to be in her handwriting ? "

" Yes. The hand is rather shaky, but, of course she was ill ; and the signature is characteristic."

" How often have you been to Flumetown ? "

"I stayed a fortnight to recuperate after the accident, and have been there once since."

"You paid her attentions?"

"Naturally. I took her out driving, or rather she took me, as we used her phaeton."

"There was no flirting?"

"We were very lively, and on thoroughly good terms with each other. Nothing more."

"Nothing which she might have construed into a declaration?"

"Nothing."

Before this conversation had ended, the lawyer had put Strongwood through a severe cross-examination, but could extract no further information.

"Excuse me, Sir," he said at last, "if I have seemed too persistent; but I wished to acquaint myself with all the facts of the case."

"I think you have succeeded. It's all right. I quite understand."

"And for my part, I can't see that you need fear a suit."

"I don't fear it in that way, but I do fear the gossip and general scandal before it comes into court."

"You'll have to stand that, unless you are willing to compromise, for it's the money that they are after."

"Yes, and that is what they shall not get."

It was arranged that Mr. Herrick should start that night for Flumetown, and investigate matters there.

"You know, Mr. Strongwood, that if the other side are unable to give better reasons for their action than you believe them to have, you will be in a position to sue them. In the meantime, I understand you to authorize me to make no terms."

" No compromise whatever."

Strongwood had now done all that he could. But his dread of Bessie hearing of the matter hung over him like a nightmare. Less serious, but still very formidable was the thought of how, with their pride of position, it would strike his mother and sisters. Then his associates ! How they would gibe at him, the studious, philosophical, correct young man, for getting into such a scrape. "Breach of Promise Case in Fashionable Society," that was how the papers would print the headlines. "A Flumetown Belle sues a Prominent Young Merchant of this City." "Galway *v*. Strongwood." The thought was sickening.

Strongwood had also another cause of anxiety. His mother's letters continued to report in glowing colours the progress of Lord Southliegh's courtship, and this troubled him not a little, for he did not share the American weakness for titles, nor did he like the unintentional hints Mrs. McPherson gave as to the young nobleman's character. It appeared to him that it was a case of title courting money, and money dazzled by the peerage, and in his present state of mind he was less disposed than ever to expect anything but unhappiness to result from such a union. He wrote seriously both to his mother and Lucy ; more to satisfy his conscience than in hopes of effecting any real good ; for the whole affair would probably be settled before his letter could reach them. But it troubled him a good deal, even more than his mother's lack of sympathy, or her continued refusal to believe that his health was seriously amiss, for he had accepted these things as inevitable.

Strongwood was now well enough to walk out, and, as he preferred to have an object, had fallen into the habit of taking whatever letters were ready in the afternoon to the post office. About three days after the conversation with Mr. Herrick, he was taking his usual walk. He felt stronger than at any time since the picnic, and he was beginning to think that it might after all be possible for him to recover sufficiently to justify him in addressing Bessie. His heart beat quicker at the thought, and his step became firmer and his head erect.

In this feeling of elation he came to the post office. Just as he was dropping the letters into the box, his eye fell upon one of them, and he started. It was for Bessie, and had been re-directed by Aunt Mary. It bore the Flumetown post mark, and the handwriting was only too familiar to him.

A great temptation seized him. He knew what that letter contained as certainly as if he had read its contents. It was from beginning to end a lie against himself. Nothing but harm could come of Bessie's receiving it. Why not quietly suppress it? He felt he could understand the feelings of the Pope he had once read about, who was called upon to sign the decree condemning himself.

All the other letters were already in the post. What should he do with this one? He became deadly pale ; his knees trembled under him, and cold perspiration stood out on his forehead—but he dropped the letter into the box.

CHAPTER XXIV.

A FEW days after Hardynge's interview with Emorie, his annual holiday began. He was greatly tempted to spend it at Flumetown, for the "affair" was not progressing to his mind. Prudence, however, prevented him. Sooner or later the plot must be discovered, and he had no mind to be mixed up with it. The next best thing would be to go to Penelve, where he felt sure that he should be able to gain information about Strongwood from Amy Wildmere. He was also attracted thither by Amy herself, who had greatly taken his fancy at the picnic.

In his first object he was entirely disappointed. Amy was not so intimate with Bessie as he supposed, and Grace Wildmere, who was intimate, knew nothing, for Bessie had never talked to her on the subject. Even if she had, Grace would not have disclosed anything. Besides, Bessie, as we know, was now away from home. Hardynge met Strongwood out walking a few days after his arrival, but apart from noticing that he looked careworn, learned nothing.

But if Hardynge's visit to Penelve was a failure in the one respect, it was a great success in the other. He found Amy much troubled about her mother's health, and at once entered sympathetically into her feelings, not only by inquiries but by delicate attentions in the way of small presents of what he discovered were the invalid's favourite flowers and fruits. He always gave as if receiving a favour, for he soon learned that the Wildmeres were very well off.

Grace was the first to suspect his intentions, and spoke to Amy about him.

"Why," answered Amy, hotly, "he is just spending his holidays at Penelve; and if he chooses to call and bring flowers to mother, I do not see why I should object."

"Well, but Amy, he has never seen aunt in his life. He cannot really be so interested in her. It's thee he's after."

"I don't see that, Grace. He has become interested in mother through what I have told him."

"Now, Amy, thee knows better than that, and I do hope thee will be careful."

"What does thee mean, Grace? Does thee think I'm going to throw myself at his head?"

"I mean that I hope thee will not encourage him. Of course, I know nothing against him; but he is a thorough man of the world, and would be no help to thee. Robert Strongwood seemed to object so much to his coming to the picnic that I feel sure there must have been some good reason."

"Robert Strongwood indeed! A man who has treated that Flunetown girl as he has, is worthy of no respect. I should think less of Mr. Hardynge if he did approve of him."

"Amy, thee knows nothing whatever about that matter except from Mr. Hardynge's second-hand reports and surmises. I should have thought that his conversation that evening would have disgusted thee."

"Well, it didn't then. It was right that we should know, and it was very entertaining."

"Are tale-bearing and detraction discouraged?" said Grace, quoting from the "Discipline."

"Mr. Hardynge isn't a Friend, so that does not apply."

"Does thee consider that a recommendation?"

"I tell thee, I'm not thinking of marrying him. Would thee have me shut the door in his face?"

"No, Amy, thee knows I should not wish that. But he is paying thee attentions. Isn't he to take thee driving this afternoon? It's not fair to him to encourage him if thee means to refuse him; and to accept him, would be, I fear, a great mistake."

"What an old fogey thee is," said Amy. "What's the harm of a little fun?"

Grace saw she had not been very wise, and that there would be nothing gained by pursuing the subject, so she diverted the conversation by asking Amy's advice about a bonnet she was trimming, preparatory to leaving Penelve the next day to join Bessie in visiting some of the other Friends' meetings in the district.

She felt, however, that she could not go without saying something about Hardynge to her aunt; but she was so afraid of its worrying her that she put it off till she went to bid her good-bye.

"Aunt," she said in a confused way, "I'm afraid Mr. Hardynge is paying a good deal of attention to Amy."

"Well, my dear, he seems like a nice young man. I always think it a good sign when young people pay attention to an old sick woman like me."

"But, aunt, we know nothing about him except that he is not a Friend."

" I'm sorry he's not a Friend. But I do not at all suppose there is anything in it, or that Amy cares for him. I shall, of course, make careful enquiries if things should become at all serious."

Grace kissed her aunt and departed. Amy was waiting for her in the hall.

"Good-bye, Grace," she said. " I hope you will have good meetings ;—and,—don't be uneasy about me, I really will be careful."

" I know thee means to be, Amy, and please don't take any step without careful thought and—prayer. Good-bye."

Amy was a thoroughly good girl at heart, and did honestly mean to be careful, but she was heedless, and as soon as she was in Hardynge's company she forgot all her resolutions and enjoyed his society to the full.

It is but justice to Hardynge to say that he was not playing a game. As far as his shallow nature would admit, he was in love with Amy, and he pressed his suit vigorously. He took her out driving, and entered into all her plans and fears about her mother, discussing whether it would be practicable to take Mrs. Wildmere to Philadelphia or New York for further advice, or whether a specialist should be sent for to see her at Penelve.

A few days before his vacation was ended he made her a formal offer of marriage. Amy was, in her own mind, prepared to accept him at once, but, being a dutiful daughter, she reserved her answer till after she should have consulted her mother.

Mrs. Wildmere was already prejudiced in Hardynge's favour, and besides, was so blindly devoted to her daughter that she would not think of refusing her anything. But she had been a good deal troubled by Grace's warning, and also by a visit from one of the elderly women "overseers" of the meeting, who had spoken pretty plainly to her after the two young people had been seen for the third time driving together. She accordingly insisted upon some inquiries being made and upon having an interview with Hardynge herself.

When Amy blushingly brought Ralph Hardynge into her mother's sunny sitting room, Mrs. Wildmere, in her deep rocking chair, with her fresh Quaker cap and white silk shawl over the intricate folds of French muslin that covered the body of her dress, looked the very impersonation of placid dignity.

After the first greetings, she said :

"And so thee wishes to take my daughter from me."

"Not in the least, madam, I assure you. So far from losing a daughter, you will be gaining a son."

"Ah, I lost a son years ago," said the old lady reflectively.

"I wish, in some measure, I might try to take his place."

Mrs. Wildmere was touched. Presently she asked :

"What is thy religious profession ?"

"I have generally attended the Episcopal Church," said Hardynge, "though, of course, I travel a great deal, and am necessarily irregular."

"Perhaps thee knows that we Friends feel it important that our children should marry members of our own Society. Families should, we believe, be united on the most important of all subjects."

"But you would not have me become a Friend without conviction."

"Assuredly not. At the same time I greatly regret thy position."

" I can assure you, madam, that I have the highest regard for the Friends, and shall never, in any way, interfere with Amy's preferences, and shall leave to her judgment all the religious questions that may present themselves in our household."

" I appreciate thy liberality of feeling, Ralph Hardynge, and while I am sorry thee cannot go further, I am willing, if Amy feels satisfied on the matter, to leave that point."

The conversation then turned on the subject of his income, and then Mrs. Wildmere reminded him of how little they knew of him, and asked him for references. He gave her three which he knew to be " safe."

Answers were received on the morning of the day of his departure from Penelve ; and when he went to pay his farewell call he found Amy in the parlour, radiant with pleasure.

After a delightful hour in her company he left. Her affectionate confidence roused the best that was in his nature, and, as he walked back to his hotel, some sight of his own real character came before him, together with a momentary sense of compunction for having passed himself off to a simple minded girl as a man worthy of her affections. A dread also fell upon him like a dark cloud, at the thought that his mean plot against Strongwood might be discovered, and he half resolved that if he once got fairly out of this "scrape," he would never offend in the same way again.

CHAPTER XXV.

AFTER a fortnight's stay with some cousins at Atlantic City, Bessie Bruce returned to Pennsylvania and joined her brother Charles, Emily Southport, an "Elder," from another town, and Grace Wildmere, in a visit to two or three country neighbourhoods. They were all members of a large standing committee appointed by the "Yearly Meeting" to visit the different congregations of Friends and to engage in such evangelistic work as "way should open for." It was not customary for the committee to direct any of its members to go to particular places ; its method was rather to suggest, and to make it easy for those who felt the call to carry out what is known among Friends as their "concern." On the whole the plan answered admirably, and nearly every year substantial growth in the membership and church work was reported.

The four were as usual warmly received, and they threw themselves heartily into the labour before them. The mornings were spent in visiting families, each visit being partly social and partly religious, often ending with a little "quiet time" before the Friends left. Each day at noon saw them at a new house for dinner, after which they would drive off again and repeat the morning's experiences, going to a fresh house for tea. In the evening a public religious meeting would be held, announced according to local usage to assemble, "at early candle light." Bessie and Grace had the most continuous work, for the women folks of the household where they lodged, who had been busy all day, would come to their room at night, not for gossip but for serious conversation on personal hopes and difficulties, and in regard to the work. The strain of all this was great, especially as the visitors entered thoroughly into each case; but the work did not last very long at a time; and when it was over, Charles Bruce would return to his counting room as if nothing had happened, and those who heard Bessie preaching felt that her words gained added force when they learned how thoroughly efficient she was in all household and domestic duties.

This series of visits was to continue about three weeks. The meetings in the various places had been large and many had acknowledged the blessing that had been received. The last day before their return had come, and, instead of separating into two parties, as usual, they were together making their farewell calls. The mail was distributed at the little country post office about 2 p.m., and, as it was on their way, they decided to stop for letters.

They were not disappointed. Bruce received several business letters, and one from his wife giving a good report of all at home, except Strongwood, who was said to be more poorly and apparently troubled about something.

Grace's letter was from Amy announcing her engagement to Ralph Hardynge. She gave a little start and exclamation, which naturally made them ask what was the matter.

" Amy is engaged to be married."

" To whom ? "

" Ralph Hardynge."

Charles and Bessie were silent, as neither were pleased.

" Who is Ralph Hardynge ? " asked Emily Southport.

" He's a travelling salesman from Philadelphia. I hardly know anything about him," answered Grace. Then she added : " Oh, Amy says it's to be a profound secret for the present. I should not have spoken."

" I don't think thee need feel troubled about that Grace," answered Mrs. Southport. " If people will write their secrets, and never say they are secrets, till the end of the letter on the second sheet, they have themselves to thank if their confidences leak out. However, I think we can all agree to say nothing."

" What do you think about it ? " asked Grace.

" Well," said Charles after a pause, " I hope it may turn out to be all right ; but I was not favourably impressed with him at the picnic. I am afraid he will take her into fashionable life."

" She writes," returned Grace, " that he promises to let her remain a Friend."

" I have heard of such promises before, and I know what they amount to," said Mrs. Southport incredulously.

Bessie said nothing. She was truly sorry for the engagement ; but she was glad that it furnished conversation and prevented any question being asked about the letter which lay unopened in her pocket. It bore the Flametown postmark, and taking this in connection with the report of Strongwood, given in her sister's letter, she felt sure that it would throw some light, possibly an unpleasant one, on the story Amy Wildmere had told her of his adventures in Flume-town. She had a strong inclination to return it unread, but felt she should hardly be justified in such a course. But until she had read it she determined that no one, not even her brother, should know that it had come.

In the meantime she tried to forget all about the matter and to turn her attention to the duties of the hour, which were pressing enough. Her power of sympathetically putting herself alongside of others was very great, and on many previous occasions when heavy anxieties had pressed upon her she had been enabled to throw them entirely off in her interest in those who claimed her help. But to-day, to her great grief, she could not do so, not even when she was seeking, not unsuccessfully, to bring comfort and hope to a sick girl.

After a long afternoon with many calls, they finally reached the Friend's house where they were to take tea. When Grace was ready to go down to the parlour, Bessie asked her to excuse her to the family, as she wished to be quiet till tea time. Grace was not surprised, for they had had a tiring day, and Bessie had been very silent during the drive home, and looked very weary. She thought she quite understood why Bessie wished to be quiet; for the meeting that evening in the Methodist Church was expected to be a crowded one, and it had been announced to be held by women ministers, Charles Bruce having an appointment elsewhere. The fact was, that, unknown to Bessie, the Methodist minister had given out that she would preach. He was well aware that she would never promise beforehand to do so, but he had said that he knew Miss Bruce and would take the risk. Grace, who had, as she said, only " a small gift," felt that the main burden of the preaching would fall on Bessie, and was very glad to be able to set her free for a quiet time to herself. In fact, they all tried, if possible, to have such times before their meetings, not to prepare what they were to say, but for communion and prayer, so that they might be, as Bruce expressed it, in tune with the Spirit of God, and thus be ready either for silence on their part or speech, as might be needed by the congregation.

But to-day, although Bessie felt the need of quiet more than ever, she could not leave her letter any longer unread.

It was as follows :—

> " Creekside,
>> " Flumetown, N.Y.
>>> " August 12th, 189—.

" Miss Bruce.

" Madam,

" You will, I trust, pardon the liberty which I, a stranger, take in addressing you. The importance of the information I have to give must be my excuse ; although to write it is perhaps more painful to me than the reading of it will be to you.

" I understand that Mr. Robert Strongwood, of New York City, has been spending some weeks at your brother's house in Penelve, on account, it is said, of his health.

" I write to warn you against him. Last winter my sister had the misfortune to be rescued by him from a blizzard. They became engaged. Now, suddenly, with no apparent reason, after the engagement has become generally known, he entirely disowns and denies it. My sister, when the news came, was travelling out west with my father, on a trip to Alaska for his health. She became utterly prostrated by this brutal treatment, and now instead of being able to care for her father in his feeble condition, she is herself lying ill, threatened with brain fever.

"You will not be surprised to hear that a suit for heavy damages is hanging over Mr. Strongwood, unless he promptly changes his attitude, or consents to give pecuniary satisfaction without a suit.

"I am, Miss Bruce, yours respectfully,

"JONATHAN GALWAY."

The effect of this letter was very different from what Hardynge expected when he arranged for Emorie to write it. Thinking that matters were much further advanced between Miss Bruce and Strongwood than they were, and judging her by himself, he expected that she would insist upon his paying the money down at once, so as to avoid scandal. He had no belief in the reality of Christian experience, and supposed that as a Quaker she would be especially careful of appearances.

As Bessie finished this letter she closed her eyes and strove to collect her thoughts. There must be some mistake. She could not believe Robert Strongwood would act in such a way. Could Miss Galway have misunderstood him? No. Bessie did not believe he was a man who would be likely to commit himself without knowing what he was about. What then was the meaning of his words on the mountain that day about choosing what was right? There had evidently been a struggle, and she had had the clear impression that the right had triumphed. Supposing him to have been engaged to Miss Galway, it was quite possible that it might be the right thing for him to break it off, but it could never be his duty to deny that he had been engaged. Perhaps Miss Galway was

deranged, and her delusion on this point the first symptom of
insanity. Or,— could there be any truth in Ralph Hardynge's
story?

She was half ashamed of feeling it so much. She had
not been aware that Strongwood had made any advances to
her, and she held the old idea pretty strongly that it is un-
maidenly for a girl to know she is in love before her lover has
in some way shown his attachment. Now she had to acknowledge that she felt the trouble more deeply than could be
explained by mere general interest in him.

"I shall say nothing about it to any one," she thought,
"and I only hope he will have strength to do right in the
matter, whatever that is."

Then she remembered the meeting. How could she face
it? She wished she had followed the example of an old
Friend from America, who, many years before had travelled
in England as a minister. Shortly before the time appointed
for a meeting a letter from home had been placed in his
hands. He began to unseal it, and then stopped: "No," he
said, "I believe this letter contains sad news"; and he went
to the meeting without reading it, that his mind might be
clear for the service. There had been, of course, no outward
sign of mourning on that letter, but it contained news of a
death in his immediate family.

"If only I had done the same thing with this letter," she
thought, and tried to turn her mind to the work before her;
but her anxiety would assert itself, and she even found herself
longing to learn the truth from Robert Strongwood's own lips.
But no! she knew she could never broach the subject to
him.

Her friends at tea time noticed how poorly she was looking, and one of them said:

"Bessie, we are working thee too hard. Thee's quite overdone."

She smiled, and succeeded in turning the conversation into pleasanter channels. But after tea, the motherly Friend at whose house they were staying, made her lie down till it was time for the last carriage from the house to start for the meeting.

"Grace," said Bessie, "I do hope thee will have a message to-night. I don't feel as if I had a ray of one."

"That is all right," Grace answered. "I have noticed that thee never preaches so well as thee does when thee goes to meeting without a ' ray.' "

"But it is different to-night, Grace. I feel as if I could not speak."

Grace saw that her friend was used up, and she said sympathetically :

"We felt clear that it was right to have this meeting, and I believe it was. They won't call us for five minutes ; shan't we have a little time of quiet together first ? "

So saying, she locked the door and they sat down. After a short silence Grace knelt and prayed for all who were to be at the meeting, and then for Bessie and herself, that each might keep her right place, and be used in the power of God. Bessie arose comforted; but the evident nervousness of the two Friends who drove with them to the meeting, as to how the motley crowd would be able to understand the silence of a Friends' meeting did not help her. They gave the plainest hints that they hoped there would be little silence and much preaching, and that the preaching would begin as soon as possible.

The crowd at the church fully equalled all expectations, both as to size and character. The beautiful summer evening and a drive through the woods after the sultry day were attractions in themselves. The novelty of a woman preaching was an additional inducement, and many a country swain had brought his sweetheart. It was just the kind of congregation that would whisper and laugh, and Bessie realized this very painfully as she entered the building.

She could not help thinking what all these people would say, if they knew that the two who had called the meeting had as little idea of what was to be said and done in it as any one in the house. It did look like temerity, and she knew that most Christians outside of Friends would condemn them as very foolish. Yet she could not act against her convictions. She could not claim to give a message from the Lord, unless she felt that she had received one from Him to deliver. If knowledge of what it was to be were given before she went to meeting, she had no predjudice against accepting it, though, as a rule, it was not so given. It seemed to be necessary for her to be face to face with the congregation before she could realize what was the needed word. Yet preaching was no idle matter with her. She studied the Bible, and kept her mind open for impressions, and tried to live in a condition of constant preparation for service, private or public.

As she took her seat with Grace and Mrs. Southport in the pulpit, and saw the packed house, and people standing at the windows, her heart almost failed her, and she cried out silently for the right message, and also for readiness to be thought a fool, rather than yield to the temptation of professing to give a message when she had none to give.

She arose and made an introductory explanation of how the meeting was to be held ; that the silence was to allow the Lord to be the first speaker, and that all hearts might draw near to Him in their own way, and pray for themselves and their neighbours, and that He might choose whom He would to speak, and direct them as to what should be said. She closed with the words, " The Lord Jesus by His Spirit is actually here ; let each one of us open our hearts to Him."

She sat down, and a solemn hush prevaded the assembly. To her own dismay, she found she could not turn her thoughts from that Flumetown letter. After a short pause the minister of the congregation prayed. Then another silence followed, rather long, when some one started a hymn. Bessie still sat in darkness. To her great relief, Grace rose and fully held the attention of the people as she spoke to them very simply and personally on the love of Christ. At the end of fifteen minutes she sat down. Bessie still had no word to say. Her mind was in deep sympathy with Strongwood, who she was sure was in some way being grossly misunderstood. After a pause Emily Southport arose, and probably, for the first time in her life spoke in a public meeting. It was a very brief endorsement of Grace's remarks.

" Oh," thought Bessie, " if I could only get that letter out of my mind, something might be given me to say, and the people do look so hungry." Then it seemed as if a voice spoke to her : " Thou hast the message already."

She saw her duty, and rising, began without a text to speak of the sorrow of being misunderstood. The subject developed, and the people were all attention. The lady seemed to know everything about them, for there had been many bickerings and misunderstandings among them. She spoke of various kinds of misunderstandings and of how they arose, and of how they could be checked. Illustration followed illustration, each more pointed than the preceding, till some felt utterly ashamed of themselves. Then, with powerful effect, making a transition so sudden as to be almost startling, she showed them how they were, many of them at least, misunderstanding their Saviour who had died for them; misunderstanding Him by doubting Him, or by being afraid of Him, or by fancying that His love would not inexorably demand righteousness of them. She pointed out how all this was grieving Him, and keeping them from His light and home. She recalled what Grace had said of His love, and besought them to yield themselves to Him who would come into their hearts with His saving power.

At the close of the meeting the good old minister, as he grasped their hands in farewell, said, while the tears rolled down his cheeks :

" The Lord's been with us sisters, the Lord's been with us. This night will tell for eternity."

Well might he say this ; for before the meeting had ended one of the notorious characters of the neighbourhood had publicly renounced his sinful life and turned to the Lord. It was afterwards found that several others, though silent, had found that meeting to be a turning point in their lives.

CHAPTER XXVI.

MISUNDERSTANDINGS.

AFTER his interview with Strongwood, Mr. Herrick lost no time in beginning his investigations at Flumetown. He was a thoroughly good lawyer, but the work that was now before him was more that of a detective, and as a detective he was deficient.

His coming was not unwelcome to Emorie, who had made his plans with special reference to such a contingency; and Herrick was much impressed with the generally prevailing belief, which Emorie's suggestions and hints had produced, that Miss Galway was really engaged to Robert Strongwood, and he began to feel grave doubts as to the strength of his client's case. The old housekeeper at Creekside, for instance, was quite convinced of the engagement, and spoke of daily letters having come from New York for the young lady. Was she sure they were from Mr. Strongwood?

"Well," she answered, "I did not read them, but when folks are engaged and the young lady gets letters every day from the place where he lives, it looks suspicious as to who they come from."

Old Mrs. Smith at the cottage had no doubts on the subject; in fact she said that Miss Galway had as good as told her so. Beyond this, Herrick found only general impressions, but was afraid to appear too curious, lest people should suspect trouble, and recognize him as Strongwood's agent.

As it was, no one knew of his errand except Emorie, who treated him with cold politeness and appeared to give him every opportunity for pursuing his inquiries.

"Here, Mr. Herrick," said he, showing him some papers, "do you want better proof than this? Here are letters from my father and sister."

Herrick read the letters, which contained positive statements against Strongwood, and authorized Emorie to proceed in their name. He looked at them carefully, compared the signatures with other specimens of their writing, and felt satisfied that they were genuine.

"There is no power of attorney here, Mr. Galway."

"No, of course not. There is no notary at the little place where they have been during my sister's illness. I am only acting as their adviser. It will be quite sufficient if Mr. Strongwood will make the draft payable to my sister."

"We have hardly reached that point yet," remarked Herrick, in his most professional tone. "You will kindly let me see the 'documentary evidence' mentioned in your father's letter to my client."

"That will be produced in court," returned Emorie stiffly. "Mr. Strongwood must have a very short memory, if he is not fully aware of its nature."

"Well, Mr. Galway, I can tell you plainly that if you think that your bluster is going to make my client pay so much as one cent in order to avoid a lawsuit, you are very much mistaken."

"And your client, Mr. Herrick, is very much mistaken, if he thinks he is helping his case by pushing us to extremes.

In the critical state of my sister's health, threatened as she is with brain fever, my father is naturally anxious to have the matter settled at once, without exposing her to the nervous strain of a suit at law. Therefore he is willing to accept a far lower sum now than he would do later. Besides this, I do not suppose that Mr. Strongwood cares to have his name dragged in such a way before the public ; and I give you fair warning, that if he does not pay up promptly, I shall keep quiet no longer ; but shall publish his villainy to the world, and especially in the New York papers."

" It is very kind of you, I am sure," said Herrick, " to be so very solicitous for my client's reputation ; but that is a matter he is fully competent to look after himself. I wish you a very good morning."

So saying, he withdrew. But, despite his words, Herrick was impressed. Emorie saw this, and was well satisfied with the progress he had made.

In fact the lawyer wrote to Strongwood that afternoon, and advised a compromise.

The letter arrived the day after Charles and Bessie Bruce returned to Penelve. Bessie, who had fallen at once into her old ways, carried it to Strongwood, who was sitting in the summer house.

She had inadvertently seen the post mark, and could not altogether conceal her embarrassment as she handed the letter to him.

" Here, Mr. Strongwood, is a letter for you."

He thanked her, but noticing her embarrassment, and that she addressed him with " you " instead of " thee," felt that she was holding him at arm's length. A glance at the envelope explained it all.

"Miss Bessie," he said, "if you can spare me a few moments, may I ask if you got a letter from Flumetown about me?"

"What make's you ask?" she answered, colouring.

"Because my correspondent in Flumetown said that he was about to write to you, and I re-mailed an envelope myself directed to you in his handwriting."

Bessie looked at him in surprise, but said nothing.

"Miss Bessie, did you believe that letter?"

"No, I did not." Then blushing at the look of pleasure and thanks Strongwood gave her, she returned to the house before Strongwood had time to say anything more.

He read the letter carefully several times and was greatly perplexed. His resolution almost wavered, and if Bessie had not already known about the matter it is not impossible that he might have consented to a compromise. Now, however, that she knew, his strongest reason for doing so was removed. The threat of publicity in New York did not impress him so much as it would have done had his mother and sisters been at home, or he himself likely soon to return to the city. As it was, he experienced a painful pleasure in determining that Bessie should know the very worst from him.

Accordingly, finding her alone in the garden that afternoon, he said to her :

"Miss Bessie, I wanted to tell you that the letter you brought me this morning was from my lawyer."

"Your lawyer?"

"Yes, I thought the case grave enough to engage one, and he is in Flumetown in hopes of being able to sift the matter."

"I hope he is succeeding."

"Not very well thus far; for he writes me advising a compromise."

It was very difficult for him to get the words out, and Bessie noticed it, but misunderstood the cause of his embarrassment.

She hardly knew what to say. He evidently wished to continue the conversation, but she found it very awkward, and was about to excuse herself and go into the house, when he added:

"I cannot imagine why she should persecute me so. I thought she was really a fine character."

"Are you sure," said Bessie,—— and then stopped.

"Sure of what?"

"Excuse me, I was about to say something without thinking."

"You mean, 'Am I sure I did not care for her?' I tell you I never loved any one in the world, but——" He checked himself. He had almost been betrayed into a declaration. Then he added more quietly: "But one, who is beyond my reach."

Bessie thought he meant that the one he referred to was dead, and felt sorry for him; but it hardly seemed the proper time to say anything about it. She paused for a moment, and then, before she could speak, the two younger children, Esther and Clarence, rushed up and began to tell her of some great joke they had played upon their grandmother.

They were so excited with laughing, and their words tumbled out so quickly and disjointedly that there was no making out what they said. Bessie was afraid that what had been fun to the children might have been the reverse to their grandmother. So she felt it was necessary to go and set matters straight, and excusing herself to Strongwood she went into the house, only to find that her fears had been groundless.

Strongwood naturally felt uncomfortable ; it seemed clear to him that Bessie would suppose he had been imprudent, and this wounded his pride terribly and made him dejected.

His one chance now of standing well with her was to allow the Galways to do their worst and trust to being able to prove his innocence. Whatever others might do he was certain Bessie would not care for the appearance of things, but for the truth.

And yet—and this caused him no small anxiety—if his own lawyer whilst investigating the matter on the spot could be deceived by appearances, what hope could he have of being vindicated in court, where the chief witnesses against him, whom Mr. Herrick had not yet seen, would be on hand ? Would his own unsupported testimony avail to clear him ?

But to pay hush money would be morally unjustifiable, and he was glad that Bessie's knowledge of the circumstances had removed the temptation to compromise. Sometimes he almost wondered whether with so much smoke there might not after all be some fire, and he would rack his memory to recall every word or look that had passed between himself and Miss Galway. He could think of nothing that could substantiate the charge.

Then he would grow angry and feel that he did well to be angry, and so he became more and more unhappy, and the light that had begun to dawn upon him grew dark.

However, he had far too healthy a mind to mope, and his thoughts were now a good deal taken up with his business.

The letters from Mr. Hansen spoke of such serious difficulties that he was expecting to be summoned to New York at any time. For the present, his partner urged him not to come, as his presence was not necessary, and the weather was so intensely sultry that there would be great risk in his going to the city.

CHAPTER XXVII.

WHO ARE YOU?

AFTER writing to Strongwood, it occurred to Mr. Herrick that it would be a good thing to write directly to Miss Galway herself, and he called on Emorie to get her address.

Emorie was out, and he was shown for the first time into the study, with apologies from Mrs. Henderson, who explained that the parlour was being papered.

As he waited his eye fell on the list which Miss Galway had written out and fastened to the wall, giving a full itinerary of their proposed journey, with the dates, so that Mrs. Henderson might know how to forward their letters. Herrick had just finished copying their present address, when Emorie entered.

"Good morning, Mr. Galway, I just called to ask if you had any objection to my writing to your sister direct."

"Not in the least, except that it is quite unnecessary. The whole matter is in my hands, and her state of health makes it very undesirable for her to be troubled."

"Still, you are willing?"

"Certainly, and I will forward any letter you may write."

"Oh I need not trouble you to do that. I suppose a letter sent to the address given here will reach her?"

Emorie started ; but hid his confusion in a laugh.

"So, Mr. Herrick, you have been playing detective, have you ? It's well I came in. It would serve you right for me to let you send your letter to that address. If it had not been for your client, they would have kept to that route. As it is, my sister's illness has altered their plans. This is their present address."

He wrote an address on a sheet of paper and handed it to Herrick, who thanked him and withdrew.

Emorie was thoroughly alarmed, and deeply regretted that in his anxiety to avoid suspicion he had allowed Mr. Herrick so much liberty. He hoped he had put him off the right track ; but he had but too good reason to fear that the lawyer would send a duplicate letter to each address.

Should Mr. Herrick do this (which as a matter of precaution he did) Emorie knew that he had only a few days longer at his disposal, and, becoming desperate, threw discretion to the winds. He had hitherto been very careful to say nothing that in any way reflected upon Miss Galway's character ; for she stood so high that he knew it would be fatal to his purpose. He had proceeded very carefully, so that none of the Flumetown people had suspected that there was any likelihood of the engagement which they imagined existed between Miss Galway and Strongwood being broken off. His hope had been to manage the affair so as to cause as little comment as possible. Now he determined to gain his end immediately if he could.

Accordingly when Mr. Herrick communicated Strongwood's positive refusal to make any terms, Emorie played his last card.

It was only an insinuation. But it was enough.

"You lie, sir," said Mr. Herrick hotly.

Emorie drew himself up.

"I allow no one to use such language to me."

"Then don't use language to call it forth."

Mr. Herrick had always been so very conciliating in his manner that Emorie hardly knew how to act. Should he appear to sacrifice his self-respect, or his last hope of getting the money?

He naturally chose the former.

"If it were not for the sake of my sister," he said, "I should have nothing further to do with you. As it is, all I have to say is, Write to your client, and you will soon see him alter his tune."

"I imagine he will, and you will find yourself defendant in a suit for libel, if you are not careful."

"You forget that what I say to you, as his counsel, is a privileged communication."

It was Herrick's turn to beat a retreat.

"If you dare repeat it to a third party, it will be actionable. And I give you fair warning that if this cause comes up for trial, and you make statements derogatory to my client's character, which you are not able to substantiate, you will suffer for it to the extent of the law."

"All right," retorted Emorie. "It's all very well for you to bluster ; 'let those laugh who win.' We'll soon see who has the best of it."

"Why did you not make this charge at first?"

"It was hardly necessary when he knew all about it, but you will find too late for your client's good that I have proofs."

Both men left each other's presence with very uncomfortable feelings. Emorie's bold manner had shaken Mr. Herrick's confidence in the strength of his case, and he determined to write a bare statement of what had passed to Strongwood.

Emorie soon recovered his spirits, and, as he walked by himself in the gathering twilight along the paths of the Creekside garden, he thought to himself :

" I've made an impression, and I'm much mistaken if Herrick doesn't write a letter that will fetch the money double quick. Let me see, to-day's Thursday. I don't think Miss Galway can get Herrick's letter till Tuesday, at the earliest, and, in that case, allowing for difference in time, no telegram can reach Flumetown before Wednesday morning. I'll be off by that time ; Miss Galway will never know what a brother she has missed."

The next morning he began to speak to his acquaintances of his intention of leaving in the following week.

This announcement was received with much regret by the little circle in Flumetown, with whom his pleasant manners had made him a favourite. He had become specially intimate with the cashier and other officers of the bank, and he had ventured on drawing two cheques for rather small amounts as a preparation for a bolder move. These had been paid without demur, and he had for some time been openly speaking of expecting a large draft from his father in aid of a business scheme in which he was about to embark. His plan was to draw the money the last thing before starting, but everything was ready, and he was only waiting for Strongwood's answer to his last threat.

Before the answer came an unexpected event happened.

The true Jonathan Galway came home.

It was on Monday morning. Emorie was in the hall about to leave the house. Just as he opened the door a man, rather shabbily dressed, but with a somewhat gentlemanly bearing, came up the steps.

" Is my father, Mr. Galway, at home ? "

Emorie was thunder-struck ; but he recovered himself almost instantly, and, after looking the new comer in the face for a little while, as if trying to make sure who he was, said : " Yes, I suppose it must be you. You must be my brother Ephraim. Well, I should never have recognized you. Are you really Ephraim ? "

" Scarcely. I'd have you know that I'm Mr. Jonathan Galway. But who in the world are you ? "

" Oh ! I understand your game," said Emorie, determined to brazen it out. " You would have been wiser, young man, to have claimed to be Ephraim. I should not have detected your trick so soon."

" Where's any trick ? "

" You are very dense, sir, if you expect me to receive a stranger who attempts to pass himself off as myself."

The unexpectedness of this remark, and the quiet effrontery with which it was uttered made the real Jonathan gasp for breath.

" Well, sir," he replied after a moment, " this is what I call cool. Here you are, a stranger in my father's house, telling me to my face that you are me. Come, now, this joke has gone far enough."

" I quite agree with you."

" Well then, where are my father and sister ? "

" I don't know who your father and sister are."

Jonathan swore.

"I mean Mr. Caleb Galway and Miss Isabel Galway. Do you know now ?"

"My father and sister are at present nearer Alaska than New York."

"What do I care where your father and sister are ?" said Jonathan with further angry expletives.

"Very much, apparently, as you claim them as your own. But if you wish to see Mr. and Miss Galway, and are sure they would recognize you, you might possibly meet them in Salt Lake City on their way east."

"Think they would recognize me, indeed. What are you doing here, I should like to know ?"

"Doubtless you would."

"Answer my question."

"A gentleman does not generally account to tramps for being in his own father's house."

"This is not your father's house," and Jonathan's language became unquotable again.

"You seem to know better than I."

"I do."

"Come, my man, say what your business is, and go."

"I won't."

"You shall."

"I shall not," and so saying he pushed Emorie aside and forced himself into the house.

Emorie caught hold of him.

"You villain, get out of this."

"I won't get out, and you dare not put me out," said Jonathan, struggling to free himself.

"Mrs. Henderson," said Emorie, for the house-keeper had appeared, and had been watching them with interest, with all her sympathies enlisted for Emorie. " Mrs. Henderson, call Bryan."

The gardener came promptly, and rescued Emorie from a very unpleasant predicament, for Jonathan was holding him by his throat against the wall, and was beginning to pummel him.

" Hold him, Bryan, while I summon the police," said Emorie, as soon as he had recovered breath.

He went to the telephone, and an officer of the law soon had the unfortunate Jonathan under arrest.

Before the magistrate the poor man had no show. His appearance was against him, and his story of having had his portmanteau and better clothing stolen was received as a tramp's lie. Curiously enough, he had actually done what Emorie had pretended to do, and had come without warning, so as to surprise his father and sister, who, he thought would now be at home ; as indeed thay would have been had they not postponed their trip a fortnight in hopes that he might join them.

The contrast presented by the two men was very striking. Jonathan Galway was not only shabby, but so violently excited as to be almost incoherent, whilst Emorie, well-dressed, and bearing himself as a gentleman, knowing how much was at stake, kept perfectly cool.

The magistrate was accustomed to see him everywhere accepted as Mr. Galway's son, and never thought of doubting his identity.

After the facts of the interview and the assault had been brought out, Emorie asked permission to put a few questions to the prisoner. During his short stay at Flumetown he had picked up a great deal of imformation about the Galways, and knew far more about what they had been doing than did Jonathan, who had never been in the place, and had often failed to keep his family informed of his address for months at a time. Emorie with his legal experience was easily able to confuse the prisoner and make him appear ridiculous.

When he had finished with his questions he turned to the magistrate and said :

" I have been examining him in order to bring out what I consider the most serious part of the case. Here is this fellow who admits that he knew that my father and sister have been away——"

" I don't admit any knowledge of your father and sister," interrupted the prisoner.

" Silence ! " commanded the magistrate.

" He admits," continued Emorie, " that he knew they were away from home. He evidently did not know that I was here. So he attempts to palm himself off as my father's son, in the hope of getting money from the house-keeper."

" You lie," roared Jonathan. " Do you think I need money ? Look at this." And he took out his pocket-book, and exhibited a sufficiently long roll of bank notes.

" This only shows how successful he has been in obtaining money elsewhere on my father's security."

The magistrate evidently thought so too.

Jonathan's indignation boiled over.

" I'll telegraph for my father, and have you arrested ; you ——"

" Certainly," said Emorie sarcastically ; " I suppose you expect him to recognize the signature ? "

" I'll send for my brother."

" Where will you find him ? "

Jonathan gave the correct address.

"That shows how much you know about his movements. He is on his holiday, and beyond the reach of telegrams or letters for three weeks to come."

Just then a messenger handed a telegram to the magistrate, who read it, and, looking at the prisoner, said :

"You wished to appeal to Mr. Caleb Galway, did you ? Well, he has telegraphed about you."

"Impossible," said Jonathan.

Emorie felt a cold shiver pass over him, but realized immediately that his only safety lay in keeping cool, and he hid his momentary confusion by turning about, and using his handkerchief, while the magistrate proceeded :

"This has, doubtless, reference to that roll of bank notes you have just showed us. Those you have imposed upon have evidently communicated with Mr. Galway. This is his telegram :

"*Arrest man passing himself off as my son Jonathan, recently returned from Europe.*"

"I hope you are satisfied."

"Entirely. The telegram has reference to that scoundrel," said Jonathan, pointing to Emorie.

"Be more careful of your remarks," said the magistrate.

Emorie, who had by this time quite recovered his equanimity, smiled and said nothing.

"In default of bail," continued the magistrate, "I must commit you to await action by the grand jury."

"On what charge ?"

"For endeavouring to force yourself into Mr. Galway's house under pretext of being his son, and for assault."

" And I shall bring action against you for false arrest and imprisonment."

"Certainly. In the meantime, officers, take charge of him."

Jonathan submitted per force, but gave a parting shot at Emorie :

" You scoundrel, I'll make you suffer for this."

" Silence," commanded the magistrate ; and the party withdrew their several ways, while he gave attention to the next case.

CHAPTER XXVIII.

SHALL WOMEN PREACH?

IF ever any man felt himself abominably ill-used, it was
Robert Strongwood when he read Mr. Herrick's last
letter.

" How Mr. Galway can have fallen so low as to risk his
own daughter's reputation for the sake of money is more than
I can understand," he said to himself. The underlying motive
of the whole proceeding had been clearly shown in the evident readiness on the part of the accuser to accept a money
compromise ; but Strongwood never once suspected that he
was the dupe of a conspiracy of which Mr. Galway was as
innocent as himself. The only explanation he could think of
was that Mr. Galway had become involved in business difficulties, and had resorted to this mode of raising money as a
last resort.

He did not write to his lawyer at once, because he had
made it a rule to write no letter when he was angry.

The next morning the question presented itself whether
he should tell Miss Bruce about this letter.

No, of course not.

But he had determined that she should know everything,
and he felt in honour bound to let her learn the worst.

It was not easy for him to find an opportunity, for
" Quarterly Meeting " was coming on, and she was very busy

with preparations for it. Susquehanna Quarterly Meeting met at different places every quarter, so that it was held only once a year at Penelve. This time it was to be a specially important occasion, for besides the annual reports which had to be prepared for the approaching Yearly Meeting, a temperance conference had been arranged, and an unusual number of ministers from other places were expected. Although it would not be, except in a relative sense, a large meeting, it required a good deal of preparation, for there were not many Friends who were able to entertain visitors, and some meals were to be served at the Meeting-house.

It so happened that Ezra Seward and Bessie Bruce were members of the committee on arrangements, and it was remarkable that, while he never called to consult her except for a good reason, good reasons seemed to present themselves continually, so that a day seldom passed without one or two interviews.

Strongwood noted all this and felt correspondingly uncomfortable, and chafed at being obliged to stand by without a word and watch some one else paying suit to the woman he loved. He saw that everybody would consider that Ezra Seward was just the man for her. It is true he was several years her senior, but he was very well off, a bank president, and officially connected either as chairman or manager with almost all the institutions of the place. Besides this, he was a staunch Friend and thoroughly in sympathy with all Bessie's aims and views of life. Even Strongwood was forced in fairness to admit that Seward was apparently more suitable for her than himself. But although he admitted it, he did feel it, and called himself a dog in the manger for being troubled because another man was doing what he himself had deliberately refrained from doing. He wished he had left Penelve before her return and not yielded to the kind pressure which Bruce and his wife had put upon him to remain over the Quarterly Meeting.

It was on a Saturday morning that the guests began to arrive. Those who stayed at Uplands were mostly from the country meetings Bruce and Bessie had just visited.

There was one guest different from the rest, who specially attracted his attention. This was Esther Longboat, a ministering Friend from the West. She wore the Friends' dress, and her face when quiet was pensive and almost sad. Her complexion was sallow and there was an underlying look of intensity about her, though she had a sweet, winning smile. She spoke little, and there was nothing specially noteworthy in her conversation, except when called upon to tell some of her experiences in Gospel work. At such times she would relate occurrences of startling interest.

"Tell me about her," Strongwood said to Bruce when they were alone together.

"Well, Rob," he replied, "she is a remarkable woman, and has, as we say, a real gift. She has had great results from her ministry ; perhaps more among the Methodists, with whom she is very popular, than among Friends."

"Has she much education ?"

"No. Perhaps you noticed how ungrammatically she talks ; but, if she preaches to-morrow her language will be almost correct. The difference in this respect is very interesting. Perhaps the most singular thing about her is that she occasionally gets into a kind of trance, during which she often says quite wonderful things. She herself attaches very little importance to these utterances, and wishes her friends to rouse her if she begins to speak in this way."

This last piece of information awakened Strongwood's curiosity and he therefore stayed in the parlour with the Friends as much as possible, which pleased the Bruces, but put some restraint upon the other guests. However, his curiosity was not gratified, as she had no trance while at Penelve.

The " Meeting on Ministry and Oversight," attended only by ministers and other official members of the Society, was held in the afternoon. As usual, much time was spent in mutual encouragement to a deeper spiritual life, and in considering how to make the work more effective. Amongst other business, a minute was read from Penelve Monthly Meeting, stating that Friends there believed that Elizabeth Bruce had received a gift in the ministry, and that the time had come to "acknowledge" her as a minister.

As the clerk ceased reading, a deep silence settled over the meeting. Then one after another of the men and women present, who wished to express a judgment on the matter, did so. All heartily approved of the proposed action, and, after another pause, the clerk prepared a minute to embody the conclusion of the meeting. It ran thus :

" The following minute has been received from Penelve Monthly Meeting. (Here followed the minute.) After a time of serious consideration Friends fully united with the judgment of Penelve Monthly Meeting, that the time has come to acknowledge our Friend Elizabeth Bruce a minister of the Gospel in our religious Society.

" The clerk is directed to forward a copy of this minute to the clerks of Penelve Monthly Meeting and of Penelve Preparative Meeting on Ministry and Oversight."

Then followed an earnest prayer for a blessing on the life and service of the newly acknowledged minister.

When Bruce returned home from meeting he found Strongwood on the porch, and, as it was not quite time to go to the Temperance Conference, he sat down beside him and told him, among other things, what had been done in regard to Bessie.

Strongwood felt it as a fresh barrier between himself and her.

" I don't know that I approve of women being preachers," he said after a pause.

" I think it is clearly scriptural," returned Bruce. " Paul's statement as to women keeping silence in the church must be taken in connection with his directions as to how they should dress when prophesying, that is, when speaking under the direct influence of the Holy Spirit. Besides, the promise is that your sons and your *daughters* shall prophesy. You remember that Philip had four daughters who prophesied."

" Well, it does not strike me as suitable."

" Don't you think my sister has a gift ? "

" Of course I do. But what I was speaking of was of women becoming professional ministers. I suppose we shall have the ceremony of ordination to-morrow."

Bruce laughed.

" Oh no, we never ordain our ministers."

" What do you do then ? "

" We believe that the Lord gives the gift and the power to exercise it, and all that man can do is to acknowledge that the gift has been conferred."

" Will it be her duty to preach after this ? "

" Only when she has the call to do so."

" What is the advantage of acknowledging her then ? "

" The custom has come down from the early days of our Society. The ideal Quaker preacher is a travelling preacher. Those that went about from place to place received a certificate that they were ministers in good standing. It simply means that the church has unity with the preacher, and believes he has a gift, and encourages him to travel if he feels called to do so. But the office as such confers no right on the minister to exercise any exclusive spiritual functions, nor to give up his ordinary calling."

" What does your sister think of this action ? "

" At first she felt very much disinclined to it, and Friends, out of deference to her feelings, postponed doing anything for several months. Then she felt that it was best to submit to their judgment."

Strongwood said nothing, but he inwardly wished she had not been willing to submit.

CHAPTER XXIX.

A DIRECT MESSAGE.

IN the pause that followed the family Bible reading next morning, Esther Longboat preached. What she said consisted of a series of short discourses, each one addressed to some particular person present. This is a form of religious service that used to be more common among Friends than it is now. Although it was somewhat of an ordeal to be thus publicly spoken to, Friend Longboat said nothing that could not suitably be expressed under the circumstances. A stranger overhearing her words might have found little that was remarkable in them, but it was very evident that several at least of those addressed recognized that she had been given wonderful insight into their condition. She was really as it were delivering cipher messages, of which only the one to whom she spoke had the key. Her manner was solemn and introverted, and her style of speaking antique.

What she said to Bessie was: " Thou hast received a precious gift in the ministry and the Lord will bless thee in it yet more, and will give thee many souls for thy hire. Only be faithful, even if He should call thee to carry the blood-stained banner of the cross to distant lands and over the tempestuous ocean. I perceive that a change is soon to come into thy life. Be not afraid. If thou art faithful thou wilt receive greater blessing through it."

The last person she addressed was Strongwood:

"Thou hast had gracious visitations of the Spirit of God, and hast not resisted the drawing cords of His love. But thou art in darkness and clouds and tempest. Nevertheless the Lord is with thee, though thou knowest it not. He has tried thee and He will try thee again, yea, as it were to seven times; yet, if thou wilt trust Him, and forgive as thou art forgiven, the word shall be fulfilled to thee, 'He knoweth the way that I take, and when He hath tried me I shall come forth as gold.' Fear not, thou shalt yet praise Him."

Strongwood was much moved. The whole scene had been quite new to him, and while he said to himself, "How can this stranger really know anything about me?" he could not help feeling both encouraged and dismayed at her words; encouraged for the hope conveyed in them; discouraged at the prospect of some more troubles.

"I have had four already," thought he, "but if three more are to come, I'm afraid there will be little time left for praising. I can never live through them."

As he thought this, a light unknown to him before seemed to break upon him in the hope of a life beyond. It was like a burst of sunshine through dark clouds—glorious for a moment and then obscured. He was not ready to forgive.

The company soon scattered. Strongwood and Bessie found themselves alone in the parlour for a few minutes. Both felt a little awkward, but presently Strongwood said:

"Mrs. Longboat is certainly a remarkable woman."

"Yes," answered Bessie, "isn't she? I thought she spoke very impressively this morning; and," she added with an effort, "I hope you felt encouraged by what she said, and that you will find the words prove true."

" I hope so too, but what she said about seven troubles is not very cheering."

" I do not think that she meant what she said to be understood literally, any more than my crossing the ocean."

" Even so, it is not encouraging, especially as there are further complications in that Flumetown matter, and if good can only come to me by forgiving those people, I am afraid my case is hopeless."

" Why cannot you forgive ? "

" They are making very serious charges against my character, and threaten to publish them if I do not pay money down."

" That of course puts it out of your power to make any compromise."

" Exactly. But what am I to do ? "

" I am hardly the person to advise with. My brother Charles——"

" Don't ask me to tell any one else about it," he interrupted. " If you could only tell me what you think."

"All I can say then, Mr. Strongwood, is that the one course open to you is to be straightforward and do what is right. What that is you alone are able to judge. But under no circumstances could the payment of money be right."

" But you certainly would not have me marry a girl I don't care for ? "

" No, of course not, unless "—and she looked him straight in the face and added slowly—" unless you really are bound to her——"

Before she had finished the sentence they heard voices drawing near. Bessie hastily went out by another door and reached her own room by the back staircase unobserved.

Strongwood retreated in good order to the summer house, so that when the guests entered the room it was empty. His outward calm by no means corresponded to his inward feelings. He was very angry with himself for introducing the subject when he might have known that they would be interrupted. He had left matters far worse than before. Miss Bruce certainly suspected that he had compromised himself, and therefore, until the matter was cleared up, she would have nothing more to do with him. Of course, he could hope great things from the trial, but at best there would be scandal, and many who heard of the charge would not hear of the acquittal. What with his uncertain health and this hanging over him, he felt that his life was practically blasted. The one way of escape that presented itself was to agree to pay a sum of money down, provided the Galways would give him a properly signed and attested document certifying that the relations between himself and Miss Galway had always been entirely satisfactory, and that there had never been any thought of marriage between them. He could then at once have something to show Miss Bruce or any one else who might hear of the matter. He was sure the Galways would consent, and the certificate would be entirely true. The temptation was strong. The stake was a tremendous one for him; he felt himself about to lose everything that made life worth having. But then, the meanness of such an act came over him, and what if it should leak out that he had done it! No, it was out of the question. What had he done to merit such persecution? And if God did care, why did He allow such trouble to come on him just as he began to wish to know the truth?

He went to his room, and sitting down to his writing

table began to write to Mr. Herrick. He had only got as far as—

"You may tell that scoundrel, Mr. Galway, that he may do his worst, but that I shall under no circumstances——," when he remembered that it was Sunday, and nearly time for meeting. He knew that Charlie had counted a good deal on his being at this meeting, and, although he felt no inclination to go, he did not care to disappoint his friend.

It was still early, but, as he knew that there would be a crowded house, and as he did not wish to have company on his walk, he started off by himself unobserved.

It was a delightful day in the latter part of August. The fresh mountain breeze kept the air from being oppressive, while the Sabbath hush over everything gave a sense of rest to which he could not be insensible, so that when he arrived at the Meeting-house the fierceness of his mood had considerably abated.

As soon as Bessie reached her room, she shut and locked her door, and sat down to compose her thoughts. Her cheeks burned at the thought that any one might have heard so much as a word of her conversation with Strongwood. She also thought that he had treated her very badly to spring such a subject upon her, and she regretted that she had opened the way for it. Both his manner and words seemed to her to amount to a half admission that he had been compromised in the matter. This she regarded as being, under the circumstances, practically equivalent to an acknowledgment, and it was a great distress to her, for she had gradually come to regard him as an almost ideal character, or rather she had allowed her ideals to approach more and more to a likeness of what she supposed him to be. It was very bitter, therefore, to be forced to acknowledge to herself that all her sympathy had gone out to one who had no real existence, except in her own imagination. The image was now rudely shattered, and by his own hand. If there had been no truth in what was charged against him would he have had any doubt as to the right course to pursue? Why did his lawyer advise a money payment? Esther Longboat's words were indeed reassuring, but Bessie, though she firmly believed in the gift of discernment of spirits and of prophecy in the church at the present day, was not in this instance sure enough of it to make it outweigh what seemed to be the hard logic of facts.

It did not occur to her that if Strongwood had been really acting badly he would probably not have spoken to her at all about it. Besides, she already knew something of the affair, and the information he had given her that morning had apparently come in accidentally in a conversation on something else.

As she began to get ready for meeting, her eye fell on the beautiful panorama of hill and valley which lay before her in clear sunshine and sharply outlined shadow, and she murmured to herself,—

> " But yet I know,
> Where'er I go,
> That there hath passed away a glory from the earth."

Though she had had many trials before, this was different; for the loss of parents, the breaking up of her early home, much as she had felt them, had had no bitterness in them, for only sin or self-will makes sorrow bitter. But here was sin.

As she passed Strongwood's door, and noticed that it was closed, she supposed he had not gone to meeting, and felt confirmed in this by seeing his best hat on the table ; for he had the unconscious habit of wearing his older hats when he was depressed.   As it was late, she concluded that he was not going to meeting that day, and was rather relieved.

CHAPTER XXX.

RIGHT ABOUT FACE.

A RRIVED at the meeting-house, Bessie cast an involuntary glance at Strongwood's accustomed seat. He was not there, and the crowd was too dense for her to see him near the front where the ushers had persuaded him to sit, in order to leave more room at the back.

On his part, he, not knowing that her "acknowledgment" as a minister would not be considered complete before official notice had been received by the Monthly Meeting, expected her to take her place on one of the raised seats facing the congregation. As she was not there, he concluded that she had remained at home, and felt sure that he had offended her. Altogether his thoughts in the early part of the meeting were anything but what one is supposed to have at such a time.

But he was soon aroused by the voice of prayer. To his astonishment it was Bessie in earnest entreaty for a rich blessing to rest upon the assembled company. The part that especially impressed Strongwood was when she prayed against wandering thoughts, and added, " But if any of us should find it impossible to put away these outward things from our minds, grant that we may have strength to think about them in accordance with Thy thoughts, so that what would otherwise be hindrances to us may become the means of showing us how we may follow Thee, and live according to Thy spirit in these matters, although in so doing we may be called to give up our most cherished hopes."

The whole prayer was unusually solemn and the congregation was deeply impressed, and none more so than Strongwood. He could not help reading between the words, and understanding that if Bessie had ever cared for him, she had now entirely given him up; nevertheless the prayer soothed him, and prepared him to listen to the discourse that followed, and which proved a turning point in his life.

Yet when the speaker—a middle-aged man with a thoughtful face – announced his subject, Strongwood was disappointed, for he thought that he had quite mastered the main points of the Quaker position in favour of the non-use of ceremonial observances, and it had struck him that their absence relieved the Christian teaching of a cumbrous impediment. He felt, therefore, that a discourse on the subject was not what he needed.

He was relieved when the preacher said that his main purpose was not to explain the position of Friends in relation to water baptism and the Supper. He would, however, briefly point out that the absence of all instructions in the New Testament as to how any rite or ceremony should be performed constitutes a strong presumptive proof that no ordinance was instituted. How can we urge a command when we know not what has been commanded? The words "baptizing them into the name of the Father and of the Son and of the Holy Ghost" form no exception to this position, for there is no proof that the Apostles ever understood them as referring to a baptismal formula. The first Council at Jerusalem, in decreeing the freedom of the Gentiles from the Mosaic ritual, established no ordinances in its place, but acted on the principles laid down by Peter in his argument for freedom, that no ceremony can be required when God shows that the baptism of the Holy Ghost is independent of it.

What we see in the churches to-day varies in form and meaning with every denomination. Historically, all that is now practical is a development. What we read of as having happened in the Corinthian Church was a development from the original conception, that made the words of Christ, " This do in remembrance of Me," apply to the daily meal. Water baptism was merely the adoption of a Jewish custom.

" But friends," continued the speaker ; " let us not allow discussion as to the use or non-use of the outward make us forget the true Baptism and the true Supper of our Lord. Six times in the New Testament are we reminded that the baptism of Christ is not with water but with the Holy Spirit. Have we come to Jesus the Baptist ? Neither the use nor the non-use of water availeth anything, but a new creation,—and faith that worketh through love. These avail. Jesus Christ does not baptize by sprinkling, no, nor even by mere immersion, from which we can arise in our waterproof clothing and resume our every-day garments. His is a baptism from which we are never to emerge. As ships that were sunk in the Tiber 2,000 years ago and remain for ever below the waves, were spoken of by ancient writers as having been baptized into the Tiber, so are we to be baptized into Christ. Or, to use another illustration, iron that is placed in the fire and kept there, is at last not only in the fire, but the fire is in it. Its very nature is changed.

" The sinner comes to Christ. Is it only to have the penalty of sin removed ? No ! Forgiveness involves the commencement of a change in character. Sin involves separation from God. Christ's work is to bring us back to God, and, therefore, to righteousness.

"All that is evil within us, our uncurbed passions, our pride, our selfishness, all are for the fire of the baptism that He gives. All that is good is to be purified. The work is not completed at once ; but our Lord does not stand off from us and say, 'You shall have no communion with Me till you are perfected.' On the contrary, as we submit to Him, we are already, to the extent of our capacity, in communion with Him. Whoever desires to live as a child of God, desires what God desires, and is to that extent in harmony with God, although his knowledge of what is implied in this may be very small. His face is set in the right direction, and he is in the line of life and growth.

" Fellowship with God means an ever increasing likeness to His character as revealed by Christ, through constant learning of His mind and accepting His choice for us, by means of the indwelling power of Christ. Friends, do you know the blessedness of thinking God's thoughts after Him ? You are in trouble ? What is your thought about it ? God's thought is that through it you may come closer to Himself. Have you sinned ? God's thought about your sin is that you should turn from it, and be saved from it by the power of your risen Saviour. Have you wronged any one ? God's thought about it is that you should confess the wrong, and so far as possible repair it. Have others wronged you? God's thought about it is that you should act towards the offender as your Saviour acts towards you. We shut the door of blessedness upon ourselves whenever, in regard to anything, we refuse to think and act in harmony with God's thought about it, so far as we know it. We are also to learn the deep meaning of being baptized with His baptism, and drinking the cup He drinks of for the sake of others.

"No fitness is needed to begin this life. Your sense of need is the invitation of the Spirit of Christ. The heart that broke for the sins of the whole world on Mount Calvary still breaks for you. He will receive you as you are, and receive you now to your home, which is His own heart of love.

"He forgives, heals and strengthens. His power coming upon you gives you new life, and by daily trust and obedience He gives you true communion."

More was said about communion with God in the service of man, and other illustrations were employed. The discourse was not eloquent and probably most of the audience were better pleased with Esther Longboat's sermon that followed, which was full of touching anecdote and impressive exhortation. But it was what Strongwood needed and he heard little of what was said later. He had never before so fully realized that faith in Christ is not a mere opinion, but the acceptance of a living Friend, as a present power within us that transforms us and enables us to live righteously. He had often heard it during the summer. But this sermon was the climax of what he had been so gradually coming to. It met his need in his distress and loneliness, and in his sense of failure. He saw his need and its supply, and understood that Christlikeness was not something commanded arbitrarily, but an essential condition for union with God, as communion was an essential for power. So in that meeting he cast himself at the feet of Christ, and became willing to forgive his enemies and to accept his difficulties in the spirit of thinking God's thoughts after Him.

When he reached home his feelings found expression in the following lines :—

> "Art Thou than man more real,
>   And is Thy tear
> More tender than a mother's ?   May I pour
> My heart out with its long imprisoned store,
>   And know that Thou dost feel ;
>   That One is here,
>   Who understands,
> And welcomes me with both His outstretched hands ?
>
>   For answering touch I long,
>   For answering word ;
> Tears rising from a heart that feels and knows,
> A human heart that feels and overflows,
>   Divine and strong.
>   Lord hast Thou heard ?
>   And can it be
> Thyself that com'st through storm and gloom to me ?"

Presently his eye fell upon the letter he had begun to Herrick that morning.   He read over the angry words, and tore up the note and wrote another in which he quietly denied the charges and refused the slightest compromise. The letter had such a tone of kindliness and patience that when Mr. Herrick read it he wondered at the change that had come over his client, and was completely convinced of his innocence.

After the letter was finished, sealed and directed, a fresh sense of light and peace broke in upon Strongwood, and a hush fell upon his spirit.   He recognized that he had truly found what he had been seeking so long, far longer than he himself had been aware of.

He knelt by his bedside in silence till the dinner bell rang.

CHAPTER XXXI.

AN UNPLEASANT SURPRISE.

ALL this time Mr. Galway and his daughter had been pursuing their trip in happy ignorance of the trouble they were supposed to be causing. They had visited various places of interest in California : had taken the voyage to Alaska, and had seen the wonderful Muir Glacier, and watched its tons of ice falling into the water below.

Until toward the end of the voyage Mr. Galway's health had improved, but he was so poorly on landing at Tacoma that his daughter induced him to go immediately to bed, while she went downstairs to ask for letters. There were quite a number waiting for them. She opened those from her fiancé first, and having enjoyed them to the full turned to the others. There was one from her brother in New Orleans, enclosing a letter to himself from Jonathan, dated from Europe. Several of her Flumetown friends had also written from their various places of summer resort. These astonished her by saying that they had heard of the return of her brother from abroad, and that he was winning golden opinions from every one. The last letter she opened was Herrick's. The information contained in it was so exceedingly surprising that at first she thought it was a joke. But on reading it more carefully she became serious. The letter was written on paper stamped with Mr. Herrick's official address. She had heard Strongwood speak of having a friend of this name who was a lawyer. Its tone was very respectful, and he laid the question before her in the way a man would do who supposed she knew all about it.

Her first thought was that she would quietly answer the letter without saying anything to her father, but further consideration convinced her that as his name had been prominently associated with the affair, it was right that he should be consulted. She would take care, however, that he should not be disturbed before dinner, nor until he had had a good rest after it. So she brought the other letters and read them to him first.

"What, has Jonathan come back!" he said. "The scamp. I'll be bound he's ruining my best horses. Has he written?"

"No!"

"Just like him. Well, I'm glad he's behaving himself, anyhow. And now what does your George say?"

Belle read some extracts.

"George is a fine fellow," resumed Mr. Galway. "But for my part I never could understand why you did not set your cap for Mr. Strongwood. It would have been more romantic, and he's a richer and abler man than George."

Belle blushed as she thought of the letter in her pocket.

"I never set my cap for any one, father," she said; "and you know there never was the least flirtation between us. I am grateful to Mr. Strongwood, but George is the only man I ever cared for."

"Poor me!" said Mr. Galway.

"Oh father, you know what I mean."

She was standing by him to arrange his pillows, and he drew down her face and kissed her.

As she moved away he looked at her lovingly.

" I declare, Belle, I think I admire you most as you are."

" That's better than admiring me as I am not.

" I mean as you are every day."

" I'm glad of that, as you see me every day."

" What's that quotation your George made the other day about beauty unadorned ? "

" Don't be foolish, father."

" Can't you help me out ? "

For answer Belle placed the tray with his dinner before him.

" Here's your dinner, father."

" Oh now I remember. ' Beauty unadorned, adorned the—— best.' No. ' Beauty unadorned, adorned the most.' That's it, isn't it ?"

" The quotation is correct, father. But you must not let your dinner get cold."

Mr. Galway liked to speak of himself as a self-made man, and the story of his early struggles was of unfailing interest to his daughter, who had caught her mother's ardent admiration for her father, and this feeling had suffered no diminution or shock on her return home from a fashionable boarding school. She accepted her father as he was, and never showed annoyance at any of the unavoidable mistakes he fell into in the society which he had entered so late in life.

He in return loved her devotedly, and a word from her had more influence than a long argument from any one else. Even when he was most irritable from his sickness, a " Now, father," from Belle would quiet him.

Later in the afternoon when he had had a good rest she came in with Mr. Herrick's letter in her hand, and began by saying :

"Jonathan appears to agree with you about Mr. Strongwood, father."

"Why, has he written to you ?"

"No, but I have a letter which says he has announced our engagement as a fact."

"Well, I never ! But that's carrying a joke too far."

"Yes, it's too bad. Whatever will George say ?"

"Perhaps," said Mr. Galway ; "it's even more to the point to know what Mr. Strongwood says."

"He denies it."

"Naturally. When I get home I shall tell Jonathan it does not do to play jokes like that. He might get us into hot water. I shall have to apologise to Mr. Strongwood as it is."

"Matters are even worse than that, father. He's actually threatened Mr. Strongwood with a law-suit for breach of promise. I've ——"

"What is that you say," said Mr. Galway, starting up from his pillows—" a lawsuit ! How do you know ?"

"I have a letter from Mr. Herrick, Mr. Strongwood's lawyer."

"Jonathan must be crazy. I'll wire at once and stop the whole thing."

"Had you not better read the letter first, father ?"

"Of course, where is it ? "

As he read his face grew graver and graver.

"It's no joke at all. Jonathan's trying to get money out of him. The boy must have lost all his senses. He knows I would have given him all he needs ; and here he must go and disgrace the family, and render himself liable to be sent to the penitentiary. It's a lasting disgrace. We'll never outlive it ! never ! never ! "

" Quietly, father. There may be some mistake."

" Mistake, of course it's a mistake. All mean and dishonest things are mistakes. But do you know anything about this Mr. Herrick ? "

" I've heard Mr. Strongwood speak of him."

" Well, I'll make sure," and he dictated a telegram to his legal adviser in New York.

Towards evening an answer came, stating that Mr. Herrick was a lawyer in good standing, and giving his address.

Mr. Galway fretted himself almost ill over the matter, and Belle occupied herself partly in trying to soothe him, and partly in writing a letter to George Coventree ; but she could not word it to suit herself.

It finally occurred to them simultaneously to examine Jonathan's letter that had been forwarded from New Orleans.

" What's its date, Belle ? "

" August 1st, from Paris."

" When did Mr. Herrick say Jonathan came home ? "

Belle examined the letter and said :

" July 14th."

Mr. Galway clapped his hands.

" It's a swindle, Belle, a blackmailing swindle."

As quickly as they could be written, two telegrams were dispatched —one to Mr. Herrick at his New York address, and one to the police magistrate at Flumetown, which was delivered, as we have seen, at a very unfortunate moment for the real Jonathan.

They worded the telegrams carefully, for they gathered from Herrick's letter that no one in Flumetown, except himself, knew as yet what the imposter was really after.

Belle destroyed her half-finished letter to Mr. Coventree and wrote a fresh one ; she also wrote to Robert Strongwood, enclosing her letter in the one her father was sending to Herrick, as she did not know Strongwood's present address.

Next day a dispatch came from Flumetown, saying that the impostor was in jail.

" Oh," said Mr. Galway, rubbing his hands, " We pricked that bubble neatly, didn't we ?   It takes a long headed man to get the better of me, I tell you."

CHAPTER XXXII

FLIGHT.

THE sense of elation with which Emorie walked out of the police court was short-lived. He had indeed scored a triumph. But he presently remembered that Mr. Herrick was still in Flumetown, and that almost certainly a telegram had been sent to him also. But he had great hopes of the effect of his last threat upon Strongwood, and was very unwilling to lose the chance of securing the hoped-for prize just as it seemed within his grasp. Besides, there was that cheque which he hoped to get cashed at the bank before leaving Flumetown.

He was debating how far he could risk a longer stay, when he felt himself grasped by the arm. Looking up, he saw Mr. Herrick.

"You are just the man I was looking for," said he.

Emorie was terribly frightened, and could not think what to say. Escape was impossible. He stood still, expecting his doom.

"Come with me, Mr. Galway," continued Herrick.

"Where to?"

"We can just step aside out of the bustle. I've something to show you."

Emorie thought he detected a hidden meaning in the words, but he could not make a scene in the street, and had no choice but to accompany the lawyer. He was greatly relieved when he found that Herrick, who had his travelling bag in his hand, was simply anxious to catch a train and to show him Strongwood's letter before he started.

As he read it Emorie had enough manliness left to feel rather ashamed of himself.

"Do you mean to tell me," said Herrick, "that any one but an innocent person could have written that letter?"

Emorie's one purpose now was to get the lawyer away from Flumetown as quickly as possible, so he answered:

"You forget, sir, that I have been only an agent in the matter, acting under orders. This letter closes the negotiations. The need for my interference is over. I shall put the matter now into the hands of a lawyer, who will work up the case under Mr. Galway's directions." Then, looking at his watch, he added, "Your train is nearly due. I will walk with you to the station."

"You will, of course, inform your father of the contents of this letter," said Herrick as they walked along.

"Certainly."

"You will no doubt consider the great injury to your sister's reputation, should all these matters be gone into in court, especially if you cannot substantiate the charges."

"I tell you, sir, that that is not my concern. If my sister can stand it, I can."

They reached the station, and found that the train was behind time, and for half-an-hour Emorie was in a fever of impatience and uncertainty. He was afraid to leave and afraid to stay. He spent most of the time on the town side of the station, so that should the telegraph boy appear he might by some means or other intercept the message without Herrick knowing of it. Finally the train came in, and, after what seemed to Emorie an endless five minutes, started again. It had just moved off when the telegraph boy rushed in with a dispatch for Herrick.

"Hurry up, Sonny, you can catch it," said one of the bystanders, "she's moving slowly yet "—

Emorie took in the situation at once, and saying quickly, "No, let me have it, I'm the boss runner," snatched the envelope from the boy and ran with a good will after the retreating train, which was every moment going at increasing speed. The brakeman was standing on the rear platform and seeing Emorie running after him holding out the telegram, leaned as far over the railing as he could. He was just saying, "All right, sir, you'll do it," when Emorie with an adroitness that deceived every one, managed to catch his foot and fall. When he got up further pursuit was hopeless, and he felt that the escape was well worth a bleeding hand.

He returned to receive the sympathy of the bystanders, and nodding pleasantly to them walked off with the telegraph boy.

" I hope," said he to the operator, when they reached the office, "that there was nothing important in this telegram."

" It referred to that fellow who was arrested this morning. As he is in jail, I suppose there's no hurry."

" All right then, I'll forward it to Mr. Herrick in a letter this evening."

So saying, he walked leisurely to Creekside, shut himself up in Mr. Galway's study, filled out the forged cheque for $1,200, the largest amount he dared to make it, and quietly presented it at the bank, where it was paid without demur. On returning to Creekside a panic seized him, and fearing to take the train lest he should be traced, he ordered the best riding horse in Mr. Galway's stable to be saddled, and galloped off.

CHAPTER XXXIII.

———

ANOTHER ASPECT.

IT is said that the announcement in Parliament of the first successful message over the Atlantic Cable interrupted a scientific member in the midst of an argument to prove its impossibility. Probably the other members lost interest in his objections. The fact disproved them and whatever force there was in his theory could be considered at leisure.

Something of the same experience had happened to Robert Strongwood. His objections to Christianity had never yet been categorically answered. But they ceased to be of importance to him. His horizon had been enlarged and facts' of experience had overcome his *a priori* objections to the existence of a personal God and to salvation through Jesus Christ. As to the doctrines which he had formerly delighted to dwell upon as grotesque and absurd, he had discovered that many of them had no place in genuine Christianity at all, and that the rest, on nearer view, were not what he had supposed. His views were still hazy enough: all he knew was that in some way he had come to God through Jesus Christ, and that his attitude towards Christ was instinctively one of worship.

Therefore constructively he believed in the divinity of Christ. But none of these things troubled him in the least at present. There would be time enough later on to work them out.

Most of the guests at Uplands dined elsewhere, their places being filled by a new set of Friends. Therefore, only the family noticed the change in Strongwood's manner. The rest took his interest in the meeting for granted.

" Doesn't thee think, Robert Strongwood," said one of the country Friends, " that Esther Longboat was greatly favoured in her ministry this morning ? "

" To tell you the truth," replied Strongwood, " I was more impressed by the first speaker."

" Well now, isn't that curious ? I thought he spoke very well. I think very highly of Samuel Nabor, but I was impressed by Esther's discourse ; I thought I never heard a more powerful sermon."

" You were helped by the one, and I by the other," said Strongwood pleasantly, " so it was well for both of us."

" Yes, something for every one," replied the visitor.

This conversation occurred just before they left the table, and Bessie, who overheard it, wondered if Strongwood could be speaking only from politeness.

It did not occur to her that she was judging him hardly ; she had been greatly disappointed in him that morning, and now she felt that he was not the man she had supposed him to be.

He noticed the change in her manner and felt it keenly, but he understood it, and knew that he must bear it till he could find a quiet opportunity for an explanation. In the meantime his new experience overshadowed everything else.

For the first time since he had been at Penelve, Strongwood decided that he would attend the evening meeting. He had become much attached to the Friends' manner of worship. The usual meetings were neither long nor dull, and there was nearly always some fresh thought in what was said, and always a degree of personal application and spiritual earnestness and power in the preaching that he had not seen in the fashionable city churches.

The meeting this evening was certainly not dull, for the chief speaker, Franklin Dashway, kept things lively. He was one of the best known ministers in the denomination in America, a man of great personal magnetism, full of the wit and readiness that takes with a crowd, a great leader in his own meeting, and if I may use the adjective, a tremendous revivalist.

As Strongwood walked home from meeting with Bruce, he remarked, in answer to a question :

" I cannot say that I liked it. This morning was quite different."

Bruce noticed the absence of the bantering tone, and said :

" I was afraid the meeting would grate on you."

" Well, Charlie, I may be wrong ; but it does seem to me that some dignity should be observed in preaching, and of all places I should have least expected to find it wanting in a Friends' meeting."

" Oh ! Franklin is a law to himself."—

" Do *you* like it ? "

" No ! but he is a man who has certainly done a great deal of good."

" That may be ; but he muddles me up."

" How ? "

" I don't understand what he means by saying that people are saved by the actual drops of physical blood which were shed on the cross. He seemed to imply that they were simply a payment of the legal penalty of our sins, and that we were accepted apart from any radical change in our character. I admit he made a great point of holiness afterwards. Now, this morning, I could understand and accept what the minister said."

His voice sounded so sincere, and he spoke so low, as if it was an effort to say it, that Bruce stopped, and laying his hand on Strongwood's arm, looked earnestly at him, although he could see nothing in the darkness.

" Can you, really ? " he said.

" Yes ; though only since this morning."

Bruce uttered an exclamation of deep thankfulness.

" If I had known that, I should have encouraged you to stay at home this evening ; for I was sure Franklin Dashway would preach."

" I do not think any harm has come of it ; only I am a little muddled. Charlie," he continued, more earnestly, " do you believe that forgiveness of sin is merely the remission of the penalty ? "

" No ! "

" Why do you allow it to be preached without protest then ? That doctrine had a great deal to do in setting me against religion, and I know that it has the same effect on others."

" There you open up a very difficult question. With the great liberty of expression allowed in our meetings they would soon degenerate into debating societies if it were our custom to answer one another publicly, therefore the discipline strongly advises against it."

" Yes, I see that difficulty."

"Let me give you an example," Bruce continued. "Some of the Friends approved as little of Samuel Nabor's sermon this morning, as you and I did of Franklin Dashway's this evening. You may not know that Franklin Dashway has done more to introduce radical changes among Friends than any other one man. For instance, he advocates water baptism, and is said to have been baptized himself. It has caused a great deal of discussion, and many thought that, as Franklin was present, the sermon this morning was in bad taste. Others thought it obscured the simple Gospel."

"I see," said Strongwood. "If they had openly objected this morning we should not have liked it, and if you had objected this evening they would have disapproved."

"Exactly. And I really believe some were helped this evening. But you must not think we let everything drift. Last evening our Elders told Franklin Dashway plainly that we are loyal members of our Yearly Meeting on the subject of baptism as well as on every other subject, and that they could only welcome him on the understanding that he had come, not to spread his special views, but to preach Christ."

"Did he accept the condition ?"

"Yes, he accepted it readily."

"I should think," said Strongwood, "that you would be having rather lively times among you with all such differences in doctrines and methods."

"Just now we are, but with it all there is a great deal of good feeling. If you should read our denominational papers you would find very little written in any discourteous or unchristian spirit."

"That is saying a good deal," said Strongwood. "Religious controversies are apt to be anything but gentle."

"I am sorry to say," returned Bruce, "that Friends have not always been free from bitter controversies in the past, and even in recent years there have been local disturbances; but our present discussion is being carried on in a very amicable spirit."

CHAPTER XXXIV.

THE QUARTERLY MEETING.

STRONGWOOD spent an almost sleepless night. The new sense of trust, and the new point of view he had obtained occupied his mind and he was trying to realize the right position to take in regard to all the questions that pressed upon him.

Not the least important of these was his business : the recent letters from his partner had been anything but reassuring. For some reason which Mr. Hanson could not understand, the credit of the firm seemed to have suffered, and though he urged Strongwood not to return to New York during the great heat, the latter knew from the tone of the last letter that he might be summoned at any time.

He went over all the misfortunes that seemed to threaten him. Then he thought of his mother and sisters. He had thus far told them nothing either of the lawsuit or of his business difficulties. If the worst came to the worst of course they would have to know, but until then no good object would be gained by telling them. He determined that his next letter should speak of his religious change.

" How they will scoff," he thought, "and say that all their predictions about my turning Quaker have come true. Perhaps Mary may understand a little, but if the lawsuit goes against me and the business fails, Mother and Lucy may disown me altogether."

Then Esther Longboat's words came back to him. All these things should turn to blessing.

He did not see how they could, but already he felt that somehow they must.

As for Bessie, she had been very busy all day with the meetings and with the visitors, not a few of whom came to her for advice and sympathy. She had no time to think of herself till she retired for the night, although through it all there had been an underlying sense of what had so troubled her in the morning.

She had no hard feelings towards Strongwood, but henceforth she must treat him kindly indeed, but with distant politeness. If he needed advice, Charlie was much better qualified to give it than she was. She said this over several times to herself, for she felt she needed strength to adhere to her resolution. It was a comfort that he would soon leave Penelve, for he was now only waiting till the intense heat in New York was over.

The meetings lasted all through Monday. They began with a "meeting for worship" in the morning, at which the speaking was on very practical lines, dealing with Christian life in the home, in politics, and in business.

Strongwood was several times reminded of things he had read in *Woolman's Journal*. He was interested also in seeing the Episcopal and Presbyterian ministers sitting on the raised seat facing the meeting. Both spoke briefly in cordial Christian fellowship with the rest. Towards the close of the meeting there were a number of short, simple testimonies to the power of Christ. These affected Strongwood greatly by their genuineness and directness. Had the meeting lasted a little longer, he too would have spoken, but he was withheld by the strangeness of it, and by a doubt as to whether it would be in order.

An invitation was given to the non-members present to stay to the business session if they cared to do so, and Strongwood was among the few who availed themselves of the permission.

The method of conducting business was new and strange to him. There was no President, only a " Clerk " to record the decisions ; which were arrived at, not by voting, but by a general consensus of opinion.

The first discussion of interest arose on the " Query " in regard to maintaining " a testimony to a free gospel ministry." Some of the visitors from the West advocated the plan of supporting a resident minister as pastor in a congregation. They claimed that this had worked well where it had been tried, that it was in no sense out of harmony with a "free Gospel ministry," and that it was in accordance with the Bible.

Others, especially Charles Bruce, maintained that the New Testament made no provision for support of resident ministers, though it did allow support for those who were moving about proclaiming (heralding) the Gospel when actually engaged on the service. He reminded them how Paul told the Ephesian Elders, many of whom preached, that they ought to work with their own hands, as he had done, and so support the weak. "A resident pastor," Bruce urged, " must soon become a professional minister, and the distinction between clergy and laity arise among Friends. He would say nothing against the devoted ministers of other denominations, but he was sure that the separation of the ministry from ordinary pursuits is a serious injury to the cause. It lessens the power of the minister to enter into other practical needs of daily life; it lessens the confidence of outsiders in the purity of his motives; it allows a lower standard of righteousness for the laity; and it interferes with the liberty of service in the congregation. "To every man his work," he concluded. "We cannot hire substitutes to do our work for us."

Strongwood had never seen his friend so worked up before.

Then Franklin Dashway arose and sarcastically described those who wished to maintain the old ways as wedded only to form. "This morning," he continued, "I passed by a harness store. In the window stood a wooden horse, fully harnessed. Now that's what Charles Bruce wants. If the harness is all right he doesn't care whether it's a wooden horse or a living one."

The sally called out an almost "audible smile," but Bruce replied, quietly:

"No. I want life; but without harness the horse would be of little value for work, and surely, Friends, we have seen enough of the growth of our meetings in numbers and spiritual life, to show us that what we need is not new methods but increased consecration." And he referred to the encouraging work done at McKendry's on the mountain, where meetings and Bible-school were being kept up by the people themselves, with the help of visits, not oftener than once a month, from Penelve.

In the midst of the discussion, the door-keeper touched Strongwood's arm and handed him a telegram. He looked at it, and immediately left the meeting.

CHAPTER XXXV

THE TELEGRAM AND ITS RESULTS.

STRONGWOOD went straight home to consult his code, for the telegram was in cipher. He found that his fears had come true. A crisis had arisen in the business, and he was needed at once.

On consulting the time tables, he saw that he could not reach New York before next morning, there was therefore no object in leaving Penelve till evening. He walked the streets restlessly for some time, and then remembering that Bruce had particularly wished him to be at the lunch at the Meeting-house, he returned thither. Bruce's object had been to introduce Strongwood to Samuel Nabor, the minister whose sermon had so impressed him the day before. This he was now able to do and he found them a quiet place where they could eat their lunch and talk at the same time. Strongwood found Samuel Nabor even more interesting on closer acquaintance, and the conversation they had was very helpful to him. Then other friends came up to speak to Samuel Nabor, and Strongwood was left to himself. He could see Bessie at the other end of the room pouring out tea and coffee. He could almost hear the friendly interchange of talk and see her bright smile as she spoke to one and another. He could not be quite sure whether it was brighter when Ezra Seward came near, as he did very often, carrying the cups to be refilled. Quiet as Seward was, and proper in his manner, Strongwood's eyes were open and he could not help noticing his unmistakeable attentions to Bessie, who, he thought, did not appear averse to them.

"It's very easy to see," he thought to himself, "what is coming. Perhaps it is just as well"—and he sighed.

There was an animated discussion on the Temperance question in the meeting that followed. It brought the whole matter before Strongwood in a new light. He had hitherto looked upon total abstainers as intemperately temperate, and noticing that the Bruces were of this class had purposely avoided the subject, though he had from incidental remarks learned to understand something of the grounds of their position. The discussion to-day was as to whether a proposal should be forwarded to the Yearly Meeting, asking that body to advise its members to vote for no political party which sanctioned the licensing of the liquor traffic. There was a warm debate, people on both sides speaking their best. The opposition was based solely on the ground that by adopting the proposal the meeting would practically ally itself with one of the national political parties, which, it was urged, it had no right to do. There were some who thought local option better than national prohibition, but all who spoke took it for granted that total abstinence was a Christian duty for the individual, and that all should work for the entire suppression of the liquor traffic. The sole difference lay in how to do it. The meeting finally adopted a minute to which they could all agree, but refrained from attempting to lay down any defined method as the only right way of working.

After his experience of yesterday, Strongwood was naturally in a receptive frame of mind, and although much that was said appeared to him wild talk and beside the mark, the combined result was to make him feel that he had been selfish and short-sighted in his own carelessness on the subject.

The business that immediately followed was unintelligible to him, and consequently uninteresting; his mind turned again to his own affairs, and he had almost forgotten where he was when he was aroused by the "Clerk" reading the "Advices." The passage,—

"*With a tender conscience, and in accordance with the precepts of the Gospel, take heed to the limitations of the Spirit of Truth, in the pursuit of the things of this life. Maintain strict integrity in your transactions in trade, and in all your outward concerns.*"

This, especially the earlier part of it, seemed to fit his case, and he felt that he must consider the various perplexing problems before him from a new point of view.

Just as the meeting closed the Clerk reminded the meeting of a public lecture on Peace to be delivered in the Town Hall that evening, and went on to encourage all to spread the notice of it.

"We wish," he added, "to show that war is not only expensive and unwise, but *evil*, and that peace founded on justice is practicable, as William Penn demonstrated under most trying circumstances. We wish to show that in any case the Christian position is to suffer wrong, not to do wrong, and that Christ has come to establish justice and peace between individuals, between classes of society, and between nations."

"I say, Charlie, how many reforms do you Friends propose to work for at once?" said Strongwood as they left the

Meeting-house. "Here's the freedom of the ministry, Temperance, Prohibition, and Peace all to the front, and I don't know how many more were hinted at as in the background."

"They are only different sides of one reform—the establishment of the Kingdom of God on the earth."

"It seems a pretty large contract for so small a handful of people."

"It is not our contract. We are only the Lord's journeymen. Besides, you know, there are thousands of others who work in one way or another for the same thing."

"But as a church organization you are unique."

"In some of our positions I fear Friends are unique. But many think we are backward on Prohibition."

"It seems to me you could not safely go any further. But, Charlie, I must be off to New York this evening."

"Why, what has happened?"

"My partner has telegraphed for me. I may say to you, confidentially, that things are not as they should be in regard to business."

"I am very sorry to hear it. What train did you think of taking?"

"The five-thirty. I've about an hour and a half."

"Come and get some tea first, and I'll help you put your things together."

All the family were on the porch to see Strongwood off, when the time came to go, even Bessie, for fear her absence might excite remark, was there, but he deeply felt the coldness of her manner. Her fingers touched his and were perfectly irresponsive as she went through the form of hand-shaking, and she did not say a word. The fact was that her

brother had simply told her that Strongwood had been
suddenly called to New York on business, and she supposed
some fresh and serious change had taken place in the trouble
with Miss Galway.

He had not realized before what a deep cloud of disapproval on her part had come between them, and it cut him
deeply, so that he hardly took in the very cordial remarks of
the rest, as they wished him a safe journey and a speedy
return.

"Only for a few days, thank you very much," he replied
as he got into the carriage. "I shall just come back to get
my things in order."

Bessie's treatment of him threw a gloom over the journey
and occupied his mind as much as the crisis in the business.
He did not blame her, and he felt sure that when he could
explain matters she would understand. He still felt that his
health would not justify him in addressing her and now business difficulties threatened to raise an additional barrier. But
he loved her, and to feel himself under her disapproval was a
great grief to him. Then his mind turned to the problem of
bringing his whole life into practical harmony with his new
found faith ; and although he himself was scarcely conscious
of it, he was even more afraid of failing in this than of failing
in business. This was shown by the resolute way in which
he decided against expedients which he had been accustomed
to consider allowable.

CHAPTER XXXVI.

"BREAKERS AHEAD!"

THE report that Hardynge had spread as to the financial unsoundness of the firm of Strongwood and Hansen had produced results much more quickly than he had expected. He had started it at a reception given by the New York head of the firm he was travelling for, and had taken pains to speak of it semi-confidentially afterwards to the different gentlemen who had manifested any interest when Strongwood's name was mentioned. One and all expressed incredulity, and several told Hardynge that they knew Strongwood better than he did. But they all felt it safe to make further inquiries, and as they largely consulted each other, and none of them cared to say just how their suspicions had been aroused, they succeeded in confirming their own doubts and spreading them to others.

In the meantime Hansen had gone on quite unconscious of danger, and had only begun to feel about ten days previous that something was wrong.

The reason for the hasty summons was that a bank which had always hitherto been very obliging to them had unexpectedly refused to renew a large note that was falling due that week. Mr. Hansen, who had not anticipated any difficulty, was only prepared with a small sum, and had been unable to raise any more, or to get any one to endorse the note.

239

"I find," said he "that there is a general impression that we are shaky. I cannot understand how it is. I thought we stood well."

"I'm sorry to hear it," replied Strongwood. " But do you really think that our affairs are as serious as all that."

" Yes, and yet, if we could only get people to believe it, we are perfectly solvent. The only difficulty is that we are short of ready money. I've tried everything I could think of," and he mentioned several firms to whom he had appealed for help.

Then ensued a series of questions on the part of Strong-wood, but to every question the reply was the same :

" I've tried them ; but it's no use."

" I only see one more hope for us," continued Hansen.

" What is it ? " said Strongwood, eagerly.

" Would not your mother's attorney be willing to advance you the money for a short time ? "

Strongwood's countenance fell.

" When Mr. McPherson set me up in business it was with the distinct understanding that I should not come on the estate to help me out if I got into difficulties."

" Was the agreement in writing ? "

" No."

" Then circumstances may alter cases. I'm sure your father-in-law would not wish you to make an assignment."

" That may be ; but a promise is a promise."

" Well then, would your mother be willing for her attorney to endorse our note if we made her a preferred creditor? It would be safe."

" I don't believe in making one's own family preferred creditors in order to get out of a tight place," replied Strongwood. "Our other creditors, in case we should fail, would have reason to think that we had not treated them fairly."

"I don't think you can understand how I feel about it," replied Hansen. "This business is all I have; but you, with your rich mother, even if you go to the wall now, have nothing to fear."

"After all my step-father did for me, it would not be fair to my sisters for her to give me much more. But I'll tell you what;—if she *should* start me again, you shall be my partner with equal shares. But now, whatever happens, let us meet the situation honestly."

His words recalled Hansen to his better self.

"You are right," he said. "I should not have suggested it."

"You did not know the circumstances, and it was quite natural for you to suggest that my mother should help us out."

Hansen was pleased at the turn this speech gave to the conversation, and they proceeded to go carefully through their books together.

After several hours thus spent, Strongwood said:

"Hansen, you are right. We are quite solvent. We ought to be able to pull through, if only these people won't be too long in paying."

A well-known public accountant of high standing was immediately engaged to audit their accounts, and to prepare a full statement of their assets and liabilities, and of the condition of their business at present as compared with the previous year.

Hansen had already written or telegraphed to most of the firms that owed them money, and the others were soon communicated with. Late on Thursday evening, after two days and a half of hard work, the accountant had everything in readiness, and signed his statement before a notary public the first thing on Friday morning.

There was no time to spare, for Friday was the last day of grace. As a final resort, Strongwood, armed with the certified statement, called on a capitalist, who had been a great friend of his step-father. This gentleman received him cordially, but his countenance fell when he learned the object of his visit.

" I should like to help you, Strongwood, but it is no use throwing good money after bad, and, unless this is merely a temporary difficulty, you'll save time and money by making an assignment. You know that it is quite the talk that you are going under."

For reply Strongwood produced the accountant's statement.

After a careful examination of it, the tone of the rich man changed. He asked many pertinent questions, and seemed to hesitate, but finally consented to go on the note.

With his endorsement the bank accepted the new note, and Strongwood returned in high glee to report his success to his partner, who had been nervously waiting the result of this last effort.

Hansen drew a long breath. " Saved by the skin of our teeth," he said, "there's the clock just striking."

" Yes," said Strongwood, " I am very thankful."

Hansen looked at him in surprise at the expression, and asked, as some one is said to have done when a well-known sceptical philosopher made a similar remark :

" Thankful to *what ?* "

" To the Lord," said Strongwood simply, and yet with an effort, for the bantering tone of the question recalled him suddenly to a sense of the old atmosphere in which he used to live.

Hansen gave a low whistle of astonishment, and turned to his desk, and they entered upon a thorough overhauling of their business, to see where they could economize, or work to greater advantage.

When the question of their travellers came up, Strongwood asked after one of them in particular, a bright young man of whom he had had great hopes.

" Poor fellow," said Hansen.   " I had to dismiss him last month for intemperance."

" This won't do, Hansen."

" Of course not.   I had warned him repeatedly."

" We must not let it happen again by our own fault."

" What do you mean ? "

" We must forbid their treating our customers."

" We can't do that ; you know yourself it's necessary for them to do it."

" But it's wrong."

" I do not think so.   Besides, all commercial travellers do it."

" That does not make it right, Hansen.   And I happen to know that all do not."

" Who told you that ? "

" I was at a meeting this week, and I heard a man whom I know to be trustworthy say that all the young men who travelled for him are teetotalers, and that they succeed admirably."

" I do not believe that ours could."

"And I do not believe that we should put temptation in the way of our young men."

"Whatever has come over you, Strongwood ; you are so changed ?"

"I hope that I am."

"What is it ?"

"I have come to see that money and success are not everything, and that we have no right to make money on what injures others."

"Have you turned a philanthropist, or a Christian ?"

"The two should be convertible terms. I trust that I am a Christian."

Hansen was silent a moment.

"Well," he said presently, "if you feel so very much about it, I'll consent to this, that we instruct our travellers to treat as little as possible."

"That won't do at all. It would make half our customers angry without relieving us of the responsibility. The gentleman whom I spoke about just now said that his drummers had observed that the men who acted on that plan always had a hard time, while those who consistently refused to treat, or to be treated, took a stand that every one understood."

A long discussion followed, but Hansen remained unconvinced, and Strongwood was obliged to leave the matter undecided for the time being.

CHAPTER XXXVII.

EFFORTS AND SCRUPLES.

EARLY impressions are lasting, and this is true not only in regard to childhood, but in regard to every great change that comes over a man's life; and in Strongwood's case two clear impressions had come almost simultaneously with his new experience. These were: the necessity of forgiving his enemies, and the importance of consistently carrying out his new principles in his business. The discussion on the Temperance Question and the words of the "Advices" about preserving a tender conscience in outward affairs had opened his eyes, and he was now continually coming across things in the business arrangements of his firm that he was not sure about.

The zeal that under other influences would have led him into public speaking, or to abandon business altogether for the ministry, prompted him to a devoted life in the world of every day affairs, and now he was examining everything with a keenness that almost suggested that he found a pleasure in the hunt after inconsistencies.

His partner at last lost patience.

"Look here, Strongwood," he said: "Do you believe the Bible?"

"I have reason to."

"Well, then, please remember that the entrance to Paradise is closed. If it weren't, you might open an establishment for wholesale drugs, if they were needed, on the bank of the River Pison, but Eden is lost."

Strongwood said, half under his breath :

"'Till one greater Man
Restore us."

"Well, however that may be," resumed Hansen, "Paradise has not been generally restored in New York yet ; and if we are to do business on these new methods of yours, we had better close our doors at once. For my part, I think it's hardly honest towards our creditors. Why, man, we must live.

"I know an old Quaker lady," Strongwood replied, "who meets objections like yours with a quotation from Cowper, and asks—Has God

' Built a brave world which cannot yet subsist,
Unless His right to rule it be dismissed ? '

I confess I answer that question in the negative."

"Strongwood, I don't care for old Quaker ladies, or for Cowper either. All I know about him is that he was half the time crazy. We must be practical. Come, you're a sensible man, sleep over the matter and you'll think differently."

"I know your game, Hansen ; you generally call me a sensible man when you think I'm foolish. However, I will sleep over it."

When he came to think quietly, Strongwood saw how clumsy he had been. He had made objections hastily, and had stuck to them after they had been fairly met. In this way he had greatly weakened his position by lessening Hansen's respect for his judgment. Yet there were some things he believed to be entirely wrong. These must be altered. Mr. Hansen was an honourable man, and yet this rather made Strongwood's position harder; for his own objections were not such as he himself two months ago would have considered valid. In all such matters as providing drugs honestly according to contract the firm was irreproachable. Every drug they sent out was what it claimed to be.

"Well, Hansen," said Strongwood, as he entered the office next morning, "I've thought over what we were talking about yesterday, and I must acknowledge that some of my objections were not well taken."

"That's just like you, old fellow; I knew you had a level head on you."

"At the same time," said Strongwood, "there are still some points I am not quite satisfied about."

"Well, think them over a little longer then."

"Yes, I shall. But there are one or two where I am certain that a change should be made at once."

"Out with them then"; and the pleased expression on Hansen's face died away.

"The first is that I don't think we should put in any more estimates to obtain Government contracts for supplying drugs to the army."

"Whew! Strongwood. This is quite new. If you keep on this way you'll be wearing a broad-brimmed Quaker hat within a week, and address us all as 'Friend.'"

"I am not joking, Hansen, I mean it. War is too great an evil for us to have anything to do with it."

"Speak for yourself. My father fought all through the Civil war, and I've heard you yourself say it was a righteous war."

"I know I did; but I did not then see that no end, however noble, can justify such wickedness."

"My father was as good a man as ever lived, and I consider what you say an insult to his memory."

"I meant no insult. You and I both consider that it is wrong to hold slaves. Yet George Washington owned slaves, and we honour him. We must separate a system from the people who belong to it. Now my position is this, that Christian ethics are the highest we know anything about, and that war opposes every principle of them."

"Of course, war is an evil. But it's necessary, and in any case aren't soldiers men?"

"Yes."

"Do you mean to tell me that if there were soldiers in New York ill with malarial fever and you were the only person in the city who had quinine you would refuse to sell it to them?"

"Of course I should supply it, and I suppose I should take money for it, though I'm not quite sure about that."

"Well, why won't you put in a bid then? The soldiers are men wherever they are."

"I am not inconsistent," replied Strongwood. "A surgeon might refuse to become an attendant at duels, and yet if called in on an emergency, he might treat a man who had been wounded in one. I don't want to put my conscience on you; but I feel the matter very strongly, because I consider that as things now stand we are practically a part of the military system."

"You were yourself the first to propose putting in the bids."

"I know I was," said Strongwood. "But I was wrong." He was beginning to realize how our past mistakes dog our footsteps, and make it more difficult for us to do right. But he would not give in on what was to him a matter of principle.

The contracts were profitable, and Hansen would not consent. At last Strongwood proposed dissolving partnership.

"I suppose," said Hansen, "you have a right to withdraw your name ; but it would be a great injury to me to have you do so just now. And I am sure that you will not ask me to let you withdraw your capital."

"Well," replied Strongwood, "I'll consider the question till Monday."

The next day, Sunday, Strongwood attended the Friends' meeting at Twentieth-street Meeting-house. He was pleased with the neat, handsome green stone front, and the well-proportioned room. But what a small congregation! He was quite disappointed, until he remembered the season of the year, and understood that every one who could would be out of town to escape the intense heat.

He came away spiritually helped and refreshed, but physically he was very tired and poorly. The week, including the Quarterly Meeting and all the business difficulties, had been a great strain on him, and he had twice been caught in heavy thunder showers, and thoroughly wet through. Notwithstanding all this he wished to stay in New York; for his old interest in his business had returned, and it was certainly now Mr. Hansen's turn to have a holiday.

That afternoon, Strongwood, tired as he was, made an effort and went to call on the young man whom his partner had discharged for drunkenness. The young man opened the door himself, and greeted him most warmly.

"Ah, Mr. Strongwood," said he, " if you had only been in the city, you would never have allowed me to be turned off."

This gave just the turn to the conversation that his visitor wished, and it was not long before they were having a very direct personal talk. The young man listened respectfully, and his young wife, with their child in her lap, every now and then put in a pitiful word of entreaty. Strongwood was thoroughly aroused, and spoke in a way that, when he came to remember it afterwards, greatly surprised himself. The young man was certainly touched ; but, say what Strongwood would, he could not be brought to acknowledge that he was in any danger. He said he knew that he had once or twice taken a little too much ; but he had quite determined to be more careful in the future, and was quite able to stop before he had gone too far. Even Strongwood's proposal to induce Mr. Hansen to engage him again if he would agree to abstain entirely was not sufficient to persuade him to give up what he called his liberty. He thanked his late employer for his interest, but assured him that he was quite mistaken in his forebodings.

Then Strongwood spoke to him of his own new faith and of the result of it. The young man was thoroughly interested, and was quite ready to enter upon a discussion of the case ; but not for any personal application to himself.

Finally his visitor left, very much discouraged. His first missionary effort seemed to have resulted in entire failure, and he could not understand why. He was bitterly disappointed, for he had hoped that he who had so often influenced his friends against Christianity might now bring its helpful light to this young man.

He sat in his room that evening by the open window and remembered that other night months before when he had sat there on the evening of the day when Dr. Sanders had given him his opinion of his condition. He had been discouraged and disappointed then. He was discouraged and disappointed now. And yet there was a great difference. Then the discouragement had been because the prop of outward hope had failed, and there was nothing within him for him to fall back upon. Now, deeper than all outward discouragement, was the inward peace, which, while not yet strong enough to enable him to rise above the difficulties about him, kept him from fearing he would sink beneath them, and gave him an undying hope.

Two letters were lying by Strongwood's plate at breakfast next morning. The first was from his mother, who wrote in glowing terms of the engagement of her daughter Lucy to Lord Southliegh. He seemed to be a paragon of all the virtues, not the least of which, in Mrs. McPherson's eyes, was his title. She also spoke with satisfaction of the attentions which " a wealthy young Englishman " was paying to Mary, and added : " He is eminently respectable, although not titled like dear Lord Southliegh ; but then, of course, you cannot expect to have everything." Strongwood could not regard the matter in the same light as his mother did ; but he had already written her his views as forcibly as he could, and he felt that he must now make the best of it.

The other letter was from Bruce, giving a lively account of the doings of the family, and remarking incidentally :

" Bessie leaves us the day after to-morrow for a visit to

Williamsport, to act as bridesmaid to a friend of hers. She has been rather run down, and we have encouraged her to accept an invitation to stay a week or so."

There followed an allusion to Ezra Seward, *apropos* of nothing, and as the letter mentioned Bessie three times, and each time Seward's name seemed to be suggested by hers, Strongwood naturally concluded that the two were connected in Bruce's mind, and drew his own inferences.

Bruce ended with hearty wishes for his return to Penelve. "You left in such a hurry, and you know you said you would at least come back to get your things."

As he went down town Strongwood thought for the twentieth time over the question as to what he should do in regard to the army contracts. This was now the chief weight on his mind; for there seemed to be a temporary lull in regard to the Flumetown trouble. Mr. Herrick, who had rejoined his family at Cresson the day after Strongwood left Penelve, had written that Mr. Jonathan Galway was about to put the whole matter into the hands of a lawyer, and that negotiations were at an end.

But what should he do in the matter of the contracts? He could neither consent to them nor honourably withdraw from the firm.

After a long discussion, it was finally agreed to put in no further bids, on the understanding that Hansen should have an increased interest in the business, so that the resulting loss should, as far as possible, fall entirely upon Strongwood.

CHAPTER XXXVIII.

AN OFFER.

ALTHOUGH Bessie Bruce had tried to persuade herself that she had never really cared for Strongwood, the thought of him kept so continually recurring to her that she had to remind herself more than once of conversations she had had on different occasions with two of her girl friends on the subject of falling in love. She had listened to their impassioned assertions of love for men whose characters were known to be undesirable, and had pointed out to them that what they felt was not, as they fancied, true, ennobling love, but mere passion ; and that while they could not help their feelings, they could resist them, and that it was from every point of view their duty to do so. She had told them that the hope of raising a man by marrying him was fallacious, because the very act of accepting him when he was morally unworthy proved that his character was a secondary consideration.

One of these girls had afterwards come to thank her for her advice, and the other had already had bitter reason to repent the neglect of it. But now Bessie felt she had never fully understood how hard a thing she had asked of them.

The coldness of her manner which had so wounded Strongwood was the result of her determination to give him no encouragement. The position was new to her ; and another twenty-four hours would have enabled her to be more natural.

But before the week was out her thoughts were suddenly turned into another channel by the following letter :

> "Maple Grove,
>> "Penelve,
>>> "9 mo. 1st., 189—.

"Elizabeth Bruce,

> "My Dear Friend :

>> "Thou wilt not, I feel assured, be surprised to receive this, nor to read what it conveys. My manner to thee must have already given thee some intimation of what has long been in my heart. I love thee, Elizabeth, but I should not have ventured to speak to thee, did I not feel satisfied to do so after earnestly seeking the best guidance.

>> "I know I am some years thy senior ; but surely this need not constitute a serious barrier, and thou knows me too well to doubt that it will be my constant happiness to contribute to thine, and to further so far as I can all thy plans so that we may be true fellow workers in life and service. I am in no haste for thy reply, but can wait as long as thou thinks it best to keep the subject under consideration. In the meantime,

>> "I remain with love, which I fear I am expressing very clumsily,

>>> "Thy friend,
>>>> "EZRA SEWARD."

This letter put Bessie into a whirl of excitement. She hardly knew whether to laugh or cry. Ezra Seward seemed so old and staid. She had looked up to him for advice and sympathy. He had sometimes indeed used expressions that had made her for a moment suspect that he might have something of this sort in his mind, and she had in consequence become more reserved and distant in her manner towards him. But she had never seriously entertained the idea. On the other hand, there was no man she so respected as she did him, and she knew that, quietly as his letter had been worded, it meant far more than extravagant expressions from the pen of many another.

Just then the dinner bell rang.

After dinner her brother called her, and they walked together to the summer house.

" Has thee heard from Ezra Seward, Bessie ? " he said.

" Why, Charlie, what makes thee ask ? "

" He told me he intended to write to thee. I hope thee does not mind my knowing ? "

" Oh no ! But what did thee tell him ? "

" I said that I had no idea what thee would say, but that feeling as he did, he had better speak to thee about it ; but he preferred to write."

" Well he has certainly written a very nice letter. Would thou like to see it ? "

" Yes, if I may."

He read it carefully.

" Well, Bessie ? "

" I feel greatly mortified."

" Mortified ! It seems to me that there is nothing to feel mortified over. I confess I feel sorry at the prospect, but only from selfish motives."

" But I do feel mortified. I ought to have understood what he was after. I do wish one could be friendly with a man, and be free to consult him on the work, without his taking every smile as an encouragement."

"Why, Bessie!"

"Yes, I do. It interferes very much indeed. I am on my guard with young men, and can make them keep their place. But Ezra Seward, I thought, was safe. He's old enough to be my father."

"Hardly, though I suppose he must be past forty-five. But is it really such a surprise to thee? It is not to me."

"I can't say that it never entered my head; but I never seriously entertained the idea. You men fancy that we girls are always thinking of getting married, and it's quite a mistake."

Bruce had his answer ready, but was afraid of injuring Seward's chances, for he really regarded him as a very suitable person for Bessie.

After a pause she continued:

"I do feel so sorry about it. I can never be really free with him again, and I shall miss the pleasant, helpful intercourse."

"So thee decides to refuse him, Bessie?"

Bessie noticed the tone of disappointment.

"Why, Charlie, does thee want me to accept him?"

"My dear Bessie," said he, kissing her, "so far as I am concerned, and all of us, it will be a sad day when thou leaves us. We should like to keep thee always. But on the other hand, while I would not, if I could, persuade thee, I cannot help seeing that Ezra Seward is a man in a thousand. He's true as steel, wise and kind. He admires thee as well as loves thee, and you are both interested in the same things, and know each other thoroughly. I think thee should not refuse him without very serious thought."

" But what if I don't love him ? "

"Of course, then thee has no choice, but do not act hastily. The offer has come unexpectedly, and thee has not yet had time for quiet, prayerful consideration."

" Well, Charlie, I think I know what my answer will be ; but I will take thy advice and think it well over first. I am going, thee knows, to Williamsport in a few days, and I shall not answer Ezra Seward till I have had time to be quiet after the wedding."

The matter, however, proved to be not so simple as she expected. She had great confidence in her brother's judgment, and his decided expression in favour of Seward had its influence. He was strongly seconded by her sister-in-law, and by Aunt Mary, who remarked that she herself could not have wished for a better husband than she had had, and yet he had been more than twenty years older than she.

Respect and affection are no poor foundation for love, and Bessie felt both towards Ezra Seward. She had never cared for marriage, nor ever, till she met Strongwood, felt personally attracted towards any man. Her brother's affection and the love in the home circle had satisfied her. Now she recognized the desire to be loved by and to love some one as her very own. She believed Strongwood had failed her, and now she had the offer of a man on whom she could lean and whom she could trust.

Throughout the excitements of the wedding, and the sober festivities which attended it, the question was constantly before her with the earnest desire for right guidance. But she made no attempt to reach a final conclusion till she had the leisure which she so much needed, and which she found in the quiet Quaker home where she was staying in the days that followed the wedding. The family retired at nine, and she had plenty of time for thought and prayer.

She re-wrote her letter several times, and finally sent the following :

" Williamsport,

" 9 mo. 8th, 189—.

" Ezra Seward,

" Dear Friend ;

" Thy letter has been very much in my thoughts since its arrival a week ago, and I have taken thee at thy word, and have waited to see clearly what was the right thing before answering.

" There is no one whom I value more highly as a friend than thyself, and thee can never know how helpful thy advice and sympathy have been to me. But the very fact of my feeling towards thee in this way only makes it more clearly my duty not to do thee the wrong of consenting to thy request without that special love for thee which is rightly implied in an engagement of marriage. Thy remark that thee was acting not without a sense of the best guidance has deeply impressed me ; for I have great faith in thy guidance, and it has had a good deal to do with my delay in coming to a decision. But I think it is very clear that thy guidance and mine are not the same thing, and that thee might rightly ask what I might rightly decline.

" I am afraid that I owe thee an apology for showing so plainly the genuine pleasure that I have felt when thee came to see me. I am truly sorry if it made thee think that I meant it for encouragement. I can only say that I did not intend to trifle with thee. Forgive me. It is, of course, too much to hope that we shall continue the same unreserved friendliness as before, but I hope we shall do so as far as possible.

"I am thy sincere friend,

"ELIZABETH BRUCE."

Bessie was dissatisfied with this letter; it was so stiff; but she knew that to write otherwise would be disrespectful to Ezra Seward. She felt also that he had some cause of complaint in the encouragement, unintentional though it had been, that she had given him.

He, on his part, was not discouraged by her answer. Its tone was so friendly, that he believed that all she needed was a little more persuasion, and this he determined to use at the first favourable opportunity.

CHAPTER XXXIX.

A NEW POINT OF VIEW.

HANSEN would not hear of taking a holiday and leaving Strongwood in charge. He said that his family had been spending the summer at a delightful place on Long Island Sound, and that he went in and out every day. Besides, if things continued to go smoothly, he could soon take a fortnight off, even if Strongwood were away.

"Look here," he said, "you're worn out ; you must get out of the city again, at least till the heated term is over."

There was no doubt that the crisis in the business was passed. The capitalist who had gone on their note had also taken pains to express in influential circles his entire confidence in the firm. Besides this, money was coming in well, and they would be able to meet their next liability in full.

Strongwood could leave with an easy mind, and Hansen finally prevailed upon him to go. In fact, he had more than one reason for urging it : he hoped that Strongwood's new scruples, which he regarded as a kind of temporary attack of morbid conscientiousness, would soon pass off, and in the meantime it would be much more convenient to have him out of the way. Hansen, in order to make Strongwood feel easy to go, even consented to instruct their travellers to discontinue treating their customers.

The fact that Strongwood knew that Bessie was not at home made him the more willing to return to Penelve.

His plan was to stay a few days quietly at Uplands, after which, should the weather become cooler, as it was likely to do, he could return to New York. If not, he could go on to some health resort before Bessie's return. He felt that it was distinctly wiser for him not to see her again. It would be time enough after he had finally left Penelve to write her a letter fully explaining the misunderstanding in regard to Miss Galway. This he felt was only right, and after that their intercourse should cease. She would remain to him a memory and an inspiration. What he would be to her he did not try to imagine.

She would probably soon be Mrs. Seward. For himself he should never marry. Bessie was the only woman he had ever loved. If his poor health prevented him from making an offer to her, he could not imagine himself ever wishing to marry any one else. He thought how much harder it would be if he and she had had to live in the same town, and he was glad that she had no acquaintances in New York ; glad also to have learned that the Friends in Penelve belonged to a different Yearly Meeting from the New York Friends ; so that he could be connected with the latter without risk of being thrown in Bessie's way. And yet he sighed to think how completely his future life would be cut off from her. It would have been such a satisfaction if he could once have told her how he loved her.

The evening before he left New York, Hansen said :

" You're going back to your Quaker friends at Penelve, aren't you ?"

" Yes," said Strongwood, " I am."

" You talk so like a Quaker yourself now-a-days, I suppose you'll be joining them next ?"

"Well, I do intend to, if they'll have me."

Hansen dropped his bantering tone and spoke seriously :

" Have you really thought it out, Strongwood ? They are such a very small denomination."

" Yes, but they have great thoughts, and high ideals."

" But they are so peculiar. I suppose they will turn you out if you are seen at a ball or theatre, or even if you wear a dress coat."

" Hardly," laughed Strongwood. " Friends do not deprive their members of individual liberty like that, and all of them do not think the same way upon these points. But a man may stop theatre-going and balls for other reasons than hard and fast rules."

" I thought you considered the theatre the great public educator."

" I know I did. But I have had time to think the matter over carefully this summer, and my conclusion from personal experience (and you know I only went to good plays) is that, at the very best, theatre-going is more than 90 per cent. mere recreation, and certainly not more than six or seven per cent. intellectually profitable ; while the small percentage of moral elevation one may receive is far more than counterbalanced by hurtful tendencies."

" But even so, recreation is good."

" True ; but the price may be too high."

" So you want the price of seats lowered," replied Hansen, a little scornfully.

" No, of course not. But you know as well as I that the assertion that there is no harm in theatre-going is wholly a mistake. Booth's attempt, and every other attempt to maintain a theatre with wholly unobjectionable plays has been an utter failure.

" Because good people don't support them."

" Suppose they did, it would simply make one theatre in a large city thoroughly satisfactory, and that one theatre would become an easy stepping stone for hundreds of persons to unsatisfactory ones."

" Why don't you stop all novel reading and everything else that is sometimes a help and sometimes an injury ? "

" Because we should have to go out of the world if we did. But the theatre is a place where amusement is provided at a fearful moral risk to those who give the pleasure. The evidence of city missionaries on this point is frightful."

" Now Strongwood, don't get prejudiced ; you know that there are as moral men and women on the stage as off it."

" Yes, I admit that. But that does not alter the fact that the profession is a dangerous one, and many succumb to its temptations. None have spoken more strongly about it than leading actors. Besides, ballet dancing cannot be refining to the character. I am not willing to get my recreation at such risk to others. I should not want my sister to be an actress."

" Well, I don't see that it's my responsibility," said Hansen. " If I looked at everything from that standpoint, life would be unbearable."

" On the contrary, while it makes life serious, it makes it far more interesting and purposeful," replied Strongwood.

" Won't you ever dance again ? "

" I don't want to."

" Don't want to ! "

"To tell the truth, I never cared for it as much as I did for the theatre. But it is like this. I am fond of strawberries. But for the past three years they have always made me ill. Now I may sometimes wish to eat them when I think of their taste; but the moment I think of their effects my appetite goes."

"Then you admit you lose something in giving up these things," said Hansen, triumphantly.

"In regard to the strawberries, yes; but in regard to these amusements, I have found something better. I have not spoken of my deepest reasons—the joy of the spiritual life— the desire for more of it. Theatre-going and balls weaken a man in these things, and keep him from what he most desires —at least I believe they do in my case."

"Well, good-bye, old fellow. I wish you a pleasant journey. I confess I cannot follow your reasons."

"Good-bye. Let me know if I'm wanted."

"All right."

So they parted, Strongwood troubled at not having made a better defence, and thinking of many things far more convincing that he might have said.

CHAPTER XL.

A SUMMONS.

THE train was late, and it was quite dark when Bruce met Strongwood at Penelve station the next evening. He was so tired that he felt he could hardly get to the carriage.

"Welcome back, Robert Strongwood," said Mrs. Bruce cheerily, as he came into the hall.   " I hope thy journey has prospered."

" Yes, Mrs. Bruce, thank you, the business has weathered the storm."

" And he himself has been wrecked," whispered Aunt Mary to Mrs. Leslie.   But she added aloud :

" I am thankful to hear it.   But thou must be very tired. Here's supper ready ; wilt thou have it at once ? "

" Thank you, I think I will."

" Robert Strongwood, here's a telegram that has come for thee this evening."

" Now, Lydia," said Aunt Mary, who had done her best by signs to prevent Mrs Leslie from giving it, " couldn't thee have waited till he had had his supper ? Don't thee see how tired he is ? "

" I always think that telegrams should be delivered at once," said Mrs. Leslie.

"It is much better that I should have it," said Strong-wood.

"Do eat first," said Aunt Mary. "Nothing can be done to-night. The telegraph office is closed now, and this mutton-chop is getting cold."

The old lady was so solicitous that Strongwood acquiesced, and laid his telegram aside. But he was too tired to do justice to what was set before him. He forced himself to eat more than he wanted, and then opened the telegram and read it.

"Is anything the matter? Has anything happened?" they asked as he leant his head on his hand with a look that alarmed them?

He silently handed the telegram to Bruce. It was dated "Lucerne" and read:

"*I need you immediately, come, cannot explain.—McPherson.*"

Every one was silent.

"What can be done?" said Aunt Mary at length.

"I must go at once."

"Well," said Bruce, "I'm sorry for your mother, but I cannot help thinking it is a good thing that it came too late for you to catch the steamer to-morrow, and the next does not sail till Saturday, so that you will have a few days rest."

"I think thou art quite unfit for such a journey," said Aunt Mary.

"I *must* go, thank you, said Strongwood; and I shall telegraph to-morrow that I come by the first steamer."

In the morning, although he was more poorly, he telegraphed, and took the necessary steps for securing his passage in the Saturday's steamer.

The hours passed heavily. He lay down most of the time, but did not seem to improve.

They persuaded him not to leave Penelve till Friday morning, which would still leave him time to have a conference with Mr. Hansen on Saturday before the steamer started.

In the meantime he tried to imagine what could be the matter. The most likely thing seemed to be a fatal or at least a serious accident to one of his sisters. It was evidently something urgent, and evidently also something his mother did not care to mention. On the whole, knowing his mother as he did, this last was encouraging. Still at the best the telegram was alarming. Then it was very awkward to go away just when the law suit was coming on. Unless his mother had a good reason that could be adduced to show why she had sent for him, his absence would make a bad impression. The whole thing was exceedingly trying. He thought of Esther Longboat's words, which he had understood to predict three more troubles for him. He certainly had had one. Was this the second?

At any rate, she had spoken with even greater emphasis of coming blessing as the fruit of sorrow rightly borne. The assurance strengthened and quieted him.

The next afternoon, as he was walking through the hall to the porch, he saw Bruce and Aunt Mary in the library, the latter was holding a letter open in her hand. Just as he passed the door he heard her saying:

"Poor Ezra, so Bessie has refused ——"

He hastened forward, his heart beating very quickly.

He did not really wish Bessie to remain unmarried; that is, he would, even if he could, have done nothing to prevent her marriage. But somehow Bessie unmarried, although he had renounced the thought of her for himself, was very different from Bessie married. What could be the reason for her refusing Seward ? Could it be—— No he would not put the thought in words even to himself. It would be pleasant to think that it was so, and yet under the circumstances he was man enough to hope sincerely that no thought of himself had influenced her to refuse the good Quaker Elder.

CHAPTER XLI.

THE SHADOW OF DEATH.

THE day came when Robert Strongwood was to leave Penelve. He had had a wretched night, kept awake by pain in his ankle, which by morning was so swollen and tender that he could hardly bear it on the ground. He came down to breakfast limping and looking very miserable.

Everything was ready. Aunt Mary, who had all along maintained that he was unfit to travel, now seemed to have changed her mind. As she wished him " Good morning," she added :

" All ready to start ? "

" Yes."

" It is a fine day for travelling," she continued.

" Yes, and I am glad of it."

" Perhaps thou art not feeling very well this morning ? "

" Not very, I have a little rheumatism or something like it in my ankle ; but it isn't much."

" Yes, and the sea air is good for rheumatism," said Aunt Mary.

The rest of the family hardly knew how to understand her ; but Strongwood took it all in earnest, and went on to enlarge on the good a sea voyage would do him.

Aunt Mary continued to humour him, until he rose from the table. The movement gave him such a sudden twinge that he sank down again on his chair with a groan.

"It's nothing," he said, in answer to questions. "It will soon go off."

But he allowed Aunt Mary to feel his pulse.

"Why, man alive," she said, "with such a pulse there is no use talking : thou *can't* go."

"I must," said Strongwood, though he groaned with pain from a fresh movement.

"Well, in any case there is a later train, and there is no reason why thee should not have a doctor prescribe for thee. Here just let Charles help thee to the sofa."

The request was so reasonable, and the pain so severe, that Strongwood consented.

"All right. Thank you, Charlie. If I must see a doctor, let it be Dr. Storey. · But I must take that later train."

"Well, thou can be quiet till the doctor comes, anyway."

The doctor came, and pronounced the case to be rheumatic fever, ordered the patient to bed, and stayed to help Bruce get him there. Strongwood submitted without a word.

The necessary telegrams were sent off, and he wrote a short affectionate letter to his mother, expressing regret and sympathy, and explaining his not coming. At the conclusion he added a few lines telling her of the new source of comfort that he had found, and closed with loving messages to Lucy and Mary.

When this letter had been dispatched he agreed to Aunt Mary's suggestion that he should allow her after this to keep his mother posted as to his condition.

Then the family settled down to a siege of nursing, for the attack was a severe one, and Strongwood was worn out to begin with by his heavy ten days in New York. The remedies that often seem to cut short the disease proved ineffective, possibly because, on account of the weak action of the heart, the doctor was afraid to give them in sufficiently large doses.

By general consent, Aunt Mary assumed the control of all matters connected with the sick room. Trained nurses were not to be had ; but a strong woman who had considerable experience was engaged to do the heavy work. The sitting up at night was willingly undertaken by a number of the younger men of the meeting, two of whom came every evening at nine o'clock, and remained till after breakfast. During the night they would take turns at watching. As no one was called upon more than once, or, at the most, twice a week, it was not a great burden, and it was a great relief to the day nurses to be ensured good nights.

Every evening Aunt Mary would hand the young men a careful list of the hours when food and medicine were to be given, repeating her directions that a pencil line should be drawn through the memorandum of each as it was attended to. Every morning she carefully inspected the night's record.

But while she was so thoughtful of the patient, she did not forget the watchers, and provided such refreshments of pears and grapes, lemonade and iced tea, not to speak of more solid sustenance, as to make the task of sitting up very popular among the young men.

The case was not progressing favourably, and Strongwood himself was quite aware of the fact.

"You do not think me so well, doctor ?" he said one morning.

" I hope you will take a turn for the better in a few days," replied the doctor.

" Am I dangerously ill ? "

" You are undoubtedly ill, and require great care, but I quite look forward to your recovery."

" I wish to make my will."

" Surely you have not put off doing that till now ! "

" No, but my present one is unsatisfactory."

" Is it really important ? "

" Yes, doctor.   It is."

" Will it take long ? "

" No, it will be very simple and short."

The doctor hesitated, but, seeing the eager look in the sick man's face, feared a refusal might injure him, and consented, with strict injunctions that the will must be short.

The lawyer was promptly summoned and Strongwood gave him the necessary directions.   His share of the business and most of his personal effects were to be left to his mother and sisters.   The small property which he inherited from his father, amounting to about $10,000, and certain keepsakes he left to Charles Bruce, to be used as he should elsewhere direct.

The will was signed, sealed and witnessed, and the lawyer departed.

Strongwood was exhausted by the effort and readily acquiesced in Aunt Mary's injunction to be quiet.   But about an hour later he felt able to make the further exertion of writing out his directions to Bruce.   He had special reasons for wishing not even his friend to know what they were till after his death.

" Mrs. Wayler," he said to the nurse, "please hand me the writing tablet with paper and envelopes."

" Now, Mr. Strongwood, you're too tired."

" I must have them."

" What will Mrs. Compton say?"

" I can't help what she would say. I must have them. It's absolutely necessary. I shan't write much. Quick or it may be too late."

The effort was far greater than he had expected, and only his strong desire to carry out what was in his heart enabled him to overcome the pain caused by the movement of writing. He made the instructions as brief as he possibly could, for, since he had made the will, a desire which had been vaguely in his mind before took shape and had now become an uncontrollable longing, to write a few personal words to Bessie herself. The note to Bruce must be written first, and he greatly feared that his strength might not hold out for both.

" Dear Charlie,

"I have just made my will. In it I have left $10,000 to you, to be used as directed. I did this because I did not feel it would be quite fair to couple your sister's name with mine so publicly without her consent. I should like her to have $7,000, keep $2,500 for yourself, and put by $500 to educate or establish in trade the son of the McKendrys who were so kind to me last summer. Send my Bible to Mr. Samuel Nabor and distribute the little keepsakes among your family here, including the children. God bless you and all for your goodness to me.

" Farewell,

" ROBERT STRONGWOOD."

He folded it with difficulty and put it into an envelope which he directed

" To Charles Bruce, Esq.,

To be opened only after my death."

This done, he leaned back and closed his eyes. The nurse came to him with some nourishment.

"May I take the tablet away now, sir?" she asked.

"Thank you, I have not quite finished."

"You had best do it some other time."

"No, I must do it at once."

She was not a trained nurse, and his tone awed her, and she let him have his way. He immediately began to write, but with ever increasing difficulty, his lips firmly compressed lest any sigh or groan might escape him, and make the nurse call Aunt Mary, who certainly would remove paper and pencil at once. His heart beat wildly, not chiefly because of the pain and effort, great as these were, but because he was personally addressing Bessie for the first and probably for the last time.

Altogether the strain was too much for him, and before he had finished what he wished to write his head dropped and he became unconscious.

CHAPTER XLII.

A FINAL PLEA.

THE day before the events spoken of in the last chapter Ezra Seward unintentionally gave his confidential clerk more than a "bad quarter of an hour," by announcing his intention of attending himself to some business of trifling importance in the neighbourhood of Williamsport. The poor fellow could think of no reason why the business had not as usual been entrusted to him except that Mr. Seward was losing confidence in him.

Seward, quite unconscious of the heart burnings he was causing, went off in high spirits, greatly pleased to have so good an opportunity of seeing Bessie. He would attend to his business first, and then walk out to the house where she was staying. He knew the old Friend and his wife well, and was sure of a warm welcome, and was sure also that they would excuse themselves after dinner for their afternoon nap, and that he would have a quiet time with Bessie.

Everything worked like a charm. They received him most warmly, and at the time he expected, retired for their naps. Seward explained that he should soon have to leave for his train, and so bade them farewell.

As soon as he and Bessie were left alone, a rather awkward silence ensued. Neither quite knew what to say. Ezra naturally was the first to speak.

"Elizabeth, I have received thy letter."

" Yes."

" I hope thou wilt be willing to reconsider the matter."

" I don't think it would be any use."

" But, Elizabeth, I am in no hurry whatever for an answer. All I ask is that thou wilt take it into consideration a little longer. Thy letter was so kind, and thou acknowledged to so much in regard to thy feelings for me, that I could not but hope that on further thought thou might take the one little step further that is needed."

" I am so sorry," returned Bessie, with rising colour in her cheeks, " to have made another mistake. My letter was meant to be final ; but I could not write as if I did not care for thee, or did not feel the value of what thee was offering me ; so I wrote just as I felt."

" That is exactly what has given me hope, Elizabeth. I know that thou meant thy answer to be final, but, excuse me for saying so, I believe that both thy manner and thy letter show thy real feelings, although thou thyself has not yet realized them ; and if thou wilt only be willing to hold thy decision in abeyance a little longer, I believe thou wilt see that I am right."

He spoke earnestly, and his request seemed so reasonable that Bessie wavered, and Seward, seeing this, continued to press his point—

" I promise thee," he continued, " not to tease thee, and I will leave it to thee to give some indication when I may again address thee."

Bessie waited a few moments before replying. Then she said slowly :

" I have such great respect for thy judgment, that it would be far easier for me to say ' Yes ' to thy proposition than ' No,' especially as it does not seem to bind me to any-thing."

"And it does not, I assure thee," interrupted Seward.

"No," resumed Bessie, " I see that in a sense it does not. But it does imply that my mind is not clearly made up. Out of regard for thee, and because Charlie wished it, I took a week before giving thee my answer. Since I wrote, my mind has been perfectly at rest on the matter. I have known thee and honoured thee for years. There is nothing to be gained by waiting; it would only raise false hopes on thy part."

"I am willing to take that risk," returned Ezra Seward eagerly.

"No, Ezra Seward, it would neither be kind nor truthful. I cannot do it."

"Still I shall continue to hope, Elizabeth."

"I hope thee will not. But why——" she hesitated.

"What wast thou about to say?"

"I think I had better not say it; it might seem impertinent."

"I wish to hear it. Nothing would be impertinent that thou, Elizabeth, could say to me."

"Well," she answered, hesitatingly, "if thee will excuse me for saying so, I have often wondered why thee does not seem to have thought of Grace Wildmere. She is a lovely character, and far more suited to thee than I am."

She was about to add, "and she is nearer thy age," but she saw she was going too far.

"I thank thee, Elizabeth, but that is a matter in which I must choose for myself. Thou art my choice."

"But that is out of the question. I am really sorry."

She made a movement which Ezra understood, and he rose to go.

"Thy refusal is a deep sorrow to me," he said. "I see that I must accept thy answer as final, for the present. But thou canst not prevent me from still hoping thou mayst alter thy decision. I hope, at any rate, that this incident may make no difference in our relations to one another in the future."

"Thank thee," said Bessie. "But apart from what is necessary in meeting work, I think thee will thyself see that, at least as long as thee continues in thy present attitude, it is best for us to see as little of each other as possible. Farewell."

She held out her hand, which he grasped, held a moment, and then departed without a word.

CHAPTER XLIII.

A DYING MESSAGE.

LATER in the day, Bessie received letters speaking of Strongwood's increased illness. Her place was clearly at home; for Aunt Mary was taken up with the nursing, Lydia Leslie was too feeble to render any effectual help, and Mrs. Bruce was not strong enough to have the responsibility of the housekeeping, under the present circumstances, as well as the care of her children and of her mother.

The Friends with whom Bessie was staying were greatly disappointed; but quite understood, and encouraged her to go.

When Bessie reached Uplands the next morning, the house seemed preternaturally quiet. No one was about. The front door was open, and she went up to her room unobserved. After all, this was not so remarkable; for the children were at school, and the others busy with their usual duties. But in view of the fact that there was illness in the house, the stillness oppressed her.

As soon as she had laid aside her things, she started to find some one, but was stopped as she was passing Strongwood's door by the nurse suddenly opening it, and crying out:

"Oh, Miss Bessie, is that you? Do come quick. He's fainted, and I'm afraid he's ——"

Bessie, without waiting for her to finish her sentence, hastily went in.

There lay Strongwood, his head fallen to one side, unconscious and apparently lifeless. Bessie was shocked at the drawn and haggard face, so different from what it had been when she had seen it last, only three weeks before. The pencil he had been writing with still lay in his hand, and her quick eye, in far less time than it takes to tell it, detected that the unfinished note on the tablet began with: " My dear Miss Bruce."

Quick as thought she transferred the note to her own pocket, and began to use means for his restoration. Aunt Mary came at once, and at her suggestion Bessie went to telephone for the doctor.

Long before he came Strongwood had recovered consciousness ; but he was still very weak and exhausted. The doctor looked grave, and ordered absolute quiet. He evidently feared complications, and gave orders that no one but the attendants should see him, and that nothing in the least degree exciting should be mentioned.

It was some time before Bessie could find a quiet moment. But as soon as she could she locked herself in her room, and sat down with a palpitating heart to read the letter. It never occurred to her not to do so. She was only sorry that her absence had prevented Strongwood from telling her verbally what was on his mind, and so had caused him to make the effort which had resulted so unfavourably.

" How glad I am," she thought, " that no one else saw the letter. I suppose it is to explain about that Flumetown matter."

Here she took the letter from her pocket. After the first sentence the writing was scarcely legible, and her tears made it still more indistinct. But she slowly made it out as follows :—

" My dear Miss Bruce,

" While my little strength remains I feel I must tell you what but for my ill health I should have told you long since.

" 'I love thee, and I love thee, and I love thee.' It satisfies me to think that you will read this, and, as I shall be gone before you see it, I do not think it can hurt you. God bless you, my dear one, and may a worthier man than I be sent to love you.

" I die in the faith of Jesus, and I wish you to know that in the last three weeks I have for His sake fully forgiven all who have injured me. I am so glad.

" As to the scandal about ——"

Here the writing ended in an unmeaning wavy line to the bottom of the paper.

Bessie let the letter fall into her lap, and buried her face in her hands. She had never suspected that he loved her. Never by word or look had he let her guess his secret. She longed to go to him, but dared not. How he must have felt her coldness all the while his very love for her was sealing his lips. She saw everything now in its true light. No further explanation was needed to vindicate him. None but a true man could have written that letter.

She sat almost without moving till she was aroused by the summons to dinner.

CHAPTER XLIV.

CONFESSIONS.

A T dinner time every one felt troubled, for Aunt Mary's report of her patient's condition was unfavourable. His temperature was rising, and his mind wandering. She had sent again for the doctor. All the family were warmly attached to their guest, and in the general anxiety no one noticed Bessie's white face.

About three o'clock, as she was at work in the library, she saw a messenger boy coming up the walk, and opened the door for him. He gave her a note addressed to Strongwood and marked "*Immediate*."

What was to be done? Strongwood was in no condition to receive or to understand any message. Charlie was at the office.

"If any one has a right to read this," she said to herself as she went back into the library, "it is I," and she opened the envelope.

It proved to be from Ralph Hardynge, and had evidently been written in a great hurry, or under great emotion. It was dated from a hotel in Penelve, and urged Strongwood to come to him without delay on pressing personal business.

Bessie answered it, explaining the state of the case, and advising Hardynge to send for her brother. In about twenty minutes another note came from Amy Wildmere.

"Dear Bessie, I am so sorry Ralph sent the note. I had not told him about Mr. Strongwood's illness, and he wrote while I was out. Thy brother will not do at all, but *thee* will. Do come for *my* sake *at once*.

"Lovingly, AMY."

Utterly mystified, Bessie felt she had no choice but to go.

As she was starting, she met the doctor who was also going out.

"How is he, doctor?"

"His temperature, for the time being, at least, is lowered," replied the doctor, cautiously.

"Is there any hope of his recovery?"

"I do not give up hope; but I have advised them to telegraph immediately to his mother. There has been a decided change for the worse since morning, and I have asked for a consultation.

Bessie went to the hotel with a very heavy heart, and so absorbed was she in her own thoughts that she had almost forgotten to wonder what the purpose of her visit might be, when she was recalled by arriving at her destination and being met at the head of the stairs by Amy, who threw her arms about Bessie's neck, and burst into tears.

"Oh, Bessie," she sobbed, "I'm so glad thee has come."

"Why, what *is* the matter?"

"Ralph got here early this morning very poorly, and the doctor tells him that his only chance is a dangerous operation, which is to be performed this evening as soon as the surgeon can come from Harrisburg."

"Why don't he call in Dr.——?" said Bessie, naming a local surgeon of repute, for her Penelve pride was touched.

"He's off on his vacation. Oh, Bessie, I'm so afraid Ralph won't get through it, and he's so unhappy. It seems that he can't have any faith. He wants to see thee, and I do hope thee will be able to help him; I can't do anything. I do wish," she continued, rather inconsequently, "that he had come to our house, but thee knows our engagement is not announced yet."

Bessie tried to say something comforting to her, but Amy hurried her on.

"Don't be very long, Bessie," she added, piteously, "the time is so short."

Bessie found Hardynge evidently in great pain, and with a scared look in his face that roused all her sympathy.

"I am sorry to see you so ill, Mr. Hardynge," she said. "Can I do anything for you?"

"Could you take a message to Mr. Strongwood?"

"Certainly."

"Oh, Bessie, do talk to him about believing," said Amy, in distress, "and please don't be long," and she, supposing this would be the main subject of conversation, left the room, for she had the feeling so common among Friends that such conferences should be private.

As soon as they were alone, Hardynge said:

"It is very kind of you to come."

"I am very pleased to do so. What message shall I take to Rob—— Mr. Strongwood?"

Hardynge covered his face with his hands.

"How can I tell you?" he said.

Bessie waited.

"Miss Bruce," said Hardynge with a great effort, "my time is short. I cannot face that operation with this on my conscience. I would have told Amy, when I found Mr. Strong-wood was so ill ; but every time I began she would stop me, saying that we are all sinners and I must ask to be forgiven. But this don't answer. Will you be patient with me ? "

He looked at her so pathetically, that Bessie felt something really serious was coming.

" Yes," she said quietly.

" Well, it's awfully hard to begin, and it's a long story. Six years ago I was in a first-rate berth in New York, a favourite with my employer, and I had great hopes of winning his daughter for my wife. But I had left my native village under a cloud. No one in the city knew of it except Mr. Strong-wood, who had been there at the time, and had given me advice on the subject, which I had not taken. But he moved in an entirely different set from the one my employer belonged to, and I thought I was safe."

Here Hardynge stopped on account of the pain.

Bessie waited.

" One evening," continued he, " I saw Mr. Strongwood introduced to my employer at a reception. My heart sank, and I made up my mind to speak to my girl at once. I did so the next day. She taxed me with the old story, and claimed that she had a right to know. I knew I should become amenable to the law if I confessed, and so I began to deny it. But she confronted me with such evidence that I was silenced and began to fear that I was about to be arrested. She intimated that even if the story were true, she might still have me, if I would confess and make what amends I could ; but she said that otherwise our intercourse must be at an end. That afternoon her father went over the same ground with me, and on my continued refusal, told me that he had no alternative but to dismiss me.

I left the city and only succeeded after great trouble in getting a foothold in Philadelphia."

He stopped a minute, struggling with the pain, and then began again:

"You may understand how I hated Mr. Strongwood, as the cause of all my misfortunes. No, don't interrupt me"— for he saw that Bessie was about to speak—"Let me go on— I was determined to be equal with him ; but for several years my business kept us apart. When I came across him here last summer I began to look out for an opportunity, and I soon found one in the story of his rescue of Miss Galway from the blizzard."

Bessie's breath came quickly.

Hardynge continued : "A chum of mine in New York and I arranged the whole matter."

"But," interrupted Bessie, "how was it possible for you to interfere without consulting Miss Galway ?"

"Miss Galway knew nothing of our proceedings, nor of her supposed engagement to Mr. Strongwood."

"Nothing ! How about her brother and the heavy damages demanded ?"

"Her brother, as you call him, is my chum, the damages were what we hoped to get out of Mr. Strongwood for ourselves as 'hush' money. There now, I've told you the worst. I suppose you'll hate me."

Bessie waited a little while without speaking.

"How could you," she said at length, "be so cruel both to Miss Galway and to him when he was so out of health ?"

"I did not care about Miss Galway, and as to Mr. Strongwood, I said, 'He robbed me of my girl and I'll rob him of his, and get a neat little sum for myself at the same time.'"

"You seem to have succeeded," said Bessie, trying to speak calmly, "in your first object."

"How?"

"He is almost at the point of death." She felt herself giving way, but controlled herself to add, "I suppose now that you are prepared to stop your persecution of him?"

"Stop it," replied Hardynge. "It is stopped. Don't you know that?"

"No, nor does Mr. Strongwood."

"Why, it's nearly three weeks since Mr. Galway found out the plot, and my chum has fled to Canada."

Bessie grasped the arms of her chair.

"May I ask if you are sure that Mr. Strongwood informed on you?"

"I have lately found out that he did not. The information came through a letter from the injured party in my village."

"Have you anything more to say?"

She spoke so quietly that Hardynge, largely engrossed as he was in his bodily pain and personal fears, did not suspect the tumult that was raging within her.

"Not much; but as I wish to make a clean breast of it, perhaps I ought to add that I did try to spread a report that his firm was financially shaky.

"Was the report true?"

"Not that I am aware of. I manufactured it to worry him. But I am glad to think that that did not do any harm."

Bessie gasped. "No harm. Why it——"

Then, checking the torrent of words that rushed to her tongue, she hastily rose, and walked to the window, her whole frame shaking with suppressed emotion.

It had been a beautiful day ; but now dark clouds were gathering in the north-west, and just hiding the sun, and there were mutterings of thunder. In her heart also a storm was gathering. The whole history of the past few months passed before her in rapidly changing, but clearly defined pictures. Strongwood's first coming, their conversations, his patience, the picnic, his finding of Bertie, his illness. And then this horrible blackmailing, her mistaken judgment of him, and consequent coldness, and, as she now felt, cruelty ; then his business troubles, resulting in his present probably fatal illness. All these pictures and more presented themselves to her mind with incredible rapidity, and each fresh one excited her more and more.

She was so outraged that she did not recognize that she was angry. Her cheeks burned, and scalding tears came to her eyes. She was too self-controlled to heap reproaches upon Hardynge, but her heart was bursting with indignation.

"If it had only been against me," she thought, "I could have borne it."

She thought of Strongwood unconscious, perhaps dying. Then she remembered how his last effort had been to write words of love to her—no, not the very last—that was to speak of his joy at having been able to forgive all his enemies for Jesus' sake. The thought brought a sudden revulsion of feeling, and her anger gave place to humiliation.

Here was she, who a few weeks ago had felt herself qualified to teach him the truths of Christianity, falling far below him in the primary duty of forgiveness.

"If he can forgive, why cannot I?" she asked herself, and then there came before her a vision of One on the cross, praying. "Father forgive them," and she bowed her head in her hands, almost saying aloud :

"Oh Lord forgive me, and enable me to forgive."

A groan from Hardynge recalled her to her immediate surroundings. He had not misinterpreted the tone of her last remark, or her action in standing silently by the window. He regretted that he had been so explicit, but he had had no idea that Strongwood's present illness was in any way traceable to what he had done. He had supposed that both his schemes had failed so completely that his confession would be simply to relieve his own mind.

As Bessie turned and sat down beside him, he saw tears in her eyes.

"Mr. Hardynge," she said, "I will tell you frankly that while I was listening to you, and as I stood by the window, I was very angry with you, for what you did has done more harm than you think. But I will say no more of that. I have a message for you from Mr. Strongwood."

"What, for me? I thought you said that he was unconscious."

"He is, but the last thing he did was to write a note, and the last sentence in that note was about you. May I read it?"

"Please do," said Hardynge eagerly.

And so she read, with a trembling voice : "I die in the faith of the Lord Jesus, and I wish you to know that in the last three weeks I have for His sake fully forgiven all who injured me. I am so glad."

Both were silent for a moment or two. Then Bessie said in a low voice :

"He had only just begun the next sentence when he fainted. See," she continued, folding down the page so that only the words she had read remained visible, "how weak he was and what an effort it must have been to write it. But you see also that he did not wait to forgive till he thought he was dying. Three weeks ago he seemed to be on the road to recovery."

Hardynge, quite overcome by this unexpected message, and at the sight of the trembling hand-writing, covered his face with his hand, and almost sobbed out :

"I don't deserve it, I don't deserve it ; but I never thought I was so wicked."

"Mr. Hardynge," said Bessie, completely herself again, "may I ask you whether, if you recover, you intend to lead a different life?"

"Indeed I do."

"Have you no duty first in regard to that—that old difficulty you spoke about awhile ago?"

"No. The man I had wronged found out the truth, but refused to prosecute and sent me his forgiveness from his death-bed."

"And except for that your conscience is clear?"

"No, no, it is not," said the poor man. "I have been very wicked. But there is nothing further I can do now. If I recover I shall try to make amends as far as I can."

"Have you," and Bessie hesitated, "have you done right by poor Amy? Did she know what she was doing when she accepted you?"

Hardynge's face flushed, and he seemed inclined to be angry ; but Bessie's sympathetic tone calmed him.

"Oh, Miss Bruce, I have deceived her. But I do love her. Must I give her up?"

"I think that she should be allowed to judge. I don't think you can come with faith to the Lord while you are acting an untruth."

"There is so little time now, but I will try to tell her. Oh, Miss Bruce, I'm afraid to die. I am so wicked."

"Cannot you trust in the Lord?"

"How can I? He'll never forgive me."

"Mr. Hardynge, do you suppose that His Spirit would have enabled Mr. Strongwood to forgive you, and enabled me to forgive you, if He were not willing to forgive you Himself?"

Hardynge said nothing, but was evidently impressed, and Bessie took advantage of this to open her Bible, and read to him the Parable of the Prodigal Son, calling attention to the points that seemed specially appropriate. While she was reading, the door opened and Amy came quietly in and sat down on the other side of Hardynge and took hold of one of his hands, occasionally raising it to her lips. Hardynge gave her a look of loving recognition, but immediately turned his attention again to the reading.

Bessie went on to read other passages illustrative of Christ's compassion for us and sufferings on our account, and with us, such as the fifty-third of Isaiah, and His invitation, "Come unto me all ye that labour and are heavy laden, and I will give you rest." As she closed the Bible she began to sing:

> "There were ninety and nine that safely lay."

And then she prayed, confessing her own sin of anger, and coupling herself with Hardynge in a joint petition that they might know in its fulness the forgiving and cleansing power of Jesus Christ to be in them, preparing them for life or for death.   In conclusion she referred to the impending operation, and to Amy, plainly but delicately.

She ceased, and the solemn silence that followed seemed to come as a seal of the Lord's blessing.

Hardynge pressed her hand as she rose to go.

"Thank you, Miss Bruce," he said, "and thank Mr. Strongwood too——   Oh if I could only feel that the Lord would forgive me as well."

"He is far more ready to forgive than any of us can be," replied Bessie.   "Remember what I said that if His Spirit enabled Mr. Strongwood to forgive you, it is because He is Himself ready to forgive you."

"But I am so afraid."

"He can't forgive you and punish you too, Ralph dear," said Amy.

Hardynge looked inquiringly at Bessie.

"I am quite sure," said Bessie, quietly, "that the Lord cannot receive you and cast you off at the same time. Just how He will deal with you I do not know. But whatever He may do He will not remove His presence and blessing. To be with Him in harmony with Him is to be in Paradise. Remember that He loves you independently of your deserving it.   The Cross of Christ proves this to us.   Your very sense of sin shows that He has come to you by His Spirit, and that He is only waiting for you to yield to Him and confide yourself to Him."

As she spoke a new look of hope seemed to dawn in Hardynge's eyes, and she added :

"Trust yourself to Him, and set about doing what you know to be right."

Hardynge motioned her to stoop nearer.

"Pray for me," he whispered, "that I may have strength to tell Amy."

"Yes, I will," she answered, "and about the operation too."

CHAPTER XLV.

AS Bessie walked home in the beautiful evening twilight, for the threatened storm had passed by, she was filled with a deep gladness of heart that only those can appreciate who have experienced it. She had not only met and forgiven the enemy of the man she loved, and therefore her own enemy also, but had been able to point out to him the way of peace. The look of hope in his eyes she took as showing that he was one more proof of the mighty power of Christ to save all that call upon Him. Then, too, she had her own joy, which in no way jarred on the higher note—the joy of knowing that there was not only no reason why she should not frankly and fully accept and return Robert Strongwood's love ; but that she would be able to vindicate him in the sight of all men. But as she entered the house the shadow of sorrow fell upon her. She longed to know just how Robert was, but dared not knock at his door. She went to her own room, but could not rest. At every sound she would start up to see if any one were going in or out of Strongwood's room. Finally she was rewarded, and hastened forward as Aunt Mary came out.

"How is he ? " she asked.

"No better, I'm afraid," replied Aunt Mary. "By the way, Bessie, won't thee carry down the cups to be washed ? "

Bessie entered the room to get them, and just then a loud noise from the children in the garden below caused Aunt

Mary and the nurse to go to the window, the latter out of curiosity, and the former to ask them to be quiet, a request that was seldom needed, for the children were fond of Strongwood, and generally remembered to be careful not to disturb him.

Bessie was thus left for a few moments practically alone by the sick man. He was unconscious and evidently very ill. This might be her last opportunity of seeing him alive. He belonged to her, though no one knew it. She gave a hasty glance at the two figures leaning out of the window, and then before she had fully made up her mind about it, stooped down and softly kissed his forehead.

Another moment and she was upright again. To her horror she fancied that she saw something like a smile on Strongwood's face. What if he were more himself than she had supposed! What would he think of her! How glad she was that the twilight had come on, so that no one would see how her cheeks were burning. She hastily caught up the tray, and was out of the room before the two had turned from the window, but she went downstairs with a very guilty feeling, and was almost certain she should find out later that Aunt Mary had seen her—and wouldn't she be scandalized!

During the next day word was brought that Hardynge had succumbed about twelve hours after the operation.

Bessie went at once to the Wildmere's.

" How is Amy ? " she asked as soon as she saw Grace.

" As well as could be expected. Of course, it is a terrible shock to her."

" Was she with him ? "

"She and I spent the night in the parlour of the hotel. The doctors said that his general condition was favourable; but after the operation they told us that the local trouble had progressed so far that there was very little chance for him. So we waited in suspense till about five in the morning, when word was brought down that there was no hope, and then Amy went up and was with him at the close. But won't thee come upstairs? Amy said she wished to see thee."

At Bessie's entrance Amy's control of herself, which had till then been remarkable, gave way, and she burst into a violent storm of weeping.

Bessie sat down in silent sympathy, and put her arm about her, drawing Amy's hand down on her shoulder. By degrees she regained quietness, and was able to talk quietly.

Bessie found that Hardynge had honestly tried to tell Amy everything, but she had refused to let him, saying that she doubtless would have done just the same things had she been in his place, and that it was enough for her to know that he had repented and was trusting the Lord. Whatever he had done Amy had told him she loved him and always would love him.

He had managed, however, to let her know enough about his treatment of Strongwood to make her say to Bessie:

"I am not at all surprised that thee was angry. I know I should have been; but I am so glad that thee came. It was such a comfort."

"I am glad too, but I was afraid it might have been too much for him."

"No, I am sure it was not," said Amy. "He was so much quieter and more natural after thee had been there. The doctor told me after the operation that the trouble had gone too far to be remedied by any human power. Oh, Bessie, I don't see how I lived through last night "; and the poor girl began to sob afresh.

" Grace told me thee was with him to the last."

" Yes, and it was such a comfort that he was so completely himself. He gave me the names and addresses of some of his friends. He wants them to be told of his repentance and change. But he said that I must not write to them myself. Does thee think that thy brother would do it ? "

" I am sure he would be glad to do anything to help thee."

Just then a telegram was handed in. It was from Hardynge's mother, giving directions for the body to be sent home.

" I know it's all right," said Amy, " but I wish the funeral could have been here."

Bessie proposed having a funeral gathering first, and Amy was deeply gratified.

" I should like it at our house," she said ; " I want every one to know that we were engaged. Bessie, would thee approve of my wearing mourning ? Friends do wear it a good deal now."

" That is something thee must decide for thyself, Amy. When my mother died, I did not put on black. It did not seem to me to be a fitting emblem for a Christian's sorrow or a Christian's hope. Thee knows that it was adopted from a paganism that had no hope."

" Still," replied Amy, " it certainly is a mark of respect, and it sometimes saves awkward questions."

" Well, Amy, I don't want to persuade thee. Just do what thee thinks best."

When Bessie reached home, she was glad to find her brother in the library. He agreed to attend to everything as Amy desired, and also to write to the young men she had spoken of.

As soon as this was settled, he went to the mantelpiece, and taking up a telegram, said :

" This has come for Rob. It may be important. Had I not better open it, it is addressed to my care ? "

Bessie could not help smiling at this evidence of her brother's caution.

" That gives thee a legal right to open it, doesn't it ? I think thee ought to do it, anyhow."

Bruce opened it and read:

" Letter received from Caleb Galway stating whole affair pure blackmail, is highly indignant, has ordered arrest of imposter at Flumetown, who is now in jail.—Herrick."

" What does this mean, Bessie ? "

" It means that some one falsely pretending to be Miss Galway's brother has endeavoured to levy blackmail on Robert Strongwood for alleged breach of promise."

" Did Rob tell thee ? "

" The imposter wrote me a letter himself. I could not help knowing."

" Why did not thee tell me ? "

" Please excuse me, Charlie, I did not know how to at the time, for the letter came the very day before we returned home from the meetings. Then after we came home, Robert Strongwood asked me not to."

" Surely thee did not tax him with it ? " and Bruce's brown eyes opened wide with astonishment.

" No, Charlie, but he had recognized the handwriting on the envelope, as he was dropping it into the letter-box, and he spoke to me."

"It is very strange," said Bruce. " However, I'm glad it was not true. Bessie," said he after a pause, " I believe Rob is a truly Christian man."

" I believe he is," said Bessie.

She would not let even her brother suspect her feelings, and in her endeavour to hide them she spoke almost coldly.

" Well, it's time for me to be off," said Bruce. " I'll just put this telegram with Rob's letters."

CHAPTER XLVI.

AUNT MARY expressed such a strong desire to attend
Hardynge's funeral that Bessie, a good deal to her own
relief, gave up going and offered to sit in Strongwood's room
during the time, and call the nurse if anything should be
wanting. He had not yet recovered consciousness, but on
the whole was stronger, and when Bessie went in, he was in
a quiet sleep.

She sat down near him, hardly daring to breathe lest she
should arouse him.

After a time he opened his eyes and looked at her and
smiled.

"Is this heaven?" he said presently.

Bessie felt like saying that it was, but answered: "Oh no.
Does thee not know me?"

"Yes, you are an angel, and this must be heaven."

Then he seemed to collect his thoughts.

"How did get here?"

"Thee has been very ill," replied Bessie. "But thee's
better now."

"I almost wish my first thought had been true," he said,
and then closed his eyes, and slept till Aunt Mary returned.

"I think he is better," said Bessie. He woke up, and
after the first moment seemed like himself."

"Yes, I think he is better," Aunt Mary agreed. His hands are cool and he is sleeping naturally. I am really glad I went to the funeral. It was a very satisfactory, solemn occasion. I gave thy note to Amy. I think that she quite understood thy not coming. She was very calm and quiet, and I was glad to see her in her usual dress."

From this time Strongwood began to improve, though at first very slowly. Bessie hardly saw him at all, and, when some necessity or other called her into the room, he never showed by word or sign that he specially cared for her. She could not understand it, and asked herself whether it could be possible that his note had been written in delirium, and he have forgotten all about it. If so, she had gone through a great deal for nothing. She did not take in that Strongwood did not know that she had seen his letter, and she never imagined that he, noticing her constrained manner, supposed that she still disapproved of him.

As he grew stronger his first interest was about his mother.

"Has anything been heard from her?" he asked Aunt Mary.

"Yes, she cabled a message of sympathy," and Aunt Mary read it to him.

"Did you get any letters?"

"Yes, I had a letter the other day."

"May I read it?"

Aunt Mary had been vexed at the coldness of the letter, and had no wish to let him see it, so she replied:

"I think thou art still too weak to be troubled with letters, but I can tell thee that they were all well, and were hoping soon to hear improved accounts of thy health. Thy mother has quite given up expecting thee."

"That is all I wished to know," said Strongwood. "I was afraid some one might be ill."

His next wish was to hear about the lawsuit.

" Miss Bruce," said he one day as she was leaving the room after bringing in some flowers, " have you heard anything more about Miss Galway ? "

" Oh yes," said Bessie.

" I suppose my illness has caused a stay in the proceedings."

" I am glad to tell you," said Bessie, " that there are no proceedings to stay."

" What did you say ? said Strongwood eagerly.

" Now Mr. Strongwood," said Bessie, "you must not excite yourself. After awhile I can tell you all about it ; but just for the present I want you to be satisfied. Everything is settled. It was all a mistake. There will be no further difficulty."

Strongwood was so weak that the news almost overcame him.

" I thought," said he, " from your manner that things were as bad as they could be." Bessie was cut to the heart.

" I am very sorry," she said. " I never meant it." Then, with sudden change to the practical, which had sufficient element of absurdity in it to make them both smile, she added: " Here, let me give you some ammonia, I'm sure you need it."

After he had taken it, Bessie proceeded to tell him that the supposed Jonathan Galway was an imposter, and that neither Miss Galway nor her father had known anything of the plot.

He was greatly relieved, and from that time began to improve more rapidly, so that he was soon able to walk into a pleasant upstairs parlour, where he would spend most of the day.

Before this, however, he had gone through the letters that were waiting for him.

Those from his partner gave encouraging reports of the business. Then there was a letter from Herrick, which explained that by some means he had missed Mr. Galway's telegram, and had in fact only heard of its existence on receiving a letter from that gentleman, which in its turn was delayed, owing to Herrick himself being off for a week's excursion into a remote part of the State. The country postmaster had delayed forwarding it to him. Strongwood was specially pleased with the letter from Miss Galway which was enclosed; and on the first opportunity handed it to Bessie to read.

His mother's letter had naturally been one of the first opened by Strongwood. It began by expressing regret at his illness, which she hoped would not prove serious, and went on to give an account of her troubles and of why she had sent for him.

"First, I must tell you," she wrote, "that Lucy and Lord Southliegh had been engaged for some time before your letter of caution arrived. It was doubtless well-meant, but considerably beside the mark. I may say, in passing, that she paid you back in your own coin by drawing a most clever caricature of you as a Quaker with Miss Bruce on your arm. It was most entertaining, but, seriously, you must be careful not to let her capture you. I have no doubt that the Bruce family are thoroughly respectable, but you know they are not in our set." Strongwood flushed up at this slight on Bessie, but read on. "Last week I had a most disquieting letter from my business adviser, telling me that my income would in future be dreadfully reduced, owing to the failure of those Western Land Mortgages to pay. I hardly know what to do, for I have already agreed with Lord S. as to the amount of Lucy's dowry, and I am seriously afraid that, notwithstanding his protestations of loving her only for her own sake, he will not feel justified in marrying her when he finds out the true state of affairs. In fact, I cannot blame him, for his own property has become greatly reduced, and he must live in a certain style, and has heavy expenses. But I cannot bear to think of poor Lucy missing such a brilliant match. I have not dared to speak of the matter to him or to any one else, except you. So I cabled to you, without telling a soul what I was doing."

Then followed vague hints and references to "poor dear Mr. McPherson," and his kindness to Robert, which made Strongwood think that his mother had hoped for something more substantial than mere advice.

"How my death would have simplified matters," he thought.

His sister Mary's letter was naturally in a different strain.

"My dear Rob,

"What an excitement you have put us all into. First, on Thursday comes a telegram telling us you are sailing by the next steamer. I cannot tell you how glad we were—at least, I can speak for myself. I think Lucy was just a little nervous as to how you and her beloved Lord Southliegh would take to each other, for she tells him everything, and had told him you did not like the nobility.

"As for mother, she was divided between her pleasure at expecting to see you, and wonder as to what could be the reason of your sudden determination.

"Now, to-day, just as we were full of plans of what we should do when you arrived, comes this wretched telegram saying you are ill. I am so sorry : I wanted to come to you at once, but mother witheld her consent, and, what was fully as important, the money. So here I am stuck, and I don't like it a bit. I feel so home-sick for you, dear boy. I do hope that this letter will find you much better.

"What dears the Bruces must be from all you say of them.

"Between you and me, I'm inclined to agree with you about Lord Southliegh. What Lucy sees in him beyond his title I cannot understand. He strikes me as an ordinary fast young man with an extra polish. But both mother and Lucy are fairly infatuated with him. If ever I marry it will be for something more than a title. I told Lucy so before they were engaged, and she was so angry that I never repeated the experiment. I simply now speak of him as '*dear* Lord Southliegh,' at which Lucy shoots fiery glances at me.

"We are having a most charming time, but I have not much prospect of settling down to work at music. However, we might as well enjoy ourselves. One is only young once.

"I do hope you'll soon be better.

"Your affectionate sister,

"MARY McPHERSON."

This letter cheered Strongwood; but his mother's perplexed him. He wished the engagement could be honourably broken off ; but on the other hand he knew how chagrined Lucy would be, and he himself felt that since his mother had given her promise, the honour of the family was involved. How far could he help them? He did not feel able to grapple with the question at present. He must wait till he was stronger, and there did not seem to be such haste that the delay of a week or two could make any very great difference, and so he would let the matter rest on his mind for the present.

A few days after this, when Bruce and his sister were with him in the upstairs parlour after dinner, Strongwood said:

"By the way, Charlie, did I not write a letter just before I became so ill?"

Bessie started and became very intent upon the flowers she was arranging. Charlie's answer was a great relief to her.

"Yes. Aunt Mary found it on the floor, and gave it to me. But, as it was only to be read in a certain contingency, which I am thankful to say did not arise, I simply sealed it up and put it away. Would you like to have it?"

"If it's not too much trouble?"

Bruce went and fetched it—

"Here it is, Rob."

"Thank you. I just thought I should like to add a few lines to it."

He opened the envelope mechanically, took out the letter, and looked perplexed."

"What's the matter, Rob?" asked Bruce.

"I thought there was an enclosure."

"It is just as Aunt Mary gave it to me. The nurse said she thought you had written something more, and they searched carefully for it, and this was all they found."

"It is very strange," said Strongwood. "I was sure I wrote another note. It must have been that I merely had it strongly on my mind ; but I would not have had it left lying about for anything."

The truth rushed upon Bessie. It was clear that she had not been intended to see those lines, except after Strongwood's death. She beat a hasty retreat to her room with feelings better imagined than described. Of course, she would have to confess, but how ?

What a humiliation it would be !

" Bessie," said Aunt Mary at tea time, " does thee think that Robert could have written a letter without our finding it ? "

Bessie desired to be quite truthful ; but was determined to keep her secret.

"Aunt Mary," said she, " does thee think it is quite suitable for us to speak of him as Robert ? "

" Why not, pray ? If an old woman like me cannot speak of a man she has been nursing for weeks, by his first name, I'd like to know why."

" The children might get to do it, and it would not be respectful."

" The children must learn not to do all their great aunt does,—at least till they're her age," she added, for she saw by their nods that the little ones were about to quote her against herself.

The question of the note came up again, however, and Bessie was only saved from the dilemma of confessing or prevaricating by a timely choking fit. She was not quite sure in her own mind whether it was altogether accidental. But before it was over, it was real enough, and it effected a complete diversion.

CHAPTER XLVII.

A TÊTE À TÊTE.

THE next afternoon Bessie and Strongwood were together in the sitting room, and Bessie was trying to think of some suitable way to explain about the letter, when Strongwood said :

" How delightful the mountains are ; I am never tired of looking at them."

" Yes," responded Bessie, in rather an absent tone, " the view is lovely."

" It is so restful," said Strongwood. " I just lie back here in my chair like a child and watch the changing shadows."

" I wonder how a child feels," said Bessie, rousing herself to take up the conversation. " How new and wonderful everything must be to it."

" I don't know about that," said Strongwood. " I often think animals have the advantage over children in that, for they acquire their powers so rapidly. When I was in the country last spring I watched the lambs. Did you ever notice the air of surprise in their faces. It is all so new to them, and they are so delighted with everything, that they cannot help jumping and bounding about for very joy. But children develop so slowly that they have become quite used to the things about them before they dream of the beauty."

" I think," said Bessie, " that you allow too much to the lambs and too little to the children."

" Of course," replied Strongwood, " it's only guesswork as far as the lambs are concerned ; but I think I am right about the children. I believe that to most of us the real enjoyment of nature comes after we are grown up."

" You don't agree with Wordsworth then—

'Heaven lies about us in our infancy' ? "

" Well, Wordsworth to the contrary notwithstanding, I know that as a boy the country attracted me chiefly as a playground. But now I can consciously enjoy the beauties of nature in a way I never thought of as a boy."

" And perhaps more than you would have done a year ago even," said Bessie.

Strongwood thought a moment, and then said :

" Yes, that is so ——"

" Of course, you have more leisure now, and besides," she added in a low voice—

" ' Heaven above is softer blue,
    Earth around is sweeter green,
  Something lives in every hue,
    Christless eyes have never seen.' "

" I believe you're right," said Strongwood, after a moment's pause. " His love in our hearts changes everything."

" I almost wonder at myself," he continued, " for being so very contented. Nothing seems to trouble me. I feel like a little child, and I must confess it's rather pleasant."

It was the first time they had spoken on serious subjects since his illness, and Strongwood wondered how she knew of his new faith, and hoped that she would pursue the subject.

But her secret was weighing on Bessie's mind, and his remark about feeling like a child suddenly suggested a way of making her explanation.

She began in a cheerful tone, but with rather a sinking heart :

" Well, if you are a child, suppose I tell you a story."

" Oh, please do," said Strongwood, fully entering into the spirit of the proposal. " Let it be something really simple, suitable for my tender years. Let it begin, as all orthodox stories do, with ' Once upon a time.' "

" Very well then, ' Once upon a time there was a little girl ' —— "

" Delightful ! " said Strongwood, " that's the very thing."

" Children shouldn't interrupt. As I was saying, Once upon a time there was a little girl who tried to be good and obey her mother."

" Capital ! "

" Hush. Well, one day when her mother had gone out, she went into the dining room."

" Was that naughty of her ? " asked Strongwood.

" No. It was quite right. As she came into the room she saw a sheet of paper lying on the floor. Now, she was an orderly little girl, and stooped to pick it up. She did not intend to read it, but she could not help seeing that the letter was in her mother's writing, and began with ' My dear Emily.' "

" Was her name Emily ? "

" Yes."

" But you said she was a little girl. Do little girls read writing ? "

" I did not say how old she was. She was about ten."

"Small for her age, I suppose. However, go on. This story just suits my capacity. I can quite understand it."

"Thank you. Well, as I was saying, she saw it was to herself from her mother. It said her mother was sorry to leave her, but that when she was gone, Emily was to go into the garden and gather some roses, and put them into vases to welcome her grandmother, who would be coming to tea."

"Emily was surprised that her mother had gone without saying 'Good-bye'; but she was very fond of her grandmother, and proud of being trusted to gather the flowers by herself; so she went at once into the garden, and had all the roses nicely arranged when who should come in but her mother.

"'Where did those roses come from?' she asked.

"'I picked them,' said Emily, 'as you told me, for grandmother.'

"'You naughty child,' said the mother. 'You know that I never told you to do any such thing.'

"'Excuse me, Mamma, you told me so in your letter.'

"'Where did you find my letter?'

"'On the floor in the dining room.'

"And her mother was very angry and boxed her ears and sent her to bed without any supper, because she had not intended Emily to see the letter till the next day, when she (the mother) was going away for a visit. But she had been called off while she was writing, and the letter had fallen on the floor."

Bessie paused, and Strongwood said:

"Please go on. I want to hear of the great ogre who came and took away the wicked mother, and gave the good little girl a necklace of rubies and pearls."

Bessie breathed more freely, though she feared that when Strongwood should hear all, the personal equation might make him reverse his judgment. But she went on bravely:

" I cannot speak of any ogre, for he did not come. In fact, you might almost make Emily spell Elizabeth."

Strongwood had so seldom heard Bessie called by this name, that it was by her tone of voice and the tell-tale blush on her cheeks, more than by her words, that he understood she was referring to herself.

" Surely, your mother was not that kind of a person," he said.

" No, Mr. Strongwood," she answered. " Let me explain. I came home the very morning you were taken so ill. As I was passing your door, the nurse ran out, saying you had fainted, and asking me to help. Of course, I went in at once, and found you unconscious. Lying before you was an unfinished note, and I saw that it was addressed to myself. Without a thought I hastily put it into my pocket. It never occurred to me till yesterday, that you did not intend to have me read it. As I had been away from home, I thought that you——"

She did not finish, for Strongwood had grown suddenly pale, and looked as if he were about to faint.

" I hope you will forgive me. I did not mean to do wrong."

Strongwood looked most distressed, but said nothing.

" I could not leave it for others to see, and I thought you intended me to read it," continued Bessie.

" Oh what weakness," said Strongwood, as if speaking to himself.

" Yes, I suppose it was. I'm very sorry," said Bessie humbly.

" Not to be trusted," continued he in the same tone.

Bessie began to feel that she hardly deserved such severity, but she only said:

" Please forgive me."

" Why, what was I saying ?" said Strongwood, rousing himself.

" You said I was not to be trusted," replied Bessie, almost crying.

" I did not mean you.   I meant myself."

" Do you forgive me ?"

" Forgive you.   What for ?"

" For taking the letter ?"

" You did perfectly right.   But I cannot forgive myself."

" Then you are sorry you wrote it ?"

" Very sorry indeed——"

" Do not let that disturb you in the least," said Bessie, drawing herself up. " You were entirely excusable under the influence of the fever.   No one but myself knows of the matter, and I shall quite understand that you did not mean it."

This speech touched Strongwood to the quick, and threw him off his guard.

" But I did mean it, and I do mean it.   That's the difficulty ; but I thought it would not hurt if you did not know it till after I was dead.   Oh, how weak I was.   Will you forgive me ?"

" It is hardly a subject for forgiveness," replied Bessie, " but I understand that you retract the letter."

" I cannot deny its truth ; but I wish I had never written it ; not because I do not love you, for I do ; but because a wreck of a man like me has no right to offer himself to such a one as you are."

Bessie, as she looked at his pale face, worn with illness and suffering, felt that she loved him all the more for what he had been through, and she said with a great effort :

" Your health is no difficulty, but—but—you know I am a Friend."

The effect of this speech was very different from what she had expected. Strongwood for a moment forgot his illness and said eagerly :

" Miss Bessie, when I was in New York I made up my mind to become a Friend—not from any hope of winning you," he added hastily—" for *then* I never expected to talk to you like this."

After a pause, he continued :

" But, Miss Bessie, I have said too much Please consider that it is as if I had not written that letter."

" Certainly, on one condition."

" What condition ? "

" That you have changed your mind."

" Changed my mind ? "

" Yes. Whenever you tell me that that letter no longer expresses your real feelings towards me, then I will accept your retraction."

" But just look at me," said Strongwood, " what business have I, a man in consumption, to think of marrying ? "

" Does thee think," said Bessie in a low voice, " that thee has a monopoly of loving, or that thy weakness is a bar to my loving thee ? "

As she said this her eyes fell, and she blushed so bewitchingly that Strongwood could resist no longer. He sprang up, and taking her hand, stooped down and kissed her cheek.

"My own love," he said.

He was never quite sure whether what followed was an embrace or not, for he suddenly became weak, and Bessie, putting her arm about him, helped him back to the sofa. There they sat together, hand in hand, as the twilight closed in, too happy for words.

CHAPTER XLVIII.

ON TRIAL.

WHEN Jonathan Galway was carried off to jail, he could hardly believe the evidence of his senses. To meet with such treatment, instead of the surprised and loving welcome home to which he had been looking forward after his years of wandering, seemed more like a nightmare than a fact. He almost expected to wake up and find it was really a dream. But the truth became more and more distressingly apparent, and his wrath increased in proportion.

The next day he wrote letters to his father and sister, and to his brother in New Orleans, all of which were duly forwarded, but did not reach the persons for whom they were intended in time to do any good; for his brother was taking his holiday beyond the reach of mails, and his father and sister were travelling about so rapidly that letters did not catch up to them.

A true bill was found against Jonathan, and in default of bail he was again committed to prison. He refused to engage counsel, saying that he should conduct his own case.

As his anger cooled he became morose and sullen. He felt that he was the victim of a plot. Why did none of his people take any notice of him? He wished now that he had paid more attention to his home letters; for he could not remember the names of any of their acquaintances in Flumetown, and this fact had told heavily against him in the examination.

In the meantime, unknown to him, there was considerable excitement as to what had became of the man whom every one regarded as the true Jonathan. He had ridden off, telling the housekeeper to expect him back not later than seven o'clock the same evening, but he had not returned. He had stopped at a country inn, given his name as Mr. J. Galway, of Flumetown, and had gone out, as he said, for a stroll in the woods, leaving his horse in the stable. That was the last that had been seen of him. The business manager at Mr. Galway's had engaged men to search the forest, and had offered a large reward for the discovery of such traces of the missing man as should lead to finding him alive or dead ; but nothing came of it. The event happening so immediately after the arrest of the fellow who had endeavoured to pass himself off as Mr. Galway's son, soon excited suspicion. People said, "Of course the prisoner had accomplices, and they have spirited poor Mr. Galway off, for revenge or for reward." When it transpired that Jonathan had had a large sum of money upon his person, the belief gained currency that he had been murdered. The Galways were important people in the place, and the occurrence cast a gloom over every one. The local paper was full of it, and published many communications giving various theories as to how the crime might have been committed. Feeling ran so high that the business manager sent off telegrams to Mr. Galway to different addresses in hopes that one of them might reach him. One did, and altered that gentleman's plans considerably. His son in New Orleans had forwarded him a letter from a friend in Europe, which spoke of Jonathan returning home. The telegram therefore alarmed him very much, and he telegraphed in reply, " Greatly distressed, spare no expense."

Thus encouraged the business manager engaged the services of a noted detective agency. The agent they sent to work up the case, as soon as he heard all the particulars and what a high character the missing man had borne, concluded that the murder theory was almost certainly the correct one, and decided to try whether he could induce the prisoner, who was described to him as a desperate man, to turn State's evidence.

He called at the jail, and tried to lead up to the subject as naturally as possible. But as soon as Jonathan Galway got an inkling of what he was after, he poured out such a storm of abuse upon the detective as almost made the latter lose his habitual coolness.

" You say that the villain has been killed, do you ?" continued Jonathan. " I can tell you I'm glad to hear it. It's nothing more than he deserved. I only wish I had done it myself."

The detective made a note of the remark, but said nothing.

This was too much for Jonathan, and he yelled out :

" Get out of this cell this instant, you cur, you dog, or I'll thrash the life out of you, and gladly take the consequences."

On the whole the detective felt that nothing would be gained by remaining, and with an exasperatingly cool bow he departed.

Poor Jonathan, as soon as the reaction came, saw what he had done, and was completely subdued and broken.

The detective, on his part, concluded that the bluster had been assumed, and was more convinced than ever of the correctness of the murder theory, but looked upon the prisoner as " game." He worked hard, and even had one or two men arrested on suspicion, but as nothing like a case could be made out against them, they were promptly released.

It must be remembered that all Mr. Galway's agents were working in the dark, for Emorie, while encouraging the report of Belle's engagement to Strongwood, had taken care never to breathe a word as to any trouble between them, and Mr. Galway had at his daughter's earnest request avoided all mention in his letter of the alleged breach of promise, or of other details.

The case, therefore, against the real Jonathan seemed very clear and very simple.

The trial was arranged to take place after Mr. Galway's return, but, owing to various unexpected delays, he and his daughter only arrived on the very morning that it opened.

Mrs. Henderson, the old housekeeper, gave them a tearful welcome.

" To think," said she, " that you should get back to such sorrow."

" Has anything been discovered ?" asked Mr. Galway, huskily.

" No, nothing at all, and those that know best, say that they are not like to learn anything now. And he was such a kind spoken gentleman. You should have seen him, Miss, standing before your mother's picture when he first came home. I couldn't help crying myself to see him."

Mr. Galway blew his nose suspiciously.

"I do not give up hope yet," he said. "Jonathan was always a queer boy. Like as not, he has run off on a tramp and may turn up any day."

The old housekeeper shook her head.

"He never would have left your favourite horse in a strange stable without a word, and taken nothing for his journey."

Mr. Galway went into the library. There was the letter of welcome he had sent to Jonathan, waiting for his return, together with letters of condolence from many friends.

Neither father nor daughter was able to do justice to the very tempting breakfast prepared for them, and Belle had no heart to go to court, but shut herself up in her room. Her father went alone, but arrived after the proceedings had begun, and so had no time for even a short interview with the prosecuting counsel.

There was an unusual crowd, for every one wished to see the bold criminal who had attempted to pass himself off as the son of the richest man in Flumetown.

The prosecuting attorney had already made a brief opening statement to the effect that the prisoner had appeared on a certain morning in August and endeavoured, first by false pretences and then by force, to effect an entrance into the house of Mr. Caleb Galway, apparently with the intention of obtaining booty, but that he had been fortunately stopped in his attempt by Mr. Jonathan Galway, who had since disappeared under distressing circumstances, for which disappearance the prisoner might or might not, be partly responsible. Evidence could be produced sufficient to justify the prisoner's being held for trial on this point also. But the evidence of unprovoked assault and battery, and of his endeavouring to obtain privileges under false pretences was so convincing that the counsel confidently expected the jury to return a verdict of guilty, although the prisoner's persistent claim to be Mr. Galway's son might lead them to call his sanity in question.

Jonathan Galway refused the offer of counsel, and simply stated that the accusation was utterly false, and that the real criminal was the man who opposed his entrance into his home. He closed with a statement that he was himself the true Jonathan Galway, and that he had landed from Europe in New York only a day or two before his arrest, and had been robbed of his baggage after landing, and had therefore no means with him for identification, but that he could now prove who he was by his own father, who, he understood, would soon be in Court.

The prosecution first called Mrs. Henderson and then the gardener, who both testified to the prisoner's attempt to enter the Creekside Mansion, and the violent assault on the gentleman of the house.

The history of the examination before the magistrate was then brought out, and certified lists were produced of all the passengers on all the European steamships reaching New York for four weeks previous to the prisoner's arrest, none of which contained the name of Galway.

This was an unexpected blow to poor Jonathan, for, not anticipating any trouble, he had come over in the steerage, because he was low in funds, and had from false pride registered an assumed name.

At last Mr. Galway entered the court-room and was called. He testified that his suspicions had been aroused by a letter from a New York lawyer dealing with matters not now before the Court, but which showed that the prisoner had been in the country much longer than he claimed.

When asked if he recognized the prisoner, Mr. Galway replied that he did not. In fact this was not surprising. His son had left him a mere youth, with a slim figure and refined face, and had returned a rough, heavy man, with fairly thick beard, and a gruff voice. His coarse, untidy clothing was also against him.

In the cross-examination, Jonathan Galway tried to make his father tell what the business was that was mentioned in the lawyer's letter. Mr. Galway refused to answer, and the court sustained him on the ground that it was an irrelevant question.

" Father," said Jonathan, " don't you know me ? "

" I have never to my knowledge seen you before."

The distress and surprise of the prisoner were so evident, that a murmur of pity ran through the court room.

" Poor fellow, he's out of his mind," was the general comment.

Then the court took a recess for dinner.

Jonathan was conducted back to his cell, broken-hearted. How could his father have forgotten him ?

" Mother would have known me," he sighed, " or Belle. Where is Belle, I wonder ? "

He had not been able to see whether she had been in court, and he supposed she was still out of town.

" What a fool I have been," he thought. " If I had acted like a man of ordinary sense, it would have been all right. I'll think twice before I travel under an assumed name again, or assault a man before I am in a position to prove my identity. I wish now I had consented to engage a lawyer. But it's all of a piece with my whole life. As it is, it's touch and go between prison and a lunatic asylum."

At the thought he bowed his head in despair—

" Oh God help me."

The court reassembled and Caleb Galway was once more in the witness box.

Jonathan, greatly subdued, endeavoured to recall to his father's mind incidents in the old home life, and matters referred to in home letters. It was all in vain.

To all his questions the invariable answer was, " Yes, I remember that perfectly."

" Then don't you see that I am Jonathan ?"

" No, all I see is that you have cleverly learned your story from hearing my son talk of his early life."

All at once the court was disturbed by a cry, and Jonathan saw to his astonishment a beautiful young lady entirely unknown to him coming towards him.

" Oh Jonathan, Jonathan," she said, " it is you after all."

" Silence !"

The officers with difficulty conducted Miss Galway back to her seat, but not before she had cried out: " O Father, take care, take care. It's Jonathan."

This testimony was, of course, not in a form to be accepted by the court, but every one was electrified by it, and Mr. Galway became very pale.

His agitation was so great that the judge assented to his request to be allowed to rest before going on with his testimony.

Jonathan asked eagerly that the young lady might be called as a witness.

" Do you know her name ? " asked the judge.

Jonathan, as we have seen, was not a man of ready resource, and answered that he did not know, but he supposed she must be his sister, Miss Isabel Galway.

Every one laughed and the judge remarked :

" If Miss Galway is correct and you are the man you claim to be, you cannot blame Mr. Galway for not recognizing you under your unfavourable surroundings, when you your-self cannot recognize your sister after she as good as told you who she was."

The prosecuting lawyer agreed that Miss Galway should be called at once.

Her first answer was a disappointment.

" You recognized the prisoner as your brother ? "

" No, I did not."

This produced a sensation.

" I was not where I could see him," she continued.

" Then why did you address him by his name."

" These letters did it," and she held up two letters she had in her hand.

" How ? "

" They are from him, and have been following us about from place to place, and I got them from the post office as I came to court, and in reading them I suddenly discovered who he was."

The letters were immediately submitted as evidence.

The prosecuting lawyer demanded that the handwriting should be further tested. This was done by dictating passages from them to the prisoner, who wrote them out and signed his name. The two were then shown to the judge, the opposing counsel, and the jury. There was no doubt about the matter.

The first was from Jonathan to his brother in New Orleans, written the day of his landing, and forwarded by the latter just before he had started on his vacation. It spoke of his voyage and his assumed name, and of his intentions of surprising his father and sister. The second letter spoke in passionate terms of his unjust imprisonment.

The passenger lists were again referred to, and Jonathan's assumed name was found on the date mentioned.

The cross-examination came very near being a conversation between Jonathan and his sister, but the judge overlooked the absence of some formalities. It only served to bring out the force of Miss Galway's testimony, and when her father was recalled he requested to be allowed to retract his former statements, and now fully identified the prisoner at the bar as his son.

The prosecuting attorney satisfied himself by explaining how he had been led into error by a very unusual combination of circumstances, after which the jury returned a verdict of acquittal without leaving their seats.

CHAPTER XLIX.

FOR CONSCIENCE SAKE.

WHEN Bessie left Strongwood the gas was lighted on the landing outside, and before she reached her own room she encountered Aunt Mary, who noticing her flushed cheeks and sparkling eyes, asked :

"Why, Bessie, what has happened ? He has not been proposing to thee, has he ? "

" Hush," said Bessie, entering her room, followed by Aunt Mary.

" Has he really ? "

As Bessie said nothing, Aunt Mary continued :

" I believe he has. What did thee say to him ? I think that he has taken a very unfair advantage of his position, I do indeed, and I hope thee was firm. The idea of his behaving in that way after all our nursing. It's too bad."

" He has behaved beautifully," said Bessie.

" Then all I have to say is that thee's as bad as he is."

" But thee's quite mistaken, Aunt Mary. He did not propose, and did not want to."

" I declare, Bessie, thee doesn't mean to say that thee proposed to him ? "

" Aunt Mary, how can thee say such a thing ? "

" I don't see how else to understand it. We never ought to have let thee be so much with him. However, all young people are alike. Still I thought ——"

"Now, Aunt Mary," said Bessie, "do be reasonable. Sit down, and I will tell thee all about it."

As she did so Aunt Mary became deeply interested, for she was really very fond of Strongwood.

"He's a fine fellow," she said. "But he's quite right. What would become of thy life-work if thee should marry him?"

"I think I can trust for that."

"Well, but the trust must be well grounded. If thy work for the next few years is to nurse him, well and good. But if it is, as I thought it was, to go about and preach, then the care of an invalid will interfere with it. It's sheer nonsense to undertake the one and trust to be able to do the other."

"Well," said Bessie, "thee knows that I always regard sickness in the family as a providential thing, and am ready to give up outside work for it."

"But thee becomes thy own providence if thee imports sickness into the family with thy eyes open."

"I can't help that. I hope he will be getting much better. In any case, I feel that he has been given to me, and that it will be all right; and oh, Aunt Mary, I am so happy."

Aunt Mary did not attempt to push the point further, and left her with her best wishes.

Although Bessie did not find Aunt Mary's remarks very exhilarating, they did not shake her determination, but prepared her for further opposition. Mrs. Bruce, however, offended none, simply saying that she had no doubt Bessie had considered the matter carefully, and that apart from his health she considered Robert Strongwood a very suitable man for her sister.

Mrs. Leslie, however, was very much concerned, and took the first opportunity after breakfast the next morning to expostulate.

"I am really surprised, Elizabeth," she said, "that thou should think of such a thing. Remember what the Advices say, 'In contemplating the important engagement of marriage, look principally to that which will help you on your heavenward journey,' and 'Bear in mind the vast importance, in such a union, of accordance in religious principles and practice.'"

"I think, Aunt Lydia, that I am living up to both the letter and spirit of that advice."

"Why, Elizabeth, how canst thou say so? He is not only not a Friend, but I doubt if he is even a religious character."

"I know that Robert Strongwood has only recently become a religious character," said Bessie, "but I believe him to be thoroughly in earnest, and he intends to join our Society."

"It's only to gain thee, Elizabeth. I have no confidence in his remaining serious after he fully recovers—if he ever should recover, which I fear is not likely."

"Aunt Lydia," said Bessie, "thee does not know him. He became a Christian before this last illness, and I really cannot have him spoken against in that way."

"Well, Elizabeth, I did not mean to do him any injustice, but I cannot but think that thou art running a serious risk, and I must say I am greatly surprised. Think of the influence of thy example on other young Friends of the meeting. Remember thou art an acknowledged minister."

"I don't see," returned Bessie, with spirit, "why being a minister should prevent my loving the best man I have ever met ; and, as for my example, if any girl of my acquaintance finds herself in a position like mine, I only hope she will act as I do."

So saying she left Mrs. Leslie and went to Charlie in the library, and told him what had passed, and added :

" I don't understand why she objects so strongly. It is a matter that concerns myself."

" I am not so sure of that, Bessie. Remember, he has consumption."

" I do."

" Well, thee knows what a strong feeling our old family doctor had about consumptives marrying, and I think thee will remember that his objection went further than the mere personal inconvenience occasioned by having an invalid husband or wife."

" I think it is really too bad, Charlie," replied Bessie, almost losing control of herself, " that thee of all others should not have sympathy with me, when he is thy friend, and thee's always praising him up to the skies."

" Why, Bessie, I do sympathise. But I cannot help having a judgment in the matter."

" I thank thee for thy sympathy," replied Bessie with an almost hysterical laugh, " but it's not exactly the variety that I appreciate."

" But, Bessie, I must say what I think, and leave it to thy own conscience."

" Oh, of course, but——"

Here Bessie checked herself, and hastily left the library. When she reached her room, she sat down by her writing table, and leant her head upon her hand. There she remained for a long time without moving. At last she said to herself :

"Yes, I'm sure that Charlie meant to be kind. But he's mistaken. It cannot be right after all we have gone through to break it off. In Robert's state of health it would be a very serious thing to do. It is an exceptional case. Besides, I told him last evening that his health made no difference. I shall not retract what I have said. We love each other, and it must be right to go on with our engagement."

Just then the clock struck ten, and she started up. It was time for her to go and teach in a sewing class for girls that she was interested in.

All the way to the school she kept saying to herself, " I am sure it is right, we have been given to each other."

When Bruce went to see Strongwood, the latter asked :

" Has she told you ? "

" Yes."

" Do you approve ? "

" I approve of *you*."

" As I am ? "

" That is a difficulty, I confess."

" I suppose you think I was very weak to write that note, and weaker still to give way to my feelings yesterday. But I just could not help it, and I confess I can't be sorry that I did."

" It is very hard on you, Rob."

" Then you don't approve ? "

" Well," said Bruce, " the truth is, my difficulty lies a good deal in the fact that you have a disease that is hereditary."

Strongwood was silent. His mind had been so completely occupied with the simple personal question between

Bessie and himself that he had quite overlooked the other side.

"I understand," said he, and fell into a deep silence.

Bruce waited a little longer, but as his friend did not speak, he arose, pressed his hand and left the room without a word. As he walked down to business he felt like a brute. What right had he to play the oracle and come between two loving hearts. And yet he could see no right way of unsaying what he had said.

As for Strongwood, he felt as if he had grown suddenly twenty years older. It seemed so hard just to have been allowed such great happiness only for an hour, and then to have it dashed to the ground. But he did not feel as Bessie did. He had thought the matter out carefully from one point of view during the summer, and now that Charlie had put it to him from another standpoint he felt clear that the manly thing to do was to set Bessie free ; but it was none the less an effort. He blamed himself severely for his own want of self-control, which had brought matters to their present pass.

Bessie was detained at the school, and only reached home after dinner had begun. She had a splitting headache, and barely managed to sit through the meal, but she could not bring her mind to go to the parlour to see Robert afterwards, for she was afraid he would think it right to follow Charlie's advice. She must be stronger before she met him. So she sent up a vase of flowers by Bertie, with a message, and went to her room to lie down.

Strongwood divined her motives and wrote on a piece of paper,

"Dearest Bessie, let us do what is right,—Robert."

He folded it and asked Bertie to take it to her.

Bessie, alone in her room, read the words as if they had been a death knell. " It is right to be engaged to him," she cried to herself ; "I shall not break it off. I *will* not."

The last three words recalled her to herself. Was it her will in the matter that made her decide what was right ? She tried to be quiet and to pray for guidance.

She knelt by her bedside in silence for a long time, and her thoughts gradually shaped themselves. Her lover had touched a chord that always responded. She had long put conscience first. Now she remembered all the good old doctor used to say on the matter. He had always spoken of it as a moral question, and his words came back with almost crushing weight upon her.

Late in the afternoon Bessie went to Strongwood in the little parlour.

He saw by her face what a severe struggle she had been going through.

She sat down near him, and for some time neither spoke. They had never seemed so near to each other as now when they were purposing to separate, and neither wished to begin the final conversation.

At last Strongwood spoke, falling naturally from its association with her into the Friendly mode of address.

" Has Charlie been speaking to thee ? "

" Yes."

Then followed another silence.

" I think he is right," said Strongwood with a voice very low from suppressed emotion.

" So do I."

Another silence.

"I wish I were well enough to travel," said Strongwood. "I am afraid that my staying on here will be very awkward for thee."

"No, Robert, please do not feel uneasy. I have thought of that, and I can easily write and arrange to finish my visit to Williamsport which was cut short."

"I suppose," said Strongwood, "that it is better that we should be away from each other."

"I think it is."

After a long pause, Strongwood continued :

"It will always be a great joy to me to know that I have had thy love."

"I shall always love thee, Robert."

"And I shall always love thee, Bessie. Promise me that if thee is ever in need or in trouble, thee will let me know."

"Yes, Robert, I will. And thee'll let me know about thyself in the same way, won't thee ? "

"Yes, and I want thee always to let me contribute to any work thee is interested in."

"We shall hear of each other sometimes through Charlie," said Bessie, and then she cried out :

"Oh Robert, if only this could have been settled before ever thee was poorly. Then it could not have been right to break it off later."

"But unless my health had failed we should never have seen each other. Bessie," he continued with an effort, "Remember I hold thee perfectly free, should any one else——"

"Don't, don't," interrupted Bessie. "I know that we are free in one sense, but in my heart——" She could not finish her sentence.

The trouble was too great for further words. Finally she arose and held out her hand to him. Strongwood grasped it and drew her down, and their lips met. Neither spoke and the one warm tear that fell on his cheek was the only outward sign of the deep emotion Bessie felt. Yet neither misunderstood the other, and each knew how the other suffered. Both knew that their only hope of adhering to their resolution was to maintain perfect self-control.

It is the ever repeated and ever fresh miracle of love by which two souls become in a short time more to each other than the whole world beside—dearer than father and mother, brother or sister. Strongwood and Bessie had become so to each other, and knew it ; but they both recognized without argument, and as a matter of course, that duty had a stronger claim still.

—

CHAPTER L

CLOUDS.

A S Bessie did not appear at tea that evening Bruce went up to her room, and found her lying on her lounge. He sat down beside her and took her hand in his.

"It's all settled," she said wearily, and then added : "I am going to write to Williamsport and see if it is convenient for them to have me finish my visit now."

"I think it's a good plan," said Bruce. "Dear Bessie, I am so sorry."

She grasped his hand without a word, and he, feeling that quietness was what she needed, left her.

Bessie was quite exhausted, and kept her bed for several days. On the evening of the second day, as her brother was sitting beside her, she said :

"Charlie, it doesn't seem right that I should feel this so much."

"Why ?"

"It seems like a want of submission."

"I think not," said her brother. "If I fell and broke my arm, I might be perfectly submissive and uncomplaining, but of course I should suffer the pain and loss of power from my injury. Now thee has received a far greater blow than that, and why should thee be surprised that thee suffers from it. Christianity, I often think, does not make us less sensitive, but more so."

" But it teaches us where to find strength to bear ; and I am not bearing this ; I'm crushed."

" Would thee recall the resolution thee has made ? "

" Of course not, it would not be right."

" Is thee angry about it and rebellious ? "

" I believe not, unless the feeling that comes over me like a flood every now and then, that I would give anything to have it different is rebellious."

" Shall I tell Rob that thee wishes to reconsider the question ? "

" No, No ! It would not be right."

" Then, Bessie, thee is not crushed but strong, and the Lord is helping thee. Now don't fret thyself any more with false accusations."

" Oh, Charlie, I was so happy."

Bruce could not find any words to answer this, and so simply stroked her hand. Bessie continued :

" Please don't let Robert worry about me. There is really nothing the matter. I'm only resting."

" All right, little sister," said he, kissing her. " I think Rob will understand."

Then he went downstairs, almost broken-hearted himself at having been the one to spoil so much happiness.

The nervous strain of the past week or two, followed by the crowning effort of renunciation, was too much for Bessie, and for some time, although she had no definite disease, she continued utterly weak.

Strongwood felt the blow no less keenly than she did, but after the first day or two it had the opposite effect upon him. After she had left him, he sat looking out at the lovely panorama before him, but seeing nothing of it. His mind seemed a blank. Then he remembered how exactly the wish he had had in New York had come true. He had said that if he could only be able to let Bessie know of his love for her he should be quite satisfied. Now he saw how mistaken he had been, and yet immediately afterwards he added aloud to himself :

" I do not regret that we went as far as we did. It is better than not knowing."

Then a feeling of utter loneliness came over him. There was no one to whom he could look for sympathy. His mother and sisters would regard the conclusion reached as a fortunate escape, and all the family at Penelve felt that the marriage would have been unsuitable. He had intimate friends in New York—a few—but none of them would sympathise with his new-found hope.

Then the words he had read in " George Fox's Journal" came to him :

" There is One, even Jesus, who can speak to thy condition."

It was a true message and he bowed his head and worshipped.

That night, when the double feeling was strong within him, first of human loneliness, then of the divine Comforter, who could speak to his condition, he wrote the following lines, which meant a great deal to him, however commonplace they might seem to a reader ignorant of the mental state in which they were composed :

> " I may not speak the grief I feel,
> The hidden pang may not reveal :
> Lord grant that I through this may gain
> Annointed eyes for silent pain,
> And haste with healing word and deed
> To hearts in unsuspected need."

Then there came to him, as never before, a sense of rest and joy in the personal love of Christ. Nevertheless he was for a day or two distinctly more poorly and Aunt Mary feared he was going to have a relapse ; but before long he roused himself. His manliness revolted at the thought that his presence should force Bessie to arrange to leave her home at a time when she most needed sympathy and love. It was his duty to get sufficiently well to go away himself, and as a preliminary step he began to busy himself over his correspondence. What should he write to his mother ?

Another letter had come from her, more discouraging than the first, in which she had referred not only to Lucy's probable disappointment, but had spoken of her own income as having been greatly reduced in a way that made Strongwood suppose that she had met with a second loss and was actually in danger of being brought, if not to poverty, at least to very straitened circumstances. Her letter had closed with remarks about "poor dear Mr. McPherson's generosity" and a direct appeal for help.

Strongwood was not a little troubled that his mother should write such a letter, when she knew that he was ill ; but it served to emphasize how urgent she felt the case to be. So he sat down at once and wrote to her attorney in New York asking for a full statement of the matter. But the lawyer had got wind of what Mrs. McPherson was after, and wrote vaguely, though with apparent frankness. He closed with the statement that he felt that he was not violating professional secrecy in saying that Mrs. McPherson had met with serious losses.

All this put an entirely new face upon the question. To give money in order that his sister might make an undesirable marriage was something that Strongwood felt he could not rightly do. But when his mother was really in embarrassed circumstances, and possibly worse, there was no question but that he should do what he could to relieve her, not only because she was his mother, but because he owed all the success that he had had in life to the aid given him by his step-father, who except for that would have given his whole fortune to his wife and daughters. After all, it did not seem to Strongwood that it mattered very much to him. He had only himself to provide for, and his health was probably permanently disabled, and he would not, at the longest, live more than a very few years, and would have to spend them very quietly.

So he wrote to his mother, telling her that he greatly sympathized with her in her losses, and wished that he could do more for her than he was about to propose, but the fact was that his firm had been in such difficulties a short time previous that it was impracticable for him to draw capital out of the business. In the meantime he hoped to be able to send her regularly two-thirds of his share of the profits as long as she was in difficulties. In case he should sell out, he hoped to hand back to her at least as much as Mr. McPherson had given him to start with.

The letter was written very cautiously, and did not legally bind him to anything whatever. Yet his mother was quite satisfied with it, for she knew about what his business was worth to him, and she knew that he would fulfill his implied promises absolutely.

"Ah!" she said to herself, as she read his letter, "I knew that what I said about my own losses would make him act: it'll prevent that Bruce girl from setting her cap

for him, when she finds that;·he has not the money she
thought, and it will enable me·to spare the dowry for Lucy
without feeling it."

Still she had in the depth of her heart some little sense
of compunction at what she had done, but she smothered it
with a laugh, and salved her conscience with the thought :

" Well, I really have lost much more than I like."

CHAPTER LI.

BRUCE had at once quietly informed the family (except, of course, the children, who knew nothing about the matter) what had happened, and how Strongwood and Bessie had felt it right on account of his health to break off their engagement. This saved Bessie the pain of going over it again with them, and she was touched and comforted by the many little ways in which they showed their sympathy. Strongwood was also conscious of a change in their attitude, which, while it emphasized the loss he had sustained, drew him closer to them.

Both he and Bessie continued to improve, but he still took his meals upstairs, more from delicacy of feeling in regard to her than from necessity.

One morning before breakfast, as Bruce was standing before his dressing table, his wife happened to remark that Dr. Storey had brought Professor Swift to see Strongwood the day before to pass opinion on the condition of his lungs, and that the report had been encouraging.

Upon hearing this a sudden thought seemed to strike Bruce, for he brought down his fist hard on the table, and said :

" What a fool I have been."

" Let me see," said his wife, " thee is just about thirty ; thee is just ten years ahead of time :

>   " At thirty, man suspects himself a fool ;
>   Knows it at forty,——"

" Come, it's no laughing matter," said he, " I may have done great harm."

" What's the difficulty ? "

But he would not tell, saying he would rather wait and see before speaking of it, even to her.

After breakfast he called on Professor Swift.

" Doctor," said he, " I am very glad you have not gone back to town yet."

" No," replied the Professor. " I was not well, and the University extended my leave of absence."

" May I ask you what you think of Mr. Strongwood, who is staying at my house ? "

" Certainly you may. I am much encouraged about him. I have seen him twice lately. His lungs are no worse than they were three months since."

" Can he recover ? "

" He may ; but, of course, it is a treacherous disease."

" What would you think of his getting married ? "

" That would certainly be undesirable at present."

" I ask you," said Bruce, " in confidence. He and my sister are deeply attached to each other, and after his late illness they became engaged, but I represented to them the serious responsibility they were taking. Was I justified in advising them to break it off ? "

" I think that if the young lady wishes to break it off, he should not try to hold her to it."

" But she don't."

" Then if they are already engaged, and neither wishes to break it off, I suppose you want me to put in my veto."

Then followed a long conversation, in which the Professor went into the matter very fully, and finally said :

"Of course, he is in no condition to marry at present. But if they are prepared to face the uncertainty, let them be engaged, with the understanding that it all depends on his health."

" Then you would not refuse it on the mere danger of heredity ? "

" I think not, if he recovers, as I hope he will ; hygienic surroundings, especially in the country, would reduce risk in that direction to a minimum."

" We can trust Mr. Strongwood to take precautions," said Bruce. The way he has carried out your directions for disinfection all the summer is evidence enough for that. I must say they were simple enough."

In the meantime Bessie and Strongwood were conversing. They had both come to the conclusion that it was weakness to avoid each other as they had been doing, and when they met accidentally in the library neither retired. It was rather hard to begin talking, but Strongwood said presently :

" Miss Bessie, I am so glad to see you better."

" Thank you," she answered, " and I am glad to see you downstairs."

" Yes, and in another week I hope to be able to travel."

Bessie was silent. Then she said :

" By the way, I have a message for you that I should have given sooner."

" From whom ? "

" From your worst enemy."

"That must be myself," said Strongwood, smiling; and the little pleasantry put them much more at their ease.

"Do you remember the last sentence you wrote in that—that little—note?" said Bessie, hesitatingly.

"No, I only remember the first."

Bessie looked troubled.

"Please excuse me," he added, hastily, "What was it?"

"You spoke of having forgiven your enemies, and the reason for it."

Strongwood thought a moment.

"Oh, yes, I do remember. Well?"

"Your enemy came to Penelve very ill, and sent for you the very day you became delirious. I saw him and found him in great distress of mind. He confessed how he had injured you, and I read him just that sentence of forgiveness from your note, and told him that writing it had been your last conscious act. Did I do right?"

"Entirely right."

"Do you know," continued Bessie, "that I believe your forgiving him had a great deal to do with his being able to trust God's forgiveness?"

"Oh, I am so glad," said Strongwood, "I was thinking only this morning that I had never been the means of helping any one to the light, and, oh, how many I led towards darkness!"

"I thought you would be glad. Do you think that you could stand hearing the whole story, names and all?"

"I believe I can; for I have forgiven them."

And so she told him. He started at the name of Hardynge, but did not interrupt her. When she had finished he looked up and said in a tone of deep feeling:

"I want to say that I do not regret, but am thankful that I wrote that note and that you found it. I am glad for the *whole* of it."

"So am I," she said, almost under her breath.

"And I believe that the time has now come," he continued, "when we should no longer make the rest uncomfortable by trying to avoid each other's society. The conclusion we have reached was from a sense of duty. For the few days that remain let us act as ordinary people—as far as possible."

"I agree with thee," she said, and held out her hand, which he grasped silently. It was to each of them as the final closing of a chapter of their lives.

They were just leaving the room, when Bruce entered.

"I am so glad to find you together," he said. Come back, I have something to say to you."

He closed the door, and while they waited in surprise, he said :

"I have made a great mistake."

"How?" they both exclaimed, and he proceeded to repeat his conversation with Professor Swift.

Strongwood and Bessie, moved by a common impulse, stood up and clasped each other's hands, while Bruce, having performed his errand, left them to themselves.

Presently, however, Strongwood sat down and covered his face.

Bessie knelt beside him and laid her hand on his shoulder.

"What is the trouble, Robert ?"

"It's too late."

"Too late !"

"Yes; I have parted with a large part of my money"; and he told her how he had practically given it to his mother. "I did not know," he went on, "that this would happen. But we cannot marry on what is left."

He spoke slowly, and without raising his head.

Bessie put her arm round his neck.

"What a dear, foolish man thee is. Why, I'm so glad to hear it. Nothing could have pleased me better."

"Glad!"

"Yes. For I was afraid thee might be rich, and I did not like it, and I am so glad that thee gave her the money. It was just like thee. I have some money of my own, and between us we shall have enough to live upon in Penelve. Thee knows thee can't live in town again. We shall have a common purse, shan't we?"

Strongwood kissed her, and made some endearing remarks, and then added:

"I suppose pride must have a fall, but I did look forward to having my wife received in some style."

"I shall be much more at home without it," she said, simply.

Then they sat down to their first real talk about plans. Both recognized the great uncertainty that hung over their future, but they were so thankful not to be separated that it was not hard to leave future possibilities in the background.

At the conclusion of their talk they fell into silence, and for the first time in his life Strongwood knelt and in the presence of another used words of his own in praise and thanksgiving.

CHAPTER LII.

BESSIE had been perfectly honest in her expression of satisfaction that Strongwood was no longer a rich man ; but before the autumn was over, she more than once regretted that he should be so cramped as to be unable to follow the advice of his physician as to the most suitable health resort. However, the event turned out better than she feared, for the winter was a very favourable one, very dry and cold, with an unusual amount of sunshine. Strongwood secured very comfortable rooms in a house a little further from Penelve than Uplands, and here, with the exception of a fortnight in New York on business, he spent the winter, glad of this effect of his reduced fortunes that it enabled him to see Bessie every day.

He became more and more interested in the work of the Friends ; he had also much time for thought, and many points in regard to Christian faith and practice became clearer to him. Towards the end of November he heard that Lucy and Lord Southliegh were married, and received the following letter from his sister Mary from the Langham Hotel, London.

" My dear Robert,

" What a dear, splendid brother you are ! John has just told me all about it ; but I forgot, I must tell you that John and I are engaged, and he is too good for anything.

347

Do you know that I was so surprised to find that he really
cared for me, that I could scarcely believe my ears when he
proposed to me, and he thought at first that I had refused
him? Just think of it! The bare possibility of his having
gone off with that idea in his head almost gives me a nightmare. And, is not it funny?—He seems to think it so strange
that I should care for him. Now Lucy was so set up with
her engagement to 'dear Lord S——.' No I won't make fun
of them, I'm too happy. But I feel I don't deserve it. Sometimes I almost dread lest John will find me out, and not care
for me, but when I tell him this he only——Well I won't go
into particulars.

"But it *was* good of you to help mother and Lucy so.
The way I know it is this: When John spoke to mother
about me, he was so simple and straightforward that she told
him all her difficulties. Then something came out which
was a great surprise to her, but none to me, for John had told
me already, and that is, that he is not rich at all. Lord S.
had somehow got it into his mind that John was a son of
Mr. Leland, a very wealthy manufacturer of Manchester, and
he is only a *distant* relation. Poor mother was quite floored
with the news; but John, just like him, said that he had
enough to be comfortable upon with reasonable economy, and
he loved me, not my dowry, and if I was willing she might give
my share to Lucy. Mother hemmed and hawed, and took
the matter into consideration. But she soon found that I did
not regard matters in the light she does; so nothing further
was said about whether he was rich or not, nor about giving
my portion to Lucy. Only John and I feel that we are as
much indebted to you as Lucy is, and we regard our share of it
as a loan, which we hope to repay if John's business prospers.

" Yesterday I went with him to see the house he has taken for us. It is such a dear, in a lovely garden, and all so bright and cheerful."

[Then followed a full description of Lucy's grand wedding, after which the letter resumed :]

" I am so glad that you are allowed to be engaged to Miss Bruce, as she seems to suit you so well, and that you are getting better. Your becoming a Christian and a Quaker was, I confess, a shock to me, and made me fear for your mind ; but do you know that somehow my happiness in John makes me wonder if it can be true that our love can only be till death. It seems such a pitiable end to it.

" Your ever loving sister,

" MARY McPHERSON."

" P.S.—Oh, I have not told you what John is like. He is tall and handsome, with lovely curly hair, and open honest eyes—but I won't go on, or you'll laugh at me. I may add that, though he has been brought up a believer, my views don't shock him at all."

As Strongwood read this letter he was inclined to be indignant. His sister evidently supposed that he had promised the money in order to help Lucy get married. His mother had hoodwinked him. He had half a mind to write to her withdrawing his offer. Did he not owe it to Bessie to do so ? But on second thoughts he decided to let matters stand, sooner than provoke a family quarrel. He would take a later opportunity to explain this matter to Mary, and he was glad to be helping her. So he wrote to her in true brotherly style. We shall only quote part of the closing paragraph.

"I don't wonder that you feel the grave to be a pitiable ending to love. Is not love the highest thing we know anything about? Can we get higher than our primal source? If not, then love is at the source of all things, and we love because love is of God, for God is love; and we may rejoice in the experience of it."

This was all he said on the subject, but the thought impressed his sister a good deal, and made her hungry for the infinite love he spoke of.

In February came an unexpected opportunity for Strongwood to retire from his New York business. It was suggested by a letter from Mr. Galway—

"Creekside,
"Flumetown, N.Y.,
"February 2nd, 189—.

"My dear Sir,

"It was very kind of you to remember my daughter in the exquisite little present you sent her for her wedding. She has, I doubt not, written to you herself. The wedding passed off satisfactorily, and the happy pair are now on their travels. It is a great comfort to me that her husband, Mr. Johnston, has decided to live in Flumetown, and has gone into partnership with me. He is a capital fellow, and will relieve me of a great deal of responsibility. They will live at Creekside with me.

"Now I come to the point of my letter. It is about Jonathan, the one who did *not* try to levy blackmail on you. By the way, I always feel that I owe you half an apology and restitution for all the annoyance that scoundrel—whatever his name may be—caused you last summer. I am so mortified

when I remember how he used our names that I hardly
know what to say. I hope you know that you were not the
only sufferer. He lived all those weeks like a fighting cock
at my expense, and I had a pretty collection of bills to pay
on my return, to say nothing of sums spent on detectives,
etc., in order to find traces of his precious body. He had
forged cheques also, and drawn considerable sums out of the
bank on my account. Of course, I was not responsible for
what he had done, but after I had sworn in court that I did
not know my own son—I don't believe that his own mother
would have recognized him—I say, after that I really felt I
could not be hard on others, and so I paid the bills, and the
bank and I shared the loss.

"But to return to my son. His month in prison has
done him no end of good. It made him think, and sobered
him completely. He told me that he saw that if he had
acted properly the mistake would never have occurred. It
made him review his past life, and under his sister's guidance
he has become, I believe, a truly changed man. Four
months ago he joined the Presbyterian Church where we
belong.

"But he does not take to the quiet life at Flumetown, and
wants to go to the city. He had a first-rate business training
in a London house, before he got into irregular habits, and,
now that he has really turned over a new leaf, I wish to set
him up in business in New York City. Could you advise
me?" . . . .

Strongwood went at once to consult Bessie and her
brother, and finally decided to write to his partner explaining
all the facts of the case and suggesting that he (Strongwood)
should sell out to Mr. Galway.

Hansen opened a correspondence with the Galways, and after many letters and interviews they came to an agreement. Hansen was sorry to lose Strongwood, whose sound business judgment, even when he was absent, was very helpful ; but there was no probability of his ever returning to New York to live, and, besides this, his scruples were sometimes awkward to Hansen. The scheme would put more money into the business, for Mr. Galway would become a " silent " partner in the firm in addition to buying part of Strongwood's share for Jonathan. The rest was taken up by Hansen himself and by the head clerk, and the firm was to be known as Hansen, Smith & Galway.

This enabled Strongwood to hand over a large part of what he had promised to his mother, and as soon as the payments should be fully made, it would, after deducting all he should give her, leave him quite a little capital of his own.

Bruce, who had a great opinion of Strongwood's business ability, suggested that they should go into partnership together.

The offer was made very delicately, for it was a decided descent in life from being the head of a New York firm. But it was so clearly the right opening, and presented such a satisfactory means of increasing his income, that he accepted it with a good grace.

It was arranged that Strongwood's share in the actual work of the business should for the present be advisory only, and Bruce insisted that he should spend the brightest part of the day as much as possible in the open air. Bessie arranged to be with him at these times, and Strongwood thought she was never so altogether bewitching as when she met him at

the gate in her snug jacket and seal-skin cap ; her cheeks
rosy with the cold and her eyes shining with pleasure.

One morning he had stopped at the post office for letters,
and was reading them as he walked up. Bessie noticed a
rather grave look on his face and asked the cause.

" I'm about to lose more money," he said. " I don't know
what we shall do."

" Well," said Bessie with a smile, " we've never had to
go to the poor house yet, and I hope we shan't have to
now."

" It is hardly that bad," he answered, " but it really is
rather serious. It amounts to five thousand dollars."

" Oh, well, money is not everything. What is the
difficulty ?"

He handed her the letter. It was from the trustee who
had the care of the money Strongwood had inherited from
his father. It ran as follows :—

"59. —— Street.
" New York,
" February 10th, 189

" Dear Sir,

"You may remember that at your request some years
ago I invested $5,000 of your funds in —— & —— R. R.
Trust Mortgage Bonds. They were considered good because
it was understood that the —— & —— R. R. Co. were
guaranteeing them. This morning I have received private
information from one of the directors of the latter Company
that this is a mistake, and that at the next meeting of the
Board they will announce it. The result will be that the
bonds you hold will fall from 90 their present value—to 10
or less. The terms of the trust do not permit me to change

the investments without your consent.   Please telegraph at once the required permission.

"Awaiting this, I am yours very truly,

"NICHOLAS REASON."

"To ROBERT STRONGWOOD, ESQ.,

"Penelve."

"I am very sorry about it, Robert," said Bessie, gravely.

"Of course, I cannot sell them," he answered.

"Of course not.   It would be the same as stealing," she answered.

"I should not have troubled thee with it, Bessie, but that was part of the money I left to thee when I was so ill, and somehow I felt it was more thine than mine, for my life is very uncertain."

"Nonsense, Robert, thee is getting better every day. But please don't keep from telling me things because thee fears it will trouble me.   It would trouble me far more if thee did not tell me."

"All right, I'll remember.   But I hate to lose the money on thy account."

Bessie laughed and sang:

"'But oh, the choice what heart can doubt,
'Of tents with love, or thrones without.'

"Why, Robert, I am so glad thee's getting better, I don't mind this at all.   Has thee sent the telegram?"

"No, not yet; the letter is only just come.   But I'm going to the office now.   Won't thee come with me?"

As they turned to leave the garden, Robert took advantage of the close hedge to snatch a kiss, and they went on quite gaily as if they were arranging to gain rather than to lose the money.

CHAPTER LIII.

CONCLUSION.

INFLUENZA prevailed in Penelve during the following spring, and all the members of the Uplands household were in turn more or less affected. They all had it rather lightly, except old Mrs. Leslie, who with her feeble vitality almost succumbed to the attack, and was left by it a confirmed invalid.

Strongwood himself in spite of all precautions was laid up for a month. He was at no time seriously ill, but his friends were naturally very uneasy about him. He was a long time gaining his strength, but as the summer came on he began to improve rapidly, and in September, Professor Swift, who had again spent the summer in Penelve, consented to his being married.

"I think that you are justified in the step, Mr. Strongwood," he said, "the disease has not only been arrested, but you are greatly improved, and there is a favourable report from my microscopist. Of course you will need care."

Arrangements for the wedding were immediately set on foot and application for permission sent to the Monthly Meeting, as the "Discipline" requires, and Strongwood wrote the good news to his mother and sisters.

In due time the following answers were received:—

"Southliegh Park,

"Bucks, Eng.

"September 18th, 189—.

" My dear Son,

" Your letter announcing Professor Swift's favourable opinion reached here day before yesterday, the very day that my first grandson—the future Lord Southliegh—was born. He is a fine healthy little fellow, and his mother is proud of him, as you may well believe. Poor girl, I hope he will prove a greater comfort to her than the present Lord does, though he is not unkind, only he is away from home so very much. I do not think she at all repents the step she has taken, for like me, she is fond of high life, and when she was presented at Court, she herself looked like a queen. She takes her place at the head of this establishment as if she was to the manner born, and enters with hearty zest into all the social claims of her new position. It is a great satisfaction to me that Lord S. approves of my making this my home. With all that is upon her, Lucy needs me much more than Mary does in her snug little house, where Mr. Leland pays her every attention that affection can suggest, and his limited means afford.

" As to your approaching marriage with Miss Bruce you know it is not just what I should have chosen for you ; but, under all the circumstances, especially as you have became a Quaker (just think of it !), it seems to be the best you can do. So I willingly sign the form of consent which you wish to present to the ' Monthly Meeting.' It seems a queer thing to require from a man of nearly thirty. I also send you a wedding present which I hope will be acceptable. Lord S. and Lucy are sending something as well, and he has also hunted up an early edition of George Fox, which he pretends to think you will value most of all. I hope you won't be offended.

"If I can leave Lucy, and can find a companion, I shall hope to come over to the wedding. How remarkable to have all my children married within a year. Hoping that your marriage may be as happy as the happiest,

"I am, your affectionate Mother,

"EMILY McPHERSON."

"P.S.—Please give my love to Miss Bruce."

This was the most affectionate letter Strongwood had had from his mother, and it pleased him accordingly.

The letter from Mary was also very welcome—

"2, Melton Villas,

"September 18th, 189—,

"My dear Robert,

"John and I are so glad to hear you have been able to fix your wedding day. If we only could come over to it we would, but the fact is that John spent too much time last year on the Continent courting me, and while he was gone the stupid clerks lost him some important orders. I tell him I am so sorry, but he says that it was the best investment he ever made, and proves it by ways better understood than expressed. Still he is obliged to stay closely at business to make up for lost time. I wish I could see Miss Bruce. You *must* give her our warm love and congratulations. I should congratulate any girl who gets you for a husband, and I congratulate you too on having her.

" I find John really is more religious than I thought he was at first. He was so quiet. We have family prayers night and morning, and he really tries to be a Christian. But he is such a conservative. I tell him I'm surprised he saw anything in a radical like me to admire, but he just smiles. I must admit he was a little shocked when he found out that I really was in earnest in my agnosticism ; but he never argues, and I don't often mention the subject. The fact is, that I don't feel quite so sure as I did. What you said in one of your letters some months ago about our love proving God's love has stuck with me, and has made me want to believe it. But how can I ? There is so much misery in the world, and then I have to believe so much. My mother-in-law tells me I should accept the Church, and believe all it teaches. But even supposing there is such a thing as revelation, what evidence have I that the Church of England is a divinely authorized exponent of it. The same feeling prevents me from accepting my sister-in-law's advice. She is a strong evangelical, and tells me I must accept the Bible *in toto*, and applies the quotation :—

' Unfaith in aught is want of faith in all.'

And she tells me I must accept Christ's imputed righteousness and vicarious sacrifice, and I don't half understand what she means. At prayers this morning John read about the sun standing still. I don't believe it, and I can't believe it, and yet it seems that my salvation depends on my believing it. Yet I do want something which I have not got. Although I am very happy in John, I can't get over the dreadful thought that if he died I should lose him for ever. Your Bessie evidently has not that feeling about you, nor you about her. But whenever John is not perfectly well I am miserable, and then again I feel so selfish when I think how happy I am (apart from this dread) and how I do nothing for others less fortunate.

"Here I have written a long letter all about myself, when I should have told you of the new Lord Southliegh—the future one I mean. But mother will have written about all that. I wish I could see Lucy often. I fear she is not very happy ; but she moves in such a different set, and lives so far off, that we have not seen each other since my marriage.

"With ever so much love to you and to Bessie, in which John joins.

"I am, as ever, your affectionate sister,

"MARY McP. LELAND."

"P.S.—I hope that the little present we are sending will not prove to be a duplicate."

Strongwood was very busy with preparations for his wedding, but he found time to write to his sister.

After thanking her for the wedding present, and expressing regret that she and her husband could not come to the wedding, and giving other news, the letter continued :

"I do wish that you could see how perfectly charming Bessie is. She is so natural, and so brave, and so cheerful. I look at her in wonder and cannot understand how such a blessing as she is should have come into my life.

"And now to your letter ; it has done me good, for it has shown me that I was mistaken in the thought that I had almost come to, that sorrow and difficulties are the only way by which men are led to long after God. I see that you are being led through happiness, and I do so hope that you will allow yourself to be led. But don't get side-tracked on secondary issues. What you are really longing for is Jesus Christ and His revelation of God. Questions of Church order, the infallibility of the Scriptures, and special doctrines can well be left for future consideration. What you need is Christ.

"But you will say to me, that this is as hard for you to accept as any of the other things that you have been told to believe and follow. I do not think so, if only you will consider Him in the light of a person. He is One who has offered to His followers more even in this world than any other teacher or prophet since the world began. Who else has promised new life and strength and comfort as He has done? He not only makes these promises but He also comes to us now with the testimony of those who down through the ages have trusted Him and found Him true. The amount and character of this testimony seem to me to compel the attention of all thoughtful persons. Those who testify to Him have belonged to many and often opposing sects, but with one voice they tell us that He gives what He has promised. Now, if you knew that such a person had lived centuries ago, but thought that He was only known through tradition, would you not say that you would be so glad if only there existed some reliable account of how He impressed the people who had access to Him? Now this is exactly what we have in the New Testament. There is the record of how He impressed His contemporaries, and of the effect which He had on their lives and characters. Will you not study the record to discover just what this impression was, and how far it appeals to you? I am sure that as you read in the spirit of a learner, you will feel that there is a message in it for you, because it will speak to your need, and the Spirit of God will impress your heart with its truth.

"If your experience is at all like mine, you will find, as you compare yourself with the standard of righteousness there presented, that you are bound to accept that standard, and to try to conform to it, for it is the true one. You will also soon find that you are bound to condemn yourself, for failing to live up to it. Do not be discouraged; this is but the preparation for what is to follow. As you read, and consider the beauty and goodness of the character of Jesus Christ, you will find the very fact of His goodness to be an evidence that it is a true revelation of what God is. Otherwise He is greater than God and better than God; the stream has risen higher than its source. I do not think that you will take this position, and therefore you can say to yourself as you read, 'God is always the same. The goodness and love and power there shown forth is still His. The same tenderness, the same readiness to suffer for those who are out of the way is in Him to this day, the same care for individuals. Therefore I can come to Him and trust Him to forgive and to receive and to help me.'

"Dear sister, will you not take my testimony as an added reason why you should come and try for yourself whether these things be true?

"With dear love to John and yourself, in which Bessie joins.

"I am, your affectionate brother,

"ROBT. STRONGWOOD."

"P.S.—The uncomfortable feeling you speak of in thinking yourself so selfish when you are so happy, is really the result of the working of the Spirit of Christ in your heart. The same Lord Jesus who is showing you your failure is waiting to show you Himself as your Saviour. Do not be satisfied with anything short of this."

As Strongwood had anticipated, Mrs. McPherson was unable to get to the wedding. Perhaps she never really intended to come. Robert was sorry, but also a little relieved, while Bessie very much regretted that none of his near relations would be present. Those that had accepted the invitation were distant cousins, whom he knew but slightly. A number of his old New York friends were also expecting to attend, attracted partly perhaps by the novelty of a Quaker wedding.

At last the day came, bright and beautiful, with fleecy clouds floating in the deep blue sky. The Meeting-house was filled with those whom affection or curiosity had brought together. But a deep hush was over all as the bride and bridegroom arose to repeat the simple ceremony. Both spoke distinctly and with feeling. As they stood, they joined hands, and Strongwood said :

" In the presence of the Lord and before this assembly, I take Elizabeth Bruce to be my wife, promising, with Divine assistance, to be unto her a loving and faithful husband, until death shall separate us."

Bessie followed ; her voice was very low but clear.

" In the presence of the Lord and before this assembly, I take Robert Strongwood to be my husband, promising, with Divine assistance, to be unto him a loving and faithful wife until death shall separate us."

Then they sat down.

We need not describe the reading of the certificate and the signing of it, nor the prayers and exhortations that followed. To the strangers present, the simplicity of the arrangements, the absence of any officiating minister and the equal promises of faithful love made alike by bride and bridegroom were unique and strange, but all were impressed with the sense of reverent quietness that was over the congregation and with the beauty and solemnity of the occasion.

The reception at Uplands afterwards was large and informal, for Bessie had been anxious to neglect no one ; so that there was a great, but good humoured, medley of Robert's city friends, including Mr. Hansen and Jonathan Galway, members of the meeting, and acquaintances at Penelve, and guests from the country meetings, among them McKendry and his wife from the mountain, and the old United Brethren exhorter.

Bessie and Robert are standing together at one end of the large parlour, receiving the congratulations and good wishes of their friends. They are a handsome couple : his face, no longer marred by the old cynical expression, has just sufficient look of delicacy to make it more interesting, while his manly bearing dispels the idea of weakness. Bessie is a lovely bride in her simple white frock with a few sprigs of myrtle in her hair and dress, her dark eyes shining and her cheeks suffused with a delicate blush.

" I know now," said Hansen to Strongwood, " what the secret charm was that has made a Quaker of you ; and," he continued, bowing to Bessie, " I cannot wonder at it."

" You are quite mistaken, Mr. Hansen," said Bessie. " Robert decided to be a Friend, before—before he——" Bessie hesitated and Robert helped her out.

" That was, before I ever thought to see a day like this, Hansen," he said.

" Of course," said that gentleman with an incredulous air, " and I suppose, Mrs. Strongwood, that you will say that you had nothing to do with his leaving New York."

"Certainly," said Bessie laughing, "for that is not my doing but the doctor's."

"And yet in neither case are you sorry."

"Of course not."

"And you must admit that appearances are against you."

"Be that as it may, appearances are deceitful."

"But in this case, 'beauty has not been in vain,'" replied Hansen with a bow and smile.

"Your conclusion is about as correct as your quotation," remarked Bessie, a little piqued at his persistence, for she did not like people to think that she had persuaded Robert to adopt her views.

Robert saw that Hansen was rather taken aback, and said pleasantly:

"But there is one point on which she will plead guilty ; I have given up smoking."

"Don't trust him, Mrs. Strongwood. He'll persuade you to grant him a dispensation."

"He's a man of his word, Mr. Hansen," said Bessie.

"Well then, Strongwood," said his friend with an air of mock reproof, "all I can say is that you've thrown away the 'Declaration of Independence,' and given in your allegiance to a Queen."

"I admit this much," returned Strongwood, "that under present circumstances, 'I am quite prepared to shout 'Victoria.'"

The joke was rather feeble, but every one was in a spirit to appreciate it, and in the laugh which followed, Mr. Hansen made way for others to come up.

Strongwood saw the McKendrys standing near, a little abashed in the crowd, and he welcomed them cordially.

" It was good of you to come, and how is my little name-sake progressing? I was afraid Mrs. McKendry could not leave him."

"Oh, Mrs. Strongwood arranged for that," said Mrs. McKendry, "and he's well looked after, Sir. He's a fine little fellow."

" Well, I shan't soon forget what I owe you," returned Strongwood, " but here's Bessie waiting for your good wishes."

" Indeed she has them then," said McKendry, shaking her hand warmly, and ably seconded by his wife. " We're hoping to see you up on the mountain before the winter sets in. We hold our school and meetings regular every First-day afternoon," he added.

"That's right," said Bessie. " We'll get up when we can. Be sure, in the meantime, to take some of the cake to our friends there."

Later on, Strongwood said with a smile as a new face appeared :

"Bessie, let me introduce Mr. Jonathan Galway."

"I am afraid," said that gentleman, "that my name, at least, will hardly be a welcome one."

"On the contrary," said Bessie, "it is ; for I am glad to put it to the right man. After all, don't you think we have each received more than we lost through your double—no, excuse me, your counterfeit presentment?"

"I am sure I have," returned Jonathan, "but do you know our housekeeper has never become reconciled to the reality, and still mourns over that man. She does not think I'm half so nice."

"He must have been an able fellow. Have you found any clue to him ?"

"None whatever.   He had too long a start."

"And how is your sister, Mrs. Johnston?"

"Oh, she's well and happy, and sends all kinds of good wishes.   She would have come, but cannot very well leave father.   He's quite feeble you know."

And so the guests came and went.   Grace Wildmere lingered till most of them had gone and then she came up to say "Farewell."

Bessie's eyes had not been idle, and in glancing round the room as she talked, she had several times noted Ezra Seward and Grace very near together ; so now, when that young lady leaned towards her for a kiss, Bessie whispered :

"May I wish thee joy?"

A tell-tale smile and blush made an answer superfluous, and soon afterwards, when Seward himself came up, Bessie found an opportunity to say with an arch smile :

"Was I not right in my advice last year?"

Seward's eyes twinkled, but he answered gravely :

"Thou knows, Elizabeth, that I have always had great confidence in thy judgment."

*   *   *   *   *

And here we leave them.   At last accounts, Professor Swift had had no reason to regret the advice he gave. Robert Strongwood smiles when he hears that his old friends in New York speak of him as "Poor Strongwood!"

THE END.